The

DARKEST
HEART

ALSO BY THEA DEVINE

Sex, Lies & Secret Lives

His Little Black Book

Bad as She Wants to Be

The

DARKEST
HEART

Thea Devine

GALLERY BOOKS

New York London Toronto Sydney

G

Gallery Books
A Division of Simon & Schuster, Inc.
1230 Avenue of the Americas
New York, NY 10020

First Gallery Books trade paperback edition June 2011

GALLERY and colophon are trademarks of Simon & Schuster, Inc.

For information about special discounts for bulk purchases,
please contact Simon & Schuster Special Sales at 1-866-506-1949
or business@simonandschuster.com.

The Simon & Schuster Speakers Bureau can bring authors to your live event. For more information or to book an event contact the Simon & Schuster Speakers Bureau at 1-866-248-3049 or visit our website at www.simonspeakers.com.

Designed by Ruth Lee-Mui

Manufactured in the United States of America

10 9 8 7 6 5 4 3 2 1

Library of Congress Cataloging-in-Publication Data

Devine, Thea.
    The darkest heart / Thea Devine.—1st Gallery Books trade paperback ed.
        p. cm.
1. Vampires—Fiction. 2. London (England)—Fiction. I. Title.
PS3554.E928175D37 2011
813'.54—dc22   2010050023

ISBN 978-1-4165-6266-5
ISBN 978-1-4165-6281-8 (ebook)

The

DARKEST
HEART

Prologue

*H*e'd never gotten used to the bloodlust. When he was first made, he'd thought maybe, after a while, the craving, the impulse, the intensity of the urge, would slake and stop tormenting him.

But it never faded. In the twenty years since he'd been turned, he'd never found a way to rein it in, keep it close, make it his own. It existed as a separate part of him that he couldn't contain or control, something that had a life, a mind, and a hunger of its own that pulled him in and swallowed him whole.

In the early days, he'd fought it hard because he really believed he didn't have to be what he'd become. He could be sane. He could maintain his humanity. He could ignore the incessant insatiable need for blood.

He instead became a monster, and he ravaged animals in his fury over becoming this *thing*, this bloodthirsty ghoul, because it hadn't been his choice or his desire. It wasn't even Fate.

It was by someone else's action.

He'd rather have died—he *would* have died if—

But his Maker wouldn't let him. His Maker dove into the roaring conflagration where he lay choking and burning, dove past the flames, the heat, and the billowing smoke, to pull what was left of him out of the fire into the night that would be his home forever.

I won't let you die—you can't die . . .

The coruscating whisper that brought him back to life—with one sharp act of physical possession deep into his heart—it was done, the blood roaring like burning-hot fire through his veins, animating his dead soul.

The mark of his Maker showed prominently on the burned skin of his chest. Three bloody *X*'s. Child of Judas. Creature of the night. Heir to the curse of the betrayer. Doomed to wander in eternity after being cast out.

The country house burning down around his sapped body as his Maker whispered in his ear. *I had to save you.* The self-justifying excuse, evanescent as the wind. *I couldn't let you die.*

I am dead, he'd wanted to howl, but his vocal cords were burned, and his throat full of smoke, blood, pain, and metallic bile.

The whomp of the flames had been like a smothering blanket obscuring sight and sound—the creak of beams unable to sustain the onslaught, the ferocity of the fire, cracking in the background . . .

He couldn't see, he could barely hear. His Maker leaned over him and whispered heavily, *Now, you—leave and never come back.*

He'd fought a hard-won battle not to return, thinking that time and distance would temper his blood rage, his need for revenge.

He'd wandered the world. He'd refined himself, taken the name Dominick Janou. He'd made himself into a gentleman, a merchant by trade to cover his ferocious bloodlust and the trail of death he left in his wake.

It had taken twenty years to perfect himself after a nether life ruled by emotion, driven by need, and consumed by blood dreams.

Anything to keep that last shred of man that he could have been. Anything to suppress the hunger for blood. Anything to make him acceptable to the world to which he meant to return as a wealthy entrepreneur to wreak his revenge.

Only when he was certain he had mastered the thing he'd become did he even think of returning. He was exhausted from the pounding urge to feed, of the hell in which he lived with that remnant of himself and what he used to be. He yearned to confront his Maker, to put an end to the eternal seeking and to find immortal rest.

Finally, he felt ripe for vengeance, ready for a different eternity.

It was time to go to London, take up residence, and infiltrate the very society he'd been denied by virtue of what his Maker had done.

Make them all sit up and take notice. Make them want him, desire him, throw themselves at him.

Lure his enemies into the open.

And then . . .

Then he would destroy them all.

The Countess was desperate for an heir. All she needed was a young, beautiful, malleable, disposable girl who could be groomed as the wife of her charming but volatile son, Charles.

She felt the weight of passing time pulling at her vitals and the tearing desire to have a grandson to carry on the family line. She also held the faint hope that a child would temper Charles's heedless ways and cool the fire in his blood.

The hard part was finding the girl.

It would be best if she was from somewhere else. That way, there would be fewer complications and fewer questions. *They* were from far away, she and Charles, having relocated to Drom Manor some twenty years before, after a fire completely destroyed the country house in which she and her late husband had settled when they'd first come to England.

Her adored eldest son, Nicolai, had died in that fire, and before that she'd lost her husband, her sister, and her only daughter. Too many losses, and too much lost time.

So there must be an heir.

Only recently had the Countess felt the pressing urgency to see it done. But there was no talking to Charles about it. He refused to listen, to be reasoned with. He would do what he would as always, subject to no one's authority.

But still, time was wasting, and the Countess didn't particularly care what *he* wanted. She was ready for the struggle between them, but she would not back down from her determination to find a suitable wife for Charles. And he would father an heir with her whether he was amenable or not.

The Countess believed in Fate. Fate had brought her to this place with this son at this particular time for this particular purpose. She fully believed that it was just a matter of time before Fate provided her with a suitable bride.

So it did not surprise her when one afternoon, as she was contemplating whether she should take a more active hand in finding this fateful bride, she received a letter that contained the perfect solution to her problem.

It was from a solicitor in London, short and to the point:

I write on behalf of Miss Senna Landseth, to whom you are distantly related by marriage on your husband's side (a cousin's daughter). Miss Landseth is 18 years of age, recently orphaned, and has no recourse but to take up residence at the Kearnsgate workhouse unless a relative might, in Christian charity, offer her a home. I appeal to you in memory of her poor deceased mother to ask that very thing. Miss Landseth has all those attributes of substance to recommend her, and you will find her, despite the hardships she has endured, an engaging young woman, willing to learn to better herself and grateful for the chance to do so among those she might consider family.

Fate was handing her the perfect bride, the generous gift of a deceased, distant, heretofore unknown relative, with all the points in her favor, particularly youth, innocence, and fertility. Hopefully she would be trainable, biddable, and grateful—ultimately she would be a rich man's wife—if, as the Countess planned, she married Charles in due course.

The Countess needed only to take this Senna Landseth in hand, educate her to be Charles's wife, and finally see the culmination of all her plans.

Such an elegant solution.

It could only be Fate, she thought.

But then she glanced up for a moment and her gaze caught the brilliantly colored painting over the fireplace in the small parlor where she sat, a portrait of her own dear sister just before she died.

The Countess hated that portrait. She hated that not much time seemed to have passed between her sister's death and this day. Yet, time seemed finite suddenly because Charles must marry and produce an heir.

Soon.

Here she had a candidate ready-made. It didn't matter who this Senna Landseth was as long as she was even remotely presentable. She would come to live with them, she'd be grateful for all she'd be given, and therefore happy to marry Charles, with all the benefits that would come to her in that position.

Several more months did not seem that long to wait.

It seemed like forever.

It would be forever if she didn't take action and respond to that letter.

The Countess impatiently rang for the butler.

"My writing case, please. And the boy. I have a missive that must make the post coach this afternoon. Hurry."

Time seemed of the essence suddenly, words felt superfluous. All she needed to write was "Come."

And hurry.

He didn't remember London ever teeming with such juicy bodies. The thrumming blood, the rush of life, the thread of death luring him, testing his resolve. The beast always lurked deep within him.

The thirst.

He almost couldn't walk through the streets, he felt so suffocated by a hunger he couldn't have conceived of and almost couldn't control.

It taunted him. It had the power to seize every inch of his body with a bestial desire to devour unto death.

Only an almost superhuman will and an iron determination kept his every bloody impulse in check. It nearly killed him not to overwhelm random bodies, drag them into secret places, and suck them dry.

It seemed like a test of the beast in the man every day since he'd arrived in London and sought to establish himself legitimately—and secretly, so he'd leave no footprints to be followed, no questions to be answered.

He inhabited the body of a merchant, an importer of objets d'art from the Far East, from primitive places he'd penetrated and explored.

He called himself Dominick Janou and cultivated an image that was exotic and exciting, elusive and aloof.

He could afford the best, and when he was in the skin of a man, it pleased him that he was returning to London so blatantly successful in his human life. And thankful for the dank, dark waterfront warehouses so necessary for business that caged and contained his secret life.

Slowly, he settled in Town and built his reputation, insinuating himself into the social strata necessary for his plans. Slowly he developed the obdurate will to overcome the lure of all those succulent bodies he knew he would encounter—those luscious women with their alabaster skin, long swan necks, and beautiful pulsating bosoms. And the men, the men, the men—lean, long, muscular—or fat and corpuscular—all of them stupid and disposable.

He knew he could not keep his presence a secret much longer. But while he had the luxury of time and all those throbbing bodies . . .

It took virtually nothing to make the women love him: he was the very embodiment of the brooding, elusive, handsome lover, and women loved him, they wanted him. He wanted them to want him. It would be so much easier later on if they wanted him.

How could he refuse them?

But for now, it was enough that they yearned for him. They flirted with him, they engaged him in layered conversations in which they had no idea what they were really telling him, what they really wanted—or what he really wanted.

He couldn't, *wouldn't,* give in to his blood-saturated nature. But keeping up the façade of a man was exhausting. It drained him, caused him to hunt at night, to take what he could find and leave the dregs.

He was aware that if he wasn't more careful, he'd become so cavalier about the hunt that he'd leave a trail and destroy himself.

That was not the plan.

He had been settled in London for four months when he finally determined he must begin to use his powers to take on his enemy on his enemy's terrain and set things in motion.

It only took a moment of fierce concentration, his will, and his domination of every instinct, and it was done.

It was too easily done, that a monster could morph into mist, a fly, a bat, and in a breath take flight. He'd inherited all the powers of his Maker in that one life-changing bite. Reconstitution, trans-shaping, transporting, hypnotism, memory implantation—powers he'd been loath to use until now. But now, they could gain him an advantage as he prepared to battle the One, who was every bit as powerful as he.

He soared aloft, tiny and dark-winged in a death-black night, heading toward vindication.

She'd found her mark. In the midst of the crowd that surrounded her as she performed magic tricks with cards and coins, Senna saw the *one*—the innocent, gullible one whose eyes went wide with every simple sleight of hand.

Or maybe he had something else in mind.

No matter, she would use that too. She needed just enough of a crowd around her to entice him and shield her as she made her escape. Everything else, she'd prepared in advance.

She beckoned the crowd. "Here, now. Who'd like to double his money?" She raised her arms and every eye followed the movements of her hands. She held up a small coin, manipulating it in her fingers, turning to show her audience. Then suddenly she snapped her fingers and it was gone.

"You there"—she stepped into the crowd and found a bemused gentleman and tapped his chest—"look in your pocket."

The crowd leaned forward. The gentleman fished out two coins, held them up, and gave them back to her as the crowd applauded.

"Now," she said as she turned to the crowd and smiled charmingly, "who'd like to offer up a shilling to double his money?" Her brilliant blue eyes locked with the bright gaze of the mark. "You?"

He nodded, came forward, and flipped a coin into her hand.

"Ladies and gentlemen . . ." Senna showed the coin, then began her magical manipulations, snapped her fingers, and the coin disappeared.

"Now, everyone, come closer." She moved toward the mark as the crowd swirled around her. "And you." She tapped the mark's chest, bracing her hand as she again commanded, "Look in your pocket." She pushed away, ducking under the bodies pressing in.

She broke into a run, pulling off her hat and shawl, as she heard the expected aggrieved howl "She stole my money!"

She heard the roar of the crowd and pounding footsteps scattering every which way as some of the onlookers took off after her.

I can't keep doing this, she thought, knowing that she would. It was how she'd lived her life for as long as she could remember. Sometimes when she was desperate, she found that a simple con yielded the quickest results. A shilling would buy a crust of bread, a sip of soup, and a bed for the night.

Sometimes that was all she needed. She was a child of the streets, accustomed to sleeping in doorways, alleyways, the poorhouse, and sometimes behind a stove if she chanced to beg some kitchen work.

Somehow, by dint of guile, luck, street-honed intelligence, and a gift for flimflam, she had managed to stay alive, clean, out of random men's beds, and sometimes to even find employment.

She was a gambler and a schemer and she knew it. She had to be to survive, and she had the wit and patience to perpetrate a con, not the least of which was her ability to perform simple magic, tell fortunes, and read palms. Those street tricks, coupled with her arresting looks, had kept her in ha'pennies for half her life, but now time was running out.

She was too old to be cute, too streetwise to be captivating, too tired to keep running.

It wasn't that the old Gypsy hadn't warned her. Mirya had not only taught Senna to read palms, but to also read the cards. And the cards clearly predicted the penurious long haul of the rest of Senna's life.

"It's time," Mirya told her. "I don't need the cards to know you'll be walking the streets faster than gilt off gingerbread if you don't do something to change your future."

Senna decided she couldn't just sit back and wait.

A day or two later, after she'd spent the precious shilling, she cobbled together a few days' work in yet another aristocratic family's kitchen, peeling potatoes and scrubbing floors. It couldn't have been a coincidence that she overheard some backstairs gossip about an indigent relation whom the family had invited to live with them.

It seemed natural that she should conceive of the ruse of claiming kinship with a wealthy family, on the assumption that one or all of them must have a poor or disgraced relative somewhere on their family tree.

They usually did.

She hadn't thought the idea would really work; she had taken her time in the planning of what was, at best, a long play. But she had nothing to lose, and it was something to do when in reality she could do little to better her situation.

She had chosen her marks carefully and enlisted Mirya's help for an address to take mail. She'd fully expected to wait for months, if not forever, for a response to her "solicitor" letter.

The Countess Lazlaric responded so quickly, Senna was caught off guard.

Suddenly and unexpectedly, everything was in play.

"Come," the Countess had written with admirable economy not three weeks after Senna had sent the fateful letter. "My husband's cousin's daughter should have a home. I'll send a carriage."

It seemed just a little too fast, a little generous to a relation seeking alms. Instantly, Senna's instincts made her wary—which warred with her feeling of triumph that her scheme had worked so expediently, and just the way she'd hoped.

Why shouldn't it? She was good at concocting stories. She ought not to be looking for a deeper reason why the Countess wanted her. The deception had worked. She had a home.

Only . . .

She had thought she was fearless. She felt utterly spineless.

Or else the long, strenuous drive to Drom Manor was working on her nerves, giving her too much time to ruminate on a litany of everything that could go wrong, including that she hadn't planned on being immured in the middle of nowhere.

Or maybe it was the darkness that spooked her. The carriage had been waiting in front of All Souls Church at four in the afternoon, as the Countess had specified. Senna had thought it would be a trip of a mere couple of hours. She hadn't expected to be traveling this deep into the night, until the moon was gauzy, the fog hovered low, and the chill in the air permeated her bones. It was a wonder the driver could even see the road.

They'd been traveling for what seemed like hours, with only a couple of wildly swinging lanterns lighting their way. And the fog seemed to be getting closer, denser, as if it would swallow the carriage whole. There was something terrifying about rumbling through the dark with no end in sight and only a wizened driver who seemed older than time to depend upon.

She could see only miles of darkness ahead of them, behind them, everywhere. She could wind up anywhere.

The dark could eat her alive. . . .

For the first time, it occurred to her she hadn't planned the usual escape route should the ruse go wrong or if she was caught.

But here, she was at the mercy of the dark, the driver, and the possibility that Drom Manor, like the Countess's husband's deceased cousin's daughter, was just a figment of her imagination.

High up on the ceiling in the small parlor of Drom Manor, Dominick had found some footing in an elaborate frieze where he could wedge his bat body comfortably without draining his energy and power.

In just a few hours, he'd found that the Countess spent a fair amount of her day in the parlor, and that conversations reverberated so that he could clearly hear everything. It was perfect for his plans.

He knew now that among her staff were a butler, a couple of maids, and a plain cook—all of whom came daily—and the stable-boy.

He knew that his brother had not changed in the twenty years since he'd gone, and that Charles was still as feckless, reckless, and explosively volatile as ever. But the heat in him was tempered now with a veneer of charm that was equally as dangerous because his bloodthirsty impulses had not abated in all this time.

Nor had he been turned into a creature of the night, a vampire of the clan Iscariot, descendant of Judas, the betrayer. No, Charles's bloodletting was all on his own, and Dominick perceived that the Countess wanted it that way for her own purposes.

Just now, the Countess seemed inordinately distracted and impatient until Charles should join her for tea.

She rang for the maid every ten minutes. "Is he here yet?"

"No, mum."

"The minute he comes in."

"Yes, mum."

She paced. She was still vigorous after twenty years. Nothing showed on her face, no lines, no worry, and she had not aged. But she was agitated today when Dominick knew that normally she was bloodlessly calm.

Charles must be up to something.

Dominick instantly felt a devil's ache to transform again, to hunt, to kill and drink of his enemy's blood.

"Charles . . ."

He heard her voice from somewhere far away in his iron determination to keep tight and compacted on the ceiling. He had no idea how much time had passed, but he saw the table was now set for tea, and that it had gotten dark.

"Such urgency," Charles murmured languidly. "The maid fair shoved me in here."

"You're only four hours late." The Countess's tone brooked no argument. "Sit. I need to talk to you."

"When don't you?" He dropped into a nearby wing chair as the Countess continued pacing.

"We're back to the question of an heir."

Charles went still. "*You* may be back to the question—"

"Exactly," the Countess interrupted. "And so I've taken matters in my own hands. There's a girl—"

Dominick felt the shock even through his compacted body.

A girl? Devil's bones—a girl?

Charles shrugged. "There's always a girl, Mother."

"I haven't met her. I'm hoping she's as young, well-bred, and well-favored as her solicitor portrayed her. If she is, then you will court her and get a child on her. If she's not, well—she's an orphan and disposable. This you will do, Charles. I will have my bloodline carried forward before it's too late. After that is done, I won't meddle again."

Old fool, Dominick thought contemptuously, *of course she will.*

"Well played, Mother," Charles said after a while. "What if I don't want her? What if we don't suit? What if she can't breed? What if she doesn't want to? This is a foolish roll of the dice."

"You can make her want to, Charles," the Countess said silkily. "And in favor of my plan—she's an orphan, she's the daughter of some distant cousin of my late husband, so she has some pedigree. And if it doesn't work out, she won't be missed. I'll attend to that personally. No blood on your hands. It cannot happen any other way."

Charles slanted a glance at her.

Up to his old tricks obviously, Dominick thought.

"So let it not happen. I'm perfectly content to go on as I am."

The Countess stopped pacing. Her expression went cold and remorseless. "I'm not. Content for you to continue on this way, I mean. I want that heir. If you don't produce—and there's no guarantee that you will," she added brutally, "rest assured, I have other ways."

Damnation—she'll never stop. What she wanted, the Countess would have, and whatever got in her way, she eliminated.

Even Charles. Who was as relentless as she was.

And now the complication of a girl.

"But I prefer that the bloodline pass through you."

And not through your monster son? Is that tainted blood, Mother?

"She arrives here tonight," the Countess added, dropping that little cannonball before she sat and poured the now cold tea. "And you will exert every one of your considerable charms to make her feel warm and wanted."

"Does she know she's to be a broodmare?" Charles murmured slyly.

"I had rather thought you might seduce her," the Countess said bluntly. "We'll seduce her. So much more acceptable than my just telling her."

"Why, Mother—such consideration is so unlike you. And how did you find this paragon?"

The Countess sipped her cold tea. "She came to me, through a solicitor, seeking relatives who might take her in. I thought it was a perfect match, need meeting need."

"I will be predisposed to dislike her immediately. And now I need a drink." Charles moved to a side table with a tantalus and unlocked it. "What shall we toast, Mother?"

The Countess gave him a slicing look over her teacup rim. "We toast the regeneration of the Lazlaric blood, of course. There *is* nothing else."

🐍

It took every ounce of will for Dominick to hold to his perch and keep his surging rage coiled deep inside him while every muscle, impulse, and drive in him yearned to explode into life and foment death.

An unknown girl to carry the seed, the blood, the life of his father's line, through Charles? No!

He forced himself to calm down, to keep the bloodlust from flooding his vision, so he could see clearly, to let the fury seep from his vitals as he suddenly comprehended the possibilities.

Here was the perfect instrument of his revenge—the girl. Through her, *he*, Dominick, would kill the line. Fill the vessel with *his* poisoned seed and give her the curse of death instead of the gift of life.

His compacted body began to shake with the pulse, the urge, the unfettered determination, to plunder and breed.

Not yet, not yet.

He focused on the Countess—the savior of Nicolai, her most beloved son who had wanted so desperately to die. The mother-destroyer. She owed him so much for the hell he'd traversed since.

Kill the blood. He felt a deep satisfaction at the thought.

It would kill *her*. It would be *his* judgment. He'd consign her to *his* hell. It would be a vindication of the death of Nicolai, and final rest at last.

It felt perfect, ordained.

He heard the sound of a deep, sonorous bell.

A call to prayer, he thought. Or a call to the blood.

The Countess looked up and Dominick almost believed she could see him hanging there.

But no. Her every sense was focused on the arrival of the girl.

A dog howled in the distance, and the bell sounded again.

The Countess put down her teacup and rose as the butler entered the parlor.

"She's here."

Chapter 2

She was beautiful.

There was no other word. Astonishingly beautiful and slender. Her clothes were work-worn but clean. Her hair shone like a raven's wing, and her skin was creamy white. Her eyes were a defiant, sparkling blue and her dainty nose made a perfectly straight line down to her well-defined lips.

She was luscious, fertile, and throbbing with life and fresh blood. Dominick stiffened. *Not for Charles—never . . .*

She looked a little dazed, as if she hadn't ever expected the journey to end and suddenly here were these strange people staring at her and no one knew quite what to say.

Charles was dumbstruck, even Dominick could see it, constricted as he was above them.

And the Countess couldn't find a word to utter for a full minute.

She was that beautiful.

Charles would desecrate that beauty and leave her a sucked-out husk of herself. And he'd get an heir out of her too.

Not if I do first, Dominick thought.

The Countess shook herself and moved toward Senna, her hands outstretched. "Senna," she said in a husky whisper. "You favor my cousin."

Senna didn't miss a beat. "So I've been told, ma'am." Her voice was clear and confident.

She has no idea what she's walked into, Dominick thought.

"My dear husband's cousin's daughter," the Countess murmured. "Where did you say she was buried?"

"St. Bartholomew's cemetery in the Cotswolds," Senna replied. "Perhaps you've visited?"

"I'm sad to say I haven't. However, I'm pleased to welcome you to Drom."

"And I'm very pleased to be here."

What cousin's daughter? Dominick had been so caught off guard by the complication of the girl, nothing else had registered.

No, wait—that was the story the Countess had told Charles moments before.

But no matter what circumstances she devised to explain the girl, it was clear the Countess had brought this little lamb for Charles to slaughter because she wanted an heir that badly.

And now she wanted to excise the taint through Charles's blood.

And if that was her plan, then she would have to excise *him*—Dominick—again. *Let her try.* Now he'd seen the vessel, and he was determined to steal her from Charles.

He'd have to stay at Drom, of course. Which meant he'd have to transform again. He couldn't keep his body this constrained much longer. He'd nearly crippled his muscles getting to Drom in the first place because he hadn't been all that certain of his transporting powers. Then, maneuvering his exhausted bat-body down the chimney had been excruciating.

He only had to hang on just a little longer.

He homed in on the Countess, who was offering food, drink, and a seat to a tired guest.

"Yes," the Countess was saying, "Charles and I are the sole occupants of the Manor. As you'll see tomorrow, there's plenty of room.

Whitton, our butler, saw to your things. Meantime, you'll have something to eat and then we'll let you rest."

Damn Charles—staring at her like she's a piece of cream cake.

Dominick felt himself ruffling with fury. *The bastard. If he follows her to her room . . . damn—I'm losing my hold.*

He felt himself falling and he heaved his body outward with immense difficulty. He swooped into a high-slicing glide, only just avoiding a free fall, a mere breath of movement in the air.

Everyone's attention had centered on the butler, who entered with a tray.

"A bowl of soup and some nice fresh-baked bread," the Countess announced. "Something light for you tonight after your travels."

Senna met her gaze head-on, then she looked at Charles.

Don't let them hypnotize you, my pretty. Be very, very careful.

After a long moment, Senna lifted her spoon. There was no escaping those eyes. She felt a shot of jubilation. The scheme had worked and her journey had ended as it should have: at this fairy tale of a country house.

She dipped her spoon into the soup. It was thick with vegetables in a nice salted broth, and after such a daunting trip, it was comforting.

But still—these people were strangers, and this was the biggest hoax she'd ever perpetrated. It had brought her straight to the middle of nowhere.

She resolutely ate and kept her focus on the food. With the two of them watching her so intently, she felt a little uneasy after the interminable journey, the unexpected son, the shadows, the fog, the cold—and all the unexpected questions. She'd thought she'd never get past questions tonight when she was too tired to embroider the lie, yet the lies rose to her lips with the fluidity of truth.

She'd made this bed herself; no choice but to sleep in it. After all, such a complicated deception offered no guarantees.

At least she'd felt welcomed by the unexpected warmth of Drom Manor as it illuminated the darkness when the carriage finally turned into the driveway. The house itself wasn't overpowering either. It stood, from what she could see in the dim light, two stories high, foursquare and symmetrical, with every window on the first floor warmly lit.

It was everything she could have wanted, an elegant house oozing wealth and the scent of beeswax from the moment she stepped into the front hall and the Countess took her hands. She had little time to notice the grand staircase, the richly hued Persian carpets on all the floors, the crystal chandeliers, and the gold-framed paintings on the walls.

It was hardly the backdrop for an orphan of the streets. It was opulent, yes, but so far away from *anything*. She wished she had known that.

The Countess was speaking now about rest from the wearying trip, and Senna tried to focus.

"I wanted to make things as easy as possible for you tonight," the Countess said, rising. "Charles will show you around tomorrow, of course, but meantime, your room . . ."

She motioned Senna up the broad staircase, with Charles right behind. Dominick trailed them, skimming the air high above their heads, watching as they escorted Senna to a room at the end of the second-floor hallway.

"Here we are," the Countess said, thrusting open the door and encouraging Senna to enter.

She stopped short on the threshold, totally beguiled by what she saw: the tester bed covered in rich velvet, the plump pillows, the tufted chairs, the lit fireplace—all unaccustomed luxury, and all for her.

She almost felt guilty. Or was it a rill of elation? She walked in slowly as Dominick swooped into the room and grabbed hold of the doorframe.

"Things will look a little brighter in the morning," the Countess promised from the threshold below. "I know it was an exhausting trip. Charles?" He lingered for a moment, his heated gaze caressing her face.

The door closed behind them.

Dominick heaved a deep breath, released the tension from his body, and spiraled down to the floor beside Senna, an incandescent mist swirling at her feet.

Senna didn't notice. She perched at the edge of the bed, stroking the coverlet. *Dear heaven.* Didn't indigent relatives sleep in the nursery or scullery or something?

And then there was Charles to wonder about. The Countess had said nothing about a son in her letter. A handsome, obviously eligible son. She'd said it was the two of them living here. The *two* of them. And now the "poor relation." Senna didn't feel all that poor enveloped in the velvet duvet of an unbelievably soft feather bed.

She must make it clear to the Countess that indigent relatives earned their keep.

But what if it turned out the Countess had something else in mind? Something to do with Charles.

She couldn't let him be an issue. The Countess had offered her a home and it was Senna's duty to discover what she could offer the Countess in return. From the look of it, she certainly wouldn't be polishing furniture or sewing in the servants' quarters.

Then what?

The question kept her awake a long time. She was almost certain she hadn't slept when a pounding at the door caused her to jolt upright, her heart thrumming.

"Miss?" a high-pitched feminine voice called to her, completely at odds with that heavy fist.

Oh, lord, morning maids too? Senna just managed to get to the door, open it a crack, and poke her head out.

"Good morning, miss." The girl was unforgivably cheery at this hour of the morning. "The Countess invites you to join her for breakfast in the small parlor, miss. Do you need some help dressing?"

"No, thank you," Senna murmured as she closed the door. This was too much—indigent relations did not rate maid service.

Nor the deliciously hot water in the ewer, which had unobtrusively been brought into her room while she'd slept. Or her second-best dress freshly pressed and hanging on the built-in cupboard door she hadn't noticed last night.

There was a lot she hadn't noticed last night, she found. She hadn't noticed the bank of windows overlooking the gardens or the little tables scattered here and there, convenient for a book or a pot of tea.

Her plan had worked too well. It worried her. Fifteen minutes face-to-face on arrival was no true test of her acceptance by the Countess. There would inevitably be more questions. There might even be subtle tests to prove Senna was whom she claimed.

Did the Countess even care?

She might see the advent of an unknown and needy relative as a means to obtaining an unpaid companion, given she was an elderly woman, more or less living alone, and irrespective of her handsome son.

That probably was the way to play it, Senna decided. She could read, so they might spend hours immersed in a good novel; she could converse on general topics of interest if necessary; and if desperate for some alternative way to entertain, as a last resort she could read the cards or the Countess's palm.

Or maybe not. That reeked of the street, and that was the last thing she wanted. It occurred to her suddenly that she had been un-usually careless about the consequences of this deception. Or maybe she'd been so giddy her long shot had worked, she wasn't thinking with her usual sharp wits about what came after.

She hadn't given the least thought to what would happen if the Countess caught her, if she needed to get away quickly and secretly. She had no way out, she realized suddenly, and the most important thing for a successful con was an alternative plan, a necessary escape route.

She knew why too: she'd been so utterly stupefied by the el-egance and wealth the furnishings in the hallway alone represented that every other concern had dissipated into a dizzying euphoria at having pulled off the deception.

And now, she'd endure the next test: breakfast with the Countess. She needed every ounce of concentration and every strategy she'd ever learned to convincingly play this role.

The maid directed her to the small parlor at the rear of the house, where the doors stood open invitingly. Senna could see it was just as opulently furnished as the rest of the house. The Countess was already seated in a wing chair that was turned away from the harsh morning sun flowing in through the windows.

Senna made certain that Charles was not present before she entered the room, a swirl of mist trailing behind her. "Ma'am?"

"Come in, come in. Everything is laid out on the table. Help yourself and come sit by me."

Everything meant warming trays with eggs, ham, bacon, toast, scones, oatmeal, jam, butter, fruit, and tea. Senna took a deep breath, dished out some food, and steeped a cup of tea. Then she gingerly made her way to the chair opposite the Countess, who was nursing a crust of toast.

Dominick swirled his way under Senna's chair, invisible as a breath.

"I hope you slept well," the Countess said.

"Tolerably well," Senna answered without thinking, busying herself with stirring sugar into her tea. "And you?"

"Of course," the Countess went on as if Senna hadn't spoken, "the first night in a new place may make one feel uncomfortable. Nothing is familiar. There are strange sounds. You don't know your way around. But"—she sipped her tea—"that will pass."

She looked up at Senna and smiled, and Senna covertly studied her face. There was nothing to fear there—the pale white, unlined face; the deep set, pale blue eyes; the somewhat prominent nose; the thin old-lady lips. She was dressed in high-collared black bombazine topped with a thin black shawl, her graying hair tucked beneath a widow's cap. She wore no jewelry, nothing superfluous.

"What if it doesn't?" Senna asked suddenly, boldly—stupidly, even. Or maybe she was looking for a way out before she even made the commitment.

Dominick swirled impatiently under the chair.

The Countess smiled again, although this time it didn't quite reach her eyes. "How can you know if you've only just arrived?" she asked gently.

No arguing that point. "Of course, you're right," Senna murmured.

There was silence for a few minutes as she ate with real gratitude. After a lifetime of awful food, the beautifully fried eggs, the perfectly browned toast, and the lovely crunchy bacon tasted heavenly. She tried not to greedily devour what was on her plate.

She suddenly became aware of the Countess watching her.

"So," the Countess said at last, "it must be comforting to be among family."

The fiction continues.

Senna's every instinct prickled. "Yes, it is."

"They were about to send you to Kearnsgate, the solicitor wrote."

"They were. Though I might not have gone."

"It's not a place for a beautiful young girl," the Countess murmured with some sympathy.

"I've always earned my keep," Senna said sharply.

"Well, of course."

"And I wonder if you've considered how I might"—Senna searched for a tactful phrase—"repay you for your kindness in taking me in."

"Had your mother ever discussed family?"

Senna went very still. The question she'd dreaded.

Maybe she hoped the paper-thin lie would become the truth without any qualifications.

"She never wanted to discuss family," Senna said finally, hoping the answer seemed probable. "There was just something about family that one didn't ask." She invented fairy tales, after all. One couldn't run a good ruse without a good story. She just had to be careful not to overdo details and hope there was just enough truth in the lie that the Countess wouldn't question any of it below the surface.

"She had made a clean break, after all," Senna went on, making it up as she went. "And in such an atmosphere, one did not ask. But, when she was dying, she . . ."

"Of course," the Countess murmured sympathetically. "She'd hope even a long-disconnected cousin might offer to help. One does have one's pride. I know how hard it was for you to ask."

"It was very hard," Senna murmured. "Truly, it was a last resort . . ."

A tear would do now, clever girl. Even the bloody Countess isn't immune to tears.

"Still, now you're here, I understand you might feel some hesitation," the Countess went on. "But, as I said, that will pass as we get to know each other better. And after all, you really have no other recourse, do you?"

The cold-blooded bitch, hemming her in with guilt.

"No," Senna said slowly, feeling the verbal smack of the ruler, a subtle reminder of what she was and to whom she was beholden. Charity always came with strings; but she mustn't forget she had willingly put herself at the Countess's mercy.

There was only one tack to take after that.

"I'm truly grateful," Senna went on. "I could have woken up in Kearnsgate this morning instead of here at the Manor. I only wish to be useful to you."

She's already planned what use you can be, my pretty.

"And so you shall be," the Countess said. "I have something very specific in mind." She held Senna's gaze for a long moment. "But you must excuse me now, my dear. I tire so easily in the morning."

She rose up, pulled her shawl over her head, and nodded to Senna. "We'll talk more later." And she glided from the room.

Senna sank back into her chair. *Just like that? A welcome, a chiding, and good-bye?* She could almost believe she'd imagined the whole conversation.

But then, there was the part about the Countess's having something "very specific" in mind for Senna.

Senna suddenly had a pulsing sense that someone was watching her. She bolted from her chair, scanning the room for something, anything, she'd missed.

The sense of a presence was so strong, so pervasive. It could be anywhere—the room was furnished wall to wall with tufted sofas, chairs, occasional tables, heavy curtains at the windows, and who knew what cubbyholes in which someone could hide.

Or perhaps someone lurked in the gardens, visible through the floor-to-ceiling windows and accessible through double glass doors.

Who could it be?

She caught a movement out of the corner of her eye as she made her way into the hallway. A shadow? Dust?

The maid. It had to be the maid. Or that butler—Whitton? And there was a cook, obviously.

Even so, the house felt eerily deserted.

This is crazy. This beautiful house. This very agreeable old lady who hardly asked any questions at all.

Senna felt as if she'd ducked an arrow.

What am I thinking?

I need a way out, just in case.

I'll just . . . go outside and see what I can see.

She pulled the door open just a crack and wedged her body out into the chill morning.

The sun glare almost blinded her. Shielding her eyes, she moved into the curve of the driveway and turned to look at the house.

In daylight, she saw it was built of brown stone, set low to the ground, and surrounded by trees, lawns, gardens, and bushes denuded now by the winter cold. An arched stone was molding over the double-door entrance, with just a faint hint of a medieval castle in the crenellated roofline at the corners.

Shadowed against the sun with the morning wind blowing dust all around, the house seemed both imposing and isolated. But surely Senna only felt that way because it was so far from London and so new.

She had nothing to fear. The Countess seemed to have accepted her story—and her—and now they'd form a routine, perhaps go to Town now and again.

As she started walking back toward the house, someone grabbed her waist from behind. She wrenched her body in the opposite direction as dust blew up all around him, obscuring his vision, hampering his breathing. His grip loosened as he coughed.

It *was* him, Charles. A split second of hesitation gave her the opening and the momentum to run. Senna went on and on until she rounded the long corner of the Manor, heading for the carriage house and stables.

Nobody there. No way out. She couldn't drive a carriage or ride a horse anyway. How could there be nobody there?

She scrambled out to the dooryard, where, suddenly, in the middle of the nearest gardens, a figure appeared, shrouded in black, hooded, and moving like a dirge across the landscape.

A gardener, surely, protecting himself against the sun. Someone who could help her. She started to run toward the figure, her feet hitting small hard objects. A rough gust of wind pushed her forward and dust swirled around her, blurring her vision.

She suddenly couldn't see.

She couldn't . . .

But I saw—and I transposed her successfully from there to here, nightmare to reality—even if she doesn't yet understand.

"She's like that in the morning," a voice said from a distance.

Senna looked up, feeling disoriented and sun-blinded, and for a moment as if she'd been in the midst of a nightmare. But, no, she was still seated in the small parlor. The Countess had just departed and Charles was lounging in the doorway.

Senna shook herself. She *was* in the house; she wasn't dreaming. It *was* Charles on the threshold, and he was as real as the figure in her dream who had grabbed her.

Except that hadn't been real, had it?

This Charles did not seem threatening in the least.

"She tends to be abrupt when she needs her nap," he added. "You'll get used to it." He dropped into the wing chair the

Countess had vacated. "Did you enjoy your breakfast? Can you cook? Our cook specializes in very plain fare. You could be very useful there. You did say you wanted to be useful?"

He was too charmingly innocent by daylight, and too handsome for his own good, with his dark, roguish hair and his direct, pale blue gaze so like the Countess's. He was too sure of himself on top of that and too ready to please.

Was this the real Charles? Or was he the Charles who had scared her witless moments ago?

She couldn't shake the sense that it had been real, that someone had chased her. But she must have imagined the whole thing.

"You eavesdropped," she accused him as she realized what he'd said.

"Did I? I should think that would be very bad manners. The Manor is not a bad place, Senna. I'll grant you it's not a great piece of architecture, and it's fairly small and isolated by country-house standards, but it came at a good price and Mother was lucky to find it. We'll take a walk after breakfast—dare I ask what there *is* for breakfast?"

Your blood and guts on a silver salver, brother betrayer.

Charles peered at her plate. "Oh, God, the usual. Cook comes from the village every morning, you know. It's the same thing every day. Ah, well, scones and tea again." He turned to her as he poured his tea.

Senna watched him carefully. He was being just as charming as cheese and exerting himself to be pleasant and reassuring.

Don't . . . trust . . . him, Dominick willed her.

All she had to do was forget the dream and put away her reservations and charm him back.

It was easy to do with the bright sun pouring in, and everything warm and cozy. Finding a way out didn't seem so critical anymore.

Don't listen to him.

She'd imagined her gut-scared dash outside, and her conversation with the Countess seemed more fraught than it had really been.

"The woman cannot make a decent pot of tea," Charles was

saying. "I think now that you're here, we must make an effort to at least find someone who can do a decent tea."

She really had pulled it off, Senna thought with just a little feeling of wonderment. Even Charles seemed convinced. The unexpected son was actually no more a threat than a puppy dog. He might even turn out to be her savior.

He took a futile sip of his tea, set it down, and held out his hand. "Come. Let me show you around the Manor."

Dominick had transfigured his body back into the bat shape in which he was most comfortable, and now he glided above them, tightly controlling his urge to take Charles and commit mayhem on him. The bastard.

Charles was coming to grips with the idea of marrying Senna and having a child with her. *Well, he could grip all he wanted,* Dominick thought grimly. Charles was in for a battle, and this was just the opening play. Sometimes being a monster had its advantages.

Charles took her first to the library, which was at the back of the house, opposite the small parlor, and filled floor to ceiling with books, comfortable chairs, and a desk anchoring the center of the room.

"Help yourself anytime. The previous owners were avid book collectors. Do you care to read?"

"I actually thought I might read to your mother," Senna said.

Dominick almost fell off the bookshelf where he'd perched.

The mother from hell creates her own fiction.

"I'm sure she'd like that," Charles said. He plucked a random book from the shelf. "Ah, Dickens. That should take forever." He opened it and a piece of paper fluttered out.

Senna reached for it before he did, but he snatched it from her hand and turned to replace the book on the shelf, his face drained of color.

She dearly wanted to ask what was printed on the piece of paper that clearly caused him such strife.

Charles took her arm and led her out into the hallway as if nothing had happened. "Come, the music room next."

It was just beyond the library and more sparsely furnished than the other rooms. There was an out-of-tune piano, and chairs lined the walls, suggesting that at one time the room had hosted musicales and guests.

Senna ran her fingers over the keyboard.

"Do you play?" Charles asked.

"I pretend," she said, yet another of her many "talents." She struck a chord and rolled out a harmonizing melody line. "You see?"

"I see," Charles murmured.

You're blind, Dominick muttered to himself.

Senna continued playing.

"What do you think the Countess has in mind for me?" she asked idly. "Besides reading novels, I mean."

Charles's pale gaze focused on her hands. "Maybe she's thinking I'd marry you and have children."

Senna crashed the keys. "Are you asking?"

Charles quickly covered himself. "No, I was jesting."

You were testing, you bastard.

She tapped out a simple melody.

"Is the thought so awful?" he asked silkily.

The blood roared in Dominick's veins, fury swelled through him, and he didn't think, he reacted. He dove down, clipped Charles's forehead, and vanished in a flit.

"Good God, what was that?" Charles touched his forehead and wiped away a pinprick of blood.

Dominick roared into the shadows. The blood he coveted, the blood of his line, his brother, his redemption, his death—he could almost see it, touch it, taste it—and he could do nothing to ameliorate the driving need to take it and avenge himself.

He could see all the considerations playing in Senna's mind as Charles stared at the smear of blood on his fingers. Her eyes darted from him to Charles's jacket pocket where he'd stuffed that mysterious paper.

It wasn't enough to hover in the shadows, waiting for the moment. Dominick needed to force the issue and manipulate the play. His first message wasn't quite enough, it seemed.

He followed closely as Charles took her outside.

"Do you ride?" Charles asked her.

"Circumstances did not permit," she answered blithely. "I would love to learn."

They walked out into the dooryard and toward the winter-bare gardens. Just as in her dream, her foot kept hitting things, rocks, she thought, until she saw that scattered all about were the bodies of small animals.

"I think I've seen enough," she murmured, tugging on Charles's arm.

He caught her hesitation, saw what made her cringe. "Oh, the damned fox again. He's been an absolute plague. I'll get after the groundskeeper. You should never have seen that."

He steered her back in the opposite direction, making light conversation as they returned to the house.

He took her through the rest of the quarters, gave her time to admire the furnishings, the paintings, the decorative items. He even knew to a farthing how much it all was worth.

Senna took careful note. She never knew what might be useful in a con, and she'd been too careless already. A small piece of rare porcelain or a silver goblet could be converted to money in a pinch. The thought emboldened her as Charles escorted her back to her room to rest.

She lay in bed, her mind racing. The idea that Charles had floated, that his mother might have it in mind that they marry, rolled around in her mind. It would be a hugely successful finish to a truly well played deception. The happiest ending, complete with handsome prince, his Cinderella delivered by her own devices right to his front door.

It made too much sense. Charles had been dead serious, even as he'd pretended he wasn't. She had to decide how far she was willing to take things.

By her own morality, as far as she could, though she'd never contemplated the idea of a husband as the final reward for her cleverness.

Although maybe she hadn't been so clever. There were things to be wary of at Drom Manor: the Countess's too ready acceptance of Senna's story, for one. The Countess could very well have her own agenda. Marriage and a grandchild might be the least of it, or, if the Countess knew Senna was lying, the whole purpose.

But that didn't wash either. A family of this social stratum would not seek out an impoverished relation as a possible bride. It didn't make sense.

Nevertheless, she'd passed the first hurdle—she'd gotten in the door. The rest would be revealed in due course.

At dinner that night, the Countess said, "I should like to tell you a little about your immediate family."

"She means us," Charles interpolated.

They were seated at one end of a long mahogany table in the elegant dining room just across the hallway from the parlor. The table was set with fine china and silver and illuminated by candlelight.

Dominick hovered in the shadows, wondering what the Countess would say.

Whitton served the meal with the help of the cheery maid who had summoned Senna to breakfast. Soup first, an elegant vichyssoise; then a leg of mutton with vegetables, steamed potatoes, and freshly baked bread.

"We've lived here for more than twenty years," the Countess began as the meal commenced. "Originally, our family occupied my husband's family seat, a very commodious country house near the coast. My sister came to live with us there. And then my husband died. And subsequently my sister. And then our daughter. I don't believe I've finished grieving for them yet.

"There's a painting of my sister in the small parlor you might have noticed. And then"—the Countess looked at Charles for a long moment—"the house burned down. My oldest son, Nicolai, died in that fire. It was almost unbearable."

"Mother adored Nicolai," Charles said. "She adores me, of course. But he was the eldest. He was golden. She had such high hopes."

"Now they're all pinned on you," the Countess added acerbically. "We never did find out how the fire started. It was very mysterious. It happened in the summer, you know. It wasn't as if there were a clogged flue or a fireplace left unattended. There was just no explanation."

Truly there was, Mother, Dominick thought viciously.

"Nor could we rebuild. The cost was prohibitive. So we had to leave"—the Countess's voice caught—"leave the ruins, leave Nicolai. My dear boy. But luckily we found Drom and we've been settled in here ever since."

"I see," Senna murmured, just a little chilled by the Countess's matter-of-fact accounting of what had to have been an immense tragedy.

"So what I had in mind for you," the Countess went on, "if you'd be so kind . . . I want to write my memoirs, and I'd like you to take my dictation and ultimately transcribe it into a manuscript."

Senna felt a letdown that was almost as sudden as falling off a cliff. *Take notes? Every day? About the Countess's dead family and burned-out life?*

"Of course," she agreed anyway. "It would be my pleasure."

"Good, then that's settled."

But as Senna got ready for bed that night after another half hour of meaningless conversation over evening tea, she felt even more disconcerted by the whole tenor of the day. She considered how Charles's suggestion of the Countess's motives had nothing to do with reality.

Taking dictation was not what she'd expected, but the task was hardly onerous. She could be of service to the Countess in a way that obligated her to no more than decent penmanship and the patience to listen. Charles's presence at Drom didn't mean anything after all.

She settled into bed, thinking she ought to be grateful. But was she truly grateful to build a new life on a falsehood? She'd done that all her life, though, so this was no time for her conscience to hiss with disapproval.

The problem was that this situation was too good to be true, and her instincts were on alert.

Was the problem the random flits of movement on the wall she'd noticed recurring? Or was she just disturbed by the thought of the kind of fire that could burn down a country estate? Or the dead husband, daughter, sister, *and* son? That many deaths in so short a time, in one family, in one place, seemed suspicious.

There was a faint scuffling sound in the hallway. Footsteps, she thought.

She was dreaming again; she had to be.

Then she heard a deep yawling sound in the distance. Eerie, like the deep keening cry of an elephant, echoing somewhere far beyond the walls, the fields, the sky.

No, she was imagining it. There was no other explanation.

Dead silence filled the room suddenly, long and protracted.

She waited, listening. Then, a papery whisper sounded faintly, high in the ceiling. Like flies, buzzing . . .

A saint couldn't sleep. She swung her legs over the edge of the bed, her feet coming down hard into a swirling mist covering the floor.

She stopped. What on earth was she doing? The Countess had told her what it was—the odd sounds and creaking and cracking of a house she didn't know.

Don't let that comfort you, Dominick thought.

And it could be the nearly invisible household help in what seemed to be an eerily empty house. Even now, maids could be taking clothes to be pressed, water to be heated, cleaning rooms like elves in the night, surreptitiously opening and closing doors so as not to wake anyone.

None of that commonsense reasoning reassured her.

Then she heard it again: the deep elephantine bawl echoing all over as if it came from the mouth of the devil.

She couldn't just lie there listening to the noises, imagining the worst, and hoping to fall asleep. She reached for the nearest candle, but hesitated.

What am I doing?

Something. I'm doing something. I can't lie here and do nothing.

A moment later, she opened her bedroom door to complete darkness.

That gave her pause. There wasn't a candle or a sconce lit anywhere. Everything was still and dead silent, as if a moment before there hadn't been a terrifying animal sound.

She propped the door open and lit another candle, which she placed on a table. Light, faint as it was, was much more comforting than anything her mind could conjure up.

And why weren't Charles and the Countess up and about investigating the noise?

It was so dark, and the sudden silence was so stark. Fear skittered along her veins as she made her way carefully down the hallway.

Doors angled inward in little alcoves along the corridor, revealing beautifully furnished bedrooms, she saw, as she opened them one after the other.

She closed another bedroom door and wheeled around abruptly at a high-pitched screaking sound.

Dear heaven. Anyone's imagination would run wild, skulking in the dark by candlelight. She should not be sneaking around like this. She felt as if shadows were watching. She felt the heavy weight of a ghostly presence again.

This was no better than huddling in the dark in bed.

She reversed direction and headed back down the hallway toward the glow emanating from her room. Dust swirled at her feet. Dust everywhere, following her, trailing after her.

Her feeling of urgency escalated. She was almost there. The thin shaft of light was a beacon straight ahead—and she barreled right into a solid body.

Her heart stopped and she dropped the candle. She heard herself scream and then felt two hands grasping her shoulders.

"Senna!"

The voice was real, the hands were corporal, and the face was sepulchral, hollowed out in shadows.

A ghost.

The dust swirled around her, choking her.

"Senna." His voice was calm. She had to stop shaking or he'd hold on to her forever.

"I'm . . ." She coughed slightly and swallowed hard. "I'm all right."

He relinquished her shoulders and picked up the candle.

"Were you looking for something?" *Or,* his tone implied, *someone?*

"I thought I heard a noise," she choked out.

"The old mausoleum creaking and groaning, maybe," Charles said easily. "Nothing to be scared of." He handed her the candle and turned her toward her room. She blinked, whirled around, and he was gone, vanished into the shadows as if he'd never been.

She held up the candle but all she saw was shadows.

She paced away from her room slowly. This was beyond strange. Drom at night was rife with mystery. Where had Charles disappeared to?

She turned back toward her room, feeling with every step that someone was watching her. Resigned, she entered her room and stopped dead in her tracks, her heart dropping to her feet.

Something was draped over the foot of her bed.

Something she recognized instantly: the shawl that the Countess had worn this morning. And caught in the fine knit was a folded piece of paper, a flash of white in the dim candlelight.

Senna froze. There was no reason for the shawl to be there unless the note tangled in the threads was meant for her to find, to read. It looked just like the note that Charles had snatched away from her in the library.

She moved forward, inch by inch by inch, listening, feeling. The palpable sense of someone in the room was almost overwhelming.

No matter. She touched the shawl and lifted up the edge closest to the note. She folded the note over so she could read it:

I'm watching you.
Nicolai

Nicolai—the Countess's adored older son. Nicolai—the son who died.

Chapter 3

I'm watching you.

A message from the dead.

Senna felt chilled to the bone. She huddled the whole night in one of the tufted chairs, the shawl and the note clenched in her hands, determined not to sleep. There were mysteries to be solved, such as where this note came from. And how, among the books he might have chosen, had Charles taken the very one with a note inside? And was this the same note? And if the dead Nicolai was writing notes, was he even really dead?

Senna could have sworn she hadn't slept, yet, in the morning, she was jolted awake once again by the cheerful maid pounding on the door, and her hands were empty. The shawl and the note were gone.

She almost asked the maid, but it occurred to her she'd be accusing the maid of taking something that obviously didn't belong to Senna in the first place.

Her best dress hung, freshly pressed, on the closet door. The water in the pitcher was hot. The maid was unfailingly helpful and willing. The Countess would be waiting in the small parlor, just as she had the day before.

Nothing was different except it was a gray and gloomy day punctuated by a distant boom of thunder now and again.

How fitting.

I'm watching you.

Nestled neatly in the folds of the curtains shrouding the tester bed, Dominick stretched out a tentative wing. *Watching you. Watching them.*

More than that, he'd scared the hell out of Charles with that note, which had its own satisfaction. Charles understood exactly what the note meant: that Dominick could be anywhere. Everywhere. And nothing he did was a secret anymore.

The Countess, of course, never wanted to know what Charles was doing, but Dominick had deliberately played upon Charles's fear that his brother's thirst for vengeance was merely waiting for the tipping point.

Charles would be on his best behavior. He wouldn't confide in the Countess about the note, preferring, Dominick was certain, to let his mother discover the return of her long-mourned son on her own.

As she would. When the girl settled in and the Countess was less distracted, she would scent his presence, feel but a sliver of his volcanic rage, and know he had not come back out of any filial devotion to her.

Be wary, Mother. Be very very wary.

He watched dispassionately as Senna searched for the shawl and the note that he had removed from her hands in the depths of the night. Her confusion was palpable, but it settled into resignation that her imagination was running rampant again and everything inexplicable was the result of her fevered dreaming.

He'd done what he'd set out to do. He'd piqued Senna's curiosity, and the Countess would stoke it still more if she continued this ridiculous charade of dictating her memoirs.

But she would, until the moment that Charles fell in wholeheartedly with her plan for an heir. His mother was nothing if not determined.

Charles was halfway there already, seeing the union as a transient normalizing of his life, which for him would be a new and unique experience.

In the usual course of events, it would last all of a week, Dominick thought caustically, by which time Charles would have expected his seed to root, and then the girl would have nine months to come to terms with her fate.

It would give Dominick no greater pleasure than to demolish that plan, destroy his mother's every hope of propagating the bloodline, while desecrating the girl's virgin body with the taint of his own blood-soaked seed.

He couldn't wait. He needed only to find the perfect moment to move in and abduct her.

He watched as Senna washed and dressed and got ready to face the Countess and today's spurious seduction. He felt her puzzlement as she looked for a mirror so she might comb her hair.

Second clue, my pretty.

But she'd never believe it. Not until he hooked her with the reality that Nicolai had not died. He didn't have all that much time either. He felt the Countess's pulsating need to get Charles mated quickly, before he began lusting after Senna for other reasons. Dominick was certain that the Countess would remind Charles day by day of the cost of not keeping her needs in sight.

So little time for either of them to perfect their plans. They were locked in combat—although she didn't know it yet—to preserve something they each needed to survive.

He wondered, as he pushed off the bedpost curtains to follow Senna, which of them would win.

Thunder rumbled as Senna tiptoed into the library and closed the door softly behind her, just missing Dominick as he flitted in above her.

She had mere minutes; perhaps that was all she needed.

All those books. Floor-to-ceiling books. Of them all, Charles had chosen a volume of Dickens—he hadn't said which book—he'd just opened it and the note fell out.

She knew the thought that nagged at her: Had he done it on purpose? Did he want her to believe Nicolai had not died?

Because how could Charles have chosen the only book in which there was a note?

You are wise to be suspicious, my pretty, Dominick thought.

Her hands turned to ice as she pulled a random book from the shelf and opened it.

A note fell out, and she dropped the book.

I'm watching you. Nicolai.

No! She took another, opened it, a note fell out. And another, and another. In every book there was a note, as if whoever had set out to scare Charles wanted to be certain he got the message.

Who had put that shower of paper into those books?

Oh, God. Her little expedition had proved nothing at all and had scared her half to death.

Now what? She didn't have time to crawl around and pick up every piece of paper. She swiped a handful and shoveled them under the rug, then decided to leave the library door closed and try to come back after breakfast.

Breakfast—could she even pretend to be calm enough to have breakfast with the Countess and Charles?

She girded herself and entered the small parlor to find that the Countess had not yet arrived. Charles fussed by the sideboard, plate in hand, obviously awaiting her appearance.

Dominick darted to the wall molding and positioned himself head down.

Charles looked up. "Good morning, Senna. I hope you slept well."

"I—" She thought of mentioning the noises, but then she'd told him all about them last night. It didn't seem he remembered that conversation or that she'd been roaming the upper hallway like a ghost.

She couldn't tell him about what she'd found in the library.

From above, Dominick read her hesitation.

Good thinking, my pretty. Never say too much; it would be so disappointing to find he doesn't remember because it wasn't Charles you encountered in the hallway last night.

But it had to be Charles she'd talked to last night, Senna thought. Of course, it was Charles. But he was acting as if nothing had happened.

Perhaps that was what aristocrats did, to avoid unpleasant topics and unwanted explanations.

"Well enough," she said finally, answering his question.

"Good. Then take your plate. It seems this morning we have a little more imagination at work. Look—shirred eggs, kedgeree, fruit, biscuits, even hot chocolate. It's a breakfast banquet."

He served them both and pulled his chair closer to hers.

"So here we are. Do you suppose Mother planned that we should be alone together this morning?"

The observation startled her, coming so close to his suggestion yesterday of the Countess's having a motive other than offering a home to an impoverished relation.

Oh, no, you son of a bitch. Things were moving much faster than Dominick had anticipated, and he felt, right then, like clipping Charles in his vitals, sucking all the blood from his body, and leaving him sapped, suppurating, and dead.

He clamped down on that impulse as Senna responded.

"I think your mother slept late this morning," she said tartly, taking an emphatic bite of her biscuit.

I think my mother is exhausted from her hunt last night.

Still, Senna wondered if the Countess could even consider a union between an unknown distant relation and her son. Charles probably just wanted to goad his mother by speaking so irresponsibly to Senna about such things.

"It's raining hard now," Charles said after a few moments. "Which means we're landlocked today, so we have to entertain ourselves. You'll play piano for us, and Mother will natter on about the family for hours, no doubt."

Which meant no time to sneak in and clean up the scattered notes. "And what will you do?" Senna asked curiously.

"Be bored. Unless you choose to entertain me."

There could be no mistaking what he meant, and the most feminine part of Senna responded. Why wouldn't she? He was the son of a countess who lived a most luxurious life deep in the country and was handsome and charming in his own right.

What woman wouldn't be flattered—at least a little—by his interest?

Maybe . . .

No maybes, my pretty. Fate has decreed it is not to be.

It was too soon to think that way. She'd accomplished enough just by the Countess's invitation to live with her. And there were no guarantees just how long it would last.

Outside, the sky had darkened still more and thunder rumbled ominously. The look in Charles's eyes deepened and he leaned forward.

"Can you think of something we could do to entertain ourselves today?"

Dominick saw blood and death, and nothing between. No thought, no temperance, nothing but a flaming urge to kill. He sped downward from his perch, as invisible as a bullet homing into its target, and dug his claws into Charles's hand, deep and hard enough to draw blood yet again, and in a flit, he landed on the window frame, where he watched the scene below like a vengeful god. A little deeper and Charles would have been his in eternity. Deeper still, and he'd be dead.

Remember me, brother dear, because if you touch her . . .

But he himself had to remember: pain all around for those who created pain without a moment's consideration of the consequences of their actions.

Still, he did enjoy watching Charles bent over, moaning in pain, his mother just entering the room, and rushing to his side, Senna calling for the maids, cold water, and compresses.

Creating chaos had its own pleasures, along with hearing Charles's so audible curses.

Finally, after his hand was slathered in salve and bandaged, Charles calmed down.

"My dear," the Countess said consolingly. "What do you think it was?"

"I don't know—an insect, a bee. Hell, it hurts."

"I will have the groundskeeper root out the hive," the Countess assured him.

"Now," Charles snarled.

"As you wish." The Countess summoned Whitton and gave instructions that the hive was to be destroyed.

No, Mother, you don't understand. The destroyer is in your house, your bosom, your blood, and intends to take apart your world as well.

"Let us adjourn to the library," the Countess said. "I wish to begin outlining my memoirs, and the things I don't want to forget."

Senna stiffened. There was no way she could dissuade the Countess from working in the library. And so, she would enter the room, see all the notes on the floor, and who knew what she would do on this evidence that Nicolai might be alive.

"Why is the door closed?" the Countess asked rhetorically as she thrust it open. "No fire? No light? Where's the maid? We have work to do."

Senna edged her way into the room, her heart nearly pounding out of her chest. But nothing was amiss. No books were awry. Every volume she had dropped was now back on the shelf. And no pieces of paper were scattered on the floor.

Dominick had the unchecked urge to laugh as he listened to his mother's expurgated memories.

She was of Middle-European descent, but she didn't specify which country. She had married the Count in her early twenties, given birth to Nicolai, and lost her husband when Nicolai was a mere five years old.

This gave Senna pause. "You were married once before?"

"Did I not mention that yesterday?" the Countess asked dismissively. "Do let me continue."

Her second husband, Mr. Sandston, had come into her life when he'd been on his grand tour. They'd fallen in love, married quickly, come to England shortly after, and settled with Nicolai in the house that had eventually burned down. She'd borne her daughter, Irina, had brought her sister to England, given birth to Charles, then seen the death of her second husband, her sister, her daughter, and her eldest son in the space of the next ten years.

At that point, she'd taken back the surname of the Count, and having found Drom Manor, had lived a quiet, contemplative life all the years since, mourning her losses, particularly her brilliant eldest son.

"Am I speaking too fast?" she asked Senna, who was seated at the desk, writing down her every word.

"That's fine," Senna said. "Go on."

"I'm bored," Charles said.

"Well, *you* know the whole history," the Countess snapped. "Do let me continue. The fire was just devastating. My husband was already gone, my daughter, my sister . . . but then I lost Nicolai and everything else that mattered. Everything burned. Everything I loved was gone. It was almost unbearable. I—still feel the weight of it."

"What was he like? Nicolai, I mean," Senna asked as she kept writing.

"He was a god," Charles answered for his mother. "He was everything good, gracious, and holy. He was a beautiful saint. Mother revered him, worshipped him, it's safe to say."

"Nonsense, I loved you both equally."

"Yes, Mother."

No, Mother, Dominick thought. Charles had the right of it. Charles had murdered his whole family because of it. Charles wanted to be the saint, but he'd never been able to rein in his homicidal nature.

Charles had killed everyone his mother loved.

He would not be patient with the girl. She probably wouldn't hold his attention longer than it took for him to spill his seed.

Dominick saw that Charles's interest was waning. It was time to jolt him back to reality again, time to make the girl understand what was really going on before he acted.

Not easy to do when you were compacted into a bat body or deconstructed into a swirling mist.

"I'm tired," the Countess said suddenly. "You'll have to excuse me."

"I'll stay here," Senna said. "I want to make a good copy of my notes."

"I'll keep you company," Charles murmured.

The Countess shot him a skeptical look.

He stared back. "I'll read a book."

Something meaningful passed between them that even Dominick could sense because the Countess nodded and left them alone.

Devil's bones. Dominick wouldn't put it past the son of a bitch to try to seduce Senna right now. Time for drastic action. He had never transformed into an insect prior to this, but his need for speed and invisibility outweighed all other considerations, including that it might well kill him.

He needed space. He needed to reshape himself into flesh before he could reconfigure himself again. Damn and damn. Leaving Senna for even one minute alone with Charles could mean disaster after all those undercurrents. Charles would take advantage of any opening, any interest, any snip of conversation that he could read as an invitation.

Nevertheless, a quick movement and Dominick flitted into the hallway, in the shadow of the staircase, out of sight, and strenuously pushed his body outward.

God, that was enervating. With worse to come.

He could hear Charles pacing. The more impatient his steps, the shorter his attention span.

Dominick pushed himself upright and began the torturous trans-shaping downward—smaller, tighter, more compacted, within gossamer wings and fragile little legs. He took a tentative lift up . . . falling, falling—damn! *No—up* . . . supported by nothing, up—

"Are you just going to pace and distract me from my work?" Senna asked as she watched Charles irritably roaming the room.

"What work?"

"I'm copying my notes so your mother can read them."

"That would take all of five minutes. She said virtually nothing."

"It's a beginning," Senna said charitably.

"We can have a beginning," Charles said, stopping abruptly before the desk.

"I'm not writing a book."

"We can write our own story."

She did not like the direction of this conversation. "Really? And how would it end?" It seemed prudent to skip to the final chapter.

"Ah, but you can guess."

"I surely can. I would be on the streets, alone in my misery."

"There are no streets here. You're thinking beyond the page now, Senna. There's no reason not to . . . entertain each other as best we can in this mausoleum."

Yes, there was. Senna looked away and began copying the first lines of her notes.

A low, irritating hum sounded in her ear. It sounded like words—*Where are the mirrors?* But it couldn't be.

She ignored Charles—and the noise—and he began pacing again.

A fly buzzed around her head, annoying her. *Mirrors,* she heard again.

She looked up finally. "Charles, where are the mirrors?"

"What do you mean?"

"I mean, there are no mirrors, anywhere."

"I never noticed," he said coolly.

"Really?"

"Truly, is my mother, at her age, going to primp in front of a mirror? Am I? They're probably in storage somewhere. I'll have Whitton find one for you."

"I'd appreciate that." She noticed a sudden stiffness in him. He would not be goading and teasing her now. And why? Because of a mirror?

"I'll leave you to your notes," he said finally, trying to cover the awkward moment. "Mother will appreciate that clean manuscript. I'll see you at dinner."

And that was that. She must've been imagining his interest, his desire. Something about this house induced dreams and nightmares, neither of which had any truth in reality.

And she still hadn't found an escape route.

The fly buzzed around her again and she slapped it away.

Odd how she'd suddenly thought about the mirrors, when she hadn't been able to find one in her room this morning. There were none in the library either, or the hall, or even the parlor or dining room, that she remembered.

Charles had certainly reacted strangely to that question.

Dominick buzzed around her hair once again. Beautiful black, glossy hair. *The notes,* he buzzed in her ear. *The notes—*

His strength to hold tight in this minuscule body was nearly gone. He could almost see her parsing the problem of that blizzard of notes, and her curiosity growing about Nicolai's death.

Good, good, keep going, my pretty. You'll be mine yet.

The notes . . . the thought seeping into her mind. From the living dead?

But the Countess had said she and Charles came here after the fire and she'd plainly indicated that Nicolai hadn't survived the fire. Besides, she'd mourned him all these years.

So who had written the notes?

Why were there no mirrors?

And what about those noises last night?

They couldn't all have been dreams.

Keep thinking, my pretty.

She got up to look out the window. The rain was still pouring down in sheets, nearly obscuring the vista of the garden. Thunder rumbled continually; she'd been so preoccupied she'd barely noticed.

None of it makes sense, does it? she thought.

Maybe the Countess knew and could explain it.

But there had been no urgency in her recounting the story of Nicolai's death, and her emotions still seemed on the surface, seemed real. If the evidence of the notes proved he was still alive, surely she would've acted differently.

Senna climbed the steps to her room as thunder rolled and lightning cracked outside.

Dominick felt himself faltering, his musculature unable to sustain the tiny, buzzing insect body his first foray out. He landed on a picture frame, the worst place ever to disengage and regenerate.

Senna forged ahead, going over everything she knew.

Nicolai was dead. The Countess by her own account had pulled his burned, ravaged body from the ruins and buried him with her own hands. Had the Countess actually said that or was she filling in the blanks?

Senna entered her room to find the bed freshly made, the furniture polished, the hearth cleaned. Everything was pristine. But there was no mirror. She must ask Whitton to find one because Charles would most likely forget.

Where would she even find Whitton? If she remembered correctly, Charles had said the kitchen and staff stayed on the level below the main floor, which could be accessed through a door under the stairs.

So while the Countess and Charles were otherwise occupied, it might be a good time to take care of that.

She took a candle to light the dark hallway, as the rain poured, heavy as concrete, on the roof.

Dominick, on a second wind, buzzed high above her, the last of his strength and power concentrated on following her.

The house seemed unnaturally quiet in juxtaposition with the storm. She rounded the bottom of the staircase where sconces lit the lower hallway. There was only one way out of here: the front door. Simple.

But the entrance to the lower level was not so simple. There were three widely spaced and unobtrusive doors fitted into the long staircase wall.

Dominick perched on a step above the lintels, watching. This was the moment, although he barely had the strength.

The last door, my pretty.

He desperately needed to transform.

Open the door—now.

Senna hesitated. Lightning snapped across the front windows. No one was around, yet she knew servants were somewhere making certain everything ran smoothly.

The third *door* . . . If she didn't make a choice soon, Dominick would transform right before her very eyes. *Go, go*—he felt himself turning. *Go.*

Senna lifted the candle, reached for the knob of the third door, turned it, and entered.

She found herself on a landing, with a short flight of stairs ahead of her. She saw a faint light below, evidence that someone was there, and she started down the stairs.

It was not far enough down to house the kitchen, she thought. Maybe the servants' quarters were down here. Or her coveted secret escape route. She came to another landing and found that the light came from under a closed door directly to her left.

There was nowhere else to go from here except through that door. Senna knocked.

No answer. Though, maybe beyond the door there was just another hallway and no one had heard her knocking.

She tried the door. It opened with a soft creak.

She peered around the edge into a small room lit by a single candle in a sconce. The room contained one thing only—a tub—filled with what looked like mud.

She pushed the door open farther.

Something was in the tub.

A naked body.

Her whole being clenched in terror, and she couldn't move. What if she could do something to help? What if—

She took a shallow breath and edged closer. To her horror, it was the Countess, immersed in the filth, deathly pale and still as stone.

Senna froze again, but she gathered up all her nerve and knelt beside the tub to try to rouse the Countess.

She started screaming: the Countess's body felt as ice-cold and lifeless as the grave.

"Well," the Countess said, having summoned Senna to the small parlor an hour later. "I owe you an explanation. I gave you quite a fright, obviously."

Nearly scared her to death, Mother.

"Indeed, Countess," Senna murmured. *Fright* wasn't the word for it. She'd thought the Countess was lying in a dirt bath, dead. She'd thought—she didn't know what she thought. She hadn't fainted—someone had come, quelled her screaming, and led her away.

Charles—yes, it had been Charles—all murmurs and sympathy and petting her as if she were hysterical.

But she knew what she saw, what she felt, what was there. Yet, here was the Countess, fresh-faced, vibrant, and brusque, dressed as always in black, her shawl—the shawl in which the note from the dead Nicolai had been wrapped—draped over her head.

"We'll be having tea," the Countess said. "Tea is calming. It slows things down. Gives one a chance to reflect. We'll wait for the tea, and we'll talk."

Talk! Dominick nearly tumbled off the frame of the landscape where he perched in bat form. *I can't wait to hear how you wiggle away from this one, Mother.* But then, he must be grateful: all these machinations kept her so preoccupied, she'd had no time to train her senses on *him.*

Senna studied the Countess covertly. She was so alive sitting there, and yet, not hours ago, she'd been freezing cold and as close to dead as a living person could be. There was no explanation for it, and Senna had the feeling the Countess would, if she could, excise the image of it from Senna's memory.

"Ah," the Countess said, "here's Whitton."

In he came, carrying a large tray with a platter of sliced gingerbread, as well as a steaming teapot. He made a great fuss of setting it down and preparing everything, pouring tea for the Countess and making certain there were napkins and teaspoons and such until Senna felt like screaming all over again.

"Are you comfortable, my dear?"

Honestly, Mother—comfortable? After what she saw?

"Yes, most excellently comfortable," Senna said tartly.

The Countess was silent for a moment as she sipped and took a bite of the gingerbread. She gave Senna a quizzical look. "You must be so confused, my dear."

"You were dead," Senna said flatly.

The Countess gave her a benign look. "Well, it's actually very simple. What you saw was something common in my native country: I was taking a mud bath, a treatment that keeps the skin soft, supple, and ageless. You'll find me there, oh, twice a week at least. It's so relaxing, I nearly go into a trance, which lowers my body temperature. That is what happened earlier. I've been doing it for years." The Countess sipped her tea then and watched Senna's reaction.

It sounded reasonable, Senna thought. What did she know of foreign customs or of what a woman would do to maintain her looks or her body. It conceivably explained why the Countess's skin was so smooth, pale, and unlined.

Senna relaxed a little.

"I'm sure it was a horrible scare for you to come upon me like that," the Countess went on. "It made sense to put the tub near a source of water—that is, near the kitchen and laundry—since the treatment requires constant wetting down of the mud so it doesn't dry out."

"I see," Senna murmured. Like her strange dreams, this too was a major to-do about nothing. It just proved she ought not go exploring around a strange house and should instead just nurse her gratitude that her deception had worked so well and that she was safe for the time being.

Except she felt almost too comfortable to really feel at ease.

"Which brings me to something else I want to discuss with you." Dominick stiffened.

Not so comfortable. The Countess's tone had hardened just a bit, as if she were now getting down to business.

"Of course, Countess."

"It's Charles. And the fact that I'm an old woman now—"

Oh, bravo, Mother. Play on her sympathy for the elderly. And don't bother telling her you'll live forever.

"Not so old," Senna murmured.

"I want an heir. And Charles hasn't been all that inclined to settle down. But you seemed to have piqued his interest . . ."

Oh, surely the Countess couldn't mean what Charles had jokingly suggested? Senna's heart started pounding. "It's only because I'm convenient, Countess. And it's barely been two days. He couldn't possibly feel that kind of interest in just two days."

"You piqued his interest," the Countess went on inexorably, "and so I wonder—since our family connection is so distant, and none of us will live forever—if you would consider Charles as a husband."

"A husband?" Senna asked faintly.

"Charles is my only child, as you know. There's no one left. Except you—and him. My dearest wish is to see the bloodline carried forward. My dear"—the Countess leaned forward and touched Senna's hand briefly—"I know you could come to like him. He surely likes you."

Senna sat in stunned silence.

"I shouldn't be the one to ask," the Countess went on, "but I will. I need to know. Would you consider marrying Charles and giving him a child?"

Chapter 4

The Countess meant it.

Senna went very still, her every nerve ending tingling with caution. This was the problem with falling in love with the ruse and not considering the consequences. Or the possible obstacles.

Such as an unexpected living son, a long-dead son who might still be alive, and a marriage proposal from a mother who desperately wanted an heir.

The Countess had perpetrated her own deception—drawing someone she didn't even know into her web in the hope that she was presentable enough to offer to her son.

Charles hadn't been jesting, but she'd met men like him along the way, and she had a strong feeling that he was one who would seduce her, use her to placate the Countess, then toss her away. And she and the Countess had both acted to the hilt, discussing relations and elaborating on a family history that didn't exist.

Senna had been so full herself about the ruse working that she'd never considered it would end any other way but with her living in

some obscure part of her benefactor's home for the rest of her life—
or until she got bored and absconded.

She had nowhere to run now. Nowhere to go. No one to save her.

The Countess watched her expectantly, waiting for an answer.

She should look at it another way, Senna thought. There was
nothing to lose. The Countess, and by extension Charles, were
wealthy, if the luxuries of Drom were any indication. Charles was
personable, if enigmatic. He was handsome enough, and charming
when he chose to be.

Why wouldn't she want to marry him?

All the niggling little questions could probably be explained
away.

This was, on the surface, a fairy-tale chance at a life she would
never otherwise experience. Give Charles and the Countess an heir,
and their world and wealth would be hers forever.

So why had the Countess solicited an impoverished stranger to
become her son's wife?

The Countess leaned forward and patted Senna's hand. "I know
I've shocked you. But it shouldn't be that difficult to find the answer. You're already kin. This is just a step beyond and will give you
the security you've always coveted."

Senna slanted a look at the Countess under her eyelashes. *Already kin.* The Countess had no compunction about skating over
that thin ice and embracing the lie to convince Senna.

The Countess wanted her to marry Charles for her own reasons,
and she counted on Senna's having no reason to decline.

Instantly Senna felt trapped. She envisioned all the angles, and
there was just no graceful way out. She had no earthly reason to
refuse. The play had been taken out of her hands and she had no
control now unless she confessed the deceit.

Senna had the quick feeling the Countess would brush it off as
inconsequential. What if she said no? What kind of bribe would the
Countess put on the table? What could the Countess offer her in
the middle of nowhere?

Or she could say yes and figure out the rest later. By the look in the Countess's eyes, she was expecting nothing less.

"This won't be a wed-and-bed union," the Countess said finally. "Charles will court you as any man should."

Here was the first inducement.

"Two days should be enough. We'll schedule the wedding for Saturday."

Senna started to speak and the Countess held up her hand. "Obviously I have to act as a parent, as well as your prospective mother-in-law. This union will be good for all of us, Senna. You'll be richly rewarded when his seed has rooted."

Inducement number two.

"You'll be allying yourself with one of the oldest families in Middle Europe, my dear, bringing forth an heir to an illustrious heritage."

Number three.

"Be proud. Say, yes, you'll marry Charles. The rest will come later."

Senna took a wild look around her, but all she saw was a shadow slicing across the sun. Pieces of paper fluttering to the floor. Nicolai dead, maybe alive.

Same as she. No way out.

She met the Countess's pale, eager eyes and she nodded yes.

"So here I am, your wounded hero"—Charles held up his reban-daged hand as he strolled into the small parlor after the Countess departed to get ready for dinner—"ready to court, woo, and win you over. I believe Mother said I had two days."

"Surely an hour would be enough for you," Senna said, her tone tinged with sarcasm. She tilted her head abruptly as her attention was caught by a faint ruffling sound overhead.

"I'm sure you're right, but I have my orders." Charles settled himself opposite her and followed her gaze.

There was nothing to see. Dominick had expended his fury and hidden himself in the chandelier with a dip and a flit.

"So romantic," Senna murmured.

"Look—cards on the table. You and I are beyond romance. This is a business arrangement. She wants an heir. You need a home, a family, a life. It's a fair exchange. A lot of women marry for less."

"And what do you want?"

Oh, yes, dear brother, do let us hear what you want.

Charles gave her a knowing smile. "My wants are the least of it, but the truth? I get to bed you and walk away."

"That should be enough to tempt me," Senna said caustically, tamping down a rising fury that even Charles had a way out, *and* all the pleasure with none of the responsibility. "But surely there are many other eligible women who would be happy to bear your seed."

"You would think, wouldn't you? But then they would require all the lengthy and time-consuming courting, good manners, and family involvement. The bane of a man's existence. It's so much easier this way. By happenstance, Fate, good fortune, whatever you want to call it, you are the one chosen to have a part in the Lazlaric destiny."

Devil's bones, my pet, if you buy that—

"Oh, nonsense," Senna snapped, bolting out of her chair. Charles rose simultaneously and blocked her way.

"Why not?" he asked, grasping her shoulders. "Why not you?"

He had the Countess's pale blue eyes, but there was nothing empathetic in them. He wanted to kiss her, and just for an instant she wanted to let him. Just to see, just to feel for a moment that she was not being manipulated.

"Why not you?" he repeated roughly, his head tilting toward hers. "Tonight can be ours. Tonight we can try each other on. And if"—he touched her lips—"if we don't—"

She knew instantly what this was: the kiss of the seducer, the kiss he would take because he could, because she'd let him just to taste, just to . . .

"—fit"—his tongue swiped pointedly inside her mouth—"if"—he pushed deeper, commanding her response, and she was shocked that she felt pure revulsion because he was operating on pure gut need.

"—I'll help you—"

"Help?" she echoed on a breath as he bore down on her again.

"—get away."

The words reverberated through her body; she heard them loud and clear, and because she knew she couldn't leave, she pushed him away, abruptly and decisively.

"But I have a feeling that won't enter into it," he added, correctly reading the fury in her eyes. "Will it? I'll come to you tonight, and we'll—practice. Fitting."

"Oh, will we?" she said acidly. "You need not exert yourself in advance of the event. After all, you don't want me."

"Oh, you could be wanted, Senna, if I had the time to cultivate you. But all I need to do is plant my seed, and the sooner the better. The ceremony is, well, for Mother and you. If I had a say, it wouldn't occur until we were certain my seed has rooted. So to increase the odds, we'll practice."

He had made his way to the door. "Tonight. And tomorrow. And on our wedding day. By then, how could you *not* be pregnant?"

All he needed to do . . . the arrogance of him! Senna shook so hard with anger, the feeling of futility, and the knowledge that she'd stupidly done this to herself that she couldn't think clearly.

And that kiss—she shuddered. It was repulsive, reptilian.

She had a bad feeling deep in her gut. She sank back into the chair. Something besides the heated and obvious rubbed her the wrong way.

The lengthy and time-consuming courting. The bane of a man's existence—

That was it. The reason why he wanted *her*. The time-consuming courting. The need for manners, morals, formality, parents, church.

Better to find a green girl, even one operating on her wits and gross lies, and all the niceties could be bypassed.

Hadn't the Countess been quick to leap on that advantage? She'd been as honest as thieves with Senna: she wanted an heir and could wait no longer.

Adhering to courting protocols would take too long. And then what if Charles and his fiancée didn't suit? So much better to dangle the prospect in front of an impecunious and allegedly distant relation who could be bought with promises of wealth and security forever.

The Countess could then say the blood was there, the connection was there, but so distant it would barely show up on the family tree. She was certain that the weight of a legitimate marriage in Senna's circumstances would outweigh any feeling of being treated like a mere possession.

The Countess had been looking for her own mark, and she'd found it. Now Senna was neatly boxed into a corner.

It made Charles's specious promise to help her, should they not suit, utterly meaningless. He'd sooner get rid of her altogether, she thought with steaming clarity. Who would know?

For the first time in her life, she was pitted against an adversary who was older, wilier, and smarter than she. Someone who had, all along, had her own reasons for fabricating lies.

That's it, my pretty. Calm down, think it through, don't let her scare you. What you don't know, you don't need to know.

Well, the outer doors at Drom weren't locked, Senna thought determinedly. She wasn't trapped without a key. At worst, she could sneak out and just walk away.

"Miss?"

The idea was not all that realistic.

"Miss?"

The voice finally penetrated her thoughts and she looked up. Whitton. "Dinner, Miss. The Countess is waiting."

The Countess will devour you if you let her, you mean.

Senna had no time to change and barely time to gather her wits and act as if nothing were out of place. But if the Countess could do it, so could she. Charles would not penetrate her room tonight—she'd kill him first.

Everything else could wait till tomorrow.

❧

Only the Countess was seated at the table. "Sit, my dear. And don't look so worried. You've been with us barely forty-eight hours. Trust me that everything will turn out for the best."

By candlelight, nothing seemed dire. The soft illumination of the rich dark wood and glowing paintings was calming. Burnished pewter serving dishes, servants presenting her with soup, roast, and vegetables. It all was quite nice. The Countess made light conversation, demanding nothing of Senna but a nod of her head.

All this could be my life from now on—or I could steal some of the silver for something to barter. Or a weapon—

The Countess could be charming, as she was tonight, feigning a legitimacy between them that didn't exist. So bent on seducing her, Senna thought, eyeing her from beneath her lashes, that she wouldn't notice if a knife went missing.

A moment's sleight of hand and Senna felt more in control, while the Countess discussed in broad terms the wedding—in two days.

And Charles was supposed to court her when his only interest was rutting in her and planting a piece of himself forever.

Senna touched the long shank of the knife tucked in the folds of her dress.

I don't think so.

From the edge of a thick-gilt-framed painting, Dominick watched them both intently. His mother was at her most dangerous right now. The Countess wanted that union, she wanted that devil child, and if she couldn't have it, she'd kill Senna as surely as she nipped decisively around the edges of a piece of her roast.

Senna seemingly didn't notice any of it. She had no questions about his mother's eating habits, why she'd had no life pulse drowning in the mud, how there could be notes from the dead Nicolai in every book in the library, or all those dead furry things littering the grounds.

Nothing. It was as if she'd answered all the questions to her satisfaction, and anything else she didn't wish to know. Maybe that was for the best.

Finally, the dinner drew to an end. Thank goodness—he'd gotten damned tired holding his position, hanging on by a claw to the rococo swirls of gilt.

"We'll continue with my memoirs tomorrow," the Countess said as she rose from the table. "Saturday, of course, we're having a wedding." She reached across and patted Senna's hand.

Touch of the devil—and who will perform the vows, Mother? How will you explain the absence of a priest?

"Come, I'll walk you to your room, my dear." The Countess looped her arm through Senna's.

"It will be so nice to have this house filled with family," the Countess went on as she propelled Senna into the hallway and toward the stairs.

Dominick followed, a flit of shadow above.

"A child in the house again," the Countess continued rapturously as they climbed the steps. "So long absent from our lives"—she looked up as she felt something brush by her hair—"how happy that makes me to think of it. I know Charles may seem reluctant, he'll come around."

She opened Senna's door and Dominick sliced by overhead. "Sleep well, my dear."

Senna shivered as she closed the door behind her. Alone at last, in this opulent bedroom, a fire burning and the outline of a warming pan lying beneath the thick duvet. Every attention had been paid, every nicety provided for her. Things a desperate and impoverished distant relation would consider favorably against any other future she might have while discounting her warring doubts.

This could be her life. If this were all there was, a lot of women would embrace the luxuries and overlook everything else.

But for Senna, it would mean all day, every day with the Countess, being stuffed with family lore, with Charles off and about doing whatever he wanted, irrespective of his *wife's* wishes.

Beginning with Charles's courting her *his* way, if tonight's torturous kisses were any example. How many nights lying with him—after the ceremony, because he wasn't getting a foot in her bedroom door without that—before she might say there was a child?

Dear God, how had the Countess cozened *her* so neatly and completely?

There was only one choice now: bluff it out and play it through, because the Countess had sequestered her in such a way that there was no escape, and no way to keep Charles out.

When she was finally alone in her room, she pulled the knife from the folds of her dress and hefted it. The blade was all sleek and silver, just sharp enough to draw blood.

Don't worry about Charles, my pretty.

Instantly, she felt a strange warmth surround her.

Sleep, my dear.

She felt tired suddenly. The bed beckoned her and she pulled back the duvet cover and, still dressed, slid underneath.

Nothing to worry about. A concealed weapon was one way out. It would be all right.

Sleep, sleep . . .

Dominick spread himself over and around her, covering her with the light, swirling mist of his essence. *Sleep,* he breathed in her ear.

She dreamed of the lovely, luxurious house with no mirrors; of paper notes signed *Nicolai* falling like snow; of the Countess, marble still, stone white in a viscous bath of mud. She dreamed of the look in Charles's eyes when Nicolai's name was mentioned, and of all the death surrounding the Countess's family.

She dreamed of a young, ascetic face very like Charles's and very not, with mesmerizing blue eyes, and an intelligence that held hers in spite of the pounding on the door, followed by Charles's voice, and then the splintering of wood as he bulled his way into her room.

He stopped abruptly at the foot of the bed as she jolted awake and shifted her body upright. Something stopped him. Something invisible, rising up out of dust and air, repelling his attack forcefully and emphatically.

There was the faint pounding of a heartbeat, then Charles disappeared.

It was like falling into a pool of cool water and floating, supported by something firm and enfolding.

Her dreams evaporated as if they'd never been, and she awakened, refreshed and with the realization that in one more day she would be Charles's brood wife.

Charles was waiting right outside her door the next morning, knocking furiously until she opened it.

"You." He grasped her arm and pulled her close. "We had an agreement. I fully expected you to be open, hot, and welcoming to your future husband."

Never.

His eyes glittered with the fury of a petulant child. He wanted what he wanted, and his veneer of charm instantly dissipated like snow in water.

"Wasn't I?" she parried.

"We're going to make *dead certain* however much seed I spill into your body *roots* there. That's the whole point of the *exercise.*"

His hand tightened on her arm. "We have one more day to make sure something sticks. Am I clear, Senna? It's what mother wants"—he eyed her like a prize horse—"and for myself, I fully want your virginity. What man wouldn't? But I'm not in the least interested in the end result."

He shoved her back into the room. "You denied me last night, so we'll start now." He yanked at the sleeve of her dress.

Never.

"Charles!" It was a futile protest as her sleeve ripped easily from her arm.

"The heir, Senna. That's all you need to care about." He grasped the bodice of her dress. "And all I care about is ramming myself in every available hole. You have to admit"—he pulled hard and the whole bodice tore away from her body—"I've been nicely restrained till now." He stared at her breasts peeking out from the shreds of her undergarments and his expression turned feral.

He backed her up to the bed until the bend of her knees caught the edge of the mattress and she tumbled backward onto it.

Never!

She couldn't swear to what happened next. It seemed as if a cloud of dust blew into Charles's eyes. He fell back cursing, hard and heavy, then blindly lumbered after her again. A moment later he was gone. A door slammed hard somewhere beyond, and she was alone, half-naked on the bed.

With a shield of warmth permeating the room, as if something was protecting her.

Nonsense, she thought.

She gathered her wits and crawled to a sitting position to assess the damage.

Dear God, if only there were a mirror. She didn't have enough of a wardrobe to be pawed at like this. And if that was a foretaste of what the first months of their marriage would be like . . . ?

She could not, *would* not marry Charles, no matter what the inducements.

Chapter 5

*S*he tucked the knife under the mattress. Or, she thought, maybe she should keep it with her, but the image of her brandishing a table knife to defend herself against the Countess seemed a little ridiculous.

The Countess was a woman of sense, even though she was blinded by her need to carry on the family name and bloodline. She surely knew Charles's faults as well as those traits she extolled. It was merely a matter of making the case that it was too soon for Senna to marry Charles.

She won't hear you.

Now why did that thought pop into her head? She smoothed her skirt and wished again there were a mirror so she could brush her hair and check her hem.

She heard a buzzing in her ears.

Notice everything.

She looked around confusedly for the voice.

Every detail.

Senna shook it off. She'd really been affected by Charles's unexpected attack this morning. She couldn't face him. She knew how things would go: they'd both pretend nothing happened, or Charles would protest that his feelings of lust and longing had gotten the best of him.

The Countess would believe him and chide Senna for not being more understanding. She'd say, how could a man on the verge of marriage be expected to control himself.

Senna had to get out. It was definitely time to come up with a strategy.

Charles could not contain his rage as he stormed around the dining room while his mother calmly sipped tea. "She is *not* biddable."

"No," the Countess said, "she is not."

"Get rid of her."

"She is all we have at the moment."

"No, she's not. There's something else that will interfere with your plans, Mother."

The Countess raised her eyebrows.

"Nicolai is here."

The Countess froze. "That can't be. I would know. He was never to return. He has to be dead."

"He's *here*."

The Countess opened her mouth to speak, but she couldn't push the words out of her throat. She swallowed, then, in a rusty voice, asked, "And you know this because?"

"We had a close encounter in the girl's room this morning."

The Countess lifted her chin. "You're mistaken. I would know."

"You've been so busy plotting my sex life and for your prospective heirs, Mother, that you know nothing. You can't sense anything but the scent of your own blood."

"He can't have returned," the Countess said impassively. "He was never to return after . . ." Her voice caught. "After."

"And you would know," Charles added sarcastically.

"I thought I would know." But she hadn't an inkling—she'd been too immersed in her mission.

"Senna can't know," she said suddenly. Her eyes widened as she shut out Charles, her surroundings, her problems, her need to propagate—everything but her sense of Nicolai. Long, lean, strong Nicolai with his all-encompassing blue eyes and chiseled face, the compassion and grace that she had rendered to death when she turned him by the light of the roaring flames devouring their home.

Her senses radiated outward in concentric circles, seeking him while he was just a flit of a shadow above her head.

She couldn't find him. She *needed* to find him.

But he knew how to hide; how to compress himself to nearly nothing so even her fine-tuned antennae couldn't ferret him out. And he'd known the danger of vanquishing Charles this morning; he'd known his brother would tell the Countess.

As if *she* could protect him. Nicolai had things to settle with Charles, but that would come later. After his mother. After he bedded and impregnated the girl.

But the problem of Senna's reluctance to have Charles, and that the Countess would probably have to kill her, superseded everything else.

Senna was on her way down to the dining room even now, and in a moment his mother's attention would be diverted once again to the problem at hand, and Nicolai's presence at Drom would be relegated to another complication to deal with later.

Senna took the knife with her after all, just to give herself something to hold on to, something to ensure she had some control. Beyond that, she had the gut feeling she was missing something, and it kept pushing at her, disturbing her.

She'd lived by her wits for years. Being aware of details was the bedrock of survival on the streets, and the foundation of every scheme she'd ever concocted. Yet, everything had slipped by her usually keen eye the moment she'd received the Countess's invitation to Drom.

What had she missed?

The Countess, stone-cold naked in her mud bath? Perfectly understandable once she'd explained it was the custom of her country.

The isolation of Drom? The missing mirrors? But the Countess wore the same thing every day—what need had she for mirrors? The strange number of dead furry animals around the grounds? That was foxes, feeding.

The notes signed *Nicolai* in all those books in the library? That one wasn't so easily explained away.

Senna paused at the bottom of the stairs. She dreaded facing Charles, the Countess, and their seemingly unrealistic expectations.

Entering the dining room, she saw immediately that, as she feared, Charles was there, and that the Countess looked a little harried.

Charles bowed tightly and said, "I apologize for my unseemly behavior this morning. The waiting is hard. I was hard."

"I appreciate the apology," Senna murmured. There wasn't much more she could say. Charles did not look chastened in the least, but obviously the Countess had demanded he do something to mitigate his lewd conduct. He wanted the thing over; the Countess wanted to keep pretending that the marriage was to be a union of two willing souls.

"Let me service—serve you," Charles said as Senna turned toward the sideboard. "I know exactly what you like."

She ignored him. She couldn't have eaten to save her life, but she seated herself across from the Countess and unfolded her napkin. The Countess was sipping tea. A small sandwich plate was beside her saucer with a half-eaten crust on it.

Why did it seem as if the only thing the Countess ever ate was toast?

Charles set Senna's plate before her. Eggs. Nauseating. How could she eat anything when all the Countess had was a crust of toast? Maybe the Countess was not as wealthy as Senna believed. What *had* the Countess eaten for dinner last night?

Senna sipped her tea and nibbled at the eggs before buttering her toast and painstakingly spreading it with jam. She took intermittent bites as she listened to the Countess's practiced conversation.

Senna focused on the details. The Countess's skin was amazingly clear and fine, no deep lines around her mouth or wrinkling above her brow. Her mouth was thin, however, but that was a family trait—so was Charles's.

The Countess was not that old, really. She dressed as if she were, always in the same black dress, always with a widow's cap covering her hair and a shawl around her shoulders. She never sat by the window in the sun—that must be why she had such lovely skin. Her hands were equally as young-looking. Graceful. She didn't smile much or eat much.

Senna took another sip of tea. She felt icy cold, as if Nicolai's ghost were watching in secret somewhere as she observed his family.

The Countess kept talking. "We'll work on the memoirs this morning, and then perhaps you and Charles can take a walk. You two should talk." The Countess sent them both a look that dared them to contradict her.

"We'll . . . talk, if you wish," Charles said.

"Then let us adjourn to the library and continue."

Senna dutifully took notes, barely registering what the Countess said.

She thought about the Countess's dead family. All those deaths after they'd come to England. One, two, three—the Countess was rambling on about them right now in a disjointed way.

And then, her second husband, Charles's father.

"He was Mr. Sandston, you remember—no title, unfortunately. A merchant of great wealth and vast reach. I'll tell you some other time how we met and about our courtship. But shortly after we moved to England, to the house that later burned down, my dear Mr. Sandston died in a hunting accident. In the days when"—she paused almost as if she were holding back tears—"and then subsequently I suffered the loss of my sister and our daughter—but I won't dwell on that yet."

Senna looked up sharply. And Nicolai. The Countess hadn't mentioned Nicolai, who had lived to write mysterious notes with threatening undertones years after he'd perished in a fire. Notes that might still be closed between the covers of books high up on the shelves where no one could reach them.

I'm watching you.

Whom was he watching, the dead Nicolai? Where was he?

"Where was I?" the Countess said suddenly.

"It's time for our walk, Mother," Charles interpolated firmly.

She looked up at him, then focused on something beyond him. Did she see Nicolai where others couldn't?

"Of course," the Countess said. "It's time to begin the court-ing."

This was the part Dominick couldn't control. Charles knew his brother could be anywhere, but that knowledge wouldn't cool Charles's ardor or decrease his desire.

The rest Dominick had plotted out, and he only wanted the right moment to implement his plans. All he could do now was grab on to the hem of Senna's dress as Charles opened the door for her and go along for the ride.

It was cool and brisk outdoors. Senna had no shawl to wrap around her shoulders, perhaps an intentional oversight on Charles's part to give him an excuse to touch her. But Senna was wary, her whole body so stiff with resistance even Charles could sense it.

"I did apologize," he said irritably.

"I believe you said something to that effect," she said. "Are we done with the talking now?"

"You agreed to this union, Senna."

Had she? It seemed like months ago that she'd tacitly agreed to the Countess's proposal, and only because she hadn't said no.

"Perhaps I was caught up in my gratitude," she hedged. "Perhaps I didn't quite think it through."

Charles's expression turned ugly. "If you deny my mother her dearest wish, you'll have to leave. Do you understand that? You will have to go. No help for ungrateful indigent relatives, Senna.

"So envision how things will go after that—and you can be certain I will make sure of it. You go directly to the workhouse, dressed in rags, where you'll be burdened with unrelenting drudgery, grow old before your time, and die young of some unsuspected disease that will take root some winter when you had nothing but a threadbare, cast-off coat to wear and some drunkard to keep you warm.

"Compare that with the comfortable life that awaits you here at Drom: servants to attend you, a fresh wardrobe every season, six months in London every year, pin money, doctors at the ready to bring your child into the world, and anything you desire after that."

He was right. Every time she got cold feet, she should remember that the bigger picture presented the only logical course under the circumstances. It was just . . . She absently stepped on a stone, then paused as she felt something give under the sole of her shoe.

"What's this?" She knelt to examine the object—then jumped upright. "It's dead."

"The fox," he reminded her.

I keep having this conversation, she thought. *It's always the* fox. "Of course. I forgot. What were you saying?"

"I was saying"—he pulled her around to face him—"we are going to make that baby."

"Charles . . ."

He grasped her arms tighter. "Starting tonight."

She fingered the handle of the knife tucked in her pocket. "You're hurting me."

"That doesn't bother me in the least."

His eyes were cold, his expression bloodless. Charles took what he wanted; he was ruthless and pitiless. He didn't want courtships, marriage, or babies. He wanted her body right now because it was within his grasp. And he'd take her, right in the middle of the field, because he could.

She'd be shackled to a man like that forever.

He pulled her closer, and she couldn't wrench away. There was no one to help. The larger picture suddenly didn't matter. As he moved in for a violent kiss, it was all she could do to withstand the heat, the dominance, his constricting embrace; if anything, this kiss was more repulsive than the first.

"There are women who beg for my kisses," he snarled as he broke away from her.

"You keep believing that's true," she snapped.

"But you're not one of them." He pulled her tighter against him. "You will be, I promise you. You will beg, Senna. You will cry. You will yearn. You will hope—and after the babe roots, it will all be in vain."

"I can live with that," she shot back.

"You ungrateful bitch, blowing all my mother's generosity and kindness back in her face. This one small thing she asks of you, and you act as if she were consigning you to a snake pit."

"I didn't say no to *her.*"

His expression changed as he comprehended what she meant. "I see."

She felt at the hard edge of danger with those two words. She felt a ruffling at her hem. She felt the knife nudging against her thigh.

When you can, slice right down to the bone.

She felt his arms tightening around her like a vise, moving in to take what she wouldn't give him willingly. She didn't think. She had the knife, and he wasn't paying attention to anything else but restraining her and ramming his kiss into her mouth.

He didn't feel the subtle maneuvering of her hand into her dress pocket, or her slipping the knife under his jacket and up against his shirt.

All she needed was the guts, gall, and strength to break the skin.

She didn't have to kill him—though she felt a potent urgency to end his life—she just had to draw blood, to disable him.

That would be enough. Disabling sounded good.

She gripped the knife, closed her eyes, and jabbed the sharp tip hard into his body.

"Son of a—!"

His grip loosened as he grabbed at his ribs, and she wheeled and ran, his curses following her, raining down in a high-pitched howl that echoed through the fields.

She ran. To the house, to Drom. Safety in the house . . .

Behind her, Dominick hesitated, torn between the lust to suck the poisonous lifeblood from his bastard of a brother forever, or implementing his larger plan of vengeance.

This was the curse. The blood called to him, leaking from a ragged slit in Charles's skin. Charles, on the ground, blotted at it helplessly with his shirt, swearing to kill the stupid whoring bitch, as Dominick flitted above him, drawn by the blood, thirsting for the blood, yearning for the blood that could destroy Charles forever.

One swipe. Just one sip and it'd be *done.*

He couldn't, he couldn't, he couldn't. He angled upward and flew recklessly, hungrily toward Drom.

Senna ran, the knife, still dripping Charles's blood, in her hand. She wasn't aware of it. She saw nothing but the doors of Drom, the symbol of safety.

Only nowhere was safe now. She had no choice but to leave, even if she had to crawl. The doors were within reach and she grasped one handle and pulled.

Dank air rushed out at her. A metallic scent was in the air.

And an emphatic ruffling sound above her head.

Just go to your room. Close the door. Shut out the danger.

Dominick landed on a chandelier.

Whitton appeared before she could move. "The Countess is at lunch."

She nodded, still rooted on the spot. Then she turned toward the dining room, feeling as if she were sleepwalking.

The Countess was indeed dining. Senna could hear her chewing, which was odd because she hadn't seen the Countess put anything in her mouth since she'd arrived.

She saw a lot more than that as she paused on the threshold.

The Countess sat at the head of the table, a platter heaped with fur and bone in front of her, blood splattered everywhere, dripping from the corners of her mouth, onto the small, squirming furry creature she held in her hands.

She looked up, saw Senna, and smiled, a gory rictus of a smile. Death's smile. Then she opened her mouth wide and, holding Senna's gaze, she chomped into the heart of the squirrelly creature, and as Senna watched in horror, she sucked its lifeblood dry.

Chapter 6

Senna fell into a black hole and then felt herself spiraling upward, enfolded in a white cloud, as if she'd died. Surely she'd died. . . .

Footsteps pounded, and the Countess shrieked, *"Kill her!"* But Senna was floating high above the table, the bloody Countess, Charles's contorted face and his bloody clothes, high above the mess she'd made of her life and her ill-considered deceits.

It was all over now. She'd never have to endure Charles or see the Countess again. She was wrapped in warmth—cushioned, contained, and safe.

Your name is Senna. They will call you Senna.

Strange—I know my name is Senna.

You will pretend to have no memory of the past.

Odder still. But why?

You will be saved.

She believed it fervently. In her dream, that austere face appeared again, those haunting blue eyes regarded her with compassion.

You will not remember what happened here.

In her dream, she obliterated the vision of the Countess's bloody mouth. Another clue she'd missed—all those desiccated little bodies all over the grounds. And the Countess sucking their blood. How much blood did a ghoul need to satisfy its lust?

It wasn't ever a fox, she realized as she sank wholly into oblivion. She had just the faintest feeling that something had happened here, but she couldn't for the life of her recall just what.

And just like that, Senna was gone and the Countess realized suddenly she was screaming at Charles through a haze of dust, mist, and murk.

She slammed her bloody hands on the table. "I will kill that girl. I will *kill* her. I will suck the life from her heart and tear her to pieces. I will drain every ounce of blood from her body. I will—"

Only, threats were futile when the victim had vanished.

Dead silence fell.

"He took her," Charles said at length, his voice shaking. "He goddamned took her."

The Countess meticulously wiped her bloody hands as she considered the idea, then she threw the napkin on the pile of bones in disgust. "Why?"

"Why didn't he show himself to you? How long do you think he's been here, eavesdropping, plotting?"

The Countess made a deep bawling sound that echoed throughout the Manor.

Charles waited. "He despises you."

"You tried to kill him."

"And you ask why. He heard all your fine plans to get an heir and he decided to thwart you. *He* may well get her with child—and then what?"

Tainted blood? The Lazlaric line desecrated forever? The Countess's face twisted, the blood rushed to her head, suffusing her with the urge to lash out at the nearest victim.

"Never!"

"But he has her now."

She forced herself to focus, to ignore the blood urge to kill. "Where?"

"London probably. Easy feeding for monsters who are untethered. Easy to be anonymous."

The Countess hated London, especially since the population had so increased that people were practically shoulder to shoulder in the streets and houses crowded side by side, eliminating narrow alleyways where it used to be easy to snatch a stray cat or a sleeping drunk and sap their vitals in secret.

Now every inch of space was occupied. No room to grab an elbow, catch a scent, trip up a mark, suck a spot of blood.

The lure of all that blood convinced her. She would have gone there too.

"Then we'll go to London. We'll find him. He's my son. I should be able to find him. And then I will kill him. You will find a way to get to Senna, and you will plant that heir. And then we'll kill her after the child is born. That's the plan now. Or"—she flicked the pile of bloody bones—"I'll have no compunction about killing you too."

Lady Madalina Augustine was a widow of wealth and social connections. She resided alone in a town house in Berkeley Square, except when her son, Peter, was in Town, which was not often. She enjoyed her life enormously. She was a great gossip; she loved salons, parties, cards, and balls. She adored that she was considered eccentric by her friends and dutifully made certain she upheld that reputation.

This particular Sunday, she was out and about in her carriage early before church, compelled for some reason to drive to Kensington Park and enjoy the solitude. It was too early for seeing and being seen; it was too early for anything but contemplating one's own thoughts.

Lady Augustine wasn't particularly reflective though. The sound of the horses' hooves irritated her, and she kept swatting at the pesky fly buzzing around her ear.

Her name is Senna. Dominick had chosen her because it was

so easy to implant memories into Lady Augustine's disingenuous mind.

Lady Augustine shook her head. She knew no one by that name.

She is your ward. You are giving her a Season, with all that it entails.

What? Whose ward? She had no ward.

Keep driving. You will find her shortly.

Why wouldn't that stupid insect leave her alone?

You will take care of her.

Lady Augustine's heart began to race, panic rising in her chest. "Driver! Go faster."

He obliged, and the carriage went careening down the park drive at a brisk clip.

There. No more flies. No more absurd thoughts.

Lady Augustine took a deep breath, then felt the carriage skittering to a stop as the driver pulled up on the reins.

"Driver!"

"Madam, there's an overturned carriage just ahead."

Lady Augustine peered out the window. "Why, so there is. And there's someone inside. Quick, we have to help."

"You stay there, madam. Let me go. We don't know how serious this is, or if—"

Lady Augustine knew exactly what he meant by *if.* She brushed the thought away.

"Hurry," she called to him, unable to see anything from her seat. The driver appeared at the opposite window, carrying a girl in his arms.

Lady Augustine thrust open the carriage door. She gasped as she glimpsed the girl's face, a face it took her more than a moment to recognize. "Is she all right?"

Lady Augustine looked more closely as the driver settled the girl on the opposite bench. "Why, it's Senna. She's been away at school. How is it possible she's here?"

It was a trifling detail, a little mystery. How fortunate that *she* had found the girl and not some stranger who'd have no idea who she was. Thank goodness. How had this happened? But there was time to ask all the questions. For now, Lady Augustine would just bring her back to Berkeley Square, make her comfortable; the details could wait till later.

And now, Senna thought, *comes the weaving of the lies.* How could this kindly stranger think that somehow Senna was her responsibility, her *ward*?

Dear God—what should she do now that Lady Augustine had brought her back to London and given her this lovely room, which she claimed was Senna's whenever she visited from school.

Senna had never seen or met this woman before in her life. But Lady Augustine obviously thought she had.

This was too confusing. Senna didn't even have a conscious memory of how she'd gotten here in the first place. The last she remembered—

Well, there was something she ought to remember, but it was like a really bad dream that she'd suppressed. She kept reaching for the details and everything just slipped away. Maybe it was for the best.

Maybe all she needed to do was decide how to handle this really confusing dream.

Simple: she'd do what she'd always done—*lie*.

It was too easy a solution. She always did that. Lying was convenient, second nature, and expedient. In this case, if she was successful, she might be able to stay with Lady Augustine indefinitely too.

No—she'd lie only until she got her bearings and figured out how she'd gotten here. And how this woman knew her.

All she had to do was pretend she didn't remember a thing.

Dear heaven, she'd already planned the deception—and the part where she pretended to have lost her memory? It was brilliant. She wouldn't have to account for anything.

But if she confessed she had no idea who Lady Augustine was, she'd have to leave. Then she'd be back on the streets scrambling for a ha'penny, begging for alms and looking for a mark.

She didn't remember a thing past the point where she . . . what? The Countess, of course. And Charles. And Drom.

But when she reached for a certain memory, it was as if a wall were in her mind and she couldn't get past it.

So the simple explanation of a loss of memory encompassed everything. But more than that, it was a way to politely refuse questioning, a way to avoid a host of potential complications that could arise.

She couldn't have devised a more perfect ruse herself.

What was the real story, after all? She'd put herself in a precarious situation with a man she didn't know, she'd managed to evade him, and—

She couldn't remember.

She glanced around the room—a graceful four-poster bed and roomy armoire. The mirrored vanity where she now sat, studying her dirt-smudged face, her troubled blue eyes, her wind-tossed hair, her wrinkled shirtwaist.

She hated herself for taking refuge in lying, but she couldn't think of another option. It wasn't fair to Lady Augustine, who'd been so kind to her thus far. Senna made up her mind right then. No more lies. No more deceptions. She would tell Lady Augustine the truth and let this ill-begotten adventure bring her back where she belonged: scrubbing floors in the scullery of some wealthy nob's town house in London for the rest of her life.

There was a knock on the door. "Senna! Senna! You're not taking a nap, are you? I've called for a bath—the tub will be up soon. Senna . . . Open the door!"

Lady Augustine rattled the knob, found the door unlocked, and bustled in.

"There you are, my dear. You must relax. I'm sure there's some good explanation for why you were coming to see me so early in the morning."

"I—"

"Never mind, it doesn't matter now. You're here, and I can pamper you all I want. Perhaps that was all you needed."

"My lady—"

"Shhh . . . a nice warm bath, a good scrubbing, and fresh clothes, and the problem will be solved."

Now Senna felt like Alice through the looking glass; everything backward, upside down, and impossible to make sense of.

"Lady Augustine?"

"Why so formal?" She tilted Senna's face and started brushing her hair. "Oh, you need a good scrubbing. I can't imagine what could have been so terrible that you had to muddy and dirty yourself to rush to Town."

"Lady Augustine—"

"Yes, dear?"

How did she even start? "I'm . . ." Maybe it *would* be better to pretend memory loss. It would give her time. It would give her distance from the Countess and Charles. It would give her a safe place for the time being.

It would only be a little lie . . . for a little while.

"I—I don't know quite how to tell you, but I don't know who you are."

Well, that wasn't a lie, for sure.

"Senna!" Lady Augustine sounded as if she were mortally wounded.

"I don't remember anything," Senna said, crossing her fingers. "I feel like a fraud."

No lie there.

"Oh, my dear. Was it that bad an accident?"

Senna did not hesitate to invoke the excellent cover-up. "I don't remember."

Lady Augustine put her arms around Senna's shoulders and hugged her. "We'll call in my doctor tonight to look you over."

Oh, lord, another hurdle. "Oh, please don't. I'm not who—you shouldn't—"

"I'll take care of everything. You just take that nice hot bath and dress for dinner. You won't remember, of course, but there are clothes in the armoire. Dinner is at six. I'll see you then."

❧

The guilt set in. She'd taken the easy way out instead of throwing herself on Lady Augustine's mercy. She told herself it was solely because she still didn't understand how she'd come to be here and why Lady Augustine, a complete stranger, kept insisting she and Senna somehow had a relationship.

Her life was turning into one big sham.

She should just leave.

But how could she?

She let in the servants with the big copper tub and sank into it gratefully, greedily, and just wallowed. A steamy bath was a luxury. The fragrant oils to soothe her skin were heaven. The maid helping her wash and dress was an angel.

The armoire was full of clothes in exactly her size. It wasn't possible in the realm of the rational. Nothing about the last day made sense. Her sojourn at Drom had ended with Charles's unforgivable advances and the Countess deceiving her. And that was a hard truth to swallow.

She sorted through the dresses in the armoire, her hands trembling.

But it wasn't only that. There was something else. Something to do with Charles—yes, she'd fled Drom because Charles wanted to bed her before the wedding, but there was more.

She didn't remember how she'd got from Drom to London and it was driving her crazy.

Nothing made sense, nothing.

And the Countess had been . . . in the dining room. And . . .

She couldn't remember. She felt as if her body were enduring aftershocks in her effort to reach for the memory. But all she could envision was the oh-so-eager Countess pretending a relationship that didn't exist for her own purposes.

As had she. What was the difference between them really?

"Senna! Oh, Senna!" Lady Augustine's fluty voice penetrated through the fog that had enveloped her.

She'd made the right decision to lie, she decided. She'd be safe here, at least for a little while, pretending to forget things she didn't know until she remembered what she'd really forgotten.

Lady Augustine called the doctor immediately when she found Senna huddled on the floor, shaking as if she had a fever.

Dominick, contracted into the body of the fly once again, paced along the frame of the vanity mirror, listening and thinking he'd done an excellent job of mesmerizing not only Lady Augustine but, through her, anyone who would come in contact with Senna so there would be no gaps in the story.

The doctor treated Senna as if he'd known her for years.

Senna valiantly did her part, protesting she remembered nothing, not Lady Augustine, not this house, not the doctor, not the room.

The doctor did find a conspicuous bump on Senna's head.

"Well, here we are. Surely she wasn't driving the carriage herself when it tumbled over. Senna?"

"I don't remember." The doctor had given her a compress and she held it against the bump. "I just don't remember."

The doctor shrugged. "This will be a slow process, Madalina. She'll either recover her memory or she won't. I don't think you should treat her like an invalid, however. It might be very beneficial to engage in the usual activities, as if she had been visiting otherwise."

"Yes, of course," Lady Augustine said, wringing her hands. "But the shaking . . ."

"A memory of the accident, perhaps. We can't know. Only Senna can tell us when she regains her memory." He patted Senna's hand. "Madalina will send up a tray and all will be better tomorrow. But I must caution you, Madalina—don't press her to remember. That will come."

Dominick hovered. *She's playing it brilliantly. But then, Senna is an expert at that. It's working just as I planned.*

Lady Augustine left with the doctor and Senna sank into the pillows with a huge sigh of relief.

The doctor believed her. That hurdle was passed.

The bed was warm and toasty—safe.

"Miss?" The maid was at the door, a tray in her hands. She set it across Senna's lap and stepped back expectantly. "Is there anything else?"

Senna shook her head and the maid withdrew.

Now what? She was nowhere near hungry, but for sure Lady Augustine would check to see whether she'd eaten.

A fly buzzed around her head.

Lady Augustine bustled in. "Oh, you haven't eaten anything. I specifically ordered your favorites."

"I'm so sorry. I'm just not hungry." Her favorites? How would Lady Augustine know her favorites?

"Oh, those things keep," Lady Augustine said cheerfully. She sat on the edge of the bed. "I've decided you'll stay for the Season, since you're here. I'll have the dressmaker in tomorrow and we'll order some new clothes. You'll stay here and you won't go back to that school. Obviously you were running away from something there. And it will come to light sooner or later. How does that sound?"

"It sounds too generous to someone who doesn't remember you."

"But you will. And you call me Aunt Madalina, you know."

Senna tried out the words. "Aunt Madalina."

"There. Almost like it used to be. Can you sleep?"

"I can try." This was so wrong. Yet—

"Maybe you'll regain some memory with a good night's sleep."

Senna gave her a grateful smile. The woman had the kindest face, carved with life lines bracketing her mouth and crinkling her eyes. Her skin showed faint wrinkling, her eyes seemed always to smile. Not like—

Oh, why can't I remember?

"We'll see tomorrow," Lady Augustine said, rising. She took the tray. "Rest now." She closed the door gently behind her.

Breathe.

She was alone. Everything was eerily still. There wasn't a sound anywhere. Like her room at Drom, but different. If she went exploring, as she had at Drom, would she stumble on an unexpected son roaming the hallway? Lady Augustine bathing in mud? Notes from the dead?

Had any of that been real? It felt like a lifetime ago that she'd come up with her indigent-relation deception. And now she'd become the cosseted ward in the home of another titled aristocrat. *How?*

At least there were mirrors in this house. Senna huddled under the covers, certain she'd never again sleep.

Death was in the air in a way he had not sensed previously since he'd returned to London. Even from Lady Augustine's rooftop, where he brooded while Senna slept, Dominick smelled ripped flesh, bloody bodies, and vampiric death.

The Countess had come to Town. He'd known she wouldn't stay contained at Drom after he'd removed Senna. She was his mother's prey now. She wouldn't rest until she'd sunk her fangs into Senna's heart and wrested the life force from her. But even now the Countess hunted and sought the dispossessed and disposable in a fury of bloodletting she hadn't allowed herself in years.

Dominick felt her movements in his bones: her intensity, her lust, her blood-born need to feed. It only momentarily deflected her unholy desire to find Senna—and him—but that was coming.

He shuddered at the echoes of the howling demises of the victims. She'd rekindled the taste. She'd suppressed her hunger too long, and now she would be at it all night, one after another, bloody bodies exsanguinated, left for trash, or drowned by the docks.

He was not immune either; he had given in to the taste, the drive, the greed, the hunger. For all his ability to restrain and constrain, the pulsing life force of the blood called to him on an ancient and primitive level he couldn't deny, defend, or defeat.

Dominick watched now because in her crazed feeding the Countess hunted Senna. The guttersnipe Senna. The flimflammer, the sharper, the consummate liar Senna.

Who would—who *must*—bear the child. The Countess had not

given up on that either. Dominick knew it as surely as he knew she was hunting. She was torn between wanting the kill and wanting the heir.

The heir first. Dominick was certain of it. Charles would have at Senna for however long it took to conceive the heir for which the Countess was rabid. They'd cage her and keep her alive just long enough to bear the child—and then the Countess would feed on her, wholly and completely until she was gone.

The child would become the golden one, the prince. He would carry on the line and return to Romania, the homeland, as the last of the Lazlarics. As Nicolai had been supposed to do before Charles nearly murdered him.

The blood welled within him.

Death was in the air. And it wasn't just the Countess.

His senses quivered. The Tepes. His first whiff was hot, strong, and metallic, tenaciously rooting where darkness bred death.

They were here. The ancient enemy rooting out the Iscariot from wherever they roamed. He smelled it, felt it. The Tepes. Hiding, stalking, hunting, foraging, sating the thirst. They were getting closer.

No more so than the Countess, though. Things were progressing more quickly than he had expected.

It was time for drastic measures.

He transformed himself out into the night as a mist that seeped into the chimney and down into Senna's room, where she tossed restively in the maw of her foggy memories.

No invitations needed for tiny insects or swirling air slipping in through chimney stacks and chinks in bricks.

He spread himself over her body, a swirling vapor fitting itself to every curve and movement of her body, waiting for her to feel his warmth, to settle her restless body under his, to sleep.

This was becoming too familiar, too necessary. Protecting Senna from the Countess had prized up human emotions that he wasn't supposed to feel, things of which he'd never taken note in any of his other dealings with women: the soft roundness of a body, the unconscious undulations of a woman's hips, the sweet scent of her hair. And the satin smoothness of her skin, particularly the wrist, wherever veins pulsed with life.

He moved to kiss her wrist and then pricked her vein—gently, minimally—just for the one drop of blood with which he would enslave her night by night.

He tasted. One drop, just to bind. Just to taste.

Mine.

The news of the murders arrived with the morning milk. Lady Augustine was in much distress as they sat down to breakfast.

"Two deaths last night. Out of nowhere. It's horrible."

Senna took the morning paper and scanned the news story. "One found on the docks, his chest shredded, his heart—oh, God—that's awful—the other, a lady of questionable repute found stabbed nearby a pub." She looked up at Lady Augustine. "Two entirely different scenes."

"But it's been so quiet and calm this pre-Season," Lady Augustine said, the tremor in her voice betraying her nerves. "Now this."

Senna didn't see what "this" was: two different murders, two different places, two different people. Nothing linked them on the surface. "It's not as if the same person was prowling the streets looking for victims. Or at least there's not enough here to say that's the case."

"I get very nervous when people die," Lady Augustine said. "There was quite enough of that when the Ripper was stalking the streets."

"Who doesn't?" Senna wondered, taking a sip of tea, and noticing for the first time a little red dot on her right wrist. "Get nervous when people die, I mean."

She was grateful for the way Lady Augustine had already made her feel at home. Except it made her feel that much more like a fraud.

She had so much to learn. This was a different world, one of manners and constraints. She'd barely begun at Drom, and she wondered if the Countess would have gone so far as to have clothed her. Spoiled her? Eaten her?

She shivered. Why would she think that about the Countess?

She looked at the scone in her hand. The thought of spreading strawberry jam and biting into it suddenly made her queasy.

She put it down gingerly, hoping Lady Augustine didn't notice.

"We'll go shopping today," Lady Augustine said. "I won't let the fact there's a fiend on the loose keep me from the things I enjoy."

"Yes, ma'am."

"Aunt Madalina. Do remember."

"Of course," Senna said.

Aunt Madalina did *love* to shop. Shortly after ten o'clock, they were off in her carriage to Oxford Street, where there was no end to specialty shops for every accessory—hats, gloves, shawls, shoes, jewelry—and every need.

Lady Augustine loved jewelry in particular. They spent the most time admiring diamond collars, emerald-encrusted bracelets, and pearl tiaras.

"Some light entertainment is in order for tonight," she mused, holding out her hand to admire a canary-yellow diamond ring. "A friend is hosting a musicale, with cards. Of course, you'll attend with me."

"Lady Augustine—" Senna started to protest.

Lady Augustine rapped Senna's hand with a narrow, suede jewelry box. "Aunt Madalina, please."

Senna swallowed. It was hard to treat this woman like some kind of extended relation and not as a stranger to whom she was beholden.

"Aunt Madalina," she said finally, obediently.

"Now you'll remember," Lady Augustine said, handing the box to the salesperson and motioning Senna to follow her. "What were you going to say?"

Senna didn't see how she could say no. This was obviously expected and normal. It just wasn't something she remembered.

She had no choice. "I'll be happy to go."

$\mathscr{I}$t turned out to be an evening of light entertainment for a close group of twenty-five friends. A string trio played while guests swirled in and out of the parlor, the card room, and the dining room where refreshments were set out.

As Lady Augustine explained, one did not arrive too early. Eight o'clock was enough time to enjoy the music, chat with friends, play a rubber of whist, and take some refreshment. At that point, Lady Augustine said, she would have heard all the gossip and they could go home.

The intimacy of the gathering soothed Senna's worry that she would make some misstep. *I'm sorry, I don't remember* was as simple a lie as there could be. The phrase just rolled off the tongue.

She'd be fine. Lady Augustine would see to it.

What Senna didn't expect was the trio of brilliantly dressed girls who reminded her of hummingbirds flittering around, sending her covert looks and subtly pointing their fans in her direction.

Lady Augustine ignored them all and propelled Senna into the refreshment room. "Take no account of those girls, my dear. They're all after Peter, and he enjoys ignoring them, as he should."

Senna froze. *Peter? Who's Peter?*

But she knew: he was the trap, the thing that was going to unmask her and reveal the lie.

"Peter?" she echoed lightly so as not to reveal her dismay.

"Peter. You know, my son, Peter." Lady Augustine's expression changed as she comprehended Senna's bewilderment. "Of course, you don't remember. Peter is my dear son, my only child, off on the Continent for business."

"There's no Mrs. Peter, is there?" Senna didn't need even more complications.

"He's not on the market," Lady Augustine said flatly. "So never mind them."

Peter Augustine. Senna rolled the name around in her mind, thinking of the possibility that he might return. It could be tonight or tomorrow or he could be waiting at Berkeley Square when they got home.

Never mind her imagining the worst thing that could happen— there were always complications when you embarked on a lie. Things for which you couldn't plan, that came out of nowhere. Peter Augustine was one of those things.

Another unexpected son. He was not wandering around dark corridors in a gloomy old manor though. He was wandering around Europe and imminently about to return. The scenario was not so different, really.

Did he even know about the Senna that his mother had taken to her bosom? Had Senna, the ward, been part of his life, as seemingly, *she* was now? It was impossible that she hadn't—but how did that make any sense?

Standing on the threshold of the parlor in the lovely silvery blue dress that Lady Augustine had found for her, Senna girded herself to play her part.

She dearly needed to answer the question of how she had gone from Drom to an overturned carriage in a park in London at dawn.

And how Lady Augustine even knew her. And why another suitor had suddenly surfaced.

It was the only thing that kept her in character—how to explain things for which there were no rational explanations.

Maybe Peter Augustine knew the answers.

Senna moved. She had to do something or the hovering hummingbirds would devour her—with words, with questions, with demands for explanations she couldn't make.

She hesitated, then made her way back to the refreshment room with the hope that Lady Augustine was there.

Immediately one of the hummingbirds accosted her.

"You're acting as if you don't know me." This one, dressed in gold and feathers, had a pleasing voice, lovely pale skin accented by her auburn hair, and expressive eyebrows.

"I'm sorry—I don't," Senna said.

The girl looked a little taken aback. "I'm Vaida."

"I'm Senna."

"I know. You're staying with Lady Augustine."

"Yes."

"I see."

Those two words alone told her Vaida knew something wasn't right. Now what? Even her simple yes could be an unforeseen trap.

"Oh, there you are, my dear." Lady Augustine pounced on them. "And Vaida! Lovely to see you. I'm afraid Senna won't remember you. She's had an accident and lost her her memory."

"So I hear," Vaida murmured. "Does Peter know?"

"That Senna's in Town and staying with me? How can he? He's not due back for weeks. Nice to see you, my dear. Come, Senna."

Weeks. He wasn't due back for—

Senna suddenly stopped, her heart dropping to her feet. Lady Augustine looked at her curiously.

"I'm sorry—" Senna scrambled for another lie. "I thought—"

She hadn't thought. She'd reacted, the worst thing she could have done, on seeing the Countess and Charles just entering the parlor. It was the last place she'd expected to encounter them.

She felt the Countess home in on her immediately. "Senna!"

If there ever was a moment to act blank and unaware, this was it. Senna collected her wits and stared at the oncomer with what she hoped was a curious expression.

"Countess!" Lady Augustine exclaimed with too much warmth. "So good to see you."

It just became worse and worse. Lady Augustine was acquainted with the Countess.

"And you," the Countess said flatly, turning. "How are you, Senna?"

"I'm sorry," Senna said, keeping her voice dry and neutral. "Do I know you?" Oh, this was the best lie. It was so easy, and it obliterated everything, past and present.

The Countess's expression registered rank disbelief, and all Senna saw was that mouth . . . and then whatever thought she tried to grasp evaporated instantly.

"Why would you? It was such a short acquaintance."

Senna turned to Lady Augustine with a helpless look, barely able to disguise her agitation.

"If I may explain," Lady Augustine rushed to say, "Senna was in an accident. She's lost her memory. She's staying with me while she's in Town."

"I see."

The short, clipped, ominous *I see*. Too many *I see*'s for Senna's comfort—what *did* they see?

"Then I expect we'll see more of Senna as the month goes on. Perhaps she'll remember my son Charles in the course of events."

Senna gave the Countess a blank look. "I'm sorry. I don't remember anyone named Charles."

"Imagine," the Countess said, the word dripping sarcasm. "Perhaps seeing him will jar your memory. He's the gentleman just by that first column."

Senna pretended to study him for a good long moment, then shook her head. "No. He doesn't look at all familiar."

"How convenient," the Countess said, her tone faintly malicious.

There's something I need to remember, Senna thought.

The Countess hadn't left Drom in years by her own admission. It seemed pretty clear she still wanted an heir and she was bent on making Senna keep to her bargain. Why else was she here? But the Countess wouldn't force the issue in public with Lady Augustine acting as guard dog and Senna claiming memory loss. Would she?

"Excuse us, Countess?" Senna murmured as she turned away. She felt the Countess's gaze follow her and Lady Augustine out of the room.

"The Countess is very intense," Senna said to Lady Augustine, feeling the Countess's eyes burning into her.

"Is she? I didn't notice."

Senna suddenly wanted to return to the safety of Berkeley Square. It was too difficult to keep up the double pretense, especially in this crowd who knew Lady Augustine so well, and with the Countess parsing Senna's every move.

"Is it too early—" she started to ask.

This proved it—she was either exhausted or living some kind of other wonderland life—because on the threshold of the parlor was the man whose face had haunted her dreams, the impassive, austere face with the blazing blue eyes, visible from nearly halfway across the room as his gaze swept the crowd and unerringly settled on her.

He's real. A wave of cold shock swept her body head to foot.

"Ready to leave?" Lady Augustine asked. "So am I. Come."

Senna looked around wildly. He'd disappeared.

I imagined him.

Senna took a deep breath. In moments the carriage would draw up, and then it was just a quick trip to Berkeley Square.

She couldn't wait to get away.

When they'd returned home, the angel maid helped Senna off with her dress, rubbed her down, then handed her a nightgown, a robe, and a warm drink.

She must have imagined him. He didn't exist. He was a dream. Except he *had* been there.

Lady Augustine slipped into the room. "See? That wasn't so difficult, telling people what the situation is. People understand. Although, the Countess—"

"She's rather formidable," Senna said after a moment. "Do you know her well?"

"She hasn't been to Town in an age. I can't remember when the last time was, actually—perhaps before her husband died?" Lady Augustine gave it some thought. "That was a time ago. Happier times. She had weekend parties at their manor, I recall. It was very far away, near nothing. I think there were some strange accidents at the time. But you know, people talk. Anything out of the ordinary, and before you know it there's an ax murderer on the loose. Of course, there certainly can be ax murderers or—" Lady Augustine shook the thought away. "Anyway, he died. Her husband. And the daughter. So . . ."

"What about Vaida?"

"She thinks she's in love with Peter, but I've been watching how she behaves around Dominick Janou, and I'll tell you, she just wants whoever is the most coveted man of the moment. And this Season, that happens to be Dominick."

Senna had an odd feeling. "Was he at the musicale tonight?"

Lady Augustine reflected for a moment. "Oh, yes—he'd just come in as we were leaving."

The feeling curdled in her vitals. She should just leave it alone. She didn't want to know. "And Vaida, is she my friend?"

"You know, I actually think you two are just acquaintances. Isn't this fun, talking over the party? Let's think about tomorrow now though. A carriage ride is mandatory, and a stop at the lending library. Do you remember anything of the city? Should we take a little tour of London?"

"A little tour. That sounds lovely."

"Then that's what we'll do. We also need to visit the dressmaker and make an appointment for you."

Senna put out a hand as if to stop her. "Please—"

"It's my pleasure. And besides, we have all the pre-Season events coming up. You must do me proud."

Lady Augustine meant it. Their succeeding days were filled with all the small errands and delights she had promised.

In the evening, there were small get-togethers: a dinner, a literary salon, small intimate groups that didn't intimidate Senna so much as render her more silent than usual. And if she thought, once or twice, that she had seen *his* face in her and Lady Augustine's trips around London—on the street, in passing through the dressmaker's shop window, browsing in a corner of the lending library—she chalked it up to imagination. Dominick Janou could not be *everywhere*.

It was enough that he was in her dreams. It was beyond enough that she imagined he'd kissed her, on the mouth, on the wrist. In her heart.

Besides, she couldn't keep worrying about him when she kept digging herself deeper and deeper into her lies. Still, Senna didn't resist Lady Augustine's summoning the dressmaker. Once Senna's measurements were taken, the patterns made, and the appointment set, a beehive of seamstresses descended on Lady Augustine's house, and several days were taken up with fittings, alterations, and accessories.

This was the life Senna could never have hoped for. She'd intended to settle for a lot less when she'd embarked on the adventure of being an indigent relative.

She'd never have predicted she'd wind up the ward of a wealthy widowed stranger.

She was perfectly willing to take what she could while she could.

But the question of how she'd gotten from Drom to Berkeley Square bedeviled her with every beautifully sewn gown, every perfect entertainment that Lady Augustine devised.

Once or twice during the day as Lady Augustine napped, Senna had searched through the house as much as she could with servants afoot. She'd gone through the desk in the library; she'd done a quick once-over of Lady Augustine's room. She'd even searched her own room—the chest of drawers, the vanity table, behind the mirror, under the bed.

What did she even expect to find? Adoption papers? Anything, *something* that proved that somewhere sometime in her life she'd known Lady Augustine? Or that she was—penny-dreadful style— her long-lost, given-up-for-dead daughter?

She found nothing in that first foray.

"Oh, Senna is doing fine, but she hasn't yet recovered her memory," Lady Augustine would announce when they entered a room, which saved Senna even more explanations, more lies.

Then, one Saturday evening they attended a crowded charity event at the theater. Senna was thankful when the first intermission came, given the overheated melodrama of the first act. Lady Augustine had a box and visitors came to her. It was, she told Senna, much easier that way.

"No, Senna hasn't remembered anything at all yet," she was saying to a friend as Senna leaned over the brass railing and scanned the crowd. She saw faces she recognized, milling, sipping, conversing. She saw the Countess, her gaze swerving toward Senna like a magnet. She saw Charles charming Vaida.

And then she saw *him,* across a half dozen private boxes, all alone. The man Lady Augustine called Dominick Janou. The face in her dreams, the touch, the kiss . . . every night for the past week. He was only a dream, yet he was real.

Close up, he was taller than she'd imagined, perfect in formal dress, lean and spare, even his face. He had an obdurate mouth and stunningly blue eyes that didn't miss a thing. Including her.

He looked at her with an intimate knowledge. But how could he know her? He was a dream.

Maybe it was time to find out.

Senna bit her lip, then eased herself up and around the guests who were gossiping with Lady Augustine. She edged her way out into the crowd that mingled in the gallery.

A half dozen doors—she counted as she made her way—and she would discover the secret of why this man, this stranger, was so prominent in her dreams.

The door to the sixth box was ajar. She hesitated, then pushed it in.

Empty. But, oh, someone had been there. The chairs were moved, and she saw a goblet tipped on the carpet and a program shoved under the brass rail.

But there was no trace of *him*.

She whirled as the lights dimmed, and the audience began to settle in for act 2. He was nowhere to be seen, even in the adjacent boxes.

She sank onto one of the chairs as a bell rang, the curtain rose, and a body, viciously gored and pouring blood, fell from the catwalk onto the stage.

Screaming, scrambling, whistles blowing, horns blaring—voices fought through the mayhem, voices demanding calm, exhorting everyone to stay where they were.

In the chaos, Senna worked her way back to Lady Augustine's box to find her nearly hysterical. "Where were you? It's the White-chapel murderer all over again. I thought—oh, I so hoped . . ."

The body, now covered, was right in their line of sight.

Senna calmed Lady Augustine as best she could until someone, in response to a dozen shouts, pulled the curtain.

It was impossible to leave the theater quite yet. The authorities had been summoned. Someone with a most commanding voice and a megaphone issued instructions and assurances that they would be safely on their way in an orderly fashion if only everyone would be patient.

They'd be questioned briefly, the voice told them, their particulars taken, and they would be allowed to leave.

As they joined the queue summoned from the loges, Senna listened to the whispered details and speculations.

"Did you see the body? D'you think it was the Ripper?"

"Nah—Whitechapel cut throats, not necks. God, it was bloody."

"No, the Ripper cut the innards out, remember? And left 'em strewn all over."

"Name please." The bobby in charge. "What did you see?"

"Just the body falling from . . ."

"Go on then. Next."

And so it went all over the theater until everyone was released.

Senna was exhausted by the time they returned to Berkeley Square. All that blood . . . but she had seen it before. She couldn't get it out of her mind, as if it were somehow familiar, but when she reached for the memory, it dissipated.

She let the maid undress her and then tumbled into bed. There she felt safe, her dreams infused by tingling moments of pleasure. He was always in her consciousness as she slept. The warmth of his body, the touch of his mouth on her wrist. A light pull, a kiss, another—and then another.

She always sighed when he relinquished her wrist. When he touched her lips, he settled in her dream, and he stayed with her till morning.

She didn't question why Dominick Janou occupied her dreams—it could be no other way. She wanted to sleep forever, if only she could be with him forever.

The room felt suffused with warmth as Senna roused herself the next morning and Dominick watched from his perch on the vanity table.

She was so beautiful, coming out of sleep with her hair all in disarray and her expression soft and yielding.

She looked as if she belonged in that bedroom, in that house. She didn't look like a street-born flimflam artist.

She didn't seem to see him, as she sat down at the vanity and examined herself in the mirror. He wondered, in an abstract way, if she saw what others saw: the thick glossy hair, the high cheekbones, the beautifully cut lips, the unusual blue eyes.

She opened a jar, swiped some cream, and rubbed it into her

hands, pausing for a moment to massage it gently into the sensitive skin of her wrist, and then on her arms and elbows.

Just the merest flick, my pretty. Just a taste, drop by drop, night by night until I own you.

The thought of having her . . . devil's bones, to be a man for just a night, just for that one moment of naked possession . . . he'd never ever thought about a woman that way until *her*. It was too seductive when he was the one who was supposed to be seducing her.

Dangerous too.

He flung himself into the air, out of her sight, out of his mind.

More was in the papers the following day.

Senna read all the news to Lady Augustine over breakfast. The victim was an extra. No one in the audience knew him. The manager of the theater company claimed the extra kept very much to himself and didn't know anyone who was friends with the poor chap.

"'The cause of death was excessive blood loss from wounds in the neck and heart, where there was a curious pattern of three *X*'s incised in the chest,'" Senna read. "'Nearly all the blood was drained from the body, as if whoever had attacked the victim had literally sucked him dry.'"

"I will tell you that seeing it firsthand was vastly different than hearing the account in the paper," Lady Augustine said feelingly. "That doesn't nearly begin to describe how horrific it was."

"'The authorities are loath to speculate on the murderer other than to say this is not the methodology of Jack the Ripper,'" Senna continued reading. "Well, this reporter isn't afraid to say what the authorities won't. He writes, 'This is the methodology of bloodsucking ghouls. Gird yourself, London, there are vampires among us.'"

Chapter 8

*L*ondon froze. Events were canceled. Theaters and music halls closed. Restaurants shut down early. People spent the succeeding evenings behind locked doors. The city was poised to hear word of the next bloody death, certain that the killer would not stop at just one.

But nothing happened.

The authorities were still investigating. There was no new evidence, no suspect. No report of vampires roaming the city. No ghouls sucking the blood of innocent victims. No dead bodies littering the streets.

Senna stopped abruptly in her reading of that day's news story. *Ghouls sucking blood.* Something stirred in her memory.

How *had* she gotten here? She still hadn't found any answers in her surreptitious searching.

"'No cause to think that anyone is in imminent danger,'" she finished the headline article. But it had only been a few days. Anything could still happen. No one should feel secure.

But that wasn't how Lady Augustine reacted. It was almost as if she *wanted* another body to be found, just for the sheer titillation of it.

She was restive, and Senna was at her wit's end trying to make conversation about things she knew nothing about and had claimed to have forgotten anyway.

This was a moment she recognized: how she'd felt at Drom, trapped, with no escape—even with the whole of London right outside the door.

Then, unexpectedly, Charles came to call.

"My dear," Lady Augustine said when Senna hesitated, "the son of a countess is not to be dismissed lightly, even if her aristocratic credentials are Middle-European. There *are* castles in Romania, after all."

"And they are medieval, cold and drafty," Senna retorted as Lady Augustine brought Charles into the parlor.

He held out his hands. "Senna."

"You have to forgive me. I just don't remember you," Senna reminded him quickly.

"So I gather from Mother. May I sit? May I refresh your memory?"

Oh, God. What would he say? How could she just sit there and listen to *his* blatant lies?

But Lady Augustine was eavesdropping; Senna couldn't be outright rude. "If you wish." She looked at his handsome face, and her time with him seemed from a different lifetime.

He'd been charming at the outset, a cad when he didn't get his way, and she had no reason to think anything had changed in the—

Her rumination stopped there as she butted up against a memory that just wasn't there. She couldn't refute anything. Her only recourse was to respond with a blank stare and reiterate that she didn't remember.

"Did my mother remind you that we were going to be married?" Charles asked with a break in his voice. He took her hand. "I treated you abominably, and I want a chance to make it right."

That was more honesty than Senna had expected. Granted it was abbreviated and sliced close to the truth with the precision of a butcher, but honest to a point.

It amused her that he thought he could convince her, that his penitence would win her over. She was so tempted to play with him and lead him on. Just a little.

"How can I say anything when I don't remember?"

"Let me court you again, properly this time. Without my mother's interference, without rushing you. I'll give you all the time you need to be certain. Could you do that, Senna?"

"You're a stranger to me," she protested.

"Then let me begin again as a stranger you met in London who is deeply attracted to you, and let's see where that leads."

"To what purpose?" she purred.

"The marriage that was meant to happen. I spoiled all of it, Senna. I almost wish you did remember so that we could start fresh from this moment."

She shook her head. "I can't promise that. I can't promise anything."

"May I call again? Request a dance at the next party? Take you to the theater? Be your escort if you need one?"

Senna took a moment to think it through. If she were memory-deprived, would she believe his story that they were to have been married? Would she be flattered by his renewed attentions? Would she have given him another chance?

She had to play it out as if it were real that she didn't remember, or that she—she *what*? Rejected him? Ran away? Neither of those sounded quite right.

And the thought of him getting close again—she suppressed a shiver.

She had to keep acting, it was the only way to stay safe.

"You might," she said finally, mainly to appease Lady Augustine, "now and again."

"That's all I ask," he said. "Now and again could lead to always."

He left her then, a little disoriented and with a deep feeling she'd forgotten something really important.

"Oh, there's nothing like a repentant man," Lady Augustine said gleefully. "This is lovely. Even though there isn't a title, there's money there. Sandston, the father, was very, very wealthy. Don't discount a man who's ready to reform."

"I couldn't possibly," Senna said. "Or count him in either."

"Senna, you don't even remember him."

"But shouldn't one pay attention to one's instincts?"

"Not where marriage is concerned," Lady Augustine retorted.

And especially if the prospective bride was an impoverished sharper, Senna thought. Worse still, Lady Augustine had just put her imprimatur on Charles's intentions.

Senna just kept digging herself deeper and deeper into the lie.

"It's time for us to get back in circulation," Lady Augustine said later that afternoon as they settled in for tea. "We can't let some invisible murderer who has a penchant for biting necks stop us from enjoying ourselves. The paper said today that all reports of ghouls, fiends, and vampires roaming the city are greatly exaggerated and totally fictional. The murderer will turn out to be an ordinary throat-slasher. It's time to resume our rounds.

"Speaking to that, what do you think came in the mail today? A most kind invitation from Lord and Lady Hartwicke, who are just as affronted as any of us that the whole city is paralyzed by this monster. So they're throwing a Vanquish the Vampire ball."

Senna shivered.

"Tomorrow night," Lady Augustine added.

"Oh." That soon? Apparently the very rich could not stand to be idle for long, especially if a trusted institution vetted and dismissed their fears.

"It's brilliant," Lady Augustine went on. "Everyone will be there; no one will want to miss this event."

Including you, Senna thought, feeling as if she were walking on eggshells. Lady Augustine was rubbing her hands in anticipation, looking wholly on the surface and acting as if Senna were her own living doll to dress up and play with as she would.

How much longer would Lady Augustine indulge Senna without asking any questions? How long did a lie last anyway?

In every deception she'd ever orchestrated, she knew there'd be a point at which she would have to walk away. Here there were no such gauges. She was feeling her way, off-balance, on the edge of a precipice every minute, where a breath could send her into free fall.

Charles and the Countess would no doubt be in attendance. Who wouldn't? The whole of society wanted not to fear vampires and other bloodletting monsters.

Little did they know.

The errant thought caught her up short. Know what?

"Senna!" Lady Augustine broke into the thought. "Where were you? Come sit by me—we need to plan what we're going to wear."

It was like emerging from a tomb, leaving the town house, stepping into the carriage, and driving to the Hartwicke mansion on the outskirts of London.

The invitation requested each guest bring the requisite protective measures—crucifixes, garlic, stakes, religious icons, vials of holy water, pouches of seeds, hawthorn, sprigs of wild rose. The Hartwickes desired that everyone be prepared should anything untoward happen.

It added a fillip of excitement to the evening, the thought of an evil monster roaming the rafters of the Hartwicke mansion, watching and choosing his prey, and the righteous masses capturing him.

The event was perfectly timed, coming in that hiatus between the upcoming Grand National and the adjournment of Parliament, when any diversion was welcome, even the possibility of catching a murderer among them.

They came, a hundred strong, arriving in waves at the brilliantly lit mansion, where just inside in the reception room the Hartwickes greeted everyone personally.

"Come in, come in. Join the party. Dancing in the ballroom, food in the court, theatrics in the parlor. Welcome, come in."

Coats, capes, and cloaks were hung in the library, where a lively discussion was in progress about whether ghouls and vampires really existed. Lord Hartwicke had had the forethought to invite the reporter from the *Tatler* who'd written the story that scared London to death to come to convince the guests in person that vampires existed.

Gird yourself—there are vampires among us.

In the parlor, a troupe of actors were performing a play about a vampire. Those who had no interest in the show made their way immediately to the ballroom to mix and mingle and trade gossip.

But the court—a space between the parlor and the ballroom—was crowded too. Tables and chairs had been brought in for those who wished to sit while they ate, and a long table full of easy-to-handle tidbits had been arranged along a lengthy wall with plates and utensils at one end and a constant stream of wine at the other.

"No monsters here," Lady Augustine whispered. "You should be dancing, Senna. Charles will surely be here."

"And Vaida?"

"She wouldn't miss it," Lady Augustine said drily.

"*They* would make an interesting couple," Senna mused as she moved in baby steps toward the crowded ballroom.

Just watching the guests was a show in itself. Everyone was opulently dressed, including her. Everywhere she looked, mirrors heightened the sense that even more guests were milling around, expanding the space so it looked as if the rooms were triple their size.

Nothing could happen here. Everything was reflected and multiplied and visible.

So why did she feel so edgy? Because the music was loud, the laughter too forced, the lights too bright, the goading of the monsters too blatant? Or because she was tightrope-walking on the precipice?

She knew she didn't look happy. She caught sight of herself in a mirror—tall, elegant, her glossy hair swept up, her shoulders and neck bared in the beautiful pale blue satin dress with intricate ruching and glittering paillettes. Her face was composed, her gaze cool and assessing, and not a glimmer of excitement coursed through her body.

There are vampires among us.

Just glimmers of fear. Visions of blood. Senna shivered.

Lady Augustine had insisted Senna wear a perfume of attar of wild rose, reputed to repel vampires. She saw others with crucifixes made of diamonds, gold, silver, and pearls prominently but tastefully displayed, and others with their preventives discreetly hidden.

She was making too much of this.

She caught sight of Vaida and the hummingbirds in the mirror. She saw Charles strolling toward the ballroom, Lady Augustine in the midst of a good gossip, people she didn't know crowded in around her.

Charles was looking for her. She felt it as surely as she sensed another presence touching her consciousness. She looked around and instantly connected with Dominick Janou, elegantly dressed and greeting the Hartwickes as they welcomed him into the foyer.

Yet, he was immediately as aware of where she was as she was of him. A rill of pleasure ran up her spine.

Insanity. She didn't know the man.

She would talk to him now, though. There were questions she needed to ask and things he needed to explain.

But when she looked again, he'd disappeared.

He smelled death. It was too crowded, too many bodies pressed against one another. Too many pulsing veins, throbbing hearts, heaving bosoms with fine, thin veins throbbing like heartbeats. Too much temptation in too close quarters. He could only hope that someone among them would injure a foot, scrape an elbow, or cut a finger and just one drop of blood would flow.

The blood coursed through him, self-imposed chains, spiked with pressure, the desire for constraint warring with the thirst. It was the essence of his being.

Then there was Senna, the raven-haired bird of paradise, all gorgeous in pale blue. She would hardly be ignored in this crowd; he must guard her carefully, continue to seduce her drop by drop, impregnate her before any other man declared his intentions . . . and before he abandoned her to her Fate.

She knew him now, felt him every time he was remotely in her sight. He was always on her mind now, as evanescent as a kiss as he siphoned her blood drop by drop, night by night, and absorbed it into his body and his control.

Soon he would reconfigure into bat shape. The crowd was rowdy already, certain to get out of control sooner rather than later. You couldn't mix wine with a vampire-themed event without something disastrous happening.

And Senna must be protected.

She was done with the mystery of Dominick Janou. He was nowhere on that first floor—Senna looked in the rooms, in the mirrors, on the balconies, and finally she signaled to Lady Augustine, nudging her toward the ballroom as Vaida and her friends started toward Senna.

She hoped they would intersect with Charles, who was purposefully heading for her now that he'd sighted her, with the intention of introducing Vaida and letting attraction take its course.

"I know what you're about," Lady Augustine whispered, rapping Senna's wrist with her fan. "Why?"

"Just a feeling," she murmured as they stopped and acknowledged Charles just as Vaida and her friends drew up to them.

"Does everyone know everyone?" Senna asked guilelessly. "Charles, you know Vaida. I'm sorry to say I don't know her friends."

They made small talk for a moment or two, then Vaida and her friends moved on, much to Senna's chagrin. "No, Charles, I don't want to dance. Vaida might like to, though."

"I can't dance with the three of them together," Charles protested. "I would have to pry them apart and they might disintegrate altogether."

"Like a vampire," Lady Augustine said, relishing the thought. "Do you really think—"

"Aunt Madalina," Senna interpolated without thinking, as if she had been chiding Lady Augustine her whole life.

Maybe it was the mere mention of vampires. There was something about . . . vampires . . .

"There's Dominick," Lady Augustine whispered.

Senna glanced in the direction Lady Augustine indicated and then felt Charles stiffen beside her as he caught sight of him. There was an instant tension. Electricity leapt through the air all the way to where they stood, and it had nothing to do with her.

She looked at Charles. He was staring at Dominick, whose expression was carved and implacable.

Then Charles bowed. "You must excuse me," he murmured before abruptly withdrawing.

"What was that about?" Lady Augustine wondered as they watched him maneuver through the crowd. "My goodness, I do believe everyone in Town is here."

"Numbers equal safety," Senna said, watching as Vaida and the hummingbirds circled the ballroom, targeting Dominick Janou like an arrow.

She watched curiously as he greeted them politely, but she—and they—could see that his attention was elsewhere. On Charles maybe? But Charles had disappeared.

Vaida blatantly sought Dominick's attention, touching his arm and flirting with her fan, seeking any excuse to keep him by her side. But he was merely hiding his impatience under the veneer of supreme politeness.

Lady Augustine tugged on Senna's arm and whispered, "The parlor." Senna pulled her gaze away from Dominick and followed Lady Augustine.

In the parlor, the theater troupe had chosen a half dozen onlookers to reprise the actors' roles in the play. Someone beautiful for the damsel. A handsome gentleman for the hero. Another for the best friend. A fourth for the ignorant innkeeper. Someone intimidating for the vampire, who would live to see another day.

Senna felt that lick of terror as she stood rooted, watching each participant reading his dialogue. The lovers, the older mentor. The horror and the danger. The lurking menace.

She sensed a presence behind her and whirled, nearly upsetting the people standing there. She searched through the reflections in the mirror but Dominick Janou was nowhere among the crowd.

Yet she felt him like a touch, watching and waiting.

On the stage before her, the hero was imprisoned. The heroine sensed something was wrong. The best friend lurked outside the window. The mentor entered to find the heroine alone.

The heroine screamed and the mentor reassured her while assessing where and when he could take the final bite.

The bite . . .

Senna's chest tightened.

The mentor, directed by the troupe, bent back the heroine, leaned in, went for her neck, opened his mouth, and—

Someone screamed.

The director shouted, "Show your weapons, show your talismans *now!*"

Immediately, an assault of stakes, garlic, crosses. The vampire was repelled out the window with much ado by the best friend, after which the best friend freed the hero to be reunited with the heroine.

The audience hooted and applauded.

A fifteen-minute intermission was announced.

"Wasn't that exciting?" a voice behind Senna asked.

Senna wheeled to find the Countess at her elbow. Senna's heart accelerated. She stepped back involuntarily. "Countess."

"Senna. Did you enjoy the drama?"

"It was quite scary, as I suppose it was meant to be."

"How else does one vanquish a vampire?" the Countess asked, her tone mockingly reasonable. "It must make everyone feel so safe."

Senna didn't feel at all safe. She felt Dominick's eyes grazing her, but he was nowhere to be seen from where she and the Countess stood making inane conversation.

Senna's hands turned icy as she averted her gaze from the Countess and stared into the never-ending mirrors. Mirrors all over Hartwicke House, reflecting a hundred guests, mirrors in her room at Berkeley Square, but no mirrors at Drom . . .

The Countess stared at her, almost if she could read her mind. The Countess wanted something. Thank heavens Lady Augustine barged in.

"Oh, wasn't that exciting? I now absolutely believe it's all made up, just like the play. Don't you agree, Countess?"

"Definitely make-believe," the Countess said, but she was looking at Senna. "And people brought protection. How quaint. What did you bring, Senna?"

"I'm awash in attar of wild rose, Countess. Very effective against vampires, I'm told."

"How easily the masses are fooled," the Countess murmured. "And Lady Augustine?" But again, Senna had the feeling the Countess's whole attention was directed at *her.*

Lady Augustine clutched her bosom. "I have the holiest of protections, Countess. What about you?"

The Countess shuddered. "I don't believe in such nonsense." She turned away from them suddenly and so abruptly that Lady Augustine was affronted.

"Well! Just because . . . !"

Senna clenched her ice-cold hands. The Countess had disappeared, just like that. How was that possible? She was nowhere to be seen, hard as Senna looked. A trick of her imagination—again?

She didn't think it was her imagination that the noise level had risen, or that with every pouring of wine, things were getting more raucous and unruly. She badly wanted to leave, but Lady Augustine was obviously nowhere near ready.

"We're just all on edge," she reassured Senna. "Something to eat?"

They made their way to the court, which was no less crowded

and much noisier due to the free-flowing libations. Hardly any food remained, and the crowd was clearly ramping up to feed on something quite different.

"Hear, hear," someone called, banging a brass plate against a glass platter. "Let's toast—a drink of the vampire's blood." He lifted his goblet, sloshing with a healthy pour of red wine.

Cheers, drinking, more pouring, more noise.

"Blood, blood, blood, blood," the crowd chanted as they drank the wine, refilled their goblets, and drank some more.

Senna's insides congealed. Lady Augustine got caught up in the excitement as the crowd marched into the ballroom and she willingly followed, grasping Senna's hand and pulling her reluctantly behind.

A grandfather clock sounded somewhere far away, sonorously counting off the hours. The crowd quieted, listening.

. . . nine . . . ten . . . eleven . . . midnight.

Another guest climbed up on the dais with the orchestra.

"It's the hour of the vampire," he intoned, lifting his goblet. "The hour when they leave the tomb for the hunt. It's the hour to vanquish the vampire. If he's in this house, we'll hunt him down, we'll get him. We have protection, we have numbers, we're safe. Who's with me?"

The crowd rumbled with purpose, ready to rout out the resident evil.

Senna felt a touch on her elbow. She whirled to a ruffling sound above her head and a slice of shadow winging upward.

It was impossible to speak, the noise was so loud now.

The guest on the dais who had designated himself the leader banged on the drum to get everyone's attention.

"We'll form two groups. I need leaders. Who isn't afraid to search hidden corners and dark cellars?"

The women held back while the men volunteered. The guest-leader chose two and, by hand signals, divided the crowd into two segments.

"Everybody protected?"

The teams held up their talismans.

"All right then—this side take the upstairs, the others follow me to the cellars."

They marched off in two different directions out of the brilliantly lit ballroom and into the shadows beyond. The orderliness lasted all of two minutes before the crowd exploded in all different directions, front to back, upstairs and downstairs, into dark corners and deep into the dank lower recesses of the house.

Lady Augustine followed the group heading to search the first floor, as Senna stood rooted, appalled by how quickly the celebration had devolved into a sinister demon hunt.

She thought she was alone. She felt utterly small in the vast room with the glittering mirrors, which now reflected the empty ballroom. The only other occupants were the orchestra members soberly stowing their instruments.

"He was here, you know." Charles's voice, Charles's fingers touching her elbow.

She reacted defensively, fueled by her feeling of desolation. Charles was the last person . . .

"Who?" she managed through a dust-dry throat.

"Nicolai."

The name caught her by surprise. She knew Charles felt her visceral response. He'd caught her off guard, as he'd intended.

She had to remember she'd claimed no memory of her sojourn at Drom, that she didn't remember Charles, his aggression, all the inconsistencies, or the notes signed *Nicolai*.

I'm watching you . . .

Nicolai watching even here?

She shook herself. "What? Who? What are you talking about?"

Charles turned her toward him. "I don't believe you've forgotten."

So here was another unfettered glimpse of the real Charles, the impatient Charles who wanted everything instantly, especially answers.

She girded herself to slip into the part. "I'm sorry, but what are you talking about?"

"There's no audience here, Senna. No one to see or hear. You're lying about your memory loss."

She saw no immediate escape from him. In the distance, they could hear the crowd noisily taking over the house. The orchestra members had disbanded and left the dais, leaving them alone in the ballroom. It would take all the guts and guile she could muster to hang on to the lie.

It seemed like a good idea to move. She headed toward the foyer, feeling that the closer she was to the front doors, the better.

"Why aren't you with them?" she asked abruptly.

"Same reason as you. There are no vampires. And because Nicolai is here."

His certainty chilled her. Everything about her sojourn at Drom came rushing back—the opulence of the house; the stark location; the Countess, motionless as death in her mud bath; the notes from the dead Nicolai; the . . . the—she reached into the fog for the thing she couldn't remember and couldn't quite catch it.

Charles was watching her closely.

She could give everything away, trying to remember. She schooled her expression and turned to him. "You don't believe in vampires? I find that interesting."

"Neither do you," Charles pointed out.

"I'm afraid I'm just a guest who is waiting for her hostess so that we can return home." She tilted her head as she heard the guests finally returning, converging from the rear of the house and streaming down the steps from above, in groups and singly, chattering and solemn.

The self-appointed leader stood midway up the staircase motioning for silence.

"We have vanquished the vampire," he pronounced loudly.

Everyone clapped wildly.

"It is safe," he began, then suddenly there was a bolt, like a lightning strike, and in that moment, to the accompaniment of shocked screams, a body tumbled from the upper landing railing, bloody at the chest and neck, falling fast as a cannonball, and landing with a sickening thud not five feet away from Senna.

Chapter 9

*S*ociety mourned Lord Hartwicke with a lavish and fitting
funeral.

Speculation ran rampant in the papers about his bloody death.
No one had seen him the night of the ball after a time, but opinion
was divided as to what hour he had seemed to vanish.

Lady Hartwicke had been with friends when on the vampire
hunt. No one recalled seeing her husband in either group. But then,
no one could remember a half dozen of those surrounding them
as they poured through the house intent on finding monsters and
surely not suspecting one was really among them.

No one had seen who had pushed Lord Hartwicke's body over
the rail. Everyone agreed the bloody wounds were definitely the
mark of a vampire.

London shut down once again after Lord Hartwicke's funeral.
Those who could decamp to the country did, including the inconsolable Lady Hartwicke, who immediately took to her bed.

It had been just several days since the ball. The authorities were
no closer to solving the murder than they had been the evening

Lord Hartwicke died. The cause of death was a complete drain of blood from the body, similar to the death at the theater.

No one could explain the bite at the heart either. Everyone knew vampires fed through the neck.

No, they took bites out of— Again Senna reached for a memory that was still shrouded in fog. Something about bites. Something that made her feel deeply afraid, something she didn't confess to the inspectors who investigated the murder scene and subsequently interviewed every guest.

Now she couldn't leave; the authorities forbade it.

To make matters worse, there wasn't a day the headlines didn't scream VAMPIRES AMONG US.

HOW TO ROOT OUT A VAMPIRE? (AND THE CONSEQUENCES OF EVEN TRYING)

WHAT TO DO WHEN A VAMPIRE STRIKES

FIVE WAYS TO CIRCUMVENT A VAMPIRE (THEY REALLY WORK)

And then it rained as if the heavens were mourning Hartwicke's untimely death, while with every passing moment, Senna felt as if her lies were unraveling.

But then there were the nights, in that deep, comforting state of warmth, of those light, succulent kisses on her wrists or sometimes the bend of her elbow, the security of *him* watching over her as she slept. The way he enfolded her completely. She wished the dream would last beyond the night, but when she finally awoke, she was always alone.

Then there was everything else: the Countess, watching her and waiting. Charles's renewed pursuit and expressed disbelief that she'd lost her memory. Skeptical Vaida and her hummingbirds, ready to peck Senna to death if she got in their way. The unknown Peter Augustine, an ambush waiting to happen. And the elusive Dominick, the object of desire of every woman in his vicinity, and the ghost who made her dreams the place she wanted to live.

How much longer could she gull Lady Augustine?

As long as Lady Augustine believed that she was her ward and responsibility. Until the murderer was caught.

&.

Lady Augustine was bored. "We've been imprisoned again by this fiend," she fretted. "Nobody is even close to determining how to apprehend him, and we, meantime, are stuck at home with nothing to do. We need activity. We need society. We'll invite friends for tea tomorrow. We'll have company at least. I'll send Puckett round."

WHERE DOES A VAMPIRE HIDE? the papers demanded to know.

THREE IRREFUTABLE THINGS THAT IDENTIFY A VAMPIRE—BY AN EXPERT.

Lady Augustine threw all the papers in the trash.

"I won't have that garbage in my house," she said resolutely as she helped set up the tea tables in the parlor. Three round tables with plates, cups, and cutlery; a tea-serving table; the piano shifted to invite an impromptu performance; chairs placed for conversation; small tables to set down a plate or a cup—all carefully organized.

"Perfect," Lady Augustine approved, but her brow was slightly furrowed. She turned to Senna suddenly. "What if the fiend is one of us? What if I'm inviting him into my home—the same way the Hartwickes must have done—and he's with us here, this afternoon?"

"That's not likely," Senna assured her. "The murderer can't be one of your friends; he must have come in with a guest. Besides, no one was checking invitations; all he had to do was mingle. In that crowd, no one would have noticed a stranger. They'd have thought he was invited."

"You're right. I'm spinning plots like a serial novel. Except it is so dreadful it makes you believe there really are vampires."

"Or, it could be someone replicating the gothic details in some popular fiction. Anything can be simulated," Senna pointed out. "Even a bite on a neck. They will likely find Lord Hartwicke was killed first and the bites came after."

Lady Augustine shivered. "Oh, I don't like to think about that scenario. The killer deliberately inflicting those wounds after?"

That thought obviously wasn't comforting. Lady Augustine would rather believe it was a vampire than someone taking advantage of their fears, Senna thought.

But the real question was, what did she believe?

&.

Four of Lady Augustine's cronies arrived first, chittering and chattering like birds, all full of the latest speculation about the vampire.

The Countess arrived soon after, and then Charles, followed by Vaida and her two closest friends on a whoosh of rain and wind.

"Well, thank you all for coming," Lady Augustine welcomed them, positioning herself by the piano so that she could look down the spacious parlor to where Charles lounged apart from the rest of the guests.

"And to answer your questions before you ask, no, Senna has not regained her memory. And Dominick Janou unfortunately had to decline my invitation. Now, we shall eat."

Lady Augustine yanked the bellpull, and a moment or two later Puckett entered, bearing the tea tray, which he deposited on the tea table. Two maids followed, bearing trays of cucumber sandwiches, herring toast, liver pâté, and slices of orange cake.

Lady Augustine sat herself at the tea table and began to pour.

They could talk of nothing else but the vampire.

"They can't enter anywhere without an invitation. That's how he got into the Hartwickes'."

"You know you can't see their reflections in the mirror."

"They don't cast a shadow either."

"Did you know the reason we put headstones on graves? To keep the vampires from escaping."

And on it went, with no dearth of interest in any telling detail, real or imagined.

"Did you hear the most ridiculous theory?" Vaida said into the babble.

Everyone stopped talking.

"Dominick Janou is the vampire."

The Countess was suddenly electric with interest.

"Really, Dominick, a vampire?" Lady Augustine repeated. "Too funny."

"Maybe not," Vaida said, delicately picking at the remains of her sandwich. "He arrived here, what, four or five months ago from nowhere we've ever heard of. He's exotic and aloof. How do we know how he spends his nights?"

"And," one of the hummingbirds added, "he was at the theater, he was at Lord Hardwicke's, and wasn't one of those random bodies found near one of his warehouses?"

Lady Augustine shivered, cupping her tea as if it would infuse her with warmth.

The Countess leaned forward. "Dominick, his name is?"

"Yes, Mother," Charles confirmed from the back of the room.

She whirled on him. "You knew this?"

"Since the Hartwickes' ball."

"And you—"

"No," Charles said, anticipating the question and cutting her off.

Everyone stared, fascinated. The Countess's mouth worked as if she wanted to say more, only Charles's expression warned her not to. This was private, between them, whatever it was.

The Countess raised her chin. "More tea, please."

A strange silence followed.

Senna felt a crashing need to change the subject, to get as far away from vampires as she could devise.

"I can read palms," she announced suddenly. "Would anyone like to have a reading?"

"Now how can you remember that and nothing else?" Charles asked skeptically.

Senna met his gaze squarely. "I don't know. I just can." She looked around. "Anyone?"

Vaida held out her right hand.

"There are three lines," Senna said, lightly drawing them with her forefinger as she interpreted each. "First, closest to your fingers, is the heart line, which is not deeply etched. It says you like to be the center of attention and that you very much want someone to spoil you. Below that is the head line. It suggests that you are very single-minded and you like to be in control. And last is the life line, which isn't very long. It tells me you like to take risks. It tells me you need to be more careful."

Senna looked into Vaida's stony face and decided not to get into crosshatching, feathering, and other details. "The lines don't predict the future, you understand. They only tell what is, and it is for you to determine how that plays out in your life."

"Really," Vaida said, snatching back her hand. "Then let's hear what her lines say about the Countess, who has hidden herself away for so long."

"I don't wish to have my palm read," the Countess said tightly.

"Oh, do," Lady Augustine coaxed her. "I will too." She tugged at the Countess's hand and pulled it forward. "Go on, Senna. Read the Countess's palm."

The look the Countess gave Senna could have burned ice. Senna looked at Lady Augustine, who nodded, then she bent over the Countess's palm.

She ought to have refused; she saw that instantly. But it was too late now. Everyone watched, everyone wanted to know, and she had to be the one to say it.

"I—" She slanted a look at the Countess, whose expression was as hard as rock.

"Senna?" Lady Augustine and everyone else leaned forward in anticipation.

"I've never seen anything like this," Senna said reluctantly. "There are no lines on the Countess's palm."

"Really," Lady Augustine said later over dinner, "do you believe her hands were injured so badly in a fire that the lines would have burned off?"

"It's not for me to believe anything," Senna said carefully. Where were the traps? Everywhere. She'd nearly revealed that she knew about the fire. "I just read what the lines tell me."

"It's a very handy thing to know," Lady Augustine mused. "Always good for changing the subject."

"Did I?" Senna asked. "Perhaps I was a little tired of all that vampire talk."

"And making a vampire out of Dominick Janou. I couldn't

believe it. You'd think he lived in a coffin, the way they were talking, when he has a perfectly respectable house in Belgravia."

"How do you know that?" Senna asked.

Lady Augustine shrugged. "Everybody knows. There's a lovely little shop on Portland Street where he sells the objects he imports. And I've seen him out and about in daylight, if you want to know. There's nothing remotely vampiric about Dominick."

"And yet . . . all those deaths . . ."

"Well, I'm sure they could find a dozen people who had it in for Lord Hartwicke," Lady Augustine said with relish. "And the bites, the blood—all theatrics designed to obscure the truth and scare everyone into hiding behind closed doors, just as you've said. They probably were all mundane murders for mundane reasons, and now everyone's in a panic, and we can't go out at night. Who wants to go to a breakfast party, for heaven's sake?"

This was the big event of the next day, a select group spontaneously invited to a restaurant to partake of breakfast after the mandatory morning ride in the park.

The invitation had only come this afternoon, as had been every invitation issued within the last few days. Everything was arranged on short notice. No one knew what the day or the evening would bring. Nobody wanted to sit at home. No one wanted to be out at night. And no one wanted to witness another ghoulish murder.

But it made things so hard to plan. And to dress for day instead of evening was almost like not going out at all.

"Why go then?"

"How can I not?" Lady Augustine said huffily. "Of course we're going to go." She tilted her head and looked at Senna. "Aren't we?"

Lady Augustine broke off suddenly, and her gaze grew vague as she stared at Senna as if she'd never seen her. "Do I know you?"

Senna's heart stopped. She couldn't move, couldn't say a word, didn't know what to say. She wished she could just sink through the floor and vanish.

She was out of lies, stories, fabrications, excuses. This was it, the end of the deceit. And with that one question, she'd lose every-thing.

Senna waited for the indictment, feeling an after-the-fact remorse that she'd carried the deception this far.

"Who are you?"

Her name would mean nothing at all to Lady Augustine now, but she told her anyway. "I'm Senna."

"Senna? Senna . . ." Lady Augustine sounded as if she were trying on the sound of the name, then her gaze sharpened. "Oh-hhhhh! Oh my goodness—*Senna.*"

Senna could barely breathe, let alone speak. What had just happened? It was as if someone had turned up the gaslight and the encroaching darkness was illuminated again.

"I don't know what I was thinking. We were talking about . . . ?"

"The breakfast party tomorrow." Senna could barely form the words, the lightning change was so confounding.

"They're expecting everyone at nine. That should be enough time for a turn in the park, don't you think?"

"Yes, ma'am."

"Aunt Madalina," Lady Augustine corrected her gently. "We won't let monsters scare us, will we?"

"No," Senna murmured, her heart still in her throat.

But Lady Augustine's lapse of memory scared Senna to death. If it happened again, it could land her right back on the streets and straight into the poorhouse.

Right back where she'd been before she wrote those cursed indigent-relation letters.

God, that was a lifetime ago. It felt as if she'd been holding her breath ever since. How long could she pretend she didn't remember anything? How long before some tattler put together that *she* was a stranger in Town and that her memory loss could be a ruse to cover up *her* secrets? How soon before someone, in private company, speculated that she might be the vampire?

She was at the endgame of a deception that she had not initiated and over which she had no control.

Tomorrow, Lady Augustine could awaken and again have no memory of who Senna was and turn her out onto the street. It was time to cut loose and leave of her own volition.

But where would she go? What would she do? She had no money, just the closetful of clothes that Lady Augustine had provided and questions that would never be answered.

She had always played a game of risk. But the stakes were higher than they'd ever been: it was a risk to leave, a risk to stay. And she hadn't yet decided which way to play it.

Everything was about risk, never more so than since Dominick had returned to London. And now, this unplanned breakfast party and the inevitable moment he would confront the Countess.

She would go, she wouldn't refuse an invitation to anyplace she might encounter Senna or come to grips with his presence in London now that she knew he was here.

It was rather ingenious of Charles to have filtered that revelation during the tea party at Lady Augustine's, so that all the Countess's frustration had vented in seething silence rather than on Charles's head.

But the confrontation was coming. Dominick watched from afar as carriages arrived at the Colborne Restaurant, which replicated a Greek temple to conceal the private dining rooms and a dozen other small venues within, solely to serve the rich with elegance and discretion.

The guests were already gathering in an anteroom, and when everyone was present, the host and hostess would march them into the dining room.

It was an interesting wait, as he identified the guests. Neither Lady Augustine nor Senna had yet arrived. Vaida and her coterie, yes. Charles, yes. A parade of lords and ladies with whom he was moderately acquainted, yes.

He would have to join them soon—it was nearly nine o'clock. He'd wait another minute. And there they were, Lady Augustine and Senna at last, just this side of being late, as usual.

Another few minutes and he roused himself and followed, as the guests were proceeding to the private dining room.

It was as big as a ballroom, columned, with a painted, arched ceiling, gilt mirrors lining the walls, and jewel-toned Persian carpets scattered on the floor. Tables seating eight each were decked out in pristine white, silver, and crystal, with sconces and cut-glass chandeliers reflecting the light.

The guests were seating themselves—fifty and more, Dominick calculated from the entrance—but the Countess was not among them.

Yet.

He waited just there. She was near. He sensed it.

Suddenly every activity, every conversation, every movement, ceased. Everybody froze where they were.

Time stopped. Life ceased. Death was in place.

Nicolai. The Countess, as expected.

Countess.

Mother! she reminded him sharply.

He raised his brows. *Enemy.*

As you wish. You should have stayed away.

I've been counting the minutes until I returned.

Do not interfere with my plans, Nicolai.

Then you won't interfere with mine.

Lightning bolts of anger flashed all over her body. They stared at each other in the dead, motionless silence.

Hours, days, years—everything fell away.

The scene around them could have been a diorama trapped in time. The guests could have stayed there forever because there was no forever for them.

The two battled each other silently, their wills clashing, their bodies elevating above the guests, high and hard to the arched ceiling and back down to the ground as his tenaciousness warred with hers.

His strength surprised her. He was shocked that her will to triumph was no less determined after all these years.

I will eat you alive, she vowed.

Monsters do try to devour their young. So be it.

She vanished in a flash of light, and everything was set in motion again: the last of the guests entering the dining room, the conversation, the waiters serving water, the meandering of couples from one table to the next as they greeted friends.

But it was as if everyone had awakened from a dream. He heard a dozen bewildered comments all at once, like flies buzzing in his ear.

He listened above the noise, a fly on the wall. He felt the pulsing of a heart, he heard the keening cry of death, and the rabid devouring at the breast. The Countess, picking off a quick victim in the dark of a back alley, in the dank maw of her soul.

He felt the urge, the drive, the hellish need to feed.

It never ended. He was forever and always a bloodsucking ghoul. Nothing he ever did changed that.

And his own mother had done this to him, heartlessly and without regrets, even now.

That moment, listening to the Countess from a great distance as she sucked and chewed on blood and bone in some secret place of horror, he wanted to die all over again. Die and take her with him, beyond eternity, and end their blood-sodden days of trolling forever.

It would come. He would find peace.

But first there would be war.

It was a sit-down, full-serve breakfast: omelets, deviled kidneys, rashers of bacon, sausages, potatoes, grilled tomatoes, black pudding, scones with butter, honey, or jam, and tea and hot chocolate.

Senna ate sparingly, her appetite suppressed by her overwhelming feeling of wariness. The crowd was huge, all richly dressed, even at that hour of the morning, and engrossed in each other more than their neighbors at other tables.

They were at a table with guests who were strangers to Senna, so she didn't feel obligated to make small talk. Lady Augustine talked enough for both of them, introducing Senna as her ward and explaining that she had lost her memory. That caused a momentary stir, then someone commented on the food and they were off to other topics of mutual interest, to which Senna listened attentively.

She saw Charles and Vaida with their heads together. She did not see the Countess or Dominick, which seemed odd because everyone else was there, all faces she recognized from the Hartwicke ball.

Who among them was a vampire, a murderer?

She poked at her eggs.

"You're not hungry?" Lady Augustine asked.

"You are," Senna said. "This is nice." Gesturing with her fork to the environs of the restaurant. It was something to say.

"I love it when we all get together," Lady Augustine said. As if they were family instead of competitors for social status.

No one mentioned vampires.

Odd.

No one talked about Hartwicke's savage death.

Strange.

A fly buzzed in her ear and she batted it away.

An hour passed slowly. Senna smiled, made comments on passing conversation, and wondered when Lady Augustine would look at her again and not remember who she was.

It was better that the Countess wasn't in attendance. But where was she?

Senna drank hot chocolate while others poured their tea. She wished she had a sweet biscuit.

She wished . . . she were back in bed, enfolded in sweet dreams.

Instead she turned to Lady Augustine, who was just finishing her tea. "Let me read your leaves."

"Senna! Really?"

"What, she reads tea leaves? Oh, do mine!" A woman sitting across from Senna held out her cup.

"And mine."

"How droll. She reads leaves?"

"And palms," Lady Augustine said, nodding imperceptibly at Senna to indicate it was quite all right to take the first woman's cup.

The required sip of tea remained on the bottom of the cup. Senna swirled the cup three times, making certain that the liquid on the bottom touched every part of the interior of the cup.

Then she tipped it over abruptly so that the remaining tea dripped into the saucer, after which she held the cup in her hands with the handle pointing toward the woman.

Inside the cup were all kinds of omens of good fortune: a key, a rose, a flower.

"I'm happy to say I see much good fortune, in love and in money, in your future," Senna said. "It will all transpire in due course; nothing imminent. Everything takes time." She handed the cup back as Lady Augustine tugged at her sleeve.

"Read mine next."

Senna took the cup warily and performed the same ritual. This time, the reading was different. A significant clot of leaves remained on the bottom, as well as a dab of liquid near the rim, which indicated trouble. Tea stalks marched opposite the handle. An hourglass. Clouds. None of it good.

She collected her thoughts to soften the message.

"Well, the leaves tell me that a gentleman is about to enter your life. There is some trouble ahead, but perhaps we're past that point with the unsolved murders. The future isn't clear because of that. The leaves say that even so there will be good news ahead and in relatively good time."

That last was a lie, but what could she do? All those bad omens discomfited her. There were just too many in one reading. But then, it was all make-believe anyway, and Lady Augustine's friends seemed entertained.

"Me next."

She read two more cups in short order, then Lady Augustine got to her feet and said, "Come, my dear. It's time to go." But it would be another half hour before Lady Augustine finished a round of gossiping with everyone she hadn't seen since the ball, and until all the carriages were brought around.

Then Charles caught up with Senna. "You should have sent for me. You didn't have to keep Lady Augustine company all this time."

"It was my pleasure," Senna said politely. "I read tea leaves. Most enlightening."

"That you remember?"

Senna smiled and turned to Lady Augustine.

Charles persisted. "And you did say you might allow me to escort you, now and again."

"Did I? Perhaps I did."

"Senna—"

"Charles. This is not the place for you to convince me that something existed that I have no memory of. In fact, it's downright unfair."

"What's unfair?" asked Vaida, joining them.

"Charles's need to be admired by every woman he meets," Senna said lightly.

Vaida took his arm. "Well, as it happens, we're going riding this afternoon." She gave Senna a bright, disingenuous look.

"I'm sure he can use the exercise," Senna said, tapping his arm and turning to look for Lady Augustine.

Thankfully she was at the door, a step away from outside, and signaling for her carriage. "Senna!" her fluty voice summoned her.

"That was lovely," Lady Augustine commented when they were settled and on their way. "Everyone seemed very positive today. Not a word about those awful deaths. And they were vastly amused by your readings. Of course, one doesn't take those things seriously."

Lady Augustine looked out the window as the carriage turned into Berkeley Square. "Oh, I do love those trees. It's so beautiful in the spring."

By then the footman had opened the carriage door and held his hand for her. "Always good to come home," she murmured. "Senna?"

Senna followed and trailed her up the steps. The butler waited, the door ajar. "Madam?"

"Just a moment. Senna?"

"I'm here." She handed her coat and gloves to the waiting maid.

"I think we'll take some tea," Lady Augustine directed.

"Madam," the butler said, a shade more insistently.

"Yes?" Lady Augustine turned.

"Mother?" a voice demanded from the parlor.

"Peter?!" Lady Augustine shrieked, whirling into his embrace. "Senna, it's Peter!" His mother looked up at him with understandable pride. He was tall, blond, and handsome, lean and pared down as if he'd only just arrived.

He gave Senna a frosty look above the top of Lady Augustine's head. "Really? Who is Senna? Mother, I don't know this woman and neither do you. Who the devil are you?"

Chapter **10**

My dear!" Lady Augustine sounded shocked and appalled. "It's *Senna*." As if he ought to know.

"*Who* is Senna?"

"Peter, really. She's . . . she was—" Lady Augustine stopped, perplexed. "She was in the carriage, all toppled over. She . . . was at school . . . but she doesn't remember anything because of the accident."

"What school?" Peter demanded.

"Why, I—" Lady Augustine turned to Senna. "What school?"

"I don't remember," Senna said promptly. She could see in Peter's eyes that he hated her already. At the moment, she hated herself.

"You're lying," Peter snapped. "Who are you?"

"But, Peter—" Lady Augustine sounded deeply distressed. "She's my ward."

"Are you deranged? You have no ward."

"Of course, she's my—she came to me for help. She was in the carriage, in the park. I recognized her immediately . . ."

"You have no ward," Peter repeated impatiently.

Lady Augustine digested that. "I have no ward . . . really? But we've had such a time. I promised her a Season. Are you sure?"

Peter turned to Senna. "You. Leave now. Take whatever you brought with you, what you're wearing now, leave anything my mother paid for, and get out."

She couldn't say a thing in her defense. This was the man, the trouble she'd foreseen in Lady Augustine's tea leaves.

Senna mounted the staircase just as she heard him calling for a maid to accompany her and make sure she adhered to his instructions. She heard him from a distance ripping off questions that Lady Augustine couldn't answer. Senna felt the hard knot of dread she'd been living with drop hard in her stomach.

She'd arrived with nothing. She'd leave with nothing. Not even a piece of silver—a knife, maybe—that she could have pawned somewhere, as she'd originally planned.

What?

Wait—originally planned?

That sounded so familiar, as if it had actually happened.

She'd taken a knife while dining with . . . the Countess. At Drom. Because . . . she'd been going to—

The memory was like a fly buzzing around her head. Incessant, familiar. Why couldn't she remember?

She shook it off. "I don't have very much to pack," she said to the maid. "A bag will do."

"I'll find something for you," the maid said tersely. "You just sit here till I get back."

Senna sank onto the chair at the vanity and stared at herself in the mirror. Her face was pale, her eyes blazed, made even more prominent by the light blue color of the suit she wore. That beautifully made suit . . . for her, who could contain the whole of her life, let alone her wardrobe, in one paper bag.

She could keep the clothes on her back, he'd said. How magnanimous of him. He'd be up here any minute to bodily lift her out of the house, she was certain of it, he was in that much of a rage.

He saw her for what she was: a sham, a swindler, a deceiver, a cheat. For all he knew, she'd stolen Lady Augustine's money and jewels. He'd probably searched the house thoroughly when he arrived.

Except how did he even know about her presence here? He wasn't due back for weeks according to Lady Augustine. Someone must have told him. But who? They all seemed to have accepted the fact of her existence. No one questioned her presence in the company of Lady Augustine. No one denounced her. No one accused her of being a fraud while she'd hidden behind the wall of memory loss while she'd tried to figure out—

Everything suddenly jumbled up in her mind—confusing the moment of Lady Augustine's discovery of her in the park with her having been at Drom mere moments before.

That just wasn't possible. Though Lady Augustine's complete acceptance of her as someone she knew hadn't made any sense either.

Who, in her situation, wouldn't have taken advantage of that moment?

She could hear Lady Augustine arguing with her son in the distance. Peter wanted Senna out. Where was that maid?

Why hadn't she thought to steal the silver?

But she had—

She took a deep breath, trying to organize her memories.

Why during this whole misadventure had she been thinking with her emotions instead of her head? Was she so happy to have a real bed that it blinded her to the things that didn't make sense?

The maid returned with a satchel about the size of a doctor's bag. "Lady Augustine says you may have this."

"I appreciate that. Thank her for me, will you?"

The maid was already rummaging in the closet. "I believe this was what you were wearing when you came?"

She held up Senna's worn shirtwaist and skirt. Senna nodded and the maid folded it and packed it away.

"Was there anything else?"

"Nothing," Senna said. The word sounded stark even to her ears.

The word *nothing* summed up her life—always trying to fill an empty space and never quite succeeding.

Nothing.

Something had propelled her from the fields of Drom to a park in London at dawn, and when she reached for a memory to account for it, she found nothing.

Peter Augustine looked through her and found nothing.

All she had was guts, guile, and the ability to devise, deceive, and lie, with a fair amount of pleasing looks to top it off. Nothing.

It was rather fitting that she'd be back on the streets again, a nothing on her way to the poorhouse and certain death sooner than later.

Someone had said that to her recently . . . hadn't they?

She preceded the maid out of the room and down the stairs, where she could hear Peter still haranguing Lady Augustine.

He wheeled around as he heard her footstep. "There's the door."

It was open as well, but as Senna moved to leave, Lady Augustine, showing some temper and backbone, barred the way.

"Enough of this. I won't be bullied. I keep telling you and telling you, Senna has no memory of who she is or of her past. *I* know who she is—she's my ward, and I will not let you throw her out on the street. Besides, you haven't seen her since she was sent to boarding school—how many years ago I don't even remember."

"I do not know this creature," Peter said flatly. "For all we know, she's a murderer or a thief. I keep telling you, you're fortunate nothing's missing. This woman is a Gypsy and she's deceived you like the expert she is. Thank God you have concerned friends."

"Oh, truly? *I* have? Who told you that barbarous lie?"

"A worried friend."

"They need not have worried," Lady Augustine snapped. "I'm not a fool, much as you—and my so-called *friends*—might think I am."

Senna's head hurt. The back-and-forth had got Lady Augustine nowhere: Peter was adamant, and Senna felt like a shuttlecock.

"I should go," she said.

"And look, the poor girl has virtually nothing in that bag, she came barreling into Town in such a hurry. Where should she go?"

Peter reached into his frock coat, removed a handful of pound notes, and tossed them at Senna. "I don't care."

Senna moved, but Lady Augustine physically stopped her.

"I won't have it."

"She's a flimflammer, Mother. How many times must I say it? There must be a half dozen people she's taken in with this scheme. Who among our friends knows her?"

Lady Augustine raised her chin. "The Countess. The Countess knows her. She specifically said so, even though Senna doesn't re-member right now. And Charles came to visit—they were to have been married, actually. He said so, and he wanted . . ."

Lady Augustine threw a confused glance at Senna and she nod-ded.

"He said he wanted to start all over with her, even if she didn't remember they had been going to be married. So there are two ac-quaintances she knows that we know."

Peter had gone very quiet. He didn't move a muscle, but Senna could have sworn that his interest was piqued.

"The Countess," he murmured finally. "Engaged to Charles Sandston, were you?" He directed the question at Senna.

Another trap. Answering questions about things she hadn't kept track of presented a different danger. What had Lady Augus-tine overheard that day? She couldn't remember what she'd told Charles. *Say as little as possible and still answer the question.*

"I don't know. He says so. I didn't remember him."

The Countess's and Charles's acquaintance with Senna had changed something; Peter turned to Lady Augustine and said abruptly, "All right, let her stay. I'll go to my club. We'll see what happens."

He looked at Senna with his inscrutable dark eyes. "I'll be watch-ing you."

Watching you . . . an echo of another place, another presence watching . . . *I'm watching you* . . .

Would she find notes in the books on the library shelves?

"I promise you, I'm only grateful for everything Lady Augustine has done."

That pretty speech didn't mollify him. "I don't trust you."

How could he? No answer for that.

"Puckett!" he shouted, and the butler came running. "I'll be staying at my club for the time being. Make sure my things are sent there."

"Yes, sir."

Wealth has its privileges, Senna thought. And it liked to make chaos when it could. It still took some time until Peter left and Lady Augustine let out a deep breath.

"He does fill up the room," she murmured. "What's in that bag? That scruffy skirt and waist you were wearing the morning we found you? Oh, my dear—" She rang for the maid and pointed to the bag. "Burn that thing." She took Senna's arm. "Come. Now I think we really need that tea."

The Countess was so furious, all she could do was pace around the parlor. For one thing, she hated the rain. She hated the wet and the slime and the scent on dreary homeless bodies when they had been roosting in wet doorways for nights on end. She hated the sluicing bites and bitter taste of rancid food and wet, filthy clothes.

She hated the limits of the hunt when it rained.

More than that, she hated that Peter Augustine had returned and that he hadn't booted Senna to the street where the Countess could have bled her dry and picked her bones.

And Charles wasn't yet home from wherever he'd gone. Which was not to charm and seduce Senna. That just stoked her anger and feeling of impotence more: she couldn't control where he went or what he did. She was so close to giving up the idea of an heir.

Senna was as safe and guarded as the crown jewels right now, and how clever of her to plead a loss of memory that no one could dispute. The lie covered a lot of ground, enough that Senna needn't answer questions or account for anything. How smart, how wily of her.

Where was Charles? Damn him.

She couldn't stop pacing. She needed, wanted, was on fire to hunt. The minute she dispatched Charles, she would—

She heard the key rattle in the lock. There he was!

She charged into him as he entered. "Peter Augustine is back."

"I know. But he's no obstruction to your plans," Charles said, removing his cape and shaking it. "Nicolai is the real problem."

"The problem is he's compressed himself to such a nothingness that he can't be found," she snapped.

"He obviously doesn't want to be found."

"He can only evade me for so long. And what about Senna? You've made no headway with her."

"I don't believe for a moment she's lost her memory," Charles said, seating himself by the fire. "It's a tricky situation with her."

"She's been very clever about that; her lie covers just about everything." The Countess started pacing again. "But she can't claim to remember what happened at Drom if she's adamant that she remembers nothing else.

"And you, you're taking too long to bed her," she added sharply, wheeling on him. "What if Peter becomes attracted to her? Or if she pretends to regain her memory, then what? You need to be there, *now*. You need to start on that heir *now*."

Charles pursed his lips. "Would that I could order an heir from Harrod's, Mother."

"Indeed. It would simplify things enormously. Go. Seduce her." She peered out the parlor window. "What else does one have to do in the rain?"

"Mother—"

"We don't have a lot of time. Nicolai is bent on vengeance and—"

"What!? Wait, what do you mean he's . . ."

The Countess didn't answer.

"You saw him? When did you see him? Where?"

"Let's just say we had an encounter," the Countess said reluctantly. "He feels no gratitude. There's no forgiveness, and it's been twenty years, twenty lifetimes . . ."

"He could get to her first," Charles said as the realization dawned. Senna seduced by Nicolai? A spawn of Nicolai with the tainted blood of the Lazlarics?

No wonder the Countess hovered on a knife's edge of desperation. The threats were real: the purity of the Lazlaric blood could be sullied. Senna pretended not to remember the bloody scene at Drom, while at any moment she could reveal all the Countess's secrets. The likelihood of arrest for murder followed hard on that revelation.

"You're wasting time," the Countess spat as she watched him parse out the possibilities. "Go to her."

He threw her an incendiary look as he grabbed his cape and left.

How did I get here?

Senna sank down at the vanity table and stared at herself in the mirror. She looked no different. In the reflection, the room looked no different. But something *was* different.

How could it be as if nothing had just happened? How could Lady Augustine chat about clothes and the breakfast party, and how good it was to get out and see everyone, when Senna had almost been thrown out on the street not an hour ago?

She felt as wrung out as if she'd been on the run. There were mysteries to be solved. She had to think.

For one thing, who had summoned Peter Augustine?

And why should her knowing the Countess be the tipping point for Peter's allowing her to stay?

Nothing made sense; there was no rational explanation for any of it.

She closed her eyes and cleared her mind. Just for a moment. Just . . .

That's right, my pretty. Close your eyes. Dominick circled above her, gliding on a wing and finally settling on the porcelain pin box in the corner of the vanity table.

Her head rested in her folded arms. He was inches from her face, those perfect features, that thick, glossy hair. *Just let me in*. He nipped at her outstretched wrist. *Just a taste, just a flick*. He savored that barest smear of her blood until there was nothing but the faintest irritation where he had licked and sucked at it.

Slowly and painstakingly he reshaped himself into a cloak of mist to shroud her body.

Soon he would take her. Soon he would be the son who would give the Countess what she had always wanted, and he'd taste the wine of vengeance.

She saw him in her dreams that night as clearly as if he were next to her in bed. She heard him, deep in her dreams—"Kiss me"—and it seemed perfectly natural to lean in and touch her lips to his, and then suddenly to feel the devouring heat of his mouth taking over, taking her in her dreams, deeper into the eroticism of his kiss, to the place where her most forbidden fantasies resided.

She wanted to subsume herself in that heat forever. She yearned for it, she reached for it, she wanted to wrap herself in it until—

She jolted awake. No one was in the room.

She could have sworn . . . She touched her lips.

Her blood burned with an unfamiliar urgency. It was all she could think about, all she wanted, to seek him out wherever he was. Everything else, all the mysteries, seemed irrelevant next to the mystery of him.

Nothing made sense. *This* didn't make sense. To feel like this after a mere dream. To so ferociously want a man she didn't even know.

She couldn't stay in her bed another minute. She got up, sank into the vanity chair, and peered in the mirror again, seeing an image that was flushed with erotic need, her eyes dilated with a strange desire, her mouth molded by his kisses and begging for more.

From a shadow, a dream.

If she returned to her dream state, she could have him again, whole and full and hers, all into the night and beyond.

She pulled the bedcovers back.

"Miss?"

The ever-cheerful maid, at the door, startled her.

Senna turned wearily. "Yes?"

"Madam says it's time for dinner."

No kisses now, no. "I'll join her shortly."

After all, dinner would be only an hour. She could plead a head-ache on account of the day's events after that. And then . . .

She could almost feel the touch of his mouth on hers.

And she could live the fantasy again.

 ady Augustine wished to play cards that night. Dominick watched as Senna tactfully and futilely tried to get out of it.

When she finally retired, he knew she sought to conjure the dreams, but he didn't wish to let her. He draped himself over her body in a fine mist as he did every night. He took his enslaving blood-nip from her wrist and let the drop sit on the tip of his tongue until it dissolved. It was never enough, and the taste, now imprinted on his tongue, only made him ache for more.

It was dangerous and one of the reasons he tempered his dream seduction of her. But in truth he punished himself more by denying them both, and he didn't like how quickly he had succumbed to a need to touch and kiss her.

Her restive body, in a thin lawn gown, twisted and turned beneath his enfolding mist. He rippled, following every languorous move, filling the hollows and curves with enfolding warmth.

Too tempting. Her neck, her breast . . . he yearned for another kiss, another drop, another taste on his tongue of that evanescent pleasure.

One bite and enslavement could become eternity, everything could change.

Devil's bones . . .

He slid off her body onto the floor. He pulled himself up and slowly, painstakingly transshaped into his bat body, flying up into the canopy of her bed, away from the temptation of her.

Now he could think. Now the taste and the feel of her diminished into nothingness. But the craving was there, the ache to possess, the burning need to take the blood. *Her* blood.

Restraint was needed; pleasures were still to be had before the ultimate coupling. He still wanted much, too much that was exciting and arousing between the blood and the promise of her innocence and her body.

That was the lure—that, and *her,* the utterly beautiful, unbelievably enticing Senna. He'd never looked at a woman quite that way before.

He watched as she awakened, as she stretched and began her morning rituals. She removed her nightgown, bathed her curvy, naked body, and dressed.

Her.

Soon.

I have to find him. I have to find some time—an hour or two—I have to know. I have to—

Senna felt unreasonably frenetic with an urgency she almost couldn't control.

Because she hadn't dreamed of kisses and body-drugging sensual heat?

Ridiculous.

Nevertheless, she had to find him, be alone with him. Soon.

She skittered into the dining room where Lady Augustine was already having breakfast.

"Senna. Do sit down. That's a lovely color on you."

She was wearing a plum-purple dress. "Thank you."

I'll be watching you.

She felt tight as a drum now in Lady Augustine's company. She was careful to be polite, to parse every word to make certain nothing could be misconstrued, and was utterly grateful that the lie was fluid enough to cover every equivocation.

She helped herself to tea and scones as Lady Augustine looked up from reading the morning paper.

"This is the worst pre-Season there ever was," she said irritably. "No one is out and about, and no one cares about anything with a monster running loose. They haven't caught him; they don't have a clue. And all we can do is hope the sun is out so we can go for a drive in the park. Shall we at least do that?"

Senna took a deep breath. "That would be delightful." God, she didn't want to drive in the park. She wanted to drive straight to . . . to . . . where had Lady Augustine said he lived?

She racked her memory. Belgravia. Wherever that was. And a shop on . . . Portland Street, was it?

"Peter might join us," Lady Augustine added as the doorbell sounded. "Ah, here he is now."

He strode in with a suspicious look on his face, as if he expected to hear that Lady Augustine had unexpectedly expired during the night. He almost seemed disappointed something like that hadn't happened.

"You are testing my patience," Lady Augustine scolded him.

"I trust no one." He took a scone and tore it in half. "If you're driving this morning, I'll go with you."

I'll be watching you.

It was the only reason he had even come for breakfast this morning, Senna knew.

They got up and out around ten o'clock. The day was clear, sunny, bright, and crisp. The carriage was open, so they wrapped themselves in fur throws before they started out. Peter rode sedately beside them.

Lady Augustine obviously reveled in the rituals: the nodding and bowing to acquaintances, the stopping to speak for a moment to dear friends, and, now, to make spontaneous plans for the day, the next evening, the weekend, given the constraints of the murder investigation.

"No, no—Senna hasn't yet regained her memory, but all is well—and Peter is back from the Continent. A gathering of friends tonight? Of course, we'd love to come." And on and on for about an hour, with Lady Augustine committing them both to social calls on succeeding afternoons, the thought of which made Senna want to hide in her room the moment they returned to Berkeley Square.

How had she gotten so tangled up with Lady Augustine? And now, with Peter watching her, she felt as if she couldn't take a breath without accounting to one of them. She ought to have just walked out the door when he'd told her to.

She would have found her way—she always found her way. It wouldn't have been easy, but at least she wouldn't feel as trapped as she did now.

As trapped as she had at Drom . . .

If only she were a woman alone, she could do things, go places—maybe even see *him*. Her breath caught.

She felt Peter's eyes on her as he sensed her impatience.

"Is something wrong, Senna?"

"Not at all." Just the flashing moment she became aware of *him*. She couldn't even see him, but she knew he was somewhere in the crowd, approaching them as the traffic allowed, tall and elegant, controlling his feisty stallion with his clever hands.

As he drew closer, she felt his attention shift from her to Lady Augustine and Peter. She felt hot, sensual things she shouldn't even think about a man she didn't know.

"Dominick!" Lady Augustine exclaimed. "Well, here you are at last. This is my son, Peter." Peter tipped his hat. "And Senna, my ward."

All polite, gracious. Edgy—just a little?

Give me your hand.

She could barely breathe; she reached out and he kissed her hand, on the glove side first, and then he turned it and placed his lips on her bare wrist.

The merest tick of feeling and he flicked a minuscule drop of blood with his tongue and kissed the wound.

"Senna." His voice was perfect, deep, sensual, and rich. His eyes were all over her, as if he knew her, as if those sensual kissing dreams had some basis in reality.

She couldn't speak. She felt the touch of his mouth on hers and yet he hadn't moved, hadn't relinquished her hand and was nowhere near her lips. He sat still as a statue while Lady Augustine rattled on about how difficult it was to see people when their social life had been so severely curtailed and didn't he miss the dinners and parties and such.

"I'm sure we'll survive," Dominick said drily. "The murderer will be found, and meantime, we'll learn to fall back on our own resources and be the better for it."

"Do you think?" Lady Augustine asked, much struck by the thought.

"If you'll pardon me . . ." Dominick bowed to Lady Augustine and Senna as he edged his horse around the carriage.

"Well!" Lady Augustine said. "Well . . ."

"We still have a long way to go," Peter said. "Driver, if you would."

The carriage moved on. Senna turned to look for Dominick, but he was nowhere in the crowd and everywhere in her thoughts.

He would come tonight, in her dreams, she was certain of it. The way he'd looked at her, the heat that coursed through her when his lips gently sucked the skin on her wrist. He felt it too, she thought, and she went breathless again, conjuring the sensation, rabid for night to fall and her dreams to come.

Lady Augustine had impulsively invited some two dozen friends to join them for tea at three, so desperate was she for company. Lunch was a mere sip of soup and bite of fried bread as the cook scrambled to provide a full menu of sandwiches, scones, and tea for company.

Senna escaped to her room, hoping to avoid even having to attend, but that thought was almost immediately dashed.

Peter had followed her up and stood glowering on the threshold as she sank onto the vanity-table chair.

"What is it, Peter? Is there a problem?"

"You're the problem. Still."

So he was spoiling for a confrontation. That was the last thing she wanted at the moment. She just wanted him to go.

"Yes, so you keep telling me." Let him bring up her leaving. It would solve every problem except the one of how she came to be there in the first place.

Perhaps that didn't matter anymore. Nothing mattered but that she be left alone with her dreams.

"I'll leave, if that will ease your mind," she offered brazenly.

"It's not my mind that needs easing. I know you're a charlatan and a fraud. I don't know how you convinced Mother that you have any claim on her whatsoever. Never forget that I'm onto you."

"I'm aware," Senna said dismissively. "You'll be counting the silver every day and the pound notes in your pocket. I'm willing to leave—"

"Would that you could," he murmured as he stared at her from the doorway. She stared back and something raw and primal flared in his eyes. It could have been a killing instinct or a sudden arousing awareness of her as a woman.

Whatever it was, it unsettled her and she didn't know quite what to do to make him leave.

"Your luck holds: I will not distress my mother," he said finally, a concession that he'd made his point and there was nothing further to discuss. "So enjoy all this as you may, Senna. Your hours here are numbered."

He left then, and she stared at herself in the mirror. There would be no end to his threats now. He didn't wish to cause Lady Augustine any distress, did he? She knew full well that would be fleeting in the aftermath of her eventual departure.

And in time—as the other night—Lady Augustine would barely remember who she was.

She barely remembered who she was, come to that—the child

of the streets, the scrounging scavenger, liar, thief, and scoundrel she had been. She had disappeared into the maw of satin-trimmed dresses, afternoon tea, a biography that didn't exist, and her yearning for a lover who lived only in her dreams.

She felt as if the punishment for every deceit, ruse, and lie were converging here, on the altar of her greatest deception, and conspiring to bring her to her just punishment.

She'd seen the look in Peter's eyes. She was a complication to be gotten rid of, sooner rather than later, any way that he could devise.

She got up to wash her face and prepare herself for the company arriving soon for tea.

Tea must go on. Everyone expected it. Lady Augustine expected her, Peter's feelings about it notwithstanding.

Senna knew what to expect too.

Night would soon come, and with it, her dreams.

Charles was among the guests and already seated beside Lady Augustine, commiserating with her about the lack of entertainment and that the whole city was holding its breath waiting to see if the murderer would be caught or if someone else would die.

Dominick drifted down the stairs, a whiff of mist that could have been the steam from the tea, the smoke from a pipe, or a swirl of dust the maid had missed. The other guests were crowding in one after the other. He settled himself at the edge of the hem of Senna's skirt as Lady Augustine's friends arrived, then Vaida and her friends, several members of Parliament just coming from sessions, and a handful of others Lady Augustine had met in the park this morning.

The food was set out on the dining room table *en buffet,* and Puckett had arranged three tables where the guests would sit. There were platters of cucumber, salmon, and watercress sandwiches, slices of orange bread and pound cake, fresh strawberries, tea, and hot chocolate.

Guests drifted in one after the other, filled their plates, and chose a table. The conversation immediately centered on the murders and why the Yard had no leads as to who had done it. The papers were still pounding the idea of a vampire.

"It makes sense," Lady Augustine said. "How do you catch a murderer who is supernatural?"

"But vampires can be caught," one of the members of Parliament pointed out. "They can be trapped, they can be killed—violently, I grant you. But you drive in a stake, you chop off a head, you burn a heart—the thing is done."

A babble of protests and suggestions greeted that statement.

"They can transform themselves, you know."

"Oh, really, into what? Birds? Bees? Hiding in the ivy, listening to this conversation?"

"Don't believe me. I just know that's true."

"I just heard Lady Hartwicke came back to Town because she's thinking of holding a séance."

"Really? Does she hope to conjure a vampire?"

"She hopes Lord Hartwicke will come through and tell her who the vampire was."

Laughter greeted that statement.

"I happen to know there've been a lot more killings than the Yard has let on."

"No!"

"Really?"

"Why not?"

"They don't want to tell you how many of those deaths were due to neck and chest bites."

There was more babble as everyone rushed to comment at once.

Charles tapped Senna's arm and motioned to the parlor. Willingly, she followed him out, disturbed by all the levity about vampiric death.

"They have no idea what they're talking about," Charles murmured, sequestering them by the window where two chairs set for conversation were on either side of a small table.

"I hate that talk," Senna said vehemently. "I just hate it."

Charles looked at her sharply. "Yes. They have no facts, no proof, no witnesses, and yet they gossip as if they know everything. But we don't have to speak of such things. Let's recall more pleasant things, like when you played the piano for me at Drom. Do you remember?"

She remembered—he'd asked, she'd protested that she knew some chords and not much more, and then she'd played a couple of improvised bars.

Always improvising. That was her life. Yes, she remembered—and then she realized he was baiting her.

"I'm sorry, I don't," she said, keeping her voice and her expression blank.

Good play, my pretty.

"What if you sat down and tried to play now?"

"But I'd interrupt all that important conversation. They're definitely going to figure out how to catch the elusive vampire killer tonight."

"You're the one who's elusive. Let me in, Senna. We were going to be married."

Thank God for the lie. "I truly don't remember any of that, Charles."

"Then can't we just start over?"

She didn't know how to answer that this time. She hadn't known about luscious kisses last time. She hadn't experienced the urgency of her own desire-driven need last time.

She couldn't say yes; how could she, when she compared *his* kisses—the ones in her dreams—against the ones she'd rejected?

A memory flashed and faded.

But her silence was telling and he immediately leapt to his own conclusion. "There's someone else."

She didn't answer.

"Who?"

"Charles . . ." She saw Peter suddenly, hovering between the dining room and parlor, just as Charles became aware of him too.

"Is it him, Augustine?"

"He only just arrived yesterday," she said mildly. "Really, Charles."

He turned back to her and grabbed her hands before she grasped what he meant to do and she suppressed a shiver at his touch; she felt his anger.

"You're mine, Senna, even if you don't remember. I'll remember for both of us. I won't let you go. I won't let him have you—or anyone who falls in love with you. This is just fair notice. I keep what's mine. And I expect you to honor your promise to marry me."

"I can't do that. I don't remember that promise."

"You will," he said furiously, whipping away from her and storming out of the room.

Peter took his place. "I wasn't wrong about you, was I? Charles Sandston, eh? Broke a promise to marry? Really? Because you thought there was someone in Town who would suit you better? Not many are that rich."

"You have it exactly right," Senna retorted.

"I've got money. How much?"

The question stunned her. She itched to slap him; he wanted her to slap him, to exhibit in front of Lady Augustine's friends the kind of ill-bred violence that would give him good reason to throw her out.

Instead she eyed him as if she were considering his offer, then she said silkily, "You can't afford me." She stood up. "Do excuse me, Peter."

I'll be watching you.

She detoured into the dining room to tell Lady Augustine that she had a headache and to please excuse her.

"Oh, but, my dear, the vampires—"

"Yes, I know. My head is pounding from all the noise and futile speculation."

"Of course. Peter will keep me company. I think Charles went out for a breath of air." Lady Augustine waved Senna away. "Go lie down, my dear."

Good she had Lady Augustine's tacit permission. No excuses

needed then. And he would be waiting for her. She could closet herself in her room forever.

She locked her door and threw herself onto the bed. She could still hear the babble of conversation, now a low hum, from below. She wrestled the cover over her body and lay still, hoping for sleep.

No sleep, of course. Her thoughts buzzed like a swarm of bees.

Peter doesn't hate you. He wants you.

What? Where did that thought come from?

From the way he'd looked at her today? His nasty assumptions? His desire to protect Lady Augustine . . .

Where are you?

He was there, a thick mist settling over her body, enfolding her. Leaning over her shoulder, enticed by her earlobe. Yet another secret spot to just pierce lightly, judiciously. Only here, he could feed on more than a drop. He could inhale, taste, rub the taste of her onto his lips, his tongue, and she'd never feel it.

Just the thought was sensual and arousing, as tasty as sex with her would be.

*Nick the lobe—just there, just—*a drop spurted onto his lips. He rubbed his lips together to spread it before he tasted. There was yet another drop that he licked. She shuddered as his hot tongue swiped her lobe and tasted her blood yet again.

Who enslaved whom really?

She knew he was there, playing with her earlobe, licking and sucking at it until she almost couldn't stand it.

Kiss me.

I am—the luscious gift of the oozing blood in your lobe . . . a banquet, an unexpected feast of you on my lips and tongue that will bind you even tighter to my desire.

Kiss me.

Let me linger here where you can feel me.

He wanted to wallow in this orgy. As little as it was, it slaked his thirst thoroughly because he could roll the drop in his mouth and let it seep into his pores, into the tip of his tongue, into his consciousness.

She was so perfect for his purposes—beautiful, malleable, virginal, ripe for planting . . . and *his*.

Sleep, my pretty.

Kiss me.

That will come and more. Sleep . . .

Her eyelids drifted downward.

He nibbled her ear until she dozed off, flicking his tongue at the last little smear of dried blood on her lobe.

It was dangerous how much he enjoyed the taste of her, but this drop-by-drop seduction was a necessary part of his physical possession of her.

She craved him now. All her senses had been heightened by his patient bloodletting, his sensual kisses, the promise of pleasures to come.

It was a matter of time and how much he felt like prolonging the dance, always being aware the appetite was whetted by what it couldn't have. Not only for her, but for him and the moment, imminent now, when he would crave her.

Nothing had changed. Charles was still in the picture and would grab whatever opportunity he could to get her alone. And now Peter Augustine, with his hot eyes and male blood dueling with her as if he hated her when he'd rather have bedded her.

Never. Dominick licked another drop. *Mine.*

She woke with a jolt at the sound of the maid knocking on the door.

"Miss—miss . . . dinner . . . the door is locked—"

Oh, God, she'd locked the door to be alone with her dreams. And he'd come, licking and sucking at her ear and lobe. But he didn't kiss her . . .

She was still dressed too, and she swung out of bed and staggered to the door to open it. "I'm going to need help. Apparently I fell asleep with my clothes on."

"Yes, miss."

The maid didn't like her, Senna thought, because of Peter's attitude and accusations. But she was efficient and got her undressed and re-dressed in short order, and Senna went down to dinner in time, a puff of mist trailing unobtrusively behind her.

Peter had stayed. "You missed some very entertaining conversation."

"Everyone had an opinion about everything," Lady Augustine added disgustedly. "Truly, it's no wonder nothing ever gets done."

What kind of bland comment could she add to that? "I'm sure that's not true," Senna said as she seated herself. She caught the look in Peter's eyes—amusement, and something else, a gleam, as if he understood her predicament and sympathized.

"If you don't mind, I'd like to eat light tonight." Even some soup and fish were too much—she found herself nibbling the edges while Peter pushed his food around and Lady Augustine ate heartily.

Senna couldn't get the feeling of Dominick's tongue licking her lobe out of her mind. It was almost as if he were right over her shoulder, right there—

The sensation in her ear intensified, and she shuddered. It felt so real.

"I received the oddest note this afternoon, after everyone left," Lady Augustine said after they'd finished eating and tea had been set out with cookies, cheese, and fruit. "It was from Lady Hartwicke, presuming on our decades-old friendship to ask a favor of me. Can you guess?"

Peter figured it out immediately. "Then it was no idle gossip today. She wants to hold a séance."

"Indeed. But here at Berkeley Square rather than the manor. She wants a neutral and more intimate setting that will be more conducive"—Peter snorted, and Lady Augustine shot him a look—"to summoning dear Lord Hartwicke's spirit. She's one of my oldest friends. I'm inclined to say yes."

"And how many is she inviting to attend this séance?" Peter asked.

"Why, she didn't say."

"And the medium?"

"She says, she says that the Countess has kindly offered to be the intermediary."

Dominick, who was hanging on a chandelier, nearly fell off.

Devil's bones. She **damned** *never stops—not stalking, not hunting until she has her way.*

"And"—Lady Augustine held up her hand—"she says she'd like to conduct the séance tomorrow."

Chapter 12

*D*ominick hated the way Peter was looking at Senna while Lady Augustine listed reasons to accede to Lady Hartwicke's request.

He transshaped into the smoke in the guttering candles, less than ten inches from Peter's shadowed face and Senna's distressed expression.

"Surely that's not enough notice," she protested.

"Well, I won't be hosting high tea, that's for certain. Just people coming in, sitting down, and the Countess calling up spirits and then everyone goes home. How much time could that take?" Lady Augustine asked reasonably, tucking away the note. "Of course I'll say yes."

You're bored, and you'll grab at anything to entertain yourself. Be wary, my lady. All is not what it seems.

"What?" Lady Augustine asked as if someone had spoken and she hadn't heard it. "I thought you said something, Peter."

"Time to leave maybe."

But dear God, a séance, Senna thought, dismayed. What was Lady

Augustine thinking? And what did the Countess know about mediums and spirits? She— A memory wafted by, just out of recognition, just out of reach.

"Will you want me to keep you company tonight?" Senna asked after Peter had taken his leave.

"Thank you, my dear, no. I have much to plan and very little time in which to do it."

Tomorrow, Senna thought, *I'll talk her out of it tomorrow.* But for now, she felt exhausted, both from keeping up her end of the conversation at dinner, and the draining feeling of *him* close to her, tugging on her earlobe, teasing her, arousing her, so all she wanted was to retreat to her room and lock the door.

If only she weren't so corseted, encased, and boned. It took a full ten minutes for the maid to undo every hook, tie, and button, and to slip off the layers of underwear and crinoline before she was naked and free under her gauzy nightgown.

She locked the door then and slipped into bed.

Dominick seeped under the door and spread himself over her body. He let himself feel the tension, the mutual need. He waited until long after it all dissipated, and her body relaxed and she slept. Tonight he decided he wanted—no, he needed—to puncture her left earlobe and taste the delights waiting for him there.

A slight roll and her ear was bared to him. A quick nick and he took the crimson drop into his mouth and savored it. One more binding drop.

And another, the tiny, tasteful drops melting into the flesh of his mouth, his tongue, his consciousness. Craving it, needing it, wanting it. Wanting *her.*

She felt the tugging at her ear. Her body undulated as he lifted her hair and scraped his teeth along the nape of her neck in a mock bite.

He rubbed his lips against her nape, tasting the residue of her blood, the ache to bite more powerful, more consuming, than the coursing desire to possess.

He reined it in ruthlessly. This was more important than slaking his unholy thirst. This first time with her naked and begging mutely for his kisses, his hands, his desire . . . his spawn.

He had never before taken this much time with a woman. He'd always taken without compunction; he'd slaked his physical hunger recklessly, ruthlessly, and with no concern for his partner. And after—if he thirsted—it was the woman's bad luck that she'd solicited him.

But this time, with this woman, he wanted to savor his vengeance, long and sweet.

He moved his mouth back to her earlobe, hoping to coax her blood onto his tongue. He wanted her to feel him tugging at her lobe, and the heat of his tongue delving into her ear. He wanted her mindless with unspeakable, voluptuous pleasure. He wanted her aching for more, opening herself willingly to him.

Her body arched into the feeling of his caressing her. She belonged to him. It was no small thing that he had imprinted himself with her blood in that nightly ritual; she was bound to him now, and he'd kill any man who tried to touch her.

Because Charles would not give up and Peter Augustine's interest had been piqued, danger lurked in places Dominick had not yet explored.

Then there was the Countess and her thirst for blood.

He had timed it exactly right. Senna writhed in his arms, seeking the pleasure of his clever fingers, her sensual response so palpable that her body shimmered with it.

No kisses needed tonight.

Remember every minute of this night with me, Senna. Remember the pleasure. Crave it, Senna, ache for it. Lust after it and don't rest until you're naked in my arms.

Mine.

Senna awakened with the memory of his sensuous whisper in her ear—*Remember*—and as she washed, as she allowed herself to be confined and corseted, she remembered.

She understood that her fantasies of Dominick Janou drove her desire and that it had all been a dream, but still, she remembered.

How could she not?

As she readied herself to go downstairs to breakfast, she felt as if her every move was a sensual testament to her memory of her night with him. She couldn't suppress the feelings, she didn't want to.

She would have stayed in that room forever, waiting for him, aching for him, yearning for him. But she had a duty to Lady Augustine.

She was also profoundly skeptical about the Countess's ability to conduct a séance. Except it was exactly the kind of flimflam Senna herself had routinely pulled. It would be interesting just to see what the Countess really intended to accomplish with her so-kind offer.

Dominick trailed behind Senna as she left the room. She couldn't hide from life, after all, or Lady Augustine for that matter. He would make certain she didn't forget last night. Or him. Or the wickedly sexual response of her body. Or anything . . .

Downstairs, everything was in chaos.

Lady Augustine, a piece of stationery in hand, was directing the rearrangement of the parlor furniture for the afternoon's séance.

She waved it at Senna as she entered. "The Countess. First thing this morning—I don't even think the servants were awake, and this was delivered. Really!"

"Exactly what was delivered?"

"Instructions! As to how *she* wishes everything to be set out for the séance."

"It's her séance," Senna said before thinking.

"It's *my* house," Lady Augustine retorted. "But then—it's Edmee . . ."

"What's Edmee?" Peter asked from the hallway.

"It's Edmee asking this favor of me, so why should I care if the Countess wants to reconfigure my whole house in service of it?"

"May I have breakfast please?" Peter asked. "Senna, join me.

There will be no talking to her until this is done to her satisfaction. I think it's a ridiculous idea anyway."

Senna didn't want to join Peter for breakfast. Reluctantly she followed him into the dining room. He already had a full plate in hand. "You will curtail her a bit, won't you?"

"Can anyone?" Senna asked, taking her own plate, some eggs, toast, and jam, and joining him at the table.

"I suppose not. We can only watch this disaster. And anyway, since when is the long-gone and not-much-missed Countess psychic?"

Senna chose not to answer that or to comment on anything to do with the Countess. She could slip up, say something about her stay at Drom. Peter was just waiting for that. Peter was being too nice, and it didn't sit well after her confrontations with him.

She shrugged and occupied herself by pouring a cup of tea.

"And when did she approach Lady Hartwicke about this? I can understand Lady Hartwicke's distress and willingness to try anything to solve the mystery of her husband's death, but afterlife communication?"

The question fell into a long stretch of silence.

"It will be a diversion," Senna said at length. "It will make Lady Hartwicke feel she's doing something to make sense of it, and it will give your mother pleasure to help her."

Peter gave her a considering look. "And what will it do for the Countess?"

She couldn't shrug off that question. She needed a neutral response. "It will put her in the forefront of things for a time, when she, by all accounts, has been long gone from society."

Senna watched him think that over for a moment and nod.

"Very true. If this even remotely turns up a clue or a lead, she'll be the sensation of the Season. How perceptive of you."

His admiring tone made her uneasy all over again.

Remember. The word buzzed in her ear.

She caught her breath and poured more tea to avoid his glittering gaze.

"Anyone could have seen that," she said finally, holding the cup to her lips so she could take a quick sip.

Peter cocked his head. "I'm beginning to think that you're more astute and intelligent and less of a charlatan than I originally believed."

Son of a bitch. I'll kill him.

"Definitely more astute," Senna said lightly. "Now excuse me while I see what Lady Augustine is up to."

Finally. She'd gotten away from those eyes that had gone from poisonous enmity to cautious interest. If only she could retreat to her room and just spend the succeeding hours remembering . . .

Crave it, ache for it . . .

She felt a tug at her ear, and her body convulsed in response. *Oh, God*—if she couldn't walk five feet without thinking about how it felt to be handled by . . . by a dream—

But was it a dream when it felt so real? The merest thought of it sent her senses spiraling.

She paused, breathless, on the threshold of the parlor.

"Lady Augustine—"

"When *will* you call me Aunt Madalina?" Lady Augustine responded testily. "What do you think, Senna? Is there enough space between the table and the parlor furniture? Do we have enough candles? Incense?"

"Mother, let's go for a ride." Peter's voice was too close behind Senna for her comfort.

"I have too much to do," Lady Augustine said distractedly. "You take Senna."

A fly suddenly buzzed around her ear. *Remember.*

"Oh—I . . ."

"Think that's a very good idea," Peter interpolated. "We'll take the brougham—no one can object, and we both can use some air at this point."

"I—"

"Go get your wrap. It's a bit chilly out there."

The carriage was brought around in a trice. Peter whirlwinded her out of the house and into it before she could protest. "Driver!"

"Peter," she finally managed to say.

"Much better. The house smells of church. We'll have enough of that all afternoon. Are you comfortable?"

She was very *un*comfortable. Alone with Peter? Nothing between them but words with which to betray herself? She could have been alone with her dreams and memories in her room right now, and she resented his intrusion and high-handedness.

"Why are you being so nice?"

"Because you're beautiful, unexpectedly kind, and because—I want to kiss you."

She opened her mouth to say no, never, not ever—and he swooped in to settle his mouth on hers so emphatically that her protests died in her sheer amazement that she actually liked his kiss.

He moved but an inch away from her mouth, giving her the space to whisper, "Oh!" before he slipped his tongue between her lips.

Oh. This was what she missed, what Dominick had withheld, what she'd needed and wanted. How did Peter know that and her dream lover didn't?

He eased away from her. "You are too tempting, and a carriage is not a very comfortable place to make love."

What?

Senna gathered her wits. Was he testing her to see if, in addition to her being a fraud, she was a strumpet too?

"Is that what you were planning?"

"My dear Senna—any man would. Do you even know how beautiful you are, how that body all encased in whalebone makes a man wonder what's under all that satin and stiffening?"

"Me. I'm under there."

"Ah, but the you that's under there—is she shy, is she sensual, does she want to be . . . touched? Kissed? Caressed?"

She reacted—just a little start of remembrance—and he noticed.

"A man wonders," he murmured with a husky break in his voice.

They rode in silence for a while, watching the passing parade but not stopping to speak to anyone.

"I know you liked that kiss," Peter said after a while.

She didn't take the goad.

He turned to her. "If you did, you'd kiss me again." He touched her lips with his, and she shook him off.

This time it felt like a betrayal. Especially after last night and everything Dominick had done that she couldn't forget.

"We need to go back to your mother."

"I'm coming after you," Peter warned. "I still want to know what's under all those hooks and buttons."

"That's your problem. Mine is to make sure that everything goes well at the séance this afternoon."

"You'd make an excellent paid companion," he murmured under his breath, and called for the driver to return to Berkeley Square.

She knew just what kind of paid companion he meant.

Lady Hartwicke looked as distressed and overwhelmed as a widow could be. She was tall, gray-haired, her face lined with grief, her clothes now loose on her formerly bulky body from days of being unable to eat anything.

She was almost pitifully grateful for both the Countess's offer to conduct the séance and Lady Augustine's ready offer of her town house for the event.

Lady Hartwicke was in the dining room taking tea with Lady Augustine when Senna and Peter arrived.

"It wasn't days after I'd retreated to the country house that the Countess wrote me a note to say that she was said to have some psychic ability and had lent aid to others in my circumstance."

She wiped away a tear. "Well, you can imagine what I thought—I barely know the Countess—what kind of help could she give to me? But she went on to say that she had had some success conducting séances in which she contacted the deceased, and those encounters so reassured their loved ones that she felt compelled to offer herself to me for that purpose."

"I expect most people would try anything to find comfort," Lady Augustine said. "I know, for myself—well, you have the use of my parlor, so that should tell you how I feel about your situation."

"Just so," Lady Hartwicke sniffled.

"So all we need to do is wait for everyone to come."

Everyone was a selected list of Lady Hartwicke's friends, a half dozen of those closest and caring, besides the Countess, Lady Augustine, Senna, and Peter.

The Countess arrived first to inspect the environment. She removed a potted plant, several pieces of porcelain, moved a lamp, drew the blinds, lit the candles. She approved of the incense and the round table that had been set in the center of the room and the high-backed chairs, ten altogether, and placed an overturned goblet in the center.

"It would help to have some relaxing music. Perhaps someone could play for a few moments as the guests settle themselves? Senna?"

"I'm sorry, Countess. I don't play."

"But you most certainly do."

"You're mistaken."

"Or perhaps," Lady Augustine rushed in, "she just doesn't remember."

"Ah, yes—the memory. So faulty. So convenient. Perhaps one of your guests . . ." the Countess suggested, as she turned down the lights in the hallway and the dining room and closed doors so that it seemed more twilight than afternoon in the parlor.

"I seek a calming atmosphere," the Countess explained. "An exotic scent. Restful music, a brief prayer, a call to purpose"—she took her place at the table—"and then we start."

Dominick was in a rage, and all the energy he expended flitting around Senna's room and up and down the stairs while the Countess ritualized the parlor did nothing to relieve his fury.

The son of a bitch kissed her. The son of a bitch *wanted* her.

Apparently memories were not enough. The blood he'd taken to bind her to him was not enough. His kisses were not enough.

And now the Countess had a moment in time when she could destroy people, ruin lives, and reveal secrets.

She was no more a psychic than the queen.

He needed to compact himself even further. The Countess must not get wind of him. The more focused she was on the event, the less likely she'd be trying to scent him out. The smaller he contained himself, the less she'd be aware of his presence and the more damage he could do.

And he was primed for it. He wanted it. But more than that, he welcomed it.

The guests arrived one at a time and seated themselves with a solemnity due a funeral service. From the dining room, they heard the ripple of the piano and a soft étude as a friend of Lady Hartwicke's obliged the Countess to provide music. The candles glowed brightly on a table set away from the one at which they sat. The room was dim. The silence was thick and expectant.

The Countess sat almost motionless, watching the newcomers through hooded eyes. When they were finally all seated around the table, and Senna, Lady Augustine, and Peter had also taken their seats, she began.

"If the spirit is with us, there should be some acknowledgment. It could be anything—a rap, a knock, the goblet or the table might move. So we will need the utmost silence. Everyone hold hands."

She waited as they fumbled their hands together, at which point Dominick attached himself to the underside of Senna's sleeve.

"And now the call to purpose." The Countess bowed her head. "Today we come together in this place of neutrality to seek guidance and help from the spirit of the late Lord Edmund Hartwicke.

"Lady Hartwicke is here. Lady Augustine is here. Beloved friends are here. Is Lord Hartwicke here?"

Silence.

"We will ask again. In the name of dear friends who seek to avenge this death, is Lord Hartwicke here?"

No response.

Obviously. The Countess had no psychic ability whatsoever, and Dominick crept up to Senna's shoulder, wondering exactly what his mother had really planned.

"Oh, please," Lady Hartwicke sniffled under her breath. "Edmund, help us . . ."

Everyone heard. In the ensuing silence, the guests reacted uncomfortably with a riffling and ruffling to her naked plea.

The Countess said nothing. She waited. And waited.

"Is Lord Hartwicke with us?" she asked again.

No one dared breathe.

"Will Lord Hartwicke respond, is he with us?"

Silence. And then a sound so faint that they almost didn't hear it.

"Lord Hartwicke?"

Again the sound—a hollow rap, faint and far away.

"Is it Lord Hartwicke? Signal once for yes, twice for no."

One rap, louder and closer this time.

"Lord Hartwicke, I am an intermediary for your family and friends, who wish to contact you. They are distressed and wanting answers. Are you willing to answer questions?"

A long silence, then *rap*.

The Countess looked around and then focused directly on Lady Hartwicke. "Madam? Do you wish to ask a question?"

Lady Hartwicke, dabbing at her eyes, shook her head. "You—"

The Countess nodded. "Lord Hartwicke, we will come to the point. Were you murdered by a vampire?"

The guests collectively gasped.

Rap.

"Do you know who it was?"

Rap.

There wasn't a movement at the table. It didn't take ten seconds for Dominick to realize what the Countess meant to do, what her agenda had been all along.

He was to be the scapegoat. She wanted to flush him out and

ruin him by having the whole of London hunt him down, catch and kill the vicious, soulless, amoral bloodsucking killer who had taken Lord Hartwicke's life.

She was playing the death card, biding her time, waiting for the right moment.

There was dead silence as they all held their breath, waiting for the next question, for the final revelation.

It is time to transshape. A faint mist then wafted over the Countess's shoulder. Did she feel it?

"If I say a name," the Countess said, "will you identify your murderer?"

Rap.

"Charles Sandston."

Rap rap.

Not yet, Dominick thought.

"Lord Clarence."

Rap rap.

"Sir Alfred Bloodgood."

Rap rap.

Now! Dominick reared up, wrapped himself around her whole body and grasped her throat so that she choked back whatever name she was about to utter next.

The silence grew fraught.

Finally, a constricted voice seemed to arc over the table and yet sounded so far away.

"It. Was. Nicolai."

The people's shock was palpable, especially Senna's. The others waited for the Countess to speak into the silence, and when she didn't, Lady Hartwicke girded herself to say, "Who killed you? It was . . . Nicolai?"

"Nicolai-i-i-i . . ." The voice—Dominick's voice—suppressing the Countess's, eddied away.

Dead silence again. Time stopped. The Countess gave up her struggle against Dominick's strength.

"It's done now," he whispered in her ear. "You can't contradict a spirit; it will ruin you to say you were wrong, to take back the name of a murderer, to tell them Lord Hartwicke was mistaken. Or you can admit your lies. It's your choice. It's done."

He shoved her away, setting everything in motion again.

Lady Hartwicke was shaking her head. "Nicolai? How odd. Does anyone know a Nicolai? There's no Nicolai in our circle." She sounded confused and not a little aggrieved. "Madalina?"

"I know of no one," Lady Augustine said. "Countess?"

"I'm at a loss," she murmured through a tight throat and tearing rage. Dominick had ruined things for her, destroyed her one chance to get at him.

"One can't predict what information will come through," she added in a mollifying tone. "There may well be a killer named Nicolai trolling the streets. Perhaps a word to the Yard in any event? I'm sorry this session didn't prove fruitful."

Lady Hartwicke made a noncommittal sound, a covert signal that Lady Augustine must get rid of the guest.

"Countess . . ." Lady Augustine took her by the arm and pressed a wad of notes into her hand.

"Please don't."

"For your time."

"It was my pleasure; I'm only disappointed we did not receive the answers we wanted."

"Just so," Lady Augustine said. "Take this in gratitude."

"Gratitude," the Countess repeated. "Yes, gratitude . . . you people do know just how to show gratitude."

Oh, she would show gratitude all right. Maybe it was fortuitous that Lady Augustine had been designated to escort her from the august company of the very upper crust. Because otherwise she would have crushed Lady Augustine and her snotty friends to a pulp and fed on their blood and bones.

Now all she wanted was to deal the final death blow to Nicolai.

Dominick hated moral dilemmas. In his nether life, he never needed to make those choices. But tonight, the Countess was in a fierce rage that she could only temper by ripping up flesh and feeding, and it was one of the times she would not be discreet on the hunt. The first ragged miscreant she came upon would feel the bite and die.

And perhaps neither would Senna choose discretion over flattery. His choices had narrowed down to one: seducing her—tonight.

Peter's audacious kiss—and her liking it too much—had complicated everything. Peter was still with her in the dining room, talking to her, looking at her, desiring her, while the dowagers ate a light dinner, drank tea, and savaged the Countess's séance.

Enough. *He* owned her, her kisses and her body.

And the week he'd planned to work her slowly, patiently, enticing her to beg for him, had just telescoped down to one night.

He had no choice but to seduce her and plant the first spend of his seed.

Come to me tonight, Senna.

She heard him, but he was nowhere in her room. She had just dismissed the maid and was now wholly undressed with only her gauze nightgown clinging to her body.

"How can I? They'll know I'm gone—"

They won't know. You don't need to do anything. Just close your eyes . . . and come to me.

She heard a great roaring wind that suddenly tapered into calm, into a void, into his voice. "Senna."

She opened her eyes, and there he was, seated in a big comfortable leather chair, in a beautifully appointed bedroom.

"I'm real," he said simply.

"I remember everything," she answered in kind.

"So do I." His lancing blue gaze swept her body, lingered momentarily on her breasts, and she had the distinct feeling he knew that Peter had kissed her.

He held out a hand. "Come, sit on my lap, Senna."

She shuddered. This time nothing would be left untouched. He would have all of her body in his hands and the freedom to touch her everywhere.

She never hesitated. She took his hand and let him ease her onto his thighs, so that she was cradled against his left arm. He tilted her head to the side, lifted her hair, immobilized her, and began nuzzling her ear.

The curve, the cup, the lobe, all his—the feast on which he would dine in mere seconds. He nicked it, the blood welled up, and he swiped it with his tongue to her sensual moan.

This time he didn't staunch it, he let the blood ooze onto his lips, his tongue, he tasted, and he sucked. She writhed and he sucked a little harder. Her whole body spasmed as he took the blood with ruthless purpose.

"You like when I suck your lobes."

"Don't stop," she whispered.

"Give me your left ear."

She shifted her body so he had free access, and she nestled her buttocks against his hips.

He tilted her head and, simultaneously, slipped his right arm around her midriff so that he could touch her breast as he sucked.

It was too much of a sensual distraction. Edgy pleasure streamed through her body as his tongue began its sensual exploration of her left earlobe.

He drew blood almost immediately this time. No seduction of this ear—just the pulsating need for those burgeoning drops, swelling like the hardness of his body as his tongue expertly caressed her blood-wet lobe.

He didn't think he could ever have enough time to feed on her, but tonight he had that much more to devour. And he didn't have much time.

She caressed and cupped his spare, careworn face, begging for his kiss.

He drew her into his mouth as she wound herself around him and willingly gave him her tongue.

This is nothing like that other kiss, she thought hazily. Then the notion drifted away as she lost herself in the moist heat of his mouth.

It was a long, wet, voluptuous kiss. He wanted his mouth, his touch, imprinted on her in such a way that she would never think to let another man kiss her. Or touch her. Or see her body. Ever.

She wouldn't want to leave his mouth. Ever.

He gave her a moment to breathe. "I don't want to go back," she whispered. "I want to be with you just like this forever."

He promised nothing. "They won't miss you."

"Good." She kissed him and he shifted her again, so that he could easily get at her left earlobe.

He took it between his lips and compressed it. A drop of blood welled up and he let it sit and ooze while he kissed her neck, her shoulder, her lips, and back to the lobe. That luscious rounded drop of enslaving blood tasted so rich, so much like her, on the tip of his tongue.

"I want you," he whispered in her ear as he flicked his tongue at her lobe. "I can't wait to have you, all mine . . . but I warn you now: I will own every part of your body."

She shivered at the words.

"You know what I mean." His hand was already there, lifting her nightgown, stroking her thighs.

She lifted her head for a kiss and he bore down on her lips with only a taste of the exultation he felt in handling her body. He eased away from her mouth after a long, lush kiss, hovering just above her eager lips.

"Let me in, Senna."

She wet her mouth. It was so secret, so private down there, a sacred space. But it was *him*. His fingers stroked her, gently pushing, probing, seeking.

"I *will* do what I want."

Her breath caught with anticipation. "Then do it," she whispered, grasping his shoulders as he slipped his fingers between her legs.

"Remember this," he whispered, taking her earlobe again and compressing it to release the blood. "You're writhing in *my* arms. You beg for my kisses and my tongue. You ache for my touch. You're mine now, Senna."

He deliberately pulled her back to the kiss, curling her up against him in his lap, his tongue barely sated by the blood. He enfolded her, she drank him in, digging into his skin, shuddering and spasming as he expertly worked her core.

"It's too much," she breathed at one point.

"Remember it. Remember who gave you this pleasure."

He resumed the kiss, giving her body a respite by sliding his free hand under her gown and over her back to stroke her hips, her buttocks, her legs. Her body jolted in the haze of the kiss as she felt him—front and back in possession of her body.

I own you completely now.

He would not relinquish the kiss. She felt the shock of his full occupation of her body. In the kiss, all of it felt different; she was utterly open for him . . . and it was all she wanted.

Her body went slack with pleasure. She moved with his thrusts, and the sensations mounded, like soft heaps of cream, deep in her core.

She wanted more.

He gave it to her, until all the feelings peaked, and she fell off the precipice into a cascade of unimaginable ecstasy.

Perfect. She was opened, softened, sated, and ready for the taking. He carried her to the bed, and the moment he had her supine, he began stroking.

"Oh, it's too much," she moaned, almost insensate with all the unfamiliar cataclysmic feelings.

"Yes," he whispered. "You're ready for me." He ripped apart his trousers and unleashed himself. "Say, 'Yes, take me.' Say it."

She rolled her head. It was too much.

He moved away and she felt bereft. She missed everything about him immediately.

Remember—

It was only that the thing he most desired meant a corruption of her body that could never be undone. And she'd spent her life dodging the certainty of a life on the streets.

But it was *him*—his hands, his body, his sex, his need.

And the things he made her feel.

His face was as impassive as if it were carved, his burning blue gaze watching, waiting, as he stroked and primed her body to accept his.

No kisses, then. No more caresses. There would be nothing more carnal until his full possession of her body.

She touched his obdurate lips.

"Touch *me*," he commanded her.

She could give him the same pleasure, she thought through the fog. There were no more secrets. She reached down tentatively and touched him, a little stunned to find he was smooth and tactile, and his shaft was thick, rigid, muscular, and, once she grasped it, utterly responsive as if it had a mind of its own.

She went breathless, imagining it sliding into her center, no pain, a perfect fit.

He felt her carnal excitement, sensed what she imagined and how it would feel. He took it as her tacit consent, and levering himself upward, he mounted her, and slowly and carefully he nudged toward the one obstacle to possessing her.

Remember this.

There would be blood . . . and the urge, the need, the hunger, twisted inside him as he jolted past every barrier, every hindrance, and he felt the trickle of virgin blood seeping from her body, blood he'd taken but could not taste.

Her body stiffened in shock at the blast of pain, and then a feeling of thick, hard heat overpowered the whole center of her being and rooted deep inside her.

He didn't allow her to inhale the wonder of it. His kisses were rough and demanding, possessive as he rocked himself in her ripe heat. He didn't even think about the blood.

It was more than he'd thought. After a lifetime of fast, transient, and bloody couplings, he had never imagined this depth of feeling for someone who was to be his dupe, his path to vengeance. He eased up and thrust gently. So much more than he imagined. More than he deserved, perhaps, for pushing her into it sooner than he'd intended.

Mine.

He was shocked that he meant it. He pushed deeper, seeking the limitations of her body, moving his mouth from hers to nuzzle her ear, seeking again.

Pleasure first, but blood was necessary. Blood bound them. He found no satisfaction in licking the dried blood on her lobe and nicked her to draw a fresh drop to the surface.

This was necessary. All of it. He didn't intend to move ever again but just to accustom her body to the feel and heft of him between her legs. He wanted to spend all night in the hot, wet innocence of her. *Hold it, hold it*—his body seized suddenly. He tensed and tried to suppress and control his lust, but nothing could stop that one muscular drive and the volcanic explosion of his body.

He collapsed onto her, sapped, then felt the trickle of his semen seeping between their bodies, mixing with and layering over her virgin blood. He knew there would be no surcease from his thrumming blood, his blinding desire, the almost overpowering animal urge to root in her always.

For one blood-blinding moment, he didn't care. She was his. He'd worked her patiently, bound her to him, seduced her in ways that were counter to his nature, and claimed her in the end.

Peter Augustine would have ravaged her by now. Charles would have eviscerated her. They were both lying in wait, biding their time.

Too late.

Mine.

He'd taken her blood, tasted her blood, and he'd possessed her body. She wouldn't betray him now. He need do nothing more than hold her through the night, even though he ached to take her again and ten times over. Hold her, stroke her, and keep those irritating tentacles of feelings submerged.

Chapter **I3**

*S*he liked watching him strip. She liked that his naked body was lean, muscular, and throbbing with tension. His nakedness covered and enfolded her as she curled up beneath him and he stroked and coaxed her body.

She liked his firm and commanding lips and how they kept moving over her breast with precise kisses and flicks of his tongue until she almost couldn't bear the sheer pleasure of it.

She thought all this in a dreamy, drowsy way as he lapped and sucked until she could deny him nothing.

He ignored his own need. She was almost there, the sensual ache deep inside her evidenced by the surging of her hips.

Almost there. She quivered with excitement as he played with her. Softening, softening . . . almost there.

He gathered her body tight against his undulating hips. He pushed her leg aside and she stiffened and then released herself to his carnal possession—soft.

Instantly, he creamed up and he drove into her emphatically, wholly, possessively.

Mine.

She was too unexpectedly potent; he almost blew his orgasm just occupying her. He fully intended to take her as many times as he could before dawn.

He levered onto his elbows and began his rhythmic dance.

The break of pleasure caught her by surprise. It crept up on her, seized her, and inundated her in a pool of molten sensation the likes of which she had never imagined.

It rippled through her body, waves of it, as he kept thrusting forcefully into her. It was like hot gold threading through her core, shocking and electric, holding her in thrall until it pooled deep in her center and melted away.

A moment later, he lifted her legs around his waist, took one hefty plunge into her depths, and blew his seed deep and hard inside her, drenching her with it, saturating her. It left him breathless, drained, and sapped—a little stunned by the violence of his orgasm.

With her.

Don't move.

She couldn't. Didn't want to do anything but stay coupled with him forever. With him pumping all that golden pleasure into her body.

His naked body, hot and pulsing, covered her completely, from her legs imprisoned between his, to her shoulder, where he rested his chin and periodically nipped and kissed her.

She loved the feeling of being utterly enveloped and occupied by him hard between her legs. It was a moment of peace, possession, and contentment.

A moment that she'd dreaded and, ultimately, a revelation, the secrets of her body, the ravishing surrender to a man. *This* man. Who kept her tight against his body and held himself taut, tense, and tenaciously deep inside her.

She touched his face. Something about the harsh lines intrigued her. It wasn't an old face—rather it was world-weary and impassive, his lips tight except when he was kissing her fingers as she explored the contours.

"I have to go," she murmured regretfully.

He made no attempt to remove himself. "Not yet. They won't miss you. I would miss you, though." He flexed himself, still long and strong inside her soaking core. Still seeping semen—he couldn't prevent it—but the night wasn't over.

"I'll miss you too," she whispered, stroking his cheek.

"Remember how well we fit, how much you need me deep inside you."

She made a little noise.

How much you need. He recited that litany deep in her mind until it was just a jumble of soothing, sleep-inducing words and her body went slack as she dozed.

He didn't want to leave her. He slipped away for a mere moment, to find a towel to blot and clean them both, and to commence the next part of the seduction.

He lay with her facing away from him so that he was able to nestle against her and caress her softly until her body began to react and stretch and reach for the evanescent pleasure he evoked.

That and the bloodletting—the nick of her earlobe, the pearl of blood, the rising excitement of stroking her most sensual body parts. *Remember this.* He kept taking and taking, his shaft throbbing and hot, compelling him to thrust and breed.

He eased her onto her belly and lifted her onto her knees so that she was seductively there for him in this obverse position.

Mine.

Remember.

This . . . was different. This was . . . so naked, the way he engulfed her wholly and completely. She bucked under the hot, penetrating suction, riding high and hard on the rigid tip of his tongue . . . until . . . until . . .

A butterfly lapping brought her down, down, down . . .

He still kept at her, inexorable as the sun.

There wasn't a detail she missed: her body rearing up against the sensation, his holding her immobile while he rooted still harder, sucking at her with an almost primitive lust to devour.

Remember.

He spurted, wasting his seed. But when he looked down at her, he surrendered to his lust, and he took her again and again with his tongue, sucking her into orgasmic oblivion.

The second binding seduction.

Mine.

The knocking woke her.

"Senna! Senna!" Lady Augustine bright and cheery on a gray morning, at least as far as Senna could see from her bed pillows, and with some semblance of coherence after the voluptuous night she'd spent with Dominick.

Remember.

Her breath caught. "I'm here," she finally had the wit to answer.

"Breakfast."

"I'm coming." Ironic word. She had come so many times last night she lost count.

Always be ready for me. I'm waiting.

How had she gotten here? She couldn't remember anything except falling into an exhausted semen-clogged sleep after hours of . . .

Hours. More. God, she wanted more. Already. She was awash in the scent and the residue of his sex and him.

Him.

Be naked. Her body squirmed.

She remembered everything.

All those parts were tender, a little sore, a little swollen from his vigorous use of her body.

But that last lapping butterfly kiss and the cataclysmic orgasm that followed . . . she caught her breath at the mere thought of it.

Remember.

She answered the succeeding summons, the maid coming to help her with her clothes. What was her name?

She dressed for Dominick, difficult though it was. Too many

buttons, ties, and pins in the way of sensual motility. It was almost as if clothes were made to restrain and confine a woman's sex so it couldn't be touched, stroked, and caressed to a peak of explosive pleasure.

Remember.

She came downstairs to a new morning furor.

The newspapers had got hold of the story; the headlines shrieked with something new to gnaw on.

WHO IS NICOLAI?

SÉANCE REVEALS MYSTERY SUSPECT.

WHO IS THE VAMPIRE AMONG US?

London buzzed with speculation. Scotland Yard kept investigating. It was the first lead of any kind that might have some substance. Not that anyone believed in spirits or their ability to communicate from the beyond. However, there were too many witnesses. It might mean something; it might not.

No one had ever heard of a Nicolai.

Except, Senna thought as she took some toast and jam, except three: Charles, the Countess, and herself. She felt a tremor of fear that Peter could read that guilty knowledge in her eyes.

Just we three.

Who told?

Someone at the séance had to have leaked the name. Lady Augustine was agitated over who had betrayed her dear friend.

"It was probably Lady Hartwicke herself," Peter said as they ate.

"I won't hear of that. Not possible."

The revelation of an unknown suspect had caused an uproar, for if there was a Nicolai, then there was an answer to the mystery of the vampiric murders and there weren't bogeymen hiding behind every hedgerow.

"None of us ought to be going out today," Lady Augustine said.

"So you're going to confine us to the prison of the house," Peter said. "I think not. I have things to do."

"I didn't mean that. You know what I meant."

She meant London was on hold, waiting for the next body to be found. She meant no one wanted to make himself the next target of the unknown Nicolai who bit his victims and tore out their hearts. He could be anywhere in the city watching and waiting to prey on *them*.

Who could be one of *them*.

She meant she—everyone—was scared.

Who is Nicolai?

I know who Nicolai is—his name was on a piece of paper tucked in a hundred books in the library at Drom. He's the brother who died but still lives . . . whose mother mourns him to this day. Does she know he's alive, writing notes, sapping blood, and taking souls?

All of that Senna remembered. But there was something she couldn't quite grasp. Didn't she have an obligation to tell what she knew about Nicolai?

Except, it didn't make sense that the Countess's long-dead son could be the murderous bloodsucking monster on the loose in London.

". . . don't you agree, Senna?" Lady Augustine was saying rather insistently.

Her fluty voice had turned a little stony. Senna, caught short, came to attention. "I'm sorry?"

"Agree that this house is hardly a prison."

Did she? When she felt as confined as she had at Drom?

"Not in the least," she said lightly. "Peter's just bored. And he can go about much more freely than can a woman. He has things to do after all. We women must sit and wait."

She could have things to do, she thought with an almost intolerable ache to have the freedom to leave and go where she would. But there was still a Yard mandate for all who had attended the Hart-wicke ball to remain in place while authorities investigated.

"Why must we?" Lady Augustine asked fretfully. "What is anyone doing? What does *investigating* mean at this point? Really! They should have this monster in hand by now. Three bloody deaths are quite enough, don't you think? Why isn't anybody doing anything?"

Her plea was met with a funny little silence.

"Somebody is doing something, Mother," Peter said finally, quietly.

"What do you mean?"

"I mean, we're going to take back our city."

Lady Augustine slanted an enigmatic look at him. "Ah."

Senna's senses prickled. "*We* meaning who?"

"We who can move around the city more freely, as you so aptly said. We who can watch and patrol the places where the Yard can't, we who can take action."

Paladins, Senna thought. It was vanquish the vampire all over again, but this was for real. "Let me go with you," she said impulsively. "A woman could be helpful."

"Senna!" Lady Augustine protested, horrified. "I mean, my dear—you did like running around with the boys when you were younger, but not like this." She shuddered at the thought.

Peter picked up from there. "This is night work. You can't be out after dark, even on patrol with a half dozen men for protection. You wouldn't be effective anyway in a bustle and whalebone."

"Of course not." Senna knew she sounded skeptical, sarcastic; she was more taken aback by Lady Augustine's memory of a time in her life of which she could have no knowledge. "A woman, after all . . ."

Peter sent her a speaking look. "Very much a woman," he murmured with that note in his voice. "And you wouldn't have it any other way." His words instantly conjured up that kiss, and she felt a faint sensual twinge attack her vitals.

What? Feelings for him? After last night?

"Meantime," Lady Augustine said, "I am called to Edmee's side this morning. She's heartsick over the public revelation of the séance and requires my company. Sadly, Senna—if you wouldn't mind—I'll ask that you not accompany me."

Alone for the first time in weeks? Senna let out a breath. "I wouldn't wish to do anything more to upset Lady Hartwicke."

"Of course, you wouldn't. Peter . . ." Lady Augustine held out her hand and he helped her to her feet, then he bowed to Senna.

"I must leave as well."

But Lady Augustine couldn't depart without issuing a raft of suggestions for the ways in which Senna could occupy herself while she was gone.

"Truly," Senna assured her, "I have much that I've neglected." She felt Peter's amused gaze on her. "Clothing concerns, for example. I need to see what needs freshening. And I could read. I won't want for things to do." She was certain she sounded frantic at this point. "And you won't be so long that I'll need to fill hours and hours. See to your friend, Aunt Madalina." Another look from Peter. "I'll be fine until you return."

Either the use of her Christian name or the certainty that she wouldn't be away that long finally reassured Lady Augustine, and with much fuss and many admonitions, she finally left for Lady Hartwicke's, with Peter following behind on horseback.

Alone—finally. Senna sank into the sofa and sighed.

"Miss?"

The maid's voice so startled her she nearly jumped from the sofa.

"Can I bring you anything else, miss?"

"Another pot of tea. I'll take it in the dining room. Thank you."

As if she'd been ordering servants around all her life.

Except it wasn't her life. How had she gotten here?

Don't think. Don't . . . remember . . .

Don't fear the monsters that roam at night.

Because the collective of aristocratic knights will charge into the void and find and destroy them? What had been said about how to kill them? Stake them? Cut their hearts out? Burn them?

I need that tea. She heard a surreptitious movement in the dining room, almost as if the maid had covertly been watching her.

Of course. Why should she think Peter would trust her, alone, in his mother's house? A kiss didn't wipe out suspicion. It just made things that much more difficult. The maid would be watching. Senna would be under constant surveillance.

Maybe she had been since she'd arrived.

She needed to think. She was too distracted by the mysteries, especially how she got here and Lady Augustine's immediate recognition of her. But it was more than that—there were the things she couldn't remember from her time at Drom. Then the bloody, heinous murders; Peter's kiss; the constant veiled threat of the Countess; Dominick's perfect seduction . . .

If she was living another reality, that might account for the irrationality of those things.

She shook herself. She should have gone when Peter had banished her on his return, taken his money and never looked back. The endgame would have been the same. She'd be just where she'd always been: on the street, destitute, and looking for another way out.

And now—*remember*. Dear heaven, she didn't want to go.

Realistically, she needed to cover every contingency. Even stealing the silver . . .

Why was that idea so familiar to her, as if she'd thought of it before? No, as if she'd done it before . . .

Tea. A bit more to eat, if anything remained, some hot tea, would make her feel better.

Because it truly seemed as if she dreamed last night in Dominick's bed as well. The only proof of her willing surrender resided in her well-used body parts and the brush of nudity beneath her clothes.

The teapot was hot, a clean cup and saucer were nearby, and a small plate of scones was covered with a napkin at one end of the meticulously polished dining table.

It was a nice high-ceilinged room, hung with framed paintings, with large windows overlooking the gardens at the back of the house. A pleasant place to sit and drink tea in the late morning.

Tea made sense. She fingered the teaspoon next to the saucer. Silver made sense, though a knife would be more useful.

Just as insurance. Just in case she had to run.

She put down the cup carefully. A flash of memory, gone in an instant, of her with a knife in her hand.

Running?

What if she had to run? What if there was nowhere to go, and she had nothing with which to barter but the clothes she wore? Everyone needed some coin, something with which to pay his or her way.

Lady Augustine would be back soon. Senna had this one opportunity to search the house for something to barter, for money, for answers.

She was a sharper after all. No conscience involved. Whatever got her where she needed to go.

A bell sounded somewhere deep in the house.

She thought about taking the spoon and resisted. The maid would surely count the silver. Senna could never sell it: someone would recognize it as Lady Augustine's. And besides, a knife would be a better weapon.

"Excuse me, miss."

The infernal maid interrupted again, just as Senna was about to begin the search. "It's the Countess, miss. She's come to call, and she's asked to see you."

He slept. He'd slaked every hunger but one last night—and that one could wait. He wrapped his sapped, naked body in a shroud impregnated with the soil of his motherland and rolled under his massive bed into the coffin-size cavity beneath where he secretly lived.

Death didn't banish life, or the hope of a future. Death made it all that much more precious. And death surrounded him still.

It wasn't only the Countess, dangerous as she was. It was the Tepes, cleverly in hiding, cloaking their dank death-scent with something impenetrable, as they watched and waited their turn.

He knew they were there somewhere, waiting, biding their time. They thought they were invisible, unaware that they radiated the aura of the grave.

But only to those who knew, who'd grappled with them in times long before. An eternity before, in fact, since time meant nothing to him.

In time, though, there would be a child. That meant something.

And to make certain of it, he'd taken Senna as many times as he could manage.

He stiffened. Something felt different. An invasion of the space surrounding his one tranquil place.

There was a knock on his bedroom door by his all-purpose butler, whom he'd hired to keep up appearances.

"Sir."

"I'll be with you shortly."

"Very good, sir."

Now he must rinse himself off and dress, or at least dress enough to give the appearance of having been lounging in his bedroom. Trousers. Shoes. A silk robe.

By the time he finished dressing, Knoll had already gone back downstairs. He was waiting in the hallway as Dominick descended the stairs, a piece of paper in hand.

"I thought you'd wish to see this, sir."

Dominick took the paper, which had been folded and fastened, and opened it.

WE ARE THE KEEPERS OF THE NIGHT

We've banded together to patrol our streets, to root out the bloody killer who's terrorizing our city, and take action if the Yard cannot, to keep our city and our citizens safe.

WE WANT YOU!!

We will be vigilant night and day. We will protect our own. We will succeed where the authorities have failed. We are hundreds strong. We will defeat the monster. This time he will NOT escape to kill again.

JOIN US!!

This was followed by a date, time, and place of meeting to form teams and map out patrol districts.

"Dangerous," Dominick murmured, tapping the sheet. "You did well to alert me."

It was a test as well. They'd targeted these notices for delivery all over the city to a particular group of like-minded aristocrats. They would take note of who joined and who didn't, count heads and parse out who among their set had declined to hunt the monster.

They would be shadows in the night, stalking the dissenter, hoping he would turn out to be the bloodsucking ghoul whom they could condemn to death, just to mete out their brand of justice.

They were gathering their minions, fomenting trouble because they now had to *do* something. They were dangerous to him too. The Tepes were waiting.

And the Countess. Just where was she? He listened for a moment, sniffing the air.

She was not hunting. There was no blood being let—yet.

She was somewhere in place, grindingly angry, close to the kill.

While grown men hunted vampires . . . and a completely unnecessary manservant blocked his move to action.

"You may take the rest of the day," he told Knoll, containing his impatience to react, to transshape. "I'll see you tomorrow." Through hooded eyes, he watched the butler leave.

Find the Countess. He felt the urgency of it in his bones. He took a precious moment to arm himself with the lifesaving sun-soaking obsidian, and he transformed, now a shadow, a wing, and he was gone.

"So," the Countess said as the maid set down yet another pot of fresh tea beside Senna in the parlor. "Lady Augustine is visiting Lady Hartwicke this morning. I can see that she would be upset. It was no one's business what transpired at the séance yesterday. And yet someone told."

Senna poured some tea for the Countess. It was best to say nothing. It was quite obvious why the Countess had come. She still didn't believe that Senna's memory of her time at Drom was gone.

"Don't you agree?" the Countess asked silkily, after a small sip.

"Of course," Senna said reluctantly.

"It does make one wonder," the Countess went on insinuatingly.

It was like waiting for the trap to snap. The Countess was baiting it, and she meant to draw blood.

"Wonder about what?" Senna finally asked.

"About who could have told that reporter about the séance. It's as if someone in attendance actually recognized the name. Don't you think?"

"How should I know?"

"Well, I wonder about that."

"Why?"

"My dear, you spent several days at my manor trying to gull me into believing you were some long-lost relative of mine. You did a fair job of it too." The Countess looked at Senna expectantly, as if she were waiting for her to contradict her version of the story.

"Countess, I dearly wish I could remember anything beyond the moment when Lady Augustine found me in the park. But none of this is familiar to me."

"I think you're lying."

"You may think what you will, Countess. Perhaps this was not a good time for a visit."

"You're lying."

"Countess," Senna said futilely as the older woman bolted up from her chair.

"You lie." The Countess's face contorted, her eyes went red with fury, and in her curved hands and thin arms a superhuman strength lifted Senna and slammed her against the nearest wall.

She hit hard, her head cracking against the plaster. Glass rattled and a painting above her head fell to the floor, narrowly missing her, breaking the elaborate gilt frame.

"You lie." It was a monster's voice. The Countess's body twisted into an inhuman clawing *thing,* her lips drawn in that rictus of a smile that Senna recognized from a nightmare long suppressed.

She tried to get up, but she felt dizzy, as if she were trapped in a nightmare. All she could see was the Countess, blood dripping from her jowls, furry creatures in her clutches, her mouth biting hard into flesh and bone and blood and heart, biting into *her*—

The Countess loomed over her, ripe for the kill. As she poised herself to leap, Senna pumped her legs upward and outward, connecting with the Countess's midriff and catching her off-balance.

But it was a futile defense. The Countess only came at her again, and Senna screamed into the darkness, certain that this time she was going to die.

Chapter 14

A sonorous bell sounded in the distance.

Senna came out of her nightmare, opening her eyes to find that she was still seated on the parlor sofa, that the Countess was still politely sipping her tea, and that Dominick was now sitting across from her, his face impassive but for his burning gaze pinned on the Countess, compelling her to put down her cup and say, "I believe I must be going."

"So nice of you to come," Senna said in kind, rising with her simultaneously and walking her to the front hallway. The maid appeared with the Countess's things. "Thank you for the visit."

"You lie," the Countess whispered. "You die."

She meant it for Senna, but the maid heard it too. She closed the door behind the Countess and stared at Senna.

"Why are you looking at me like that?"

"What—what she said," the maid stammered.

"You're mistaken. She merely said good-bye." *I lie.* But what course had she? The maid would spread stories, embarrass Lady Augustine, cause questions to be asked.

"Twice," Senna added. "It's the custom of her country."

"Yes, miss." The maid clearly didn't believe her.

"Bring a pot of fresh tea for Mr. Janou, please."

"Who, miss?"

"Mr. Janou," Senna repeated, but even she heard the note of uncertainty that crept into her tone.

"Miss?"

Senna wheeled around and flew into the parlor, her heart pounding. Her sense of living in a separate reality was so overwhelming that it didn't shock her to find the parlor was empty.

And now Dominick followed on the heels of the Keepers of the Night, pulling down their broadsheets and narrowing their numbers simply by removing their call to congregate.

He was no hero. They were after the likes of him, the blood-drenched vampire who fed on the innocents. Just as the possibility of the creation of life could temper his unholy drive to die.

But the Countess had no such constraints. She'd brazenly attempted to try to kill Senna today—she'd been close, her fangs grazing Senna's neck . . . a scratch, a tiny staggered line of blood . . .

He'd wiped the incident from Senna's memory; he'd turned back the clock to those few minutes before, when the Countess had been sipping tea and pretending to be the genteel aristocrat.

He'd transshaped before he could prevent the Countess's parting threat, and now he needed to excise it from the maid's memory as well. All those petty little things that interfered with what he most wanted to do, take Senna again—all day, all night, forever—and create life out of the chaos of death.

Soon. He'd caught up to Peter Augustine and the men assisting him. Now it was a matter of blowing up a wind to blast the broadsheets out of their hands, up and out to paper London in places beyond where aristocrats congregated.

They'd be picked up and read by women, by day workers, by drunks, and by the poor and the destitute. If any undesirables thought there was some money to be made by joining the Keepers and scouring the streets at night, that might put paid the idea altogether.

He floated above the wind-whipped papers, exulting in Peter Augustine's anger and frustration. He'd have to cancel the meeting. The Keepers would not be stalking vampires tonight.

The house was quiet. Senna sat still as stone in the parlor, trying to make sense of what had happened. Only she could remember nothing past the Countess's arrival, and her seeming urgency to leave only minutes after Dominick appeared.

Only Dominick wasn't even there.

The Countess had come to talk about the séance.

The Countess had . . . she couldn't remember. They'd had a conversation—no, the maid had served tea.

Her shoulders and the back of her head ached, but she didn't know why.

Lady Augustine would be returning at any moment, and she'd meant to . . .

Senna got slowly to her feet. She'd meant to search the house. She felt just a little unsteady right now.

Maybe she should lie down. Just for a moment. Lady Hartwicke probably felt vulnerable after the gossip about the séance. Lady Augustine would probably be with her friend far longer than Senna thought.

So she'd just lie down, just for a moment.

Warm. Calm. Floating.

Senna opened her eyes. Dominick was beside her in bed. She had to be dreaming.

Don't go away.

I won't. I'm here. You're safe.

Safe. She didn't feel unsafe, not even when the Countess had threatened her. *You lie. You die,* she'd threatened.

Senna remembered that part concisely and clearly.

She felt him folding her in his arms as time and space fell away.

They'll be back soon. They'll miss me.

They won't. They won't know. Come with me.

She didn't question him. How could she refuse?

Now that she was released from the constraints of Lady Augustine's protection, she felt free to feel, to be, to let him take her body wherever he would.

She found herself curled on his lap, cuddled tight in his arms in that big leather chair in his bedroom as he murmured soothing sounds in her ear.

She could stay just like that forever, enveloped in an overwhelming rush of pleasure and the pure consciousness of her body beneath her clothes.

She didn't have to think. She felt no fear. She had all she needed right here. He had not moved to seduce her or kiss her or—anything.

That would come. They had all night; they had eternity, if he chose. If he wanted. If he cared, if he . . .

She suddenly lost her train of thought. She had more immediate things to think about such as burrowing against his shoulder, such as his mouth so close to hers.

He pushed aside her thick fall of hair. She felt his whole body tighten with anticipation.

He took her ear, licking, tugging, kissing, pushing himself to the extreme edge of his need not to nick her lobe and taste the welling drop.

The sensuality of it was almost too much for her. She wanted to strip off her clothes, to feel him naked and pulsing in her hand, fitting himself to her body with exquisite precision.

Damned constraining clothes.

She felt as if they'd been apart forever, and it had barely been a day. Her whole body flared with arousal just being this close to him. All she could think was *more*.

Too much time spent maneuvering out of clothes. Too much time until his hands explored those sweet spots on her body that melted her bones.

Hurry.

Wait.

She could wait. Just that little bit of time with her body pressed tight against his hard, hot body . . . she could wait.

He couldn't. Blood-blinded, he was slammed with the realization that he walked a thin tightrope on this side of his humanity and that she could easily become a victim in his hands. The taste of her blood, even that minuscule drop, skewed his throbbing desire into a primitive drive to bite, to feed, to drain every last . . .

No! He grasped her hips and pushed her facedown on the bed so her upper torso was at a distance where he couldn't bite. He hiked her onto her knees, and in one ferocious thrust, he suppressed his lust to feed into coupling with her, focusing with supernatural intensity on subsuming his bloodlust in the act of procreation. The tainted blood that would course through the Lazlarics' heir. The thing that would kill his mother.

His sensual fury heightened the urgency Senna felt. Facing the headboard, with her only connection to him the length and strength of his shaft, she felt as if he were the center of the world.

Her world.

He rode her hard, taking out all his blood-born feelings on her, his body seizing with the pressure to rip and release all the pent-up force of his nature.

The waiting was pure torture: he lusted for blood. Her body would suffice. All he needed was to bend over. Her ripe, curvy buttocks would do for now; he could make his mark on her heart later.

He throbbed with the agony of his need; every nerve, vein, muscle, and instinct bulged with it.

He had to get out, get away, get blood, get . . . *Now!*

He let go with a silent howl to the heavens, his head thrown back, his hands savagely clutching her buttocks, his hips bucking as he reached his spuming release.

No soothing covering of her body with his in the aftermath. No pure moment of feeling his skin hot against hers, melting into hers. Or rocking languorously inside her.

He gave her a violent push down onto the bed. Startled, she turned to look at him—and he wasn't there.

What?

She turned over and sat up. The room was empty, cold, dank almost, and she shivered. She felt a touch, like a feather, or a bird's wing, brush against her cheek. A comforting warmth suffused her body.

I was rough with you.

She heard him say the words, but she couldn't see him, not in the dim recesses of the room where shadows lurked.

I don't care.

Be careful who you care about.

I care about you.

I know.

Where are you?

For the moment, I'm where I can't hurt you.

You could never hurt me.

He said nothing. He could hurt her and worse, and the only thing right now that curbed those appetites was that he'd left her and fed, grabbing the first red-blooded living thing he came upon, to slake his roaring, unrequited need for *her*.

Where are you?

Close. Closer than you know. But not so close that I'll hurt you.

Do I have any say?

He didn't answer. He should just return her to Lady Augustine's and forget plans of vengeance and progeny altogether, because if he gave in for one second to the fiery blood-hunger in him, he'd kill her.

He couldn't. But he couldn't give her up either. He'd let this go too far. Her need rivaled his on some level. He shouldn't have seduced her. He shouldn't have . . . tasted, lain with her, had feelings for her.

It was too late now. Now he wanted like a human, like a man, but also like the animal, the ghoul, he was. The divide was sharp, agonizing. He needed, a man for a woman, and more, he couldn't deny her. He didn't want to deny her.

He understood he was in far deeper than she.

He emerged from the shadows, naked, erect, ready. "On your belly again, Senna. It's the only way tonight."

She didn't question his sudden reappearance or his command; she turned on her stomach and hiked up her hips, mutely telling him she wanted more of him in that delicious moment of entry, more of him penetrating inch by inch, more of his hands guiding her, his hips churning against her as he fit himself to her body.

He couldn't go deep enough. He wanted to fuse with her and infuse her whole body with his size, his shape, his lust, his juices.

His blood.

His seed.

His need.

It was always about the blood. But this way, his blood would live, and he could finally rest. His body pulsated with every rhythmic thrust, reaching for the very center of her being.

Time stopped. He couldn't move, didn't want to; he stilled the subtle undulation of her hips with his hands.

This was good. There was no temptation to bite, to taste, to inhale. It would be too awkward anyway, bending his upper torso that way over her. He could manage this, if he fed first, and if he weren't body-on-body with her and that close to those deliciously sanguineous earlobes.

Don't—

He wanted her like this anyway. All that potent seed contained. He felt it. He wanted it. If he kept taking her, he could have her like this forever: young, beautiful, sexual, ripe, open, *his*.

Don't . . .

The point was to avenge himself on the Countess and to end the bloodletting. If he took Senna and turned her, he wouldn't ask permission. It would be for his own selfish purposes, and he'd be no better than the Countess.

She'd be just another victim, another bloodbath, another murderous monster unleashed to roam through eternity.

But why should he have any compunction about that? Those wicked bloody lobes called to him. He was a monster, after all.

What was left of his humanity was drowning fast in a tide of urgency to taste.

His body seized with the overwhelming compulsion to bite and drink of her fully. Even naked and wedged tight in her, he could not override the clamorous call of his nature by embedding himself in her body.

His desire had transmuted into something feral and bloodbound. He could do nothing more tonight other than destroy her. But neither could he give her up, and that schism in him nearly tore him apart.

He hadn't expected it would happen this quickly. He'd been unprepared for the feelings. He pulled himself from her body with an abruptness that he regretted the moment he was free.

She sensed something was not right.

He didn't answer immediately. He couldn't. Then: *Lie down. I'll join you in a minute or two. Sleep . . .*

Her eyes closed.

He couldn't go near her now. She was too open to suggestion.

He toyed with the idea of implanting the memory of a full night of raw unbridled coupling in her mind, but it would resound in his memory too, along with the feel and the taste of her.

He couldn't afford that distraction when he was so suffused with the bloodlust to turn her. He could barely control himself now; he felt crazed with need and want and he had the perfect body, the tastiest blood at his disposal, here, now, and it could be . . .

Forever.

He could give her the choice . . .

But it would be a deluded choice because all she would see were the endless nights with him. Not the cold reality of her death, rebirth, and then the endless cycle of killing and feeding; not the bloodlust that would ultimately turn her into a monster; not the fact that even with her consent, she would still be a victim.

But could he take the chance his seed hadn't rooted in her?

Could he kill his own blood? Was he walking that thin a line?

He looked down at her curvy body—the vessel, the receptacle.

Her function and purpose had been solely to be an instrument, to bear his seed, to bring the tainted blood to fruition and destroy the Countess.

It was all simple when he wasn't inside her, when his blood-gut feelings weren't warring with his still-human lust to couple with a desirable woman.

That she had been the Countess's choice for Charles did add a certain provocation to his sexual possession of her.

He couldn't give her up—wouldn't.

He'd just have to learn to control the blood-greed; he'd relinquish his blood-binding on her earlobes. He'd keep her sated until his seed took. He'd keep her naked with him even afterward.

She belonged to him now, inside and out.

He'd contain his voracious blood hunger. Somehow.

Just not now.

His body corded with those opposing tensions that were impossible to resolve. He couldn't touch her now; he was lethal, dangerous, inhaling scent, pulsing for the hunt.

Death was in the air once more.

He had only one choice—to return her to the moment before he swirled in and took her off to bed. Only then would he allow himself to surrender to his darker heart.

It felt to Senna as if no time at all had passed and yet suddenly Lady Augustine was at the door, happy to see her ward with a book and a cup of tea in the parlor.

Had she been reading? Senna reached for the memory. She'd been there, and the Countess had come to apologize for the uproar over the séance. She'd not stayed long. She'd said good-bye.

You lie, you die. The words wafted up into her consciousness just as Lady Augustine entered the parlor.

"Senna. Well, I see I needn't have worried. Here you are, tea in hand, a book on your lap—"

"How does Lady Hartwicke?" Senna asked to forestall Lady

Augustine's inquisition of what she might have been doing to occupy herself.

"She runs the gamut of feelings," Lady Augustine said, sinking with relief into a chair opposite the sofa. "She's humiliated that her commissioning a séance should have become public knowledge, but hopeful that perhaps this mysterious Nicolai is a possible suspect. Though she fears that no one believes an intermediary at a séance could produce the name of a murderer. It made her inconsolable all over again."

"No wonder," Senna murmured, glancing at the window. It was dark outside now, and she couldn't quite remember what she'd done between Lady Augustine's departure and her return.

"Just the idea that it might have been Lord Hartwicke speaking from the grave, and then it wasn't." Lady Augustine shook her head in disgust. "I blame the Countess for this. She made it out she could deliver something that she could not. And we were all gullible enough to want it to be so."

"Indeed." The reassuring words were easy to find. What wasn't easy was accounting for what had happened today. The Countess had definitely visited—again, a vague memory floated up that Senna couldn't quite grasp.

The Countess in a fury?

Good-bye, good-bye—

You lie, you die . . .

"I absolutely agree," Senna said in response to something Lady Augustine had asked, even though she had no idea what it was.

"And the other thing—Peter and this new idea of his . . . they're meeting here, by the park. I'm adamantly against his doing this. It's dangerous. They don't know what they're up against. They should leave it to the Yard."

"They need to feel they're doing something," Senna said to reassure her. "Or perhaps that they might prevent something."

"The city is too big to patrol. It's folly. I should ring for dinner." Lady Augustine got up abruptly and went to the window. "Look, they've already started congregating. Well, now I won't be able to eat for worrying."

"You'll feel better after dinner." Senna rose herself and went to the window. "After all, it must have been very emotional today with Lady Hartwicke."

"Indeed. But that's done, so let's freshen up. I'll ring for Puckett."

Still, it was hard for Lady Augustine not to keep peeking out the window as the crowd got bigger. Senna left her there and went up to her room to wash.

She needed to be alone, to think, to remember.

Nothing made sense. Dominick acting so oddly. The Countess's visit. *You lie, you die.*

She splashed water on her face, but it was no help.

How had she gotten here in the first place? Why couldn't she remember these salient details?

She sank onto the bed. Last she remembered, she was on her knees, with Dominick deeply rooted inside her. That memory she could re-create, she could feel the push, the fill, the fit, and . . .

I'm going mad. Or he was a ghost lover she'd conjured in her imagination because she couldn't fathom how she'd gotten from his bed to dressed in Lady Augustine's parlor reading a book.

The commotion outside was growing louder. She heard Peter's voice and she opened the window just at the moment he began addressing the crowd.

"We're gathered here as citizens whose sole purpose is to take our city back from the evil that has permeated its very vitals. Thank you for coming, for answering the call for volunteers to patrol the streets and keep them safe. We are not mandated to accuse, capture, judge, or punish likely suspects. We are at most a preventive. If we are vigilant on the streets, the monsters will not kill. If we become the sentries of the city, the vampires will die for lack of victims. Are you with me?"

There was a rousing "Aye" and a cheer.

"Then pair off and take your places. We'll reconvene back here at sunrise."

They did as he asked, and at a signal they marched off by twos and threes into the darkness in a hum of anticipation.

Senna felt short of breath. Disaster was in the air. They'd find a scapegoat just to prove the point. They would accuse, capture, and judge.

Punish.

She raced down the stairs to find Lady Augustine at the open door.

"The fool," she spat, watching the crowd disperse and Peter follow them. "The unutterable fool . . ."

Her venomous tone shocked Senna enough that she didn't make her presence known, and so she startled Lady Augustine as she closed the door and turned. "Senna! I didn't know you were there."

"I—heard Peter's speech."

"So did the whole of the Square," Lady Augustine said drily. "Come. I had a light supper set out. Obviously, my opinion in this matter counts for nothing." She took Senna's arm and propelled her to the dining room. "So tell me, how are you enjoying that book?"

Dominick watched from the rooftop, his focus on Peter Augustine, his thoughts on Senna and everything he would do to her voluptuously pliant body when he took her to bed later.

Because he *would* take her later. After he followed this rabbling mob who were out for a vampire's blood.

They reeked of death. They wanted death, they would make death if they had to, to prove that they were necessary and that the authorities were deficient.

They were looking for Nicolai. And his interfering with the distribution of the broadsides hadn't deterred them.

It was Nicolai who watched them, Augustine especially, with a skeptical eye.

Up and down the streets, squares, and main thoroughfares they went for hours, searching behind bushes, trees, fences, and unlocked doors. They were quiet in their concentration, circling around to the waterfront, the docks, where anything could happen, even rooting out a likely candidate for a marauding vampire.

It took no time at all.

"Here! Here!"

Their shouts echoed over the water. Footsteps pounded. The patrols converged. A half dozen men dived into the fray, and after a fierce struggle the crowd parted and Peter Augustine hauled the culprit out from the mound of bodies surrounding them.

Devil's bones—Charles! Bloody, drunk, combative Charles, shouting curses, demanding explanations, a rag-doll body at his feet, a blood-smeared knife in his hand.

Charles. Took on one too many drabs. One too many drinks and his homicidal instincts roared to life and compelled him to action.

Nicolai would not intervene; he felt no filial loyalty. The Countess would be notified soon enough and race to save him. Charles had survived all these years, his murderous tendencies under control, without Nicolai's interference—but not this time, not this unfortunate night.

It was not his problem. He still felt the aura of death around him. Charles's apprehension was merely a diversion from whatever was to come.

Nothing more would happen tonight though. It was enough they'd found a mark, their vampire. Charles didn't drink blood, but he loved spilling it. They'd deliver him to the Yard, and they'd continue their hunt.

One vampire wouldn't be nearly enough to sate their thirst to execute someone, something.

Especially if someone else died.

Chapter I 5

*S*ometime deep in the night, Dominick finally seeped down the chimney and into Senna's room. He stood for a moment watching her, remembering. Last night had been torture, and tonight was a punishment, because he couldn't stay away.

Because wanting her had compelled him to feed and staunch his blood-thirst, in ways no one should know, in order for him to have her and protect her. His feelings for her had driven him to her bed when it was the last thing—and everything—he wanted.

She slept soundly, unaware of his presence, curled under the sheet draped loosely over her body. It was a mere matter of insinuating himself underneath and fitting himself tightly into her every curve and hollow.

This time, he wasn't content to make her feel safe. He wanted her to feel him, all of him, covering her all over, dangerous and unleashed.

Everywhere . . . hot and pounding . . . her body slick from her dreams, his ferocious desire calling to her, inexorably waking her.

He watched as she stretched and undulated, responding to his thrusts and—

Dominick, on a pleasurable sigh.

His body totally covered and enveloped hers, his chin resting on her shoulder, her hair brushing his face, tickling his nose, his lips.

Her ear was that close. He'd sworn not to, but how could he not? He'd fed. He was sated. She loved it, his tongue licking, his teeth nipping—

It was just a taste . . . the necessary binding.

Just—

He nicked the lobe and the drop welled up right onto the tip of his tongue. His whole body stiffened with a voluptuously sensual twinge.

Everything suddenly was different. It suddenly was sexual; he craved it now, he couldn't go on without the taste of it, hot and sweet on his tongue.

And it would get worse. He'd pillaged it before, but not with this aching, demanding urgency, or this knowledge that if she was to be his, this luscious drop of blood was as necessary to him as breathing.

She wouldn't deny him either, if she knew, but he meant for her not to be aware of any of it, to give her pleasure with his marauding tongue as he licked his fill of her.

In the midst of that, he felt her shift and lift herself to position herself so she could feel him more intensely within her body.

He felt delirious with a burning lust for all of it—her body, her blood. *Devil's bones.* He started seizing and spurting and he couldn't stop, he didn't want to. He couldn't even thrust. His body surged of its own volition, he had no control, no desire to constrain himself, and he came, jamming himself tighter and harder into her body, so that not a drop of his seed would seep out.

Don't move.

He went tense with the effort to keep from licking her ear. It would be better to shift her to a position where he could pleasure her and feed on the other ear while keeping himself tightly plugged inside her.

He slipped his right arm around her, and his left hand under her knees, and rolled until he was on his right side, and she was back to front against his thighs.

He moved to her breast and touched the nipple. A bolt of pleasure shot right to her groin.

She wanted more. He wanted more. He thrust in short, tight spurts, all that heat enfolding him, surrounding him, hot and soaked to the core with his semen, and ripe for more.

He went even more rigid at the thought. More. There was no containing him now that his pleasure peaked. His body stiffened and he blew, taking her with him into his molten slide of an orgasm.

A long, hazy silence fell, in which they intermittently dozed.

He'd covered her breasts with his palms. She grasped his wrists as if she needed to hold on. He began nipping at her shoulder, he kissed her jaw, her cheek, her ear, moving slowly and inexorably to her lobe, and then inexplicably holding back.

She couldn't imagine anything more perfect than this moment of utter pleasure, of being soaked with his essence, and with him stiff, hot, and still embedded inside her.

Don't think, don't wonder, don't speculate beyond the moment. It was so tempting to want to ask questions, parse a future, acknowledge her feelings.

She wouldn't do that. This was still that other inexplicable reality where everything was possible, including a lover like this, a life like this—

She caught her breath as he began licking her ear. Something about his sensual concentration on her ears was so carnal. Something that aroused her beyond what he did with his hands.

She turned and leaned her ear into his tongue's wicked teasing, its heat, the way it aroused her, made her crave sex, crave *him*. Any way he wanted to take her. Anything he wanted to do to her. As long as he kept up the seduction of that hot, magic tongue. It was hypnotic, it created sensations in her body in places she didn't know felt these things.

He licked and sucked, and he stiffened and spewed.

She did that to him.

She burrowed more tightly against him and pulled his arms around her, twining her hands in his. What he did with those hands . . . she kissed the backs, one and then the other, and turned them palm forward and brushed them with her lips.

So smooth. Too smooth. She rubbed her lips against the flat palm. Smooth as if there were no lines at all.

She went very still. She was imagining it. It was dark. There was no way to know for certain. She shouldn't jump to conclusions. But how had she not noticed? His hands were all over her all the time. It was inconceivable she wouldn't have noticed.

She felt panic setting in. There couldn't be two people in her world whose hands had been damaged in exactly the same way. It made no sense.

Unless . . .

She eased herself away from the seductive heat of his body.

. . . somehow they were connected.

Her hands went cold, her body went weak. *Oh, Lord. Oh no.*

The Countess and Dominick? Please no . . .

She moved to the vanity just to give herself some distance, some perspective. After all, it was dark; she couldn't really see his hands. What could she tell with her mouth, really?

All this vampire talk and Peter's rallying his friends to patrol the streets had obviously spooked her so that she saw ghouls where there weren't any.

Dominick, for heaven's sake. Thinking for one moment that her delicious secret lover could be some kind of monster.

"Senna?" His sleep-clogged voice penetrated her panic.

"I'm here."

She turned up the gaslight on the wall beside the vanity table.

"Why there? Why aren't you here?"

She had no choice but to lie, to say she was taking care of physical necessities. She didn't want to have to do that.

He assumed it anyway. "Come back to bed if you're done."

"It must be nearly dawn," she countered without thinking.

Which meant what? That she still felt uncertain? That there was even a question in her mind about something she hadn't even seen? "The maid, Lady Augustine—"

"I don't particularly care." He held out his hand. "Come."

She took it. She could tell nothing from the feel of his palm against hers. She'd imagined it. Yet, she slipped her hand away from his in the next instant.

She stared at herself in the vanity mirror, disquieted by her hesitation.

"She doesn't know," he said finally, swinging out of bed and heading to the washbasin.

He should have passed behind her.

The thought struck her like a lightning bolt at least a minute later. She should have seen him reflected in the vanity mirror. Granted, it wasn't a large mirror, but she should at least have seen his shadow.

She moved her head slightly. She heard water splashing. She knew he was there. She closed her eyes. He was just out of the margins of the mirror.

She swallowed hard.

No mirrors. A shard of a memory sliced through her disquiet. And something beyond that . . . only she couldn't grasp it.

Some other place or time she'd taken note of *no mirrors,* but when, why?

Still, she felt his presence, felt him behind her suddenly, his hands on her shoulders, his kiss on her head.

But his reflection is not in the mirror.

She heard a faint ruffling sound, then nothing.

A persistent knocking on her door woke her. She opened her eyes to find herself in bed, naked and alone, on a bright sunny morning.

Lady Augustine was at the door all flurried with the stunning news that Charles Sandston had been apprehended last night—and that he had been the vampire killer all along.

❧

Lady Augustine just relished the details, particularly over breakfast.

"Charles Sandston, can you imagine! Peter's Keepers actually found him, all bloody, with a victim right at his feet . . . Charles!" She bit into a scone. "A man I received into my own house."

Charles—something about Charles and blood sounded familiar.

"And the Countess—what must I think now? I was the one who brought her to Edmee. Oh, she will be prostrate over this news. She may require my company today as well."

Lady Augustine shook her head. "But Charles . . ." She sighed. "I feel responsible. We treated them like one of us."

Senna could barely manage a piece of toast and some tea as Lady Augustine bemoaned her gullibility and reiterated the gory particulars.

"He had a knife too. Do you suppose he stabbed them before he bit them, or after? Oh, it's too awful to think about."

A knife . . . blood . . . bite . . . no mirrors. Senna put down her toast, her appetite diminishing by the minute.

All of it was connected somehow.

Charles, a murderer? The vampire? Did she not remember something about that, about the Countess's family? The husband. The daughter. The sister. All dead.

And . . . Nicolai.

I'm watching you.

They'd forgotten all about Nicolai. Charles was not Nicolai. Nicolai had sent that warning to Charles. If Nicolai was even alive. They were gone, the Countess's family, all of them. Except Charles.

Who wrote the notes and put them in all the books in the library at Drom?

"And I encouraged you to treat him with favor," Lady Augustine was saying regretfully. "Dear Senna, how do I apologize?"

Senna barely caught the tail end of that self-flagellation. "Please, don't even think about it. I never considered it, not once."

"But before you lost your memory—"

Senna felt a lick of irritation. It was enough she really couldn't remember; having to pretend memory loss on two levels exhausted her. "Who can say? I don't remember, so to me, it's as if it never happened."

"I wager we won't see the Countess again; she's probably on her way to that mausoleum where she's been hiding all these years. Ah well. At least we can rest easy. The vampire killer is finally in the authorities' hands. And here's Peter, finally." He strolled into the dining room holding an envelope in one hand.

Lady Augustine took it warily. "Edmee, I warrant. She's one who won't be happy at the news about Charles." She opened the envelope with a quick flick of her letter opener and read the note. "Indeed. She wishes that I would visit today so we can talk over these unsettling events. And so I must. But I'm certain Peter can entertain you. We aren't housebound anymore now that Charles is in custody."

Lady Augustine flashed a smile at Peter. "I must ready myself. Peter, if you'd be good enough to take me? Senna, I must leave you to your own devices for a while—not as long as yesterday, I promise. Peter, while I freshen and change, you might take Senna for our customary morning ride in the park. I should be no more than a half hour."

"Excellent thought. I do feel the need for some fresh air after last night."

It was the last thing Senna wanted. She tried to deflect him.

"You'll be quite the hero now, Peter. You don't need to do this. I could just go alone later, while your mother is attending to Lady Hartwicke."

"Please don't go by yourself," Lady Augustine interpolated as she made her way upstairs. "I'd feel so much better if Peter took you driving this morning."

Senna gave her a speculative look. Senna was too aware that Peter didn't hate her now, that he'd liked their kiss. It seemed long ago too.

But that was before Dominick . . .

Before everything changed.

"If it pleases Lady Augustine . . ." she murmured. No use fighting her benefactress. The whole thing about Charles was unsettling enough.

"I'll behave," Peter whispered as they waited for the brougham to be brought around.

That hardly reassured her. "So will I," Senna murmured. Still, this seemed like an exercise in futility unless—*dear God*—unless Lady Augustine meant to throw them together?

"Why did your mother insist we drive out together?" she asked him as they got under way a few minutes later.

"Did she? Well, frankly, I think we should make this a daily outing."

She didn't think he was jesting either. She so badly didn't want to be there with him, not today, not any day. She wanted to be alone, to remember last night, to savor her body's capacity for pleasure, to find answers to all her questions.

"After all," he continued, "what else do you have to do?"

She froze. Not only because of the viciousness of the question, but from something in his tone.

"Yes, yes, I know. Mother. We do want to keep Mother happy. But in the course of making that happen, you should also want to make me happy. Because after all, you have nowhere else to go."

She waited, tensed and cold. The rest was obvious and crystal clear.

"I see I don't need to elaborate. There's really no choice, Senna."

After last night? After diving into that fathomless ocean of pleasure with Dominick? With her body still saturated with his essence? *Remember* . . .

How could she ever do that with Peter? It was inconceivable.

Did it matter actually? She'd wind up on the streets eventually anyway.

Peter's blackmail was akin to death. It was hardly the way she'd have planned the ruse, but she obviously was not as masterful. While she'd been wallowing in sexual excess with her secret lover, she'd been outwitted—again.

She'd never know how she'd gotten from Drom to London, never remember the things that she'd forgotten, never discover the answers to the inexplicable things she'd experienced.

But none of that was important now.

"Think of all you'd lose," Peter went on. "Safety, security, everything provided, entrée to the highest circles, of which you've already had a taste, a beautiful home in the heart of London, and a dotty old lady who for some reason thinks she's responsible for you and is willing to give you everything.

"Contrast that with what would happen if you left us. You have no friends, no family, no one willing to help you. I'd wager you've been on your own a long time and have always depended on your beauty and your ability to charm and deceive your victims."

She knew this story; she'd heard it once before a long time ago. Another man's voice bloodlessly outlined virtually the same putrid future for her if she didn't give him what he wanted.

"But, you know, when you're on the street for just a little while, your beauty goes and your satin turns to rags. You're begging for money, you're sleeping with drunks, living on the dole, headed for the poorhouse and a life of penury, thankless work, gruel, and death."

It was always about death. This time it was blackmail by death, with the same threats and unspoken calamities waiting to befall her.

"I know which life I'd choose, if I were you."

Yes, the life she'd tried to gull out of some trusting, unsuspecting, well-to-do dupe so long ago she had almost forgotten how it all started.

And look how that had turned out.

She had to leave, there just was no choice, no matter what the consequences.

"Whatever you want," she said wearily.

"A kiss for now," he coaxed her, touching her chin and then her lips.

She felt nothing. But then, she didn't have to feel anything. She just had to let him kiss her.

Which, before Dominick, had not been all that unpleasant.

What am I doing?

Why hadn't she seen that this was his play from the moment he'd agreed she could stay at Berkeley Square?

She couldn't prevent her body from tensing up as his lips touched hers a second time.

He gave her a sly look. "You're not that innocent."

"Nor that experienced," she retorted.

He looked at her speculatively. "You know, I almost believe that. *Almost.* We'll deal very well together, Senna. You have only to be as generous to me as you are to my mother."

She wished she had a weapon right then—a knife would have done, even a table knife—and she would have stabbed him in his heart, without qualm, without compunction.

What?

Blood . . . she saw blood seeping from wounds . . .

She couldn't breathe. She was on the verge of panic.

"You're very comfortable here," Peter added as the carriage pulled up in front of Lady Augustine's town house, where she was waiting and watching just inside the threshold. "A smart woman wouldn't cavalierly turn that down. And," he added, as he helped her out, "I *am* a hero."

Lady Augustine bustled down the steps, spouting instructions.

"Ring for Puckett if you need anything. Lunch at noon. I'm not expecting callers today. I should return well before dinner."

"And I, well before noon," Peter said meaningfully, before he hoisted himself into the driver's seat.

"Point taken," Senna murmured. *Don't show panic. Be calm. Get out as soon as possible.* "My regards to Lady Hartwicke."

"Of course. So kind," Lady Augustine said into the wind as the carriage rolled off.

Calm. Walk up the steps slowly. Through the door. Acknowledge Puckett and go up the steps to your room.

Sit at the cursed vanity table without thinking about last night.

No lines, no mirrors . . .

Bloody knives.
Breathe.
Blackmail.

She needed currency. It didn't matter what it was—money, jewelry, silver, small salable items. God, she'd lost all her street guile during these weeks in another world. She'd forgotten this too: how to turn whatever she had at hand into a means of survival.

She'd gotten too comfortable, so she'd sloughed off the inconsistencies and overlooked the irrational.

All she needed was a small stash. She didn't have to resort to making money on her back. She'd peel potatoes again, read palms, swab floors, tell fortunes.

She'd be fine.

Oh, God, the thought of leaving . . .

She'd gotten too accustomed to luxury. Luxury had made her soft, enough so that she'd even considered Peter's blackmail. For a mere minute, but still.

She stared at herself in the mirror and thought of Dominick.

She'd never couple with him again. Suddenly there was no point to it: all of it seemed dark and meaningless.

She had to get out of here. Where could she look to even find something she could convert to money? Lady Augustine's room first, which was in a wing across the hall from her room.

She was unaware of the tears streaming down her face as she rummaged through drawers and looked in chests and tabletop boxes.

How could she steal anything from the kindly Lady Augustine? What wouldn't she miss?

Some jewelry was in one of the boxes, silver vanity-table accessories, a pearl-encrusted comb, a silk fan, a gold locket, a beaded reticule. Inside, a silk lining, a handkerchief, a gold-plated mirror—oh, and wait—some pound notes, perhaps for a gratuity to someone who'd been particularly helpful.

Seven. She could take six of them and fold the remaining note to look as if the roll were still intact.

She darted back to her room, where she collapsed on the bed, her heart pounding, astounded that she even had any qualms about taking the money, shocked by her crisis of conscience.

And her tears. For Lady Augustine? Who'd lived like this her entire life and knew nothing else? Really?

She blew out a deep breath. Think. She had some jewelry as well—earrings, bracelets, and a necklace that Lady Augustine had provided to accessorize Senna's new clothes. She could sell her dress and perhaps find a bag so she could take several more items of clothing that she could barter.

The armoire was always full. She herself had never carefully gone through the contents. The maid always looked after, chose, and laid out her clothes.

She opened the armoire door. The interior was crammed with dresses, most of which she'd never worn, and divided so that daywear was to the right, and eveningwear to the left. Below, shoes. Above, accessories, including more jewelry, hats, hair ornaments, and bags. One large carry bag, in which she might fit one evening dress and a handful of the smaller items. That, and the money, would be enough.

She pulled the bag off the shelf and emptied it of the tissue paper stuffed in it. *Now for one elaborate evening dress. Just grab one.*

She took out one at random. Not fancy enough to command any money. She grabbed another. And another . . .

Stop wasting time. And another—at which point, she felt something that wasn't a hanger or a shelf. She let the next dress fall to the floor as she groped in the recesses of the interior.

It was a hook of some sort, or a handle. But nothing was hanging on it.

Maybe it was a lever of some kind. What if she pulled it? The whole interior would probably collapse. And Peter would find her, scrambling among the dresses, trying to steal them.

He'd be back soon—too soon.

She bit her lip, grasped the handle, and pulled it.

The back wall of the armoire slid open just wide enough for a body to fit through. Steps led downward into stygian darkness.

There was a sharp rap on her door, and her heart nearly stopped.

"Miss," the maid spoke, loudly, her tone urgent.

She didn't open the door, not with all the dresses piled on her bed like that and the mystery space behind the armoire open to view.

"What is it?"

"Miss Vaida's come to call."

"I'll—I'll be there in a few minutes."

"Very good, miss."

More than a few minutes.

She had no time to replace the dresses. She grabbed two of them, folded them hurriedly as best she could, and stuffed them into the bag, along with any of the accessories that might command some money.

All she needed was the bag at the ready, and the few pounds she'd taken from Lady Augustine's room that she'd tucked into her cuff.

What could be down those stairs?

She hesitated even stepping inside the armoire—then climbed in. How far down could the staircase go? This was not a large house. She started down, one step at a time, always mindful that Vaida was waiting, that the armoire door was open, and that dresses were strewn all over the bed and slipping onto the floor.

She counted steps—seventeen, eighteen . . . twenty . . .

A door. Dead darkness. Her heart pounded so hard she thought she'd collapse. She noticed a not-so-easily discernible hand pull well above her head.

She pulled it, and a creaking sound echoed as the door moved, just a little. A dank scent and a thick, heavy wave of air choked her.

The knocking at her bedroom door had become hard and insistent.

"Miss!" the maid called again loudly and insistently.

Senna scrambled back up the steps and tumbled out of the armoire, feeling a shudder of relief.

212 {♣ Thea Devine

"I'm coming right now."

She couldn't take the bag with the maid following behind her. The best she could do now was emphatically close the door behind her and head downstairs.

"In the parlor, miss."

The double doors were closed for some reason. Senna waited until the maid withdrew, girded herself to exchange the usual meaningless pleasantries, and flung open the doors.

"Vaida?"

She didn't know what registered first: the blood sprayed copiously on the furniture, rugs, and walls, or the body propped against the sofa with its ripped neck and its bared bitten and bloody bosom. Vaida couldn't possibly be alive.

Or was it the feral fear that no one else had been home except her and the servants, which meant there were not many suspects, and the only one for whom no one could really vouch was *her*.

Chapter 16

She felt as if she were sleepwalking as she closed the parlor doors softly behind her, pulled a cloak out of the hallway closet, grabbed the letter opener from the silver salver on the console, and walked straight out the door without looking back.

Don't think, don't assume, don't speculate. Just get away without arousing anyone's suspicion.

She folded her arms across her midriff as she walked and felt for the money tucked up her sleeve. At least she had that.

And the letter opener. It was a truly puny defense—against what? Monsters? In daylight?

Someone had just killed Vaida in daylight. Senna slipped the implement into the cloak pocket. All she could think about was the blood. All that blood. She felt her body give as she envisioned it seeping from Vaida's neck and chest, bleeding all over the sofa, the carpet, sapping a life.

Don't think. Just go.

But where?

Her mind wasn't functioning properly. It was early. Lady Augustine would be gone for hours, but Peter would soon be back and find Vaida's poor bitten, blood-soaked body—and then what?

He'd demand to see her—and he'd find the mess she'd left behind. The secret panel in the armoire, the packed carry bag, the dresses tossed all over the bed and the floor. He'd discover that no one had seen her leave.

She'd be the first suspect, the one who fled, who had no convincing story or alibi or excuse for why she hadn't instantly called for help, secured a witness, stayed with Vaida's body, notified the authorities.

She stopped in the middle of the street, breathless with fear. She didn't know what to do or where to go. The air was thick and threatening. The thoroughfare was crowded with carriages and cabs, and shops with their wares advertised on the building fronts and spilling onto the sidewalk. People swirled around her on their way somewhere, and she felt as if they were all looking at her.

But no one knew a vampire was on the loose this morning. Except her.

She was nowhere near Berkeley Square now, and she had no memory of even coming this far in her fashionable shoes that were hardly made for walking. A cab would cost her and she had no idea where to go. She'd relinquished every contact, every connection, when she'd set off for Drom.

The Countess was conceivably the only other person she could ask for help. But beg the Countess for mercy? Confess that she remembered all of her time at Drom and just not some of it?

You lie, you die.

She'd told too many lies already. She started walking again just to keep moving. Things couldn't get any worse. She'd gotten too complacent, her senses dulled, her wits lulled into thinking that she could be one of them after all. It was too seductive, being someone you weren't, clothed in all the luxuries. It had been so easy to fall into the traps, and she had fallen, hard and fast.

She wasn't yet flat on her back, but judging by the looks of some of the male passersby, she could be—soon. She wouldn't get far on six pounds, or pay for very much by way of shelter or food.

She quelled her panic. The street urchin in her didn't exist anymore. The girl who had begged, picked pockets, scavenged trash, and read palms when she got desperate—that girl was gone. She was too old now. She'd been other places, seen a different world, and she couldn't go back.

The realization stopped her cold for a long moment.

She couldn't go back. She wondered if she'd had an inkling of that when she'd conceived her indigent-relative scheme. Or if, in her heart of hearts, she'd really wanted that much more.

It was too late for all that now. Realizations always hit the moment you knew you could never have what you wanted.

She'd just never comprehended how much she wanted and how much she'd suppressed just to keep moving, to survive.

And then her heart sank: *Dominick.*

He was her secret, her pleasure, her evanescent lover who didn't exist in her real world. But he did live. He was an importer of goods, a wealthy merchant by day, eligible and embraced by society, sought after and welcomed in the best homes by night.

In the real world, he was above and beyond her touch, even with her impeccable sponsor into society. Yet, he'd chosen her to take to his bed. In her deepest dreams, she wanted to run to him. But in the real world, she had no claim on him at all.

She didn't know how much time had passed since she'd left the town house, but by now Peter must have found the body and raised the alarm. The Yard could be looking for her right now. She wasn't safe anywhere.

Finding Dominick was her only sane next step.

She had to start thinking like a street thief now, like the sharper she used to be. That Senna would do anything, use anyone, to get what she needed. She wouldn't have needed to con Dominick. She had everything he wanted, everything she'd willingly given him.

And now, she thought callously, a little desperately, as she hailed a hansom cab, it was time for him to give back.

&.

If anyone knew about the comings and goings of a household, it was a servant. Servants knew who lived where, who was in residence, who was at his club, who had gone shopping, who was having an illicit liaison in the afternoon.

Senna had worked in this world, she knew it well, and she knew how to work any belowstairs domestic to get information.

With some subtle questioning of passing servants and by encouraging them to think that she was in a certain kind of trouble, she discovered which was Dominick's town house and found out that he'd gone out early to attend to business and still hadn't returned.

Pretending to be pregnant was the perfect strategy for someone who was dressed in elegant daywear prowling the streets of Belgravia, rooting around for information. It was exactly the way a desperate woman on the fringes of society would act. It gave her credibility and sympathy in equal measure. But that was only with the servants. She had no idea what to expect when she finally rang the bell to Dominick's town house later that afternoon.

The butler opened the door and looked down his nose at her.

Senna lifted her chin. "Mr. Janou, please."

"Mr. Janou is not presently available." The voice was starchy and disapproving.

"May I wait?"

"I cannot say when he will return."

"May I wait?" she pressed. "Mr. Janou would wish me to wait." Would he? The butler's impassive expression and haughty air were nerve-racking. It was as if he scented her desperation. He was clearly close to turning her away, but he relented after a moment.

"As you wish, miss. But you must leave when I do. Mr. Janou is quite clear on that."

He showed her to a small parlor, an anteroom. "I'll send the maid with some tea."

God, yes. "Thank you."

He withdrew and she looked around curiously as she slipped off her cloak. The small, pleasant room was divided from the parlor by walnut sliding doors and was comfortably furnished with a sofa, chairs, and tables set conveniently around the room. The fireplace had a carved walnut surround with the fire now banked low. The windows overlooking the street were curtained in opaque ivory silk.

She slid open the dividing doors to reveal a long room bathed in shadows and similarly furnished. She darted back to the sofa as she heard footsteps coming down the hallway. A maid entered carrying a small tray with a teapot and a plate with some cookies.

She could barely stop from gobbling them down. Then, while she sipped her tea, she forced herself to focus. What did the butler mean by saying she must leave when he did?

It didn't matter. She meant to be here when Dominick returned even if it meant hiding somewhere in the house.

In the meantime, she'd explore. The parlor first, all dark and cavernous. She stepped inside and closed the sliding doors behind her. The only light came from the windows on the fireplace wall, which were shrouded in that sheer silk.

Still, it was obviously a showpiece room, with gilt-framed paintings on every wall, parquet floors beneath a lush Persian carpet, handsomely upholstered furniture, and a great rectangular mural over the elaborately carved fireplace.

In the far corner, against the hallway wall, stood a grand piano.

It was a room for entertaining, for music and mingling. For elegant conversation, beautiful gowns, handsome men, and illicit love affairs.

She slipped back into the anteroom. Perhaps a half hour had passed. The butler would soon leave, if she understood him correctly.

She had to find a way to stay.

She slipped her cloak on and tiptoed out into the hallway, closing the door behind her. The stairs were right there, and if she left the front door ajar, perhaps the butler would think she'd just gotten tired of waiting and left.

She followed thought with action, unlocking and pulling the

door open a crack just as she heard voices in the distance: the butler and maid.

Why did this remind her of Drom? Wandering in the hallway, bumping into things, mysterious notes, no mirrors . . . *Stop it!*

No mirrors. She had no time to assess why that thought had suddenly flashed into her mind. She darted upstairs just as the butler and the maid appeared down the far end of the long hallway.

"I can't imagine what that lady wants of Mr. Janou," the butler was saying as they came closer to the anteroom. "But it's time for her to go." He opened the door to the anteroom. "She's not here."

The maid noticed the front door. "Perhaps she got tired of waiting—the outer door is ajar."

"Or perhaps not," the butler said, irritation tingeing his previously impassive tone. "You close up. I'm going to search."

He started up the steps.

Senna hadn't expected that; she'd been lurking in the shadows in the upstairs hallway, and now he was halfway up the steps. She had one choice of where to hide, one door within reach.

It was directly to her right. She opened it stealthily and slipped inside only seconds before the butler stepped onto the landing.

Everything was dark. She was so tired of darkness. All she could see was the shadow of the bed in the center of the room. The butler's footsteps padded just outside the door and her heart pounded so hard she thought it would explode.

As she heard the door creak open, she reacted instinctively: she dropped to her knees, slid under the bed, and found herself rolling into a hidden cavity beneath and onto a living, breathing body shrouded in the dank underground stench of dirt and death.

She didn't scream. She *wanted* to scream. But she held her breath in the deadly silence as a sliver of light permeated the room. Then, she heard a step inside the threshold, a light brightening the details, floor to ceiling, seeking a hint that she was there.

The door closed.

Silence.

She swallowed her horror, not daring to move or react. Cold permeated her body, like death, and she started shivering uncontrollably. The stench was almost unbearable. The sense of a sentient being in the same space was so terrifying, she nearly vomited as fear and disgust welled up like bile.

Her body contracted, as if she could minimize contact with the rot and decay. It was like lying with a corpse. Stone dead in a sea of mud, but still alive. No lines, no mirrors, no reflections.

You lie, you die.

Senna's whole body jolted at the thought and she felt for the letter opener in her cloak pocket. A sharp tip. A bloody weapon. *Just work it free and jam it up against . . .*

What? Death?

Don't move.

The corpselike body was still there with her. The butler's footsteps had receded. It was only a question of getting out from under the desiccation. There was nowhere to hide. Ghouls were everywhere, especially under beds, everyone's worst nightmare.

Don't move. She needed all her wits, and she felt as if they were scattered nineteen to the dozen all over London. The silence choked her. She inhaled the rancid scent of death and exhaled her soul along with all she'd given away.

She should have stayed with Vaida's body.

Why was everything soaked in blood?

The tension in her body almost killed her. She had to do something, anything, to get out of there. She felt for the edge of the cavity, inches away from where she lay. The depth was a different story. Figuring it out meant levering herself up in a hunched position and pulling herself out while pushing against the thing that occupied the space.

What if it was a dead body and it disintegrated? What if it reached for her to pull her back into the dust of the grave.

Breathe.

She moved on instinct, twisting up onto her knees and thrusting, pushing against the solidity of the shrouded body that suddenly evaporated as she hoisted herself out of the cavity and fell flat on the floor.

Oh, God . . . oh, God . . . Now she felt faint and boneless. She couldn't move, certain her heart had stopped. Just a matter of time and death would overtake her.

Breathe.

Get out NOW.

Galvanized, she wriggled out from under the side rail and onto her shaking knees, then her feet, still unsteady, her heart thrumming, her clothes streaked with dirt. Certain the thing would come after her—

There was a ruffling sound, a breath, and the gaslights turned up suddenly as if by some unseen hand. The door creaked open as she reached for the knob.

She pulled back as if she'd been burned, her heart plummeting.

No shadow lay beyond the edge of the door, no way to know if someone was there.

She wrenched it open the rest of the way, her heart nearly stopping at the sight of the figure looming on the threshold, barely dressed in trousers, boots, and a shirt just covering the faded scars on his chest.

Dominick.

The scent of blood ran thick and fast in the air, in his veins, in this throbbing moment when he stood confronting Senna as Dominick, as himself, and saw the fear and disgust shimmering in her eyes.

"Vaida's dead," she said flatly.

"I know."

"I found her. They're looking for me."

"I know."

"What else do you know?" she demanded testily.

"You're here."

And trapped, between the elusive him and the thing under the bed in that room. The stench, the body, the blood, and the memories that didn't quite connect.

"As are you, finally." But as she said the words, she suddenly saw a kaleidoscope of images wheeling through her mind—the inexplicable mysteries, the journey from Drom, the nights in his bed, sex and death, no lines, no mirrors—and it struck her hard that the answers to all her questions resided in him. And that she already knew the response to the most important one.

"You're the vampire," she whispered.

"I'm your savior," he contradicted, holding out his hand.

Here was the test, if she would take it . . .

If she would trust where he would take her while knowing viscerally that he was the body under the bed, the rancid, decaying corpse, the vile bloodsucking monster, a killer . . . her lover . . .

But a savior?

She took his hand, the hand without lines, life lines, heart lines, heartless, lifeless, a vampire in his soul. How could she follow him? How could she have thought she could love him?

She followed him downstairs into the parlor anteroom, where one gaslit wall sconce burned low. The tray with the remains of her tea and cookies was gone, and the fire was out. Dominick quickly moved to light it up again.

"There's no one to bring tea or food," he said in a casual tone as he struck a match and put it to the logs he'd rearranged. "There is food—appearances must be preserved—but everyone leaves by five o'clock. I'm sure Knoll made that clear."

He pulled a nearby chair close to the fire. "Take off that awful cloak and sit."

She sat, slipping the cloak against the back of the chair, keeping the folds close around her so she could feel the letter opener. He eased himself down to the floor, leaning his back against the chair opposite.

"Did you kill them?" she asked quietly.

"Which them?"

"All of them, any of them. Lord Hartwicke."

"No, no, and no."

"How do I believe that?"

"One takes a savior on faith."

"Don't jest." She leaned forward, then hesitated.

"Ask your questions, Senna."

"Lady Augustine . . ."

He hesitated for a moment. "I brought you to her."

"Why? How?"

"She was in the right place at the right time to intercede for you."

"She didn't know me."

"But she did," Dominick pointed out. "I made certain of that."

She saw he would not explain that cryptic statement.

"The Countess is not a patient woman," he added. "As you probably discovered, she wants what she wants and sooner than humanly possible. Whatever your purpose at Drom, you were really serving her needs. Once you ceased being of use, she fully intended to destroy you."

"And so . . . you saved me? Why?"

"For my own purposes."

"For a child, you mean."

Not a muscle moved on his face. "She was the one who wanted an heir."

"And you wanted—"

He reached across and grasped her wrist. "I wound up wanting *you.*"

She stared at his face, those hypnotic blue eyes, the world-weary lines cut around his mouth that she knew so well, too well. The awareness leaped between them like a firecracker.

Douse the flame. Stiffen the spine. Run if you can. He's a vampire.

"What are you?"

He considered the question for a moment. "I am a vampire of the clan Iscariot, who are descendants of Judas and heir to the curse of his betrayal. I was made, not born, a victim of another's desire that I survive as a bloodsucking fiend. That's what I am. That's *who* I am."

She unconsciously shook her head at every word. None of that had she ever seen in him. Or felt. Surely she would have sensed the bloodless murderer in him, surely she could not have coupled with the monster he claimed to be.

He was the answer to everything—a being with supernatural powers who transported her from a house of horrors to a comfortable life beyond her imagining; from her bedroom to his bed; from virgin to—whatever she had been to him besides the potential breeder of his blood.

"You were under the bed with me in that . . . that . . ."

He nodded. "Coffin. It's a coffin-shaped cavity where I sleep in a shroud infused with the soil of the Countess's mother country. In sunlight, I wear obsidian, a rock which absorbs the sun's rays and prevents incineration. I have fangs, hidden beneath a double palate. You discovered there are no life or heart lines in my palm. I'm condemned to eternal life as the monster I've become."

Was he? A monster? Here, in a civilized setting, he was Dominick, her secret lover who owned her soul. Under that bed, he was a secret monster who could destroy her altogether just with a bite.

She shuddered, her blood running cold.

"Exactly. You can't reconcile the monster with the man."

"The Countess, she said all you cared about was making a child."

"It was not all I cared about," Dominick said, and she believed him. Or she wanted to believe him. She wanted to blot out the monster and be with the man. She wanted to tell him it didn't matter, that only their nights together made sense and she cared only about that.

But she didn't. The monster was insidious. It seeped in right between her ballooning desire and her horror and disgust at what he really was, what he had the power to do.

"Now you know. A monster can't claim a princess. It can't live a normal, moral, social life. It doesn't know love. It cares about nothing except sustaining itself. It knows only violence and death."

Not him—she knew it in her bones. She looked into his eyes. Not a monster. Not a man. And yet, he was both, and she had to distance herself from all he had been with her.

"I think it really was about making a child," she said finally.

"Is there a child?"

She hesitated. "It's too soon to know."

He held her eyes. "Is it? Would you tell me?"

". . . I don't know."

"There's still danger out there. There are others—and patrols and weapons won't stop them."

"Can you stop them?"

"Why would I want to?"

"So they don't blame you or come after you."

He shook his head. "I don't care. Those in charge have limited means to prevent the death. Vampires have powers. They can and do kill and feed at will. No one can capture them. No one can contain them."

"You mean *you*," she said pointedly.

"Them. Any of them, yes—myself included."

She went silent. His hand on her wrist was warm, enfolding, natural, and she made no move to withdraw it, or the human connection.

"Peter Augustine roused up the city for his own purposes," he continued. "They arrested Charles Sandston. They'll take into custody anyone who remotely seems like a killer. It will be mayhem out there. People will be judged. People will die. Other people will pay."

His voice was cold, bloodless. She shivered again.

"They'll come looking for you here, you know."

"Why? No one could possibly—" She broke off abruptly. "The Countess."

"Be prepared. They march in the streets even now." He squeezed her wrist. "They are getting closer. I didn't think it would be this soon."

She listened as she gazed at him. He didn't avoid her eyes. He was what he was and she couldn't believe it. When she looked at him, he was exactly the same as he'd always been.

And yet, she thought, maybe she'd always known, despite there being no mark of the vampire on him. No telltale blood dripping from his mouth. No sign of fangs. No decay on his body. His gaze was clear and steady. Nothing different, nothing changed, except that an hour earlier, she'd lain in that coffin of a cavity body-to-body with the remorseless monster he really was.

She made a keening sound.

And the doorbell rang.

"Shhh. Stay here." He rose up in one lithe movement.

She heard Peter's voice, and the murmur of the crowd with him, saw the light of torches flaming into the sky, heard Dominick saying, "Be my guest."

She blinked, and she suddenly found herself back under the bed, in the squalid dirt of the coffin cavity, wrapped in her cloak. Her skin crawled. Her body turned to ice, and her heart stopped.

She heard the cadre of Keepers thundering throughout the house, looking in closets, behind curtains, tearing apart beds, in the attic, in the unused servants' quarters, hunting a vampire.

She made a move to crawl out of the cavity, but something pushed her back down, hard. A moment later a half dozen of the Keepers of the Night invaded the room.

She held her breath and sank back into the rot and dirt, as she heard sounds of the patrol shouting back and forth to each other, rifling drawers, closets, ripping into the mattress right above her head.

Any minute one of them would look under the bed. Best to be prepared. She untangled the letter opener from the pocket of her cloak to have it at the ready.

Where was Dominick, letting these lawless people loose in his house?

But he didn't care, he'd said, and that probably applied to anything in the human realm. All this—the house, the fairy tale about his being a wealthy merchant, his courting society—all just trappings, a cover.

And she was trapped too.

In a moldering coffin full of rotted dirt.

And possibly with child.

Oh, God . . .

She should give herself up to the Keepers. Anything made more sense than depending on a vampire who could kill her with one bite—

Or give you eternal life . . .

Oh, dear Lord, don't think that . . . don't even . . .

She started shaking uncontrollably.

The noise of the search had not abated.

"Anyone look under the beds?" one of them shouted.

Immediately, the light from a lantern flashed under the bed.

Senna braced herself.

"Clear!"

What?

They'd found nothing anywhere in the house, but they were still determined to catch a vampire. It was just like that night at the Hartwicke ball—there was no stopping them. The notoriety was worth the mistakes, the wrongful arrests, to attract gossip and adulation.

She heard shouts of "Clear!" from all over the house, and the thunder of footsteps racing down the stairs.

Nothing was clear. She levered herself up and out of the cavity and crawled onto the floor. She was covered in the filth of the pit, clutching her letter opener as if it were the key to life, or death. Maybe both.

Death was a footstep away whether in the rabid Keepers or the danger of Dominick's true nature.

Savior or devil?

Who was Dominick, really?

She'd been happier not knowing. Or pretending she didn't know.

Fear consumed her like the echo of a heartbeat.

The reality was barely a foot away from where she lay. It was not a man. It was a fiend, a ghoul. It was evil. It killed. It lived forever.

She closed her eyes on a shuddery breath.

It had to be a nightmare.

They're gone.

She didn't know if he said it out loud or she heard it somewhere in the recesses of her despair. But she felt his hands grasp her arms at her elbows and propel her forward and up onto her feet.

She sank onto the bed, still clutching the letter opener. Her cloak, she noted in an abstract way, was still in the pit. Her soul was in that pit. He could kill her now and who would know or care?

"They'll watch the house," he said, watching her. "They won't give up. Vaida was one of them. Her death hits home. It could just as easily have been one of them."

She clutched at the shredded duvet. "You know how she died."

"That doesn't matter, does it? Whether it was Iscariot or Tepes, someone always dies."

She shuddered. She didn't quite know what he meant, but it didn't matter. The vampire hunters did not differentiate. They wanted—they *needed*—to assign blame.

"They're still holding Charles Sandston," he added. "It doesn't matter that he was in custody when Vaida died."

She digested this in silence, thinking how odd it was she was in the very room where he had made such ravishing love to her.

Sitting across from her was the man, the man who had made love to her.

Under the bed, sometimes, lay the monster, the corpse, the murderer.

She jumped to her feet. "And I'm the one who found her. I'm not safe here either."

"Safer than anywhere else right now," he said. "There's nowhere to go, at least not yet."

She felt edgy and scared at the thought of being alone with him all night.

"So what do you suggest? We sleep together?"

"That's not going to happen."

She felt no relief. "Then what?"

"We're going to get you some clean clothes first."

"How?"

"Well, put down the weapon first . . ."

"I don't think so."

"Tuck it away then."

She slipped it into her waistband.

"Close your eyes."

She blinked and opened her eyes to find she was back in her room at Lady Augustine's house.

Everything was exactly as she'd left it, including the bag she'd packed with items to sell, the clothes all over the bed and the floor, the armoire door ajar, and the opening in the back wall just visible in the dimmed light.

"The maid must have been occupied elsewhere," Dominick murmured. "I wonder what you were thinking."

She was staring at the armoire. "I was look—"

He bent his long frame and poked his head into the armoire and found the lever. He pulled it and the back wall slid farther open.

She watched him disappear into the opening, and she followed him into the armoire and, hesitantly, down the narrow steps.

He turned. "Shhh."

At the bottom, at the door, he felt for a latch, and finding it, he cautiously pulled it. Senna hovered behind him, waiting for that choking wave of dank air.

Dominick swung open the door.

The air was fresh, clean. No dankness, no choking thickness. What had she imagined?

Dominick peered into the opening. "It's another bedroom," he whispered. "Back up. We have very little time."

"But—" She'd had such a foreboding feeling when she'd nearly opened that door before. It had been like the scent of a tomb.

She pivoted and climbed carefully back up the steps and out of the armoire, with him close behind.

"Go change your clothes," he directed.

"There was something down there," she protested. "It smelled like—"

"It's a bedroom," Dominick said firmly. "There's no time to play guessing games. You need to change. Lady Augustine could return at any moment, even if Peter is out all night."

Senna grabbed a dress and slipped behind the changing screen. "Where is she?"

"With Lady Hartwicke, of course."

Of course. She tore the dirt-encrusted dress from her body. She needed to wash badly. The water in the ewer was cold, but it would do to remove the muck on her arms and face. She'd randomly chosen one of the simpler day dresses that Lady Augustine had had made for her, two pieces, a darker blue waist over a lighter blue skirt. Everything taken into consideration to match her eyes, enhance her body, to make her seductive and desirable.

God, how she'd loved being measured and complimented by the seamstresses and having someone else pay for the extravagance. No use denying even that.

It seemed so long ago now.

She rounded the screen to find Dominick rummaging in one of the drawers.

"Packing," he drawled, inferring her question and gesturing to the carry bag. "What was in there was not practical."

"For a street thief it was," she retorted. "And there *was* something awful at the bottom of those steps when I went down there—"

"I don't disbelieve that, but— Shhh . . . someone's coming."

He pushed her behind the screen, a flimsy cover at best but enough to shield them from a casual scan of the room.

No one knocked this time. It was the maid, and she paused on the threshold, gave the room a sweeping look, then shut the door, went to the armoire, climbed in, and disappeared.

Senna made a move to follow; Dominick held her back. "Don't. We can't make ourselves known."

"Why would she go down there? Why would she even know about that secret door—"

"It doesn't matter. It won't help you."

"You don't know that." Senna wheeled away from him and climbed into the armoire. She started down the steps and Dominick followed, pausing to transshape himself before he entered.

She wasn't aware of him flitting above her. All she could think about was that all that time she'd been with Lady Augustine, the maid had known about the secret door.

How many times when she and Lady Augustine were out and about had the maid entered Senna's room and taken those stairs?

She was nearing the door; she knew because she'd counted the steps, and because she knew evil lurked in the dark and beyond closed doors.

She had only to pull the latch and all the secrets would be revealed.

And she hesitated. She heard a sound—a ruffle—someone behind her? Dear heaven was she trapped again?

She pulled the latch in a panic now. The door swung open a few inches. That cloying, choking wave of air assaulted her just as before. She took a deep breath and held her nose.

This time, she was going in. This time, she wanted to see the innocuous bedroom she'd caught a glimpse of over Dominick's shoulder. This time . . .

She pushed open the door and stepped into moldy, rancid dirt and the foul smell of the grave. She looked up and saw the maid, saw her face change, twist into a deranged mask, her eyes turn red, her hands become claws, her mouth pull back into the death smile of a monster, open and ready to feed.

For one death-defying moment, they stared at each other, and then the maid leapt at Senna and attacked.

Chapter 17

*H*e killed the maid.

He killed without a qualm because it was the only choice.

He left her body in the parlor where Vaida had been found, a reference certain to enrage the Keepers of the Night, and Peter Augustine in particular.

He didn't know why that gave him such satisfaction.

The other side of it was, Senna was still in danger. And the maid had inflicted some damage. That thin line of red marking Senna's neck, bleeding ever so slightly, shouldn't nearly torment a man, except if he had tasted her as he had.

He wanted more. He wanted full-on possession.

And he wanted it so much that he'd fed. After all, there was no point to wasting a useless blood-soaked dead body.

He hadn't expected the maid, but she was the elegant solution to Vaida's death. They'd find her, they'd draw a conclusion, they'd question Lady Augustine, who probably would lie, and the thing would be done.

The Keepers of the Night would be vigilant in prosecuting their mission. But that didn't mean more people weren't going to die.

The air was redolent of death. People were dying now. The Tepes were on the move. The Countess prowled with the insatiable hunger to hunt.

Even he had slaked his bloodthirst tonight on a convenient death.

That was his hell to suffer with what was left of his conscience.

The Countess didn't care; she'd eat her own son as soon as a vagrant on the streets if she had to.

His mother.

He'd lied to Senna about not sleeping with her. He'd hypnotized her so that putrid-smelling tomb of a room had looked like an ordinary bedroom in that brief glimpse he'd allowed her.

He was addicted to the blood-binding with her, and he couldn't stop even if he applied all his superhuman will to the task.

He didn't want to; he wanted that child.

The reckoning was coming.

He wanted all of it—whatever he had to do.

She remembered nothing, not even how she came to be sitting on the sofa in the anteroom in Dominick's town house, drinking tea, with Dominick on the floor beside her, his hand still on her wrist.

She was wearing that two-piece blue dress—there were stains on it already. She put her cup down angrily. "What just happened?"

Dominick stared into her eyes, letting some of her memory seep back.

Her eyes widened. "Oh! The maid. She—she killed Vaida?"

He nodded.

"When I think of all the times she was in my room—dear heaven, who is *not* a vampire?"

"You," Dominick said quietly.

I could be . . .

No!

She picked up the teacup again so she didn't have to look at him. He'd read it in her eyes, in her soul.

"Can I attend Vaida's funeral?" she asked into the teacup.

"No. It's too soon and they're still investigating."

"Then I want to go back to Lady Augustine."

He went quiet for a moment. "Do you?"

"What else is there?" She felt that desperation. If she didn't have that, she'd have nothing, and everything she'd done to get to this point had been futile. "Or do you think Lady Augustine would refuse to see me?"

"Officially, they're not sure who committed the murder. But who most likely murdered the maid?"

She went cold. "Murdered? Or mauled?"

"You choose the word."

"And so they still think I did it."

"More motive. As you said, she was in and out of the room all the time. Perhaps she saw something she shouldn't have . . . or she could have testified she saw you attack Vaida."

Her heart sank. There was no defense for that when they were making her out to be the vampire. She might just as well be—

Kill that thought.

"So we—"

"Stay here as long as we can."

"I'm not sleeping in that bedroom."

"No, we'll be in the second bedroom."

"We? I thought that wasn't going to happen."

"I changed my mind."

She looked away. This Dominick would not be denied, and if she just didn't think about the thing under the bed, she wouldn't want to. It still didn't mesh in her mind. She couldn't see him as a feral animal, much less a vampire or a killer.

Maybe the Countess in her fury had not been off the mark about his wanting to have a child with her. He hadn't abandoned her. She felt protected. Even now, knowing what she knew, she felt an ineffable surge of desire. When she was with him, she never wanted to leave him.

That was inevitable sometime, but perhaps a child was the way to bind him to her. If there was a child, maybe he would stay.

"I think you've had enough shocks for today," Dominick said. "You should lie down."

"Alone? Upstairs? In that room?"

"In the second bedroom."

"Not until you show me there's nothing under that bed."

"There's nothing under the bed."

She looked at him with pleading eyes.

"I know. Come—" He levered himself upright and took the lamp out of the wall sconce. She set aside the teacup and followed him upstairs. He motioned to his bedroom. "I'll put a lock on that door if it will make you feel better." He paused at the door across the landing from his bedroom and opened it. "Now, you get on your knees and check."

He held the lamp close to the floor so she could see. The floor beneath the bed was flat, well polished even.

"No secret doors?" she asked, climbing into bed.

"Not a one." He lowered the light and joined her, tucking her body against his. "In this room."

But it wasn't enough. He needed her naked; he needed the blood. He'd intended to leave her tonight, to monitor the Keepers. He hadn't expected she'd want to come to bed with him. But since she had—

Sometimes a physical connection, a binding, could be comforting in the face of adversity. All he needed was her ear. His tongue started on her lobe, her body squirming sensuously as he nipped and pulled, slowly and gently. Time stopped. Nothing but the binding drop of blood.

It had been too long since he'd sipped. A tremor coursed through him. He needed this. Just this little lick and taste, to watch the delicious red drop pearl up again and again, to tempt him.

He had an eternity to sip and nick. And kiss. And undress.

Slowly, taking his time, taking each droplet and savoring it like wine.

She fell into a miasma of sensations—his hands on her breasts, his tongue at her ear, their bodies rocking in unison, seeking, teasing, tormenting. And then he swooped and shifted her onto her knees.

It was safer that way. He was close to losing control. It had been too many hours since he sated his bloodlust with the maid, and Senna's blood was so luscious, so giving from as small an aperture as a nick in her lobe.

Even sex wasn't better than licking her blood from that one obscure body part.

Except for the possibility of a child. It was the only thing that kept his craving in check right now. He needed to plant his seed hard and fast tonight and keep his mind on her voluptuously writhing body and not think about biting into her.

He held her hips tight, thrusting and pumping, focusing on the heat of her, the honey wet, the fit, the depth . . . the blood.

He could just cover her, take the other lobe. She'd never know, it was all foreplay and pleasure for her.

But then—her neck, the nape, her shoulders, her breasts . . .

He could not focus his mind on anything but the blood.

Blood was orgasmic; blood was life.

His seed was life. He only needed to ejaculate . . . before the other uncontrollable lust gained control.

Now.

He pushed away violently and it was done.

He fed. He left her sleeping and flew out into the night and hunted every bit as rabidly as his mother, as any vampire, and he fed, hot and hard, with no compassion, compunction, or conscience.

He fed because he couldn't feed on her. Because the binding drops were not enough anymore. Because he couldn't have what he wanted of her because he wanted his seed to root.

He would *not* turn her.

He planned to have another go at her before the night was over.

But not before he fed again, not before he was certain he wouldn't drink her too seductive blood.

He winged his way over the city. He saw the torches of the Keepers wending in and out of streets and squares. He heard the howl of death in the air. He saw secret places where monsters fed. He saw vampires on the move and no one to stop them. Death roamed the city tonight. The lonely, the destitute, the drunk, the damaged, the deranged. None of it mattered but the blood, and that no one cared about the lost and the lonely.

It was too easy to find blood in the city. Not her blood, but enough of someone's blood to fill his need and slake his thirst for a night.

Blood to live. Blood for life.

After he'd cleaned himself up, he found Senna, dozing, drowsy.

"I'm here."

"Where were you?"

"Close by," he whispered. "Closer now." He slipped his hand between her legs. She was still moist, coated with the essence of him.

"I want it." Barely a breath as he began removing his clothes.

"Take it," she whispered.

He spread her legs wide, pushing her onto her back. Her deep, guttural moan as he took her nearly sent him over the edge. His cravings, for blood, anyone's blood, and for her, felt as if they were spiraling into obsession.

He needed, he wanted, he couldn't get enough—it didn't matter that he'd fed—she was there, beneath him, swallowing him into her body, soaked in his lust for her, for a child in her, for her blood.

He kept his hands occupied and his thrusts at a steady rhythm so he had something to focus on. He kept his mind on the child, so he wouldn't be tempted by her body beneath him coursing with the blood that could nourish him forever.

Now, now, now—before his instincts overrode his sense—*now*—he flooded her body with his lust, his seed, and his need.

"Don't move." He tilted her body farther back. He was still rigid and hot, still suffused with lust, still fighting the savage desire to bite and taste the bounty of her neck and her heart.

The tension flayed him, each side warring to suppress the other.

Did a man need sex more than life? Did a vampire need blood more than life? Or was the possibility of life enough to stave off the seduction of death?

He died a little each time he spent his seed, but only with the knowledge it would be reborn. She was the means, spread out before him, a feast of woman flesh and pulsing life. He had only to bend over her, lean into her, and her heart and her blood could be his forever.

He shifted his body over hers. Trust—love even—shimmered in her eyes. A mere minute, and he could own her blood, her body, her soul.

Take it.

She'd invited him, she'd said it, whispered it in the heat of lust. Surely she'd demand it in the heat of blood.

And she'd die. And become a monster.

It took every ounce of will to wrench himself away from her, far away, transshaping distance, high above the bed, where she couldn't see him, couldn't want him, couldn't . . .

And he wouldn't do it.

He still tasted it—the pearly red drop that had melted into nothingness on his tongue. He still savored it.

It was too dangerous. Every cell in his body screamed to bite and feed and kill and suck.

No more. His bloodlust had escalated in ways he'd never imagined and faster than he'd have predicted. Or was it her?

It didn't matter. He couldn't allow himself now. He was her savior; he must now practice denial. Confess his sins. Do penance. Seek absolution. The irony was killing.

He flew low over her body, brushing a wing against her cheek, commanding her to sleep, without dreams or desire.

Then he transshaped again and crawled into his own bed, inside the coffin cavity, wrapping himself in the shroud of the decayed and the dead, steeping his senses in the fetid home soil of the one who had made him.

I slept with a monster.

It wasn't a sudden, jarring realization. It seeped slowly into her consciousness as she awakened the next morning cold and alone.

He wasn't a monster though. Again, she felt that divide. The man in bed with her last night seemed tortured and anguished. But not a—

She still couldn't grasp the idea. And where was he, anyway?

She scrambled out of bed and retrieved her clothes.

Out in the hallway, nothing seemed out of place. No sense that anyone was around, not even the few servants who came daily.

Everything was quiet as a tomb.

Senna had a sinking feeling where she might find Dominick. She eased open the door of his bedroom and slipped in.

The bed was empty. The room was dimly lit and cold. She got down on her hands and knees and peered under the bed. Her breath caught. A body lay there, shrouded and still, the stench hovering over it like a cloud, its consciousness fully aware of her presence.

She felt it, and she recoiled. She scrambled to her feet and dove out of the room, back to her bedroom, and locked the door behind her.

Oh, God. She sank onto the bed. The bed where he'd—she'd— She shook off the memory. Even after she'd named what he was; even after he'd—

The monster under the bed was Dominick. The man in her bed was Dominick. She still couldn't reconcile the two faces.

She curved her palm around her belly. She felt nothing; her tummy was still flat, still empty. Or maybe a seed was just burgeoning. Something that would bind them together forever.

Eternally.

She shook her head violently to dislodge the thought; instead she washed with the cool water still in the ewer to cool her burning face.

She needed tea and something to eat. Hadn't Dominick said something about maintaining appearances? Because monsters didn't need food?

She edged her way out of the bedroom. All clear on the landing.

She made her way downstairs slowly, cautiously, pausing at the curve of the staircase as she saw that the parlor anteroom door was open.

A breakfast tray was set out and Dominick was already there. It was as if the monster under the bed didn't exist, and all was normal again.

He'd hunted. After the crucifying torment of sex with her, he'd transshaped, he'd left her, and he'd hunted the rest of the night.

And he'd fed, body after body. Like a heartless fiend, he'd remorselessly sucked them dry, the dregs of society, the rolling drunks, the ragged homeless, the feckless bar girls.

And it wasn't enough. It shocked him that it wasn't enough. Because of her, and those binding blood drops dripping onto his tongue for so many nights as he'd seduced her, he coveted her and only her.

This was his mortification of the flesh. Not to take her. To hold himself apart from her, even as he joined with her. If he could control himself enough for that—

Last night was proof he couldn't. His lust for her corporal body, and his compulsion to turn her, compelled him in equal measure, and he'd controlled neither impulse successfully.

Sitting across from her this morning, watching her eat the light breakfast he'd prepared, he wanted nothing more than to bite and bed her.

It was getting worse now they were in close quarters, and now that she knew everything. Nearly everything.

"Do you not eat at all?" she asked as she bit into toast and he thought about sinking himself into her.

"Not necessary." He didn't elaborate and he saw she comprehended why.

"What do you do with the food they serve you?" She hardly needed to ask that either; he probably buried it with the bodies he sapped in the dim hours of the night when no one was watching.

The monster in the guise of a man. Living a life eternal, always on the thin edge of a blood line.

Looking at him sitting there all vibrant with life and disturbingly male, she wondered if it could really be so bad.

She caught herself. It was so bad—Vaida's body, ravaged and bloody—an eternal vampire had done that to her with no compunction whatsoever. Just ripped into her neck and chest and turned her into a bloody mass of death and horror.

Senna put down her toast. Dominick was perfectly capable of doing that to someone.

To her . . .

Only she was the only possible suspect who might be the vampire who'd savaged Vaida. The authorities were looking for her; Peter now hunted her. Dominick still shielded her as if she were the monster they sought.

So why not become that creature of the night?

"I gave the servants a holiday," he said casually. "They believe I'll be traveling, a buying trip to the Far East. So it will just be us here, alone, until some of the craziness dies down."

She chose not to hear the *us, here,* and *alone* part.

"What craziness?"

"Peter's monster patrol. People are dying and they don't know if it's just plain murder or if he unleashed some unholy war. It's just safer for both of us to stay out of sight right now."

"Doing what?"

"My dear Senna," he murmured, and a sensual quiver shot through her body.

This was so dangerous. He obviously was lust-crazed, not thinking clearly. He just craved, ached for, *had* to have her.

"Senna . . ."

No mistaking the hunger in him or her response.

His first instinct was to take her, sitting on his lap. But her neck, her ears, would be so temptingly close. Even after his bloodbath last night, he couldn't take the chance. The ache to bite was too close to the desire to root now.

"Go upstairs," he ordered her, on the knife-edge of losing control. "I'll follow in a moment."

After he scavenged, after he slaked—anything, anyone.

He never thought he'd want sex and surcease with one person in equal measure like this. He couldn't help it, control it, or stop it. It just *was*. He would take every opportunity to inseminate her during these few cloistered days with her.

When he entered the second bedroom, she was lying on the bed, naked, soft, pliant, hungry.

He stripped off his trousers and reached for her across the foot of the bed, pulled her to the edge of the mattress, and lifted her legs to brace them against his shoulders. The move canted her body upward, aligning her hips and his, and putting the most seductive part of her far from his reach.

For now, he only wanted to sow, and he wanted to be swift and certain of his push, his aim, his pleasure. Except he didn't know how he would do it without the blood.

She hated that she couldn't touch him. That she could only watch and experience the hard thrusts that he kept centered and deep.

Another chance to conceive. Time to lie with him, have endless sex with him. She'd never envisioned having a child before this; probably it was inevitable she'd eventually have borne some stranger's bastard.

Why not his?

Here, with him embedded that deep within her, it was the most powerful connection she'd ever imagined.

And the pleasure. To watch that impassive, ascetic face soften in sex. To see emotion ripple in his eyes, on his mouth—it was like a deep, perfect kiss when he came, pouring himself into her, his hands clenching her legs tightly, the tremor in them mirroring his emotion.

He kept her coupled with him for a long, hot moment, then he lowered her body and without a word withdrew.

"Dominick?"

"I'm here."

"But you're not *here*."

"I'll come soon." Only he could barely contain himself. Lying next to her, with all that luscious flesh and no one around was a moment made for a vampire, for the thing he'd become, for the feral conscience that was fast losing what was left of its humanity.

"I'll be there soon." He had transshaped already and hovered high over her head. But he wouldn't be there soon. He had to get out of there, away from her alluring blood and body. He had to stop, stay away. There was just no other choice.

She heard a faint, now familiar ruffling sound, then the sense that she was not alone dissipated. He'd gone—somehow, some way. He'd left the room, left her, and gone beyond her.

She took a deep breath and pulled the duvet over her body. She felt cold and bereft. That intense and profound connection with him obviously meant nothing to him. Yet again, she'd seen his callousness in play. She was nothing special; just another passing trull with nothing to offer except her body.

It struck her forcefully just how alone she was. She had no family, no siblings, no cousins, no aunts, no grandparents. It was almost as if the streets had given birth to her, she'd been alone that long.

And she'd be alone when she died, she thought. Even if there was a child. She couldn't go back to the streets. She couldn't go back anywhere.

So why not—

She stifled that thought by jumping out of bed, washing, and getting dressed. There had to be more she could do than spread her legs for him for the next few days. The possibility of a child was definitely the ace up her sleeve. Surely they'd done it enough that she might be pregnant.

And if she was—it was a link, a tie . . . forever.

She had, perhaps, a week to make it happen. If it hadn't already.

🦢

She found him in the parlor anteroom staring out the window.

It was midafternoon by then, the quiet broken only now and then by the rumble of a carriage going by.

He didn't look at her. He couldn't look at her. "I can't do this anymore."

"Do what?"

"Do what we've been doing."

"Tell me why."

He turned to her then, his eyes burning blue. "I can't control my compulsion to feed on you."

She found she couldn't breathe. "You? When?"

"Your earlobes. They bleed. Just enough. Just that taste—and now I need it too much. It's not enough—I want to drain you. But I could kill you, and I can't take the chance. I won't."

The implication chilled her and excited her.

"What if—"

"Don't say it."

"But—"

"I won't."

"Even if I want—"

"You don't. You don't know. You don't see the ghoul lurking behind the romance. You've never witnessed that ugly moment when you slice into skin and veins and life, and blood spurts into your mouth and down your throat—hot and pulsing—and you pull and suck and siphon it all every way you can think of and leave a husk in place of a life.

"And then, it becomes your life, your reason for being. To kill and feed. Forever. So, no, I won't be your angel of death and resurrection, Senna. I won't make you a victim. I won't be your sire."

"What if there's nothing else?"

"Then I'm sorry for that."

"What if there's a child?"

"It will be yours."

Now everything felt futile, as if she'd come to the end of a long, twisting road that led to a steep cliff and she had just stepped over the edge into oblivion.

"How?" She didn't hear the defeat in that one word. "I love you."

"Then I'll be your savior—again."

She heard that sound, the ruffle, and suddenly he was gone. Like a magician, he just disappeared into nowhere.

"Dominick!"

The bastard. Her savior. Dooming her one way or the other. Eternal life sounded much more alluring than scrounging on the streets with a babe in arms and rags for its clothes and cradle.

She had time on her side at the moment; the Keepers still hunted, even as society readied for the annual weekend at the Grand National. Dominick still wanted to keep her safe. He wouldn't leave her, not yet.

And now she had the key to seducing him: his deliciously arousing tongue in her ear had been more than foreplay. It had been a lifeline.

And now she'd make it hers.

Because the more they had sex, the more there was a chance of a child, and the more connected he'd become. And if she gave up her blood?

Life everlasting.

Chapter 18

The Countess had finally secured Charles's release from Scotland Yard. It had not been easy, with Peter Augustine thwarting her at every turn. The evidence of the bloody knife. The wounds in his victim's neck. The bloodthirsty desire to kill. Charles's habitual nocturnal prowling. All of it used in testimony against him.

But he lacked the fangs, the one indisputable trait of a vampire, an irrefutable fact verified by a half dozen dentists who examined him and testified for him.

He'd been in prison for days, though it felt like years. And meantime, the Countess had been feasting on the city's underground populace as if they were a banquet laid out especially for her, waiting for her son's release.

"Peter Augustine is still hunting for the killer," she said disgustedly as they hailed a hansom cab. "He'll never come close to catching me. I can't believe how much I've denied myself all these years."

And how many more murders she could still commit. "It's time to return to Drom," Charles said, keeping his tone neutral.

"Oh, indeed. I plan to dismiss the servants and close it up."

"What?"

"London is my hunting ground now. I'm coming back here. You may do as you wish—stay at Drom, live with me . . ."

He felt a muscular trembling in her, a signal that the hunger was creeping up in her. "What about Senna?"

"She soiled herself with the taint of the vampire. She deliberately defiled her purity, and she's of no use to me now."

"Even if she carries Nicolai's child?"

"*Dominick* has disavowed his Lazlaric heritage," the Countess said coldly. "Nicolai chose to be Dominick and thus chose his revenge. Therefore, I will destroy Dominick and with him Nicolai. Soon."

She sounded utterly remorseless.

Charles wondered what she'd do when he became of no use to her. As of this moment, with no heir in sight, and no prospective vessel to conceive one, he was nothing more than an appendage, hanging on by a hair simply because he was her son.

"I might return to Drom," he said, shaking off the thought. "I wish we knew if Senna conceived."

"It doesn't matter."

"He's your son."

"He chose to become Dominick. My *son* was Nicolai."

Her obdurate tone precluded any protests. Charles felt like killing her at that very moment. It was easy to forget she was a monster, and that she would conceivably have no compunction about feeding on *him*.

Maybe that was his destiny. He knew all the ways. Maybe when they were both back at Drom, isolated from the world, with no one to see, he'd finally end his own nightmare of blood and filial duty in a fury of death and damnation. Perfect, for her. Redemption, for him.

Dominick couldn't stay away. Not all the blood in London could temper his craving for Senna. He'd done that to himself. He'd played with her, protected her, seduced her, fed on her, and maybe even made a child with her.

A child was the least of it. He didn't think in terms of death and destruction now. He might not define what he felt as love, but something bound him to her—an awakening, perhaps, that his eternity didn't have to be lived alone in the grave.

It would be so easy to bring her with him. She wanted it, she'd begged for it, she was exactly a vampire's prey: young, juicy, vulnerable, needy, alone, desperate.

She was all of that and none of it. And as a result, he felt it even more keenly as the pieces of his humanity slipped away and he avidly embraced the life, the powers, the lust, of the monster in him.

Soon, he would have no compunction about turning her. No contrition, no conscience, no guilt.

He was almost there. In another life, he could have loved her, but vampires didn't love. That was a human emotion and he was no longer human.

Yet he desperately wanted the child—more than he ever imagined—and that sliver of the human still fighting in him provided a rare and momentary understanding of his mother's drive to propagate an heir.

But still, none of that mitigated that he walked a dangerously fine line, clinging to an all-too-human need to procreate that clashed with his vampiric drive to death.

Two opposing forces, never to be united. He could only have her in one world and not the other.

He still was in no shape to return to the town house. He kept circling high above London, listening to the sounds of the night, watching the Keepers prowl the streets with their torches and their determination until they doused the light and dawn was imminent.

By then, he'd fed, near to his return to the town house; he felt calm, sated, in control.

He thought.

Until he opened the bedroom door and found Senna there waiting for him, dressed only in her undergarments, her arms outstretched, and blood smeared on her bared shoulders, welling from deliberate punctures in her ears.

He took her offering; there was just no stopping the hunger, the need. *Just this once. Just this time.* Without sex, without connection. Just the pure taste of the blood on his tongue, under his skin, and the taste of what she'd given for wanting him.

He lay with her, front to back, which gave him access to her ears and her shoulders. He took his time with it. He wanted to savor it, make it last as long as the blood oozed so delicately, deliciously.

But he knew, as he took full advantage, it would never be enough. As he scraped his teeth across her shoulder to bring up a line of droplets, he promised himself it would be enough.

It was her sacrifice, her desire to give him what he needed. She knew what it meant. But to him, it meant he would soon have to leave her because neither of them could go on like this.

Finally, after he sapped her, over and over, gently and insistently, she slept. Then, he just watched her. He'd exhausted her, drained her so much that the hunger rose in him again, the dangerous, horrible, unstoppable, uncontrollable hunger.

He wrenched himself away, before he could act, before he did something irreparable and wrong, and he turned his attention to transshaping for the time it took to get himself out of that room.

He gave her this gift in return for his selfishness in taking her blood.

He left her because in that moment it became clear he could easily pack away his conscience and kill her.

He winged his way out into the night through the fireplace flue. Down below, he saw the torches marching again in the distance, heading for the waterfront in lockstep, looking for monsters.

They were as committed as clergy. They never tired of the quest. They'd been out every night since the formation of the Keepers. They prevented nothing, if the rate of random deaths was anything to go by. And yet there they were, marching.

He idly wondered why. He decided to follow them, to keep

himself from feeding too soon, to keep himself from her. He banked and swooped down lower, following the swath of smoke from the torches.

A heaviness in the air dragged him down. He dove to get under the haze and the smoky fog. Lower, the air was clearer, the visibility better.

He watched as the mob rooted out vagrants from dark corners and drabs from behind piles of trash. He watched as they questioned their victims, searched their persons, and tossed them away.

But then they doused their torches, and under the cover of the shadows, they attacked their prey. Behind barrels and trash, in doorways, and up against streetlights, they pulled the dregs of the city, and they sliced into their necks and they fed—the Tepes, hiding behind the morality of finding a killer, decimating society's most disposable at the behest of Peter Augustine, the self-proclaimed most moral of them all.

Taking the itinerant with the signature bite at the neck, into skin and bone, the blood flowing into the Tepes like a drug to an addict, then eviscerating their bodies before dumping them into the holy water of the river.

Augustine—clever as sin, disguising the telltale redolence of the Tepes behind the false leadership of a supernatural demagogue.

The revelation stunned Dominick. But he should have known. By the devil's bones, he should have guessed. He'd felt them, heavy in the air, but there was nothing suspicious to set Augustine apart with his proper-mannered mother and his social reputation.

Augustine would keep after Senna—she was his shroud, his cover. If he apprehended her, the murders would be solved, the vampire would be off the streets, and he'd be a hero. He and his followers would have the freedom of the city in the guise of public service.

Dominick felt trouble brewing in his bones. There had been some outcry that the Yard wasn't acting fast enough to solve the so-called vampire murders, despite the investigation and the nightly patrols.

Augustine must be feeling pressure to find a scapegoat.

Yet they fed with no discrimination, no thought to discretion, and with a recklessness that didn't bode well.

Dominick flitted in still closer, the scent of blood stinging his senses.

Tepes. The ancient enemy. Killers and bloodletters. Cursed and doomed. Fouled by the scent of the tomb, by the desecration of souls. No salvation was possible.

But Judas had tried. Even if he had been rejected, Judas had at least sought redemption and begged forgiveness. Because of that, the Iscariot survived.

Now, Senna must survive. They were coming for her—tonight, tomorrow—something was in the air. The feeding had not sated the body. Augustine's desperation ringed around him like an aura. Soon he'd be knocking on doors, pulling people out of their beds, methodically working his way toward Dominick's town house.

He meant to break Senna. He wanted to settle other scores.

Dominick wheeled and winged away from the carnage. He'd had enough of Augustine's machinations.

But what was Lady Augustine's role? How ripe that Dominick had chosen her to be Senna's benefactress when she might well be the Countess's counterpart.

Damn to the devil—he had to get Senna out of London. Some-where beyond Augustine's immediate reach, someplace remote . . .

Drom. The Countess hadn't made a move to return there. Nor was it likely she would since she had the whole of the city in which to sink her fangs. No more isolation. No more mourning. No more hiding her true nature for the sake of Charles. No more thoughts of an heir.

Drom would be uninhabited from now on, as much his as it ever was Charles's. He could have been the favored son had he stayed, had he become the son the Countess yearned for.

That son was Nicolai. And Nicolai died the moment she sunk her fangs into him in an act of mercy and resurrection. From then on, Nicolai had lived solely to destroy her. Had become Dominick to save what was left of his humanity. And now everything was up-ended because of Senna.

Everyone wanted Senna, no one more than he.

He found her still in bed, luxuriating in a different kind of morning after. Her skin looked fresh, infused, her body light and buoyant as she swung off the bed, dressed only in her undergarments.

He measured the distance between them to make certain he was not that close.

"It didn't hurt," she murmured. "I'd do it again, every night, every day—just for you."

"We're *not* going to do that again," he said sharply.

"No?" She'd felt that deep gut need in him; she knew if she bled, he would feed.

"No."

She clearly didn't believe him.

"Senna."

"You're lying. I want it, you want it, I want you. Why can't we—"

"Truth?"

She cocked her head. "Tell me."

"It's not enough."

She digested the implication of what he said and her breath caught.

"Then turn me."

"No." He was emphatic, angry.

"Dominick—"

"No."

She bit her lower lip. "Does that mean no sex?"

"How can we? I can't be near you."

"And yet there you are." She took a step toward him. "I'm willing to risk it, all of it."

"I'm not. I won't."

"Not even the way we coupled yesterday? Was there not enough distance between us then? And last night, you couldn't get any closer. I'm confused. You want both and neither."

"I can't want you like a man when the needs of the monster under the bed override everything. He's not controllable."

"Yet you control him when you want it." Senna backed up against the bed and sat. "What happens when I want it?"

"Senna . . ."

She wriggled out of her pantaloons. "I want it."

His instinct urged him to leave, but his body told him otherwise. It had been hours since he'd fed. The taste of her, luscious and arousing, was still on him, even with that.

She eyed him, waiting on him, wanting him. All he had to do was strip, sink himself into her, just as she lay, and spend more seed.

So dangerous.

A man had no choice but to succumb to the potent lure of the elusive and unknowable feminine.

He came at her abruptly, against his will, plunging into her heat with a fierce possessiveness. Sex now was too intertwined with his blood-binding and he was an addict, craving it as much as he needed sex with her.

He would always be her secret lover, unheeding of her pleasure this morning, aiming to get things done expediently and to the point.

He rolled her upward, so he had a more direct angle into her body. He braced her legs once again against his chest, to balance her body against his for optimum penetration.

She loved watching every undulation, every thrust, she loved feeling his body's thunderous response to hers, she could see every time the hard lines of his face dissolve and soften with . . .

With love?

She'd goaded him today, but it was worth it. Tonight—the blood, the binding. He wouldn't refuse. Maybe he already anticipated it as his orgasm came suddenly, hard and slow.

His withdrawal was difficult to bear. To not have him covering her in the aftermath—her skin yearned for the touch of his, ached for the weight of him all over her. It was her sacrifice to prove this point: he could not exempt sex, he could not deny the blood.

He could remove himself to oblivion and he would still want, need, and come to her.

She turned to face him, the expression in her eyes telling him everything.

"I will not turn you."

"All right, then don't."

"It's inevitable, if I'm with you."

"You haven't abandoned me yet."

"Because you're still in danger."

"And you're still my savior." Bitterness laced her voice. "Lest I not forget, you say none of this matters to you."

"It matters to the man. The monster, not so much. So the man will always have sex with you, and the monster will deny that it means anything."

It was so tempting to think of killing off the monster, the other who kept the man from her. But then, she'd be killing Dominick too.

No resurrections, no rebirth, no afterlife.

She shivered. There was no hope any which way. Except if there was a child. The only control she had over that was to have sex with him every hour of every day. Just to make sure.

She liked that thought, even if it was near impossible. Maybe she'd try again in an hour. Maybe she could seduce him in the parlor. The big showy room with a nice number of chairs where he could easily take her on her back, on the floor, from behind.

Foolish thought.

How could she not want more?

It seemed much too quiet suddenly.

"Are you there?" she demanded.

"I'm here." But again, he sounded far away. "You dress, I'll make you some tea."

"Come back to bed instead."

"No." This time he was adamant.

"Not yet," she murmured under her breath. Then she sensed the room was empty. "Not yet," she said louder, as she swung her legs over the mattress and sat up.

They still had time. A day, a week—it didn't matter. It was enough. At that moment, it seemed like forever.

He liked doing human things—brewing tea, serving food, making love. Making a child. But it was dangerous even for that now. She didn't need a child to weigh her down or to raise on her own.

Particularly if she was seeking a husband. And why wouldn't she?

He didn't like that thought either, but he saw no solution that didn't revolve around death and victimization.

She appeared suddenly on the threshold, her blue dress a little the worse for wear, her hair tousled and her blue eyes glowing.

He felt the pain then—incisive like a knife, slicing hard and hot into the schism in what was left of his soul with the absolute knowledge he must relinquish any hold he had on her, forever.

She sat on the small sofa and poured her tea. He'd found some fruit and a muffin. He said nothing and let her eat, and then: "Let me see your ears."

"No need. I was careful, I washed the pinpoint before I did it. You said you shouldn't—"

But he did, sliding in next to her even as every nerve ending tingled with warning. "Tilt your head." He brushed the tumble of hair away from her ear. He saw the barest pinprick on either lobe, a neat trick with no mirror to guide her.

"It's not hard to do. I'll do it now. Here's a whole kettle of hot water with which to cleanse the tip." She started unfastening a small brooch on her collar.

He grasped her hand and took the pin, a small golden oval with a black center stone. Obsidian.

"A gift from Lady Augustine," Senna murmured. "Something to wear with one of the dresses we'd ordered. It was one of the things I could sell, when I thought to run away."

"You should have," he said dampingly, holding the pin up in the diffused light from the window.

The point, so delicate and fine, would barely hurt her, she'd hardly feel the prick. She'd just said so.

And he wanted it so much. Sitting next to her tight and close like this, holding the implement with which she'd pricked her ears and drawn her blood, her gift, last night . . .

"Let me show you," she whispered. "Let me give you what you most desire." She held out her hand. "Let me . . ."

He felt every tendon tighten in denial, every muscle in his body go stiff. She was so close, her dancing eyes so coaxing, he could nick her himself and take what he wanted and she'd barely feel a thing.

But that wouldn't quite be the same as a gift: her willingness to bleed to slake his need.

He dropped the pin into her palm.

She poured some more tea into her cup and dipped the entire pin into it. He'd provided a cloth napkin, and she retrieved the pin and wiped it all over, then dipped the point into the hot tea once again.

"And now," she murmured, "you just feel for the center of the lobe, and . . . one quick *jab*." It hurt—just a little. She couldn't tell if she'd drawn blood, but the look in his eyes confirmed it. "And the other—"

He grasped her hand. "Just the one."

"You could go back and forth between them."

"Just one." Even one bleeding lobe was too much, in the parlor anteroom in broad daylight, with his blood-hunger so naked.

"Take it," Senna whispered, "take me. Again."

He watched it well up, a perfect drop of blood. It was not enough, not nearly enough—she didn't understand. Or maybe she did, and this seduction was meant to lure him into opening the door to vampiric eternity.

The bead of blood mesmerized him. How many nights he'd spent rooting around for just that licking taste of her blood, to nick and take it in the guise of his seducing her. And now the tables were turned. She enticed him, by her willingness, by her inventiveness, by understanding it was her blood, as minimal as it was, that was his downfall.

The droplet dripped onto her shoulder.

She waited, watched, certain that the waste of her blood would finally break him. He grasped the cloth and sucked the residue from it, then tore it from her shoulder.

She smiled knowingly and shifted her body to ease his way. He bit voraciously at the skin on her shoulder, licked the drops as they fell little by little from the welling blood from the pinprick, felt every instinct screaming for immersion in her blood.

"This was a bad idea." His voice was so hoarse she didn't recognize it. His tongue in her ear was rough as he tugged on the lobe, eking out more blood. His teeth grazing down her neck to her shoulder, a tiny bite and then another, and another. Any blood, the endlessly exuding earlobe—

If he just yanked that portion of the dress he'd already torn away, he could bite into her naked chest, her pulsing heart and veins, and bury his face and his senses in the geyser of her blood and make her his forever.

He was that close. Just a movement of his mouth there, pull the impeding cloth away, bare her heaving breast, and sink his fangs into the soft flesh, the thundering heart, the blood, the bone, the meat. He could almost taste it, the succulent orgasm of blood and death.

Was that her thundering heart or banging at the door?

For a moment he didn't know where he was or who he was, except that the monster in him was bent on sending them all to hell.

The thumping grew louder. He stared at Senna as if he'd never seen her before, looked at her torn dress, her blood-smeared earlobe—the heart, the blood, the bite . . .

Not now—by the devil's bones . . .

He twisted away and off the sofa, falling onto his knees in agony. The man, the man, the man—he was still the man and not the monster.

He shoved away Senna's hand. "Don't."

The pounding grew louder. Someone was at the door.

He looked up at Senna, who was bending over him.

"Someone at the door?" His voice was ragged, stripped to the back of his throat so he didn't sound like himself.

She nodded. "I'll go."

"You get into the parlor. Now."

"But—"

"They're still after you. Who else could it be?" Good. Concentrating on the danger made him feel more in control. "Do as I say, Senna."

She nodded and slipped into the parlor.

He hauled himself upright. He hated that he felt so unsteady on his feet. It would pass now that he'd suppressed the monster. Now he had to deal with the monster outside.

He gathered himself together enough to look out the window.

The Keepers. Augustine. The Vampire brigade, in the guise of protectors of the innocent and preyed upon.

Damn them to hell.

It was time to protect Senna.

He edged into the parlor where she'd been listening.

"We have to go." He spoke barely above a whisper.

The pounding grew louder. They were going to break down the door.

"Where? Why?"

"The Keepers." The banging had grown louder still, more insistent. They called his name loudly, derisively.

"Senna—time to go."

Maybe it was too late. With an earsplitting crack, the thick front door fell inward, crashing against the banister and staircase. Senna caught sight of Peter Augustine as the Keepers flooded in, their faces the masks of monsters, their bodies in an animal crouch, at the ready to attack, their mouths baring vampiric fangs.

"Peter?" Senna whispered his name in shock as Dominick thrust her away from the oncoming swarm.

She fell into a whirling pool of nothingness, tethered only by Dominick's arms and body surrounding her, and when she opened her eyes moments later, she found that they were as far from London as the moon, in the small parlor at Drom. Alone.

*L*ady Augustine stood at the window in her parlor, looking out at the street. The rabble of the Keepers had finally dispersed and Peter was slumped on the sofa, exhausted.

"So he's gone," she said grimly. That was the thing about vampires—they could just disappear, as Peter had abandoned her to go ravage the Continent.

"For the moment." Peter offered no excuses, he'd been that close to killing the bastard—blast his formidable powers. The Iscariot were mandated to be eliminated, wherever he found them. It had been the only reason he'd let that street trull, Senna, stay in his mother's house: to keep a closer eye on both the Iscariot enemy.

"He can't have gone far," Lady Augustine said thoughtfully. Her job was to restrain and advise Peter after he got into that ugly mess at Oxford just after he'd been turned. What else could a mother do? He was her only son; she felt fiercely protective of him and could foresee the dangers on the path he'd chosen. Sometimes she could even avert them.

The fiasco with Senna? She could find no explanation for it. She felt as if her head had been fogged up. But now her senses were clear, and Senna was as much her enemy as the Countess and Dominick Janou.

"Janou's been in London less than a year," she added. "He's aloof and elusive, charming to the bone, commits to nothing. He has no one in Town."

"The Iscariot give off the scent of self-righteousness. They think they are superior to us."

"You emulated the Judas bite quite nicely," Lady Augustine said, "though I wish you hadn't eaten Hartwicke. Edmee complicated things enormously, soliciting the Countess for a séance. I still haven't recovered from the ramifications of that or her constant mewling about it. And the whole thing about Nicolai—it came to nothing in the end. A waste of everyone's time.

"But the authorities still believe that whore Senna is the most likely suspect since she was on the scene at each of the murders. Senna—a vampire?" Lady Augustine shook her head in wonder. "They still think all vampires are the same."

"It's to our advantage," Peter said. "The Keepers have only to apprehend her, and the city will be wide-open to us again."

"You shouldn't have gone so public with the Keepers."

"It was necessary."

"Dominick Janou saw you," Lady Augustine said flatly.

"You don't know that."

"He is not so superior that he's cured the hunger. He's been feeding."

"And the Countess has been hunting," Peter said.

"The Countess? Really."

"She's been isolated too long. The Iscariot, as superior as they feel they are, still must feed. Unfortunately, Charles is not vampiric. Believe me, I tried my hardest to pin that prostitute's death on him, but she died from a bite, not from knife wounds, so they released him.

"He just may have been born with the heart and soul of a murderous maniac," Peter continued. "Nevertheless, Charles is vulnerable. He was to have married Senna, didn't you say? And the Countess claimed to know her?

"Yet Senna kept feigning memory loss. So if we can't find Senna, we now have the convenient alternative of the Countess on whom to pin the murders. It's time to get them out of the public consciousness; people are still running scared and it's soured the whole beginning of the Season. I should pay a visit to Charles. And I think, if he's not forthcoming, it might be interesting to turn him."

Charles had sworn he was never going back to Drom. He was adamant about that even as he watched the Countess packing to spend several days there to close up the house and ease out the servants and staff.

"You need do nothing," the Countess said. "I'll take care of everything. You might search for your own quarters while I'm gone. I do feel us living together places undue constraints on my inclination to hunt."

"Of course." But he was stunned at how her words hit him.

Go away. I don't need you. You're on your own.

He'd never lived without her. He'd always known what she was, but she'd been circumspect about it, and never as blatant as she had since they'd come to London.

Often, he thought about ending her eternal life and breaking the curse that had destroyed his. After all, that was why he'd gotten rid of his father, his sister, his aunt, and his half brother—almost. To save them from the horror and disgust of discovering what she was, and to be the only one on whom she depended.

The Sandston fortune was the least of it. The Countess controlled a fair portion of it. But now that she wanted him out of the way, it became a major consideration. A percentage had been, by his father's design, allocated to Charles for his expenses; the rest was in trust until he attained his thirty-fifth year, by which time he was supposed to have curbed his feckless ways, matured, and perhaps married.

But never mind all that. The important thing was, the Countess had no compunction about lopping him off like a dead tree limb because he hadn't produced that heir.

He watched with cold eyes as her carriage was brought around and the footman helped her climb inside.

"Surely you have a more efficient means to travel than this."

"Indeed. But a leisurely trip, with stops now and then to admire the countryside and feed on the peasants seems like a delightful prospect to me."

He waved her off, chilled to the bone as he made his way back into the house.

It was time to arm himself against her. He needed to be prepared for every contingency. She had no motherly instinct except when it came to Nicolai, and nothing Charles ever did to try to please her diminished her love for her firstborn son.

He'd best not forget that. He had always been *the other one.* The unwanted child of a union of title and convenience. His only saving grace was his homicidal tendencies—his mother enjoyed that he wallowed in bloodletting even without the family curse.

He understood what he had to do. He'd vacate the house— today—and make certain the Countess couldn't find him.

"Charles."

A familiar voice spoke behind him just as he crossed the threshold. He wheeled around, his nerves jangling, to find Peter Augustine in the doorway, nearly nose-to-nose with him.

"What the hell, Peter . . ."

"May I come in?"

Over my dead body, Charles thought. Goddamned bastard had been ready to have him jailed for life; he wasn't feeling too charitable about Peter's life right now.

"Are you crazy?"

Peter shrugged. "Fine. So you're not a vampire. My mistake. I thought because the Countess *is . . .*"

That shocked Charles. Peter knew? Who else knew? And she'd thought she was so circumspect.

"Where is she?"

"Not here," Charles spat out. He swung the door into Peter's face, but Peter stopped it with his boot.

"Where?"

Charles stared at him. Icy-cold bastard. But why was he protecting the Countess? "Where else? Drom. Are we done now?"

"Drom," Peter repeated, eyeing him as if trying to come to a decision. "Of course . . ."

Charles's nerve endings jangled again. He shouldn't have told Peter. He grasped Peter's arm as the man turned to leave. "She'll be back day after tomorrow. If you can wait that long."

"If . . ." Peter said insinuatingly. He gave Charles another long look. There was time to take care of Charles. Turning wasn't exactly a five-minute process, although Peter was sorely tempted at the moment.

He kept staring until Charles relinquished his arm.

I have to go to Drom, he thought as Peter left. Whatever Peter wanted, Charles couldn't take the chance Peter wouldn't set out for Drom sooner rather than later.

Son of a bitch. It wasn't as if the Countess couldn't take care of herself. She'd eat Peter as soon as talk to him. They had no common ground between them that he should want or need to see her.

Unless he intended to put the blame for the murders on her now that he knew her secret. Then the Keepers could trumpet that they had succeeded in keeping London safe once again.

Shit. The last place he wanted to go was Drom. All those dreary miles. All that barren countryside . . . and a wake of dead bodies to follow, if the Countess was to be believed.

He believed.

Peter Augustine was dangerous and arrogant, a lethal combination that even a vampire might not be capable of combating.

The Countess needed Charles. Whether she knew it or not.

The nightmare was not over; she really was back in the small parlor at Drom, and it was Dominick pacing around the room, not Charles.

Everything seemed different and yet the same. Senna felt both as if years had gone by since the day she'd left, and as if it were yesterday.

But she hadn't walked away of her own volition. She remembered she'd been intending to leave because Charles had become aggressive and impatient to produce the much wanted heir with or without marriage. She remembered feeling trapped and as if there were no way out of the situation that she herself had created.

She shook her head to clear it. Surely that was a lifetime ago, her running from Charles after she'd—

She'd—pulling the memory from nowhere—she'd stabbed him. She'd stolen a knife, and she'd stabbed Charles, the elusive memory suddenly full-blown in her mind.

She'd tried to kill Charles. Or just immobilize him so he couldn't come after her and force her to look at the realities of the situation.

She remembered. And the Countess had tried to pretty it all up with all kinds of inducements to marry him.

After her own too successful scheme to be taken in as an indigent relation.

Senna couldn't believe how naive she'd been, and how well the Countess had played her for her own benefit. Only in the end, neither of them had gotten what they wanted.

And now Senna was back at Drom, her feelings of dread intensifying as she watched Dominick moving edgily around the room.

She didn't feel any safer here than in London, and she'd have wagered anything neither did he. She thought if she moved from where she sat, the whole of Drom and all her lies would come crashing in on her.

"You're depending on the Countess remaining in London," she said suddenly.

"I depend on nothing, actually. This could be just a respite. Someone could come, but Drom is just far enough from London that they might think twice about making the journey."

"I would have thought twice," Senna murmured.

"It's not the first place they'll think to look for you."

"You found me here."

"*Find* isn't quite the word," he said. "You happened to be here."

"I never saw you."

"You weren't meant to."

She had an odd feeling. He'd been here when she arrived but not visible. Yet she'd felt safe, protected, especially at night. That day that Charles importuned her and she'd stabbed him—she shuddered just thinking about it—and now she'd lost the train of the memory.

No, Charles had kissed her, she remembered that. And she hadn't liked it. He'd reacted badly and he'd harangued her about the awful fate that awaited her did she not accept his offer of marriage.

With blood on the knife, she ran—had she run? The memory eluded her again.

She had the distinct feeling Dominick knew exactly what had happened, that he knew everything she couldn't remember.

The house felt oppressive, as if it retained all its blood memory, even though Dominick had made certain candles and lamps were lit everywhere to relieve the gloom.

It was early evening by then. The servants, who worked only by day, she remembered, were gone before they arrived, and she couldn't imagine how they'd explain their presence tomorrow.

But that was tomorrow. Not that long ago, she'd sat in this room with the Countess when she'd suggested that Senna marry Charles, make an heir, and live happily ever after free from want.

The moment of triumph she'd felt was followed by the fall from the rush of having successfully gulled the Countess to the low of the reality of her response to Charles. She'd bolted from her chair, as if that could keep what had happened at bay. That second night, in the darkened hallway, returning to her room to find that disturbing note pinned to the Countess's shawl . . .

She wheeled toward the door and headed to the library.

The room was just as she remembered it. Nothing had been touched, not even the notebook in which she'd been transcribing the Countess's memories.

She opened it curiously, scanned the lines written in her own hand about the Countess's tragic life, blighted by deaths, burned by fire, Nicolai.

She moved to one of the bookcases, reached as high she could, removed a random book, and opened it.

A small square of paper fell to the floor. She picked it up.

I'm watching you.

The threatening message in every book, any book, as a ghostly reminder. Dominick wouldn't let them forget that Nicolai was always with them.

The Countess hadn't lost him to *death*.

She looked up and saw Dominick in the doorway.

"You're Nicolai," she whispered into the tense silence.

"I was," he said at length.

But there was something else, something that had to do with the things she couldn't remember. They stood staring at each other, then she moved toward the door, pushing him out of the way as she barreled her way into the hallway.

Dominick pivoted to watch her, but he made no attempt to detain her.

She headed toward the parlor, then whirled away. Whatever she sought was not in the parlor, and more than that, she sensed that Dominick knew what it was. And that she didn't want to know.

Shadows were everywhere as she approached the dining room. Here, she felt a massive reluctance to enter the room. Something had happened here. She had the keening feeling that when she remembered, it would change things forever.

A flashing memory hit her hard: herself running into the house, the bloody knife in hand, and into the dining room, and—

And—why did everything stop short right there?

She took a step into the room. A feeling of rank horror washed over her and she froze. She sensed Dominick behind her so she couldn't turn and run away.

She wanted to. She felt desperate to leave. Something in that room—she could almost feel the knife in her hand, see herself standing just where she was now, coming to a hard, terrified halt as she—

—at the sight of—

The Countess . . .

The memory revealed itself like a curtain slowly rising.

Bloody hands holding . . . sharp teeth biting . . . into flesh. Animal flesh. Small, furry, bloody . . .

She heard a feral howl that couldn't be her—couldn't—as she turned and charged at Dominick, her hands beating at his chest violently, as she screamed and denied the memory.

And he let her, he let that memory back into her consciousness, until many minutes later, he just picked her up and carried her away upstairs to one of the spare bedrooms.

Oh my God, oh my God, oh my God . . .

He let her cry or mourn or whatever it was she was doing until, exhausted, she slept. There were only so many tears, and a body, a mind, could only take so much replay of the horror of that night.

When she awakened, hours later, she found him slumped in a chair at the foot of the bed, and her first thought was, even these answers to her questions centered in him.

"So you remembered," he said.

Her head felt foggy. The moment seemed so distant. The Countess at the table and then what? "What happened after I stumbled in on her?" she asked groggily.

"I took you away."

She tried to connect that to something concrete. But she didn't know he was there.

He was supposed to have died. She couldn't align what she knew of the Countess's history with what had happened, and she needed to make sense of everything now.

She propped some pillows against the headboard and levered herself upright against them. "Nicolai died in that fire," she said.

"He nearly did," Dominick said. "She saved him. She saved me."

"The Countess."

"My mother. The vampire. Saved Nicolai. Saved me."

He said it so matter of factly. His mother. The vampire. The Countess was his mother. Nicolai was Dominick. Which meant Charles was his brother.

She ought to have seen where the stories meshed. She should have known. He'd made it harder by referring to Nicolai as if he were another person.

She dreaded asking the next question. "How?"

"She turned him with the eternal bite. It was the only way, she claimed. He was too badly burned, but that, as you've seen, has healed and faded over the years. He hated her for it, by the way."

"You hated her."

"Hate her still. I wanted to destroy her. I'd planned for years. I didn't quite know how. Then I returned, you showed up, and she was looking for a receptacle to bear an heir. A perfect confluence of need."

Senna swallowed. She didn't want to know the rest. So much she didn't want to know. "Charles?"

"Is not. He's a homicidal maniac and loves to kill, but he's not a vampire. Sorry to say I'm related to him. But his blood is pure, she made certain of that. My deduction is that her second husband, Sandston, was turned sometime after Charles was born, and he in turn sired her. And she wanted, she *demanded*, Charles get an heir to carry on the Lazlaric name, honor, blood—whatever you want to call it."

"And there I was," Senna said, her tone bitter. "And I couldn't love Charles."

"Who could? Not even she."

"And you saved me—"

"Took you away, erased the memories, gave you to Lady Augustine along with a trove of memories she could draw on, and then gradually seduced you, so that you would give *me* a child."

He held her dismayed gaze as he continued, "My vengeance— because *I* am the last of the Lazlarics—was to give her an heir with the tainted blood of my father . . . and with the woman she'd chosen for Charles."

"No . . ." A heartbroken sound.

"It was so. Then. When you came."

"No." She kept shaking her head as each awful detail piled up. Those languorous, sensual nights, the explosive sex, all for revenge?

"That was the plan. That she would die, knowing that the Lazlaric heir still carried the blood of a vampire. It's a terrible vengeance."

The Countess, sly and infernal, following Senna to London, waiting and watching to see if she would reveal the secret she couldn't remember.

The Countess at the séance—calling Nicolai's name—

"And so we come to who committed those vampire murders."

"Not she. Not I. Not you."

Senna waited, her patience stretched to a thin thread but willing herself not to dwell on how he'd used her.

"Peter Augustine."

She stared at him in shock. "Peter?" But then she'd seen his face as the Keepers had pounded down the door, the monster face with the thick monster fangs . . .

"He's Tepes, a vampire clan that's violent and indiscriminate and the enemy of the Iscariot. They meant for all the blame to fall on the Countess originally. The first death, in the theater, was pure opportunity.

"The city came to a standstill during the investigation of that death. What murderer wouldn't use it to his advantage—especially a vampire. Without even trying, Peter stumbled on a way to continue his murderous path. And then he thought, if he'd killed someone prominent, like Lord Hartwicke, he could legitimately form a citizens' patrol, and then find a scapegoat whose apprehension would allow his kind to continue on as they had in the guise of keeping London safe. Thus the Keepers, all of whom are Tepes. And all of London is grateful."

No. She thought she said it out loud. *Peter* . . .

She couldn't breathe. Monsters all around her and Dominick was protecting her from them? But was he? They were alone here, for the very reason that the authorities and the Keepers were searching for her.

But maybe he had another purpose.

He'd already said he was dangerous to her, that he couldn't be near her because he wanted her blood, that he could kill her.

Maybe he meant to turn her.

She hadn't been all that averse to the thought. She couldn't imagine life beyond this moment anyway. Not without him, at any rate.

Whatever he was, she wanted him. She didn't need him to keep her safe. She needed him to want her with him forever.

She was so tired. Too many revelations. Too many vampires. But not him. Nothing about him was vampiric. He was so austere, so restrained—except when he was aroused and—

Don't.

"Dominick . . ."

"No." His tone was adamant.

"I didn't ask a question."

"You don't have to. I won't. Turn you. Ever. Period."

"You'll just save me."

"That's a wholly different matter."

"And leave."

"It's inevitable."

Now, everything seemed too much. All the explanations he'd thrown at her, the revelation that the Countess was a vampire, of Peter as the vampire murderer, of Dominick's callous plan to get her with child.

He wasn't her savior. He couldn't be.

She nestled down into the pillows feeling bereft and alone.

The silence felt empty. Dominick remained immobile, unreachable, as noises in the house magnified as the hours crawled by. She couldn't sleep, and she doubted Dominick ever did.

There were no coffin cavities here.

Wait then, where would Dominick revitalize his body?

She bolted upright suddenly to find that Dominick wasn't there.

The shadows pressed down on her. Where would anyone find a vampire deep in the night? On the hunt? Wrapped in a shroud? Bathing in mud?

God, she hated being alone. Lamps were burning low so she wasn't entirely enveloped in darkness, but it felt as if ghosts were lurking in every corner.

She'd walked this house deep in the night. It was spooky, even when the Countess and Charles were in residence. Spookier still that she thought she heard hoofbeats in the distance.

She wasn't nearly dressed to go ghost hunting. She was still clothed in that torn dress, but she couldn't do anything about that now.

She slipped out of bed and grabbed a kerosene lamp. As she edged onto the bedroom-floor landing, she had the feeling she'd played this scene before.

She crept down the steps to the front door in near darkness. She could die of fright, she thought, and there would be only vampires to feed on her.

It was a carriage—she heard the wheels rumbling, crackling on the drive, in tandem with the horses' hooves. Someone had driven nearly all night to come here.

Not a vampire, but that didn't reassure her.

She paused on the bottom step. There she was halfway between retreating to her room and knocking down an intruder and running away.

Even in the dark, she'd do anything.

Muffled voices. The door opened several inches. A suitcase appeared. And then—

"Countess," Dominick's voice came from behind her.

She looked up and saw both of them on the first and second steps respectively.

"Mother, you mean."

"Enemy," Dominick corrected tightly.

"And yet you're *here*."

"It seemed like a good idea at the time."

"I'd rethink it, if I were you."

The enmity between them crackled like a spitting fire. He truly hated her. She despised him. The tension was thick and explosive. They were in a particular kind of war: the Countess truly believed she'd saved him; he'd never forgiven her for not letting him die.

Which was why, Senna thought suddenly, he wouldn't turn her.

The Countess slanted a look at him as she picked up her small suitcase. "I'm closing up Drom. You need to leave. Now."

She headed toward the staircase at the other end of the hallway.

To the room with the mud bath, Senna thought. Because where else would she sleep? She wondered if that was where Dominick had disappeared to.

"Not very hospitable of you, Countess." A new voice sounded, Peter's, on the threshold. "How nice. We're all gathered together in one place. May I come in?"

"You can leave," the Countess barked.

Peter made a tsking sound. "Of course you'll invite us to stay the night. By then, the authorities should be here, we'll get everything straightened away so we can all go on with our lives. Senna," he acknowledged her. "Dominick."

In a sudden silence they stood frozen, as if they were in a tableau, as they heard still more hoofbeats in the distance.

The Countess uttered a curse. The moment shifted, a panting horse, the thump of a dismount, and Charles, elbowing Peter aside, blew in through the open door.

"Where's the party?"

Again, everything stopped dead. No one made a move.

The Countess spat, "What the hell are you doing here? Just leave, all of you. *Now.*" She disappeared around the far side of the staircase.

Charles and Dominick stared at each other.

"I'll just . . . find someplace to put my head," Peter said. "A tree branch will do. An anthill . . ."

"Sorry, old man," Charles murmured unrepentantly as he headed up to his room.

Dominick shut the front door in Peter's face.

"Upstairs, now." He pushed Senna's boneless body toward the landing. "Go on, into bed."

"What about you?"

"I'm going to play a game of chess."

"Don't go. I'm scared to death. I'd be so much happier if I could do this with you. If I could be with you—"

"No." He pushed her onto the bed.

She reached for him, pulling him toward her.

"Don't make it more difficult."

"They could—"

"They could," he agreed. "But I won't let them. I'm not going anywhere right now. We all know where we all are. And *what* we are. It's a matter of who makes the first move."

"And then?"

His flat tone chilled her. "Someone dies."

Chapter **20**

*D*ominick knew, even if Senna didn't, that a locked door would not deter a vampire. Perhaps it was better she didn't know.

There were few choices. He'd inherited all the powers of the Countess with that one life-changing bite, but they all had those powers and Senna had no defense against any of it.

What Peter didn't have was an invitation to enter Drom. Then there was Charles. Amusing to think of using Charles as a weapon against their mother, against Peter Augustine.

Two humans, three vampires. Not an acceptable equation, even if one of them was isolated for the moment outside the manor.

It all just meant he couldn't leave Senna alone.

Unless he enlisted Charles's help.

What were he and Peter doing here anyway?

The Countess was closing up Drom and moving her killing field to London.

Peter was after Senna. Or was he?

And Charles—his bloodthirsty half brother. As cold-blooded as any vampire. As murderous. As heartless.

But he could be certain of one thing: Charles wouldn't devour Senna.

And he couldn't walk an inch outside the door to find Charles and be certain the Countess wasn't lurking, with the mindless hunger of a bloodsucking organism, waiting to pounce.

Checkmate.

Peter was almost irrelevant. The Countess was threat enough; it was time to help Charles decide he didn't like the odds.

First, Dominick had to neutralize Peter.

There was a rapping at the door. Senna whipped around to look at Dominick.

"Open the door," he said calmly.

Charles stood on the threshold, his suitcase in hand.

He looked at Senna. "We should join forces. Against *them*." He did not look at Dominick. "I have everything we need."

"What do you mean, everything?" Senna asked.

"I mean crucifixes, holy water, icons. Stakes. Knives. Whatever we need for protection. You realize there are two of us and three of them."

She had, but she wasn't quite as terrified as he until this moment.

Two of us, three of them.

Dominick was one of *them*.

She should not believe she was safe with a vampire. She looked at Dominick.

"We all have similar powers. Neither you nor he are immune to them, so Charles was very wise to come prepared."

"Oh, yes," Charles said. "I'm prepared. And while I didn't expect to see Senna here, I would hate to see her die."

"Do you have someone else in mind?"

"You."

There was a faint ruffling sound and Dominick vanished.

"Good luck." His voice, disembodied, floated at them from somewhere in the room.

"Bastard," Charles muttered. He slammed the door. "The problem with those sons of bitches is that they can infiltrate anywhere just by reconstituting into smoke. No one is safe, and if you ever thought you were"—he whirled on Senna—"you're as naive as a baby."

He tossed the suitcase on the bed and unlatched it. "Here." He tossed a crucifix and chain at her. "Don't take that off. And carry this at all times." It was a vial of holy water. "Throw it in their eyes and it'll burn them to eternity."

She peered over his shoulder. There was more—the icons, knives, a gun, bullets. He handed her several of the icons. "Put them around the room."

Dominick can never come back to this room, she thought as she placed one each on the bed, the chair, and the floor near the door.

"The knives and the bullets are silver," Charles went on as he loaded the guns one after the other. "Everything harmful to the Iscariot comes back to the thirty pieces of silver Judas was paid for his betrayal. The Iscariot bite—three *X*'s—mark those thirty pieces of silver on their victims forever. They are every bit as vicious killers as the Tepes. The clans are ancient enemies. They're always at war. Peter has to die, you know."

"I don't care," Senna said, not even shocked by her heartlessness.

"Well, that's something."

"Are we protected enough to leave the room?"

"It's a matter of degree. How much do you want to die?"

If I can be with Dominick . . .

She suppressed the thought and sidestepped the question. "What can I do?"

Charles looked grim. "Wait."

He'd always underestimated Charles, Dominick thought. Charles was the perfect combination of his mother and his upbringing. The second son, always not quite the best, not quite up to snuff, not quite . . . and even the murders he'd committed so long ago had never elevated him beyond "other son" status.

Eliminating the competition just hadn't worked. And there had always been that absent immortal biblical brother in his way.

At least this time, Charles had been honest enough to name his target.

Too bad *he* had to die.

Right now, however, he was a useful bodyguard. He'd trapped up the whole room with all the relics and ritualistic preventives he'd brought, and he and Senna had hunkered down to wait.

Senna would not put up with that for long. She'd figure out that Peter had been bluffing about the arrival of the authorities in the morning, and that would galvanize her.

Meantime Dominick had already checked on the Countess. She was not at rest; she was probably prowling somewhere around the house or the grounds, seeking to root out Peter, the interloper.

And Peter had probably already transmogrified into mist so he no longer needed an invitation to cross a threshold. Peter could be anywhere in the house right now. The Countess could be a fly in the shadows.

It was now a game of hide-and-seek and who would show first. Dominick winged a circuit of the parlor, the small parlor, the library, the dining room, staying high in the shadows. Matte silence. Not a movement. Not a breath. Just the latent sense of waiting, watching.

All those books he'd filled with the note *I'm watching you*. It had been meant as a warning to Charles that he was now accountable to someone. Charles, who thought when Nicolai disappeared, it was for good, forever. But Dominick wasn't one to let a bloody-minded half sibling get too comfortable.

Vampires didn't forgive—or forget—an attempted murder when there was an eternity to gnaw on the past.

The recent past felt an eternity away.

Somewhere on this floor, the Countess and Peter bided their time.

One of them would trigger the confrontation. Just not yet. Everyone was jockeying for the best position, the optimum time, the sweet moment to move in for the kill.

The minutes crawled by.

Damned Charles always needed a nudge, except when it came to murdering his family.

Come downstairs.

Something had to tip the balance, and Dominick wasn't averse to challenging Charles to do it. Charles wanted to be a hero. Charles wanted his story to be the right story, and that every death at his hands the result of his holy cause.

Now was the time. Charles had at his hands the opportunity to come out from under his mother's yoke and his brother's immortality.

It's time to show your mettle.

If Charles didn't take the goad, they could be here for days. Only Dominick didn't think Senna would have the patience. Charles, however, would be cautious, wary. He'd want the advantage. He'd use his weapons. He wouldn't care about Senna, only about preserving his own neck.

Soft footsteps sounded. With subtle sound of wings, Dominick slipped into the shadows and transshaped back to human form. So silent. The house was too lit up—he'd wanted to banish the darkness when they arrived—but now, the light gave him too little room to maneuver, and no way to rectify it without revealing his position.

A hissing whisper. "Senna!"

A distraction. He closed his eyes and the lamps dimmed down.

A finger of light shot down the staircase, a looming shadow moved downward step by hesitant step.

"Senna!" Charles hissed even more urgently.

An eerie echo: "Senna . . ."

It stopped her. Silence dropped like a stone. The whip of a wing. The hiss of drawn-in breath. Senna, like a statue, froze in place a third of the way down the staircase.

Dominick watched in the shadows, calculating which sound was the Countess, which one Peter, which one was hungry, which one hadn't fed.

Peter wanted Senna, to bring her to justice, to pave the way for the Keepers of the Night to continue their murderous course.

Charles was another matter altogether. He'd always been devoted to the Countess, in his way. But that filial loyalty had never been reciprocated. Charles was tired, he longed to be free from the shackles of the Countess's secrets, and his own bloody past.

He could bury everything with one well-timed aim of a dagger, of a gun. Here, in the deep of the night, in the isolated backcountry of a sparsely inhabited shire, no one would care who died at Drom.

And someone *would* die.

A footstep. An impatient sigh. Senna moved down another step, silent as a mouse. Charles, the coward, hovered on the landing, peering over the banister. The tension ratcheted to the boiling point.

"What do you see?" he mouthed to Senna.

"Shadows," she whispered back.

"Vampires don't throw shadows."

I'm watching you.

She swallowed hard. She felt as if she were walking into a miasma of evil. Neither Peter nor the Countess would hesitate to kill, and right now she even had her doubts about Dominick.

But she was safe—she wore a crucifix, she carried the vial of holy water, and she was perfectly prepared to use it.

She went down another step silently, holding her breath. For all she knew, Peter Augustine had transformed himself into the dust under her feet or the smoke wafting from the lamps.

She moved cautiously down another step, into a thick, evil silence; no one breathed, no one moved.

Something had to give.

She edged down three more steps, aware that the lamp she carried cast a long shadow behind her, touching Charles, who stood behind her at the head of the stairs.

She sensed Charles move closer.

"I can't see anything," he whispered.

"They're down there. They're waiting." But for what?

"Do something," she hissed.

"I'll tell you what—you create a diversion and I will. I'll do something."

She felt a tremor of fear. What could she do? And what would they do to her if she wasn't successful?

Did she care, if it meant—

Don't . . .

Charles pushed her slightly. "We've got to distract them."

She nodded.

The only possibility was the lamp she carried. She'd have to heave it far enough down the hall that she and Charles could get out with their lives.

Vampires could do anything, even kill them on the spot. So how much of a distraction would it be?

Fire wouldn't impede a vampire, but it was the only thing she had.

It was all *they* had, she and Charles. They could die standing on the steps; they could be pushed, tripped, trapped, surrounded, bitten, burned . . .

Or turned.

She bit her lip and touched the crucifix. There was little hope. She and Charles would both die, unlikely allies at the end. Why not wrest her one chance at eternity from an enemy who would kill her anyway?

The silence grew more ominous. Charles touched her shoulder.

"In case you're rethinking it, don't—"

She nodded. "They *will* kill us."

"I'd wager on it."

It was the moment to take action, not the time to think of ramifications or life beyond death or even what it was like to die.

It was time to heave the kerosene lamp as far as she could throw it, watch it arc through the air as she raced down the steps, hear the unholy whomp as it landed on the carpet and spilled flame and kerosene and caught fire.

She felt a pull at the chain around her neck and then the lift and shove of something grabbing her, and suddenly she found herself on her back on the drive, watching the roar of flames racing through the first floor.

Dear God, Charles.

She saw him then, silhouetted in the glow of the fire, stabbing over and over.

Dominick!

She crawled to her feet. *Dominick!*

Suddenly someone jumped at Charles, howling like an animal. The Countess.

Charles turned abruptly and impaled her on the knife that still streamed with Dominick's blood.

She screamed, she fell on him, on Dominick, and Charles rolled her off and over. Then Peter grabbed him, flying out from the shadows and seizing his neck in his mouth and taking him. His fangs were so deeply embedded in his neck that Charles dropped his knife and gave himself up to the bloodlust of the beast because he could do nothing else.

Senna watched in horror while she tried to staunch the blood streaming from Dominick's wounds. She didn't know what to do or how to help him. His blood flowed all over her hands, her skirt, mixing with Charles's blood flowing from his neck and shoulder, and the Countess's, pooling under her body.

Save Dominick.

With what? How? How did you stop a vampire from dying?

Stop the blood. Anything, wrap it up somehow.

She wiped her bloody hands on her skirt, pulled her petticoat out from under her, and tore at the thin cotton, pulling at it until she had enough to wrap around Dominick's body. She shifted and lifted and got the material under and around him and tied it tight just under his breastbone.

A horrible, awful deathly thud—*Charles.*

She looked up. Peter loomed over her. At his feet, Charles lay dead.

No chance, no choice.

She dove for the bloody knife and just barely got a grip on it before Peter came after her, his jaws still dripping with Charles's blood.

She scrabbled backward, at a great disadvantage because she couldn't get to her feet.

"It's just you and me now," Peter said coaxingly. "It won't hurt—much."

There was no point trying to reason with a bloody vampire either.

She reached for her crucifix to protect her—but it was gone.

Her heart jumped.

Oh, God. That tug at her neck as Dominick whirled her out of danger . . . he'd pulled the chain from around her neck so he could save her.

He'd left her without protection. Left her altogether, was dying on the ground, inches away from her blood-spattered feet.

"Don't fight it," Peter coaxed. "It's inevitable. You can die, or you can choose life everlasting."

"Don't . . ." It was a scratchy whisper. Dominick, barely sentient. "No. Tepes. No." He choked as blood welled up in his throat. "Don't . . . " he said on a long, rattling breath.

Don't—in her mind, in her heart.

Peter didn't want her. Peter just wanted to take her out of vicious malice while Dominick was still alive and could bear witness.

She still had the bloody knife clenched in her hand, like a scene she'd played before, just with not quite as much at stake.

Peter was close, down on his knees now, certain of his power and dismissing that the puny human had a weapon.

He leapt from his kneeling position right onto her body, rocking her backward, her arms outstretched as his teeth pulled at the skin of her neck, and the nick of his fangs shafted through her like poison.

Noooooooooooo!

The instinct to survive overpowered her sudden desire to just give in and give herself up to him. She still had the knife, clutched like death in her hand. She worked her arm free, and she sliced it around and jammed the knife up into his side, under his ribs with every ounce of dwindling strength she could muster.

She knew his reaction: he'd be startled, the tip of the knife would have penetrated his jacket, his shirt, perhaps his skin. She thought so because he paused as he felt it skim into his body.

She needed another shot—the thing wouldn't move. She'd pierced the skin—*oh, God, was it stuck?* She pulled again, with all her strength, and his body convulsed as the tip twisted in the wound.

This is my life—

She yanked again, tears streaming. Peter's monster face was above her, ugly, deadly, vicious in its animal hate, its vampiric lust to kill.

A knife wound under his ribs wouldn't stop him. He bent to her neck again, his leering mouth wide-open. She swung her arm again with all her might, aiming for his neck, his jugular, with faith she'd damage him somehow or disable him enough so she could get away.

Her arm wasn't quite long enough to get at his neck but she sliced at his face, and with him cursing, howling, she attacked blindly, slicing, stabbing, hefting the blade upward when she felt contact with something solid, twisting and pushing the blade deeper into his hollow soul. And when he fell away, she scrambled to find something hard and heavy to heave at him.

Heat radiated all around her. The whole manor house was up in flames.

Drom was burning and no one cared.

She found a slab of a rock and turned toward Peter, who was still moving, still with the will to kill her no matter what he suffered, no matter how much of his blood he would shed.

She heaved the slab at his face and he fell backward again.

She slipped to her knees.

"Don't rest until you kill him." A ghostly voice came from the flames.

No, it was her imagination.

"Cut off his head."

Oh, dear God, she must be dead. This nightmare . . .

"Senna!"

A ghost couldn't know her name.

She crawled to Dominick's body and the blood-soaked petticoat she'd wrapped around him. His pulse was thready, he was barely breathing, and he'd lost so much blood, too much blood soaking into the ground.

"Senna . . ." the Countess said, not even a whisper.

Senna crawled to her.

"Save Nicolai and I will turn you."

A chill swept Senna, head to toe.

Here was her endgame, her moment of decision. Live forever or live.

"How?"

"My blood. Nicolai. Feed. At my wound. Get me to him."

Senna's heart started hammering. To live was to die. To die was to be buried for eternity. To live for eternity was to die.

"Turn me first."

"Save Nicolai."

"Then quick . . . tell me what to do."

"You know."

She knew. She must give her heart and her life to the Countess so the Countess could give her heart and her life to Dominick.

But she wanted to give her heart and her life to Dominick. If she did it, she had an eternity to win him over.

She had no time to weigh her decision. Dominick was dying and the Countess's strength was waning. Only her indomitable will kept her alive.

And Peter was moving, which meant she wasn't done with him yet.

There was no time to weigh the cost of any decision she made. Instinctively she knelt close to the Countess's face, cradled her head against her breast, and girded herself for the bite.

It was worse than ever she'd imagined. Deep, hard, screamingly, deathly painful, an eternity, never ending—and then, suddenly, in the end, a red flood of ecstasy.

"And now," the Countess whispered, "take me to Nicolai."

Sapped as she was, she managed to lift the Countess by her arms and slowly maneuver her body over to Dominick.

"Don't," he breathed. "Let me die."

"Heart to mouth," the Countess whispered. "Hurry."

How? She couldn't move him, she had to shift the Countess onto his body, with her breast directly over his face so he could feed from her.

It was the most horrific moment, manipulating that nearly dead body onto Dominick's and positioning her chest so that he could siphon her copiously flowing blood.

He didn't want to, he wouldn't take it, he refused to feed.

"Charles is dead," Senna whispered in his ear. "The Countess is dying. You have to live, you have to . . . you'll choke if you don't feed, you'll die . . . please don't die."

"Senna," the Countess breathed in a thin, papery voice as Dominick's instinct to feed took over from his will to die, "you need to take of my blood. From my wrist. *Now.*"

"How?"

"Bite," the Countess commanded. *"Now."*

Senna lifted the Countess's limp wrist to her mouth. She couldn't. She couldn't. This was why Dominick had refused her. Because of this—the hot vampiric instinct to take of the blood. The ugly, vicious act of biting into someone's skin, veins, flesh . . . she'd opened herself to this. She'd willingly acceded to this. Eternity meant this awful, ugly bloody act of ingesting another's soul.

She put the Countess's veiny wrist to her mouth.

"You must," the Countess hissed. "You must. To complete the act, you must. Or you'll die."

The abyss loomed. She didn't want to die, to end, never to see Dominick, or her baby—there was only one choice: Senna closed her eyes and bit, hard, into the thin-pulsing wrist, and the Countess's warm blood flooded her mouth, her tongue, her throat.

"Kill him," the Countess whispered on her last breath.

And so they remained until the Countess died, Dominick feeding at her breast, Senna sucking at her wrist, the wild crackling flames racing through Drom the only witness to the bloody exchange.

Chapter 21

It was a nightmare suffused with blood. She dreamed that the Countess had given her the eternal bite, and that she'd fed on the Countess's blood. That Dominick had drowned in it. That Drom had burned to the ground.

And she had done all of it.

And everyone had died.

Everyone.

Only she'd gone into a great dark hole and succumbed to the blood. She'd willingly turned her only existence into a life of the damned.

She had nothing else, and now she didn't have that either.

She hurt. A burning pain clawed at her chest, as if her heart had been pulled from her body, as if her blood had been drained from her veins.

She felt weak, hot, hurt, slightly delirious, dizzy, thirsty.

Peter—she had a mandate to kill Peter.

She jolted awake to find herself in the shadow of the burned brown stone walls of Drom, a piece of black rock folded tight in her hand.

She was alone, curled up against the ash-stained black hole that had been Drom.

She drew in a deep, anguished breath and pushed herself upright against the burned stone. A black rock fell at her feet, and on a wave of dizziness, she bent and picked it up and turned it in her fingers as she stared at the barren landscape.

There were no bodies: no Peter, no Charles, no Dominick, no Countess.

But the ground was saturated with blood, dried, nearly absorbed by the earth.

Like a body, like death.

If she didn't move, she'd be sucked in, and she too would finally die.

Only she felt so alive.

And so alone. The bodies were gone, the house was gone, and she was the sole living creature in the landscape.

The servants would come soon, though. How would she explain the destruction of Drom? *I don't*, she thought. *I have to get out of here.*

Because on top of those vampiric murders, she'd be blamed for the fire too.

She needed time to think, to plan. She was in no shape to take action.

Neither the stables nor the carriage house had burned. She could tuck away in the stables, the closer of the two buildings, rest some more, feel secure until the servants left.

But then what? If she revealed herself, she could leave with them.

No. Not a good idea when she was barely aware of her needs or her powers.

Clutching the black stone, she stumbled into the sunlight. Heat flashed on her face and sizzled into the black stone, and she comprehended that this was the stone that absorbed sunlight. The stone that had permitted Dominick to walk among them now protected her as his last act of compassion.

She held it face up in her palm as she made her way to the stables, and she collapsed just inside the door as the sound of a carriage rumbling down the drive broke the eerie morning silence.

Senna lay slumped on the ground, listening. The servants' agitation over the destruction of Drom was nearly hysterical. She'd been right to hide, to just rest and gird herself for what came next.

She was stranded here, now the servants had gone, but that had been a conscious decision. She should just start walking. Later, when the sun was going down. The thought exhausted her.

Her blood memories exhausted her, and that she didn't know whether the Countess's sacrifice had saved Dominick.

Nicolai.

And she hadn't cut off Peter's head.

How had everyone vanished?

She didn't know what to do. She did nothing, just sat on the floor and felt her throbbing blood and her broken heart.

She'd been warned.

She looked at the rock in her hand, remembering what Dominick had said. It was obsidian, and it kept him from burning up in the sun.

Thank goodness she'd have it with her when she started walking. Because she saw no other option to get away from the ruins of Drom—and her life.

She had no idea where to go. The old Senna no longer had a mission, a place, or a pulsing drive to deceive.

Her fate had been sealed from birth. No matter what happened to her, she was destined to return to the streets, to that deathly future in the poorhouse predicted by both Charles and Peter.

She picked herself up and started toward the ruined manor. It was still smoking in places, and she wondered that a small kerosene lamp could so easily destroy such a large house.

Nothing was left. Not even a depression in the ground where Charles and Peter had fallen. Just that slab of rock she'd thrown at him, bloodied with bits of his skin.

There were no prayers for the damned.

She started down the drive, her shoes crunching on the gravel. Her dress, torn at the shoulder, was bathed in blood, which had also dried on her hands, face, and chest. Even without a mirror, she felt the tug of dried blood when she moved her mouth or her arm.

When she breathed.

If she could even see herself in a mirror—

No mirrors.

What had she done?

She kept walking, clutching the black rock.

Who would notify Lady Augustine that Peter was gone?

Dust and dirt whipped up around her suddenly, abruptly, and before she caught her breath, she was standing in Berkeley Square, at the bottom of the steps of Lady Augustine's town house.

She shivered. *Surely that thought didn't precipitate an action.*

She had all the answers now, and they all had to do with supernatural powers.

The door opened, and Lady Augustine appeared.

"I've been expecting you, my dear. Come."

"Peter's gone," Senna said blankly. She might as well give Lady Augustine the awful news before she set foot in the house.

"I know. Come in."

Vampires knew everything. Senna wondered if Lady Augustine was a vampire. After all her own tension and fear over vampires among them, becoming one didn't seem all that onerous once the deed was done.

But she hadn't yet felt the throbbing urge to feed.

She wanted a bath and clean clothes. She wanted to run as far away from Lady Augustine as her powers would take her.

Did vampires even bathe? she wondered. Or did she require a tub of dirt, a shroud in a coffin under a bed?

By all that was damned, she hadn't thought this out, wished she'd listened more closely to Dominick's warnings. She couldn't remember all that had terrified her before.

"Where's Dominick?" she demanded.

"I wouldn't know. He's Iscariot."

Yes, he'd told her that.

"And you're Tepes now," Lady Augustine added with just the faintest tone of malice.

"*What?* No, no . . . the Countess took me . . . the Countess turned me—"

"Peter had you first, Senna. So, of course, you came here."

"I'm Iscariot," she insisted.

"What you are right now is exhausted, filthy, needing a bath and fresh clothes. Let's do that first, and then we'll sort out who did what to whom," Lady Augustine said as she called for the tub. "Your room remains as it was. All your clothes are there. The room below awaits you when you need to revivify yourself."

"When I—*what?*"

"The secret room below yours. You will need to rest there when you're not out and about. I know. I prepared it for Peter."

Horror shot through her like an arrow. "I won't—I'm not . . . I—"

"It takes a little time to get used to the idea. You won't want to sleep in a bed."

Instantly she saw an image of a bed. The bed in which Dominick had seduced her. Of course she wanted to sleep in a bed.

"Your bath is ready, Senna. Your clothes are laid out. Take your time. We'll talk more later."

Senna felt as if all the scrubbing in the world would not rub out the blood or the feeling of it dried on her skin.

Then she lay wrapped in a robe and curled on the bed where— she clamped down on the memories. She moved to the vanity and turned slowly to look at herself in the mirror, her heart pounding wildly.

She wasn't there.

She looked at her palms and caught her breath.

No lines.

As if they'd been erased by the blood. No heart line. No life line. No life. She was alive *and* dead and she didn't know how to come to grips with it.

Nor did she want to believe it even when she looked down at her naked breasts and saw the livid X-shaped bite marks still healing where the Countess had fed from her heart.

She touched her neck. She couldn't see how deep Peter's fangs had punctured her skin. She only knew it hurt. She still hurt, all over.

But that secret dirt-filled room awaited her should she need surcease.

She hadn't yet felt the pulsating drive to kill, to feed. It curled around the edges of her consciousness, and she felt it unfurling deep in her being. It was coming, creeping up on her as much as she tried to suppress it.

She grabbed a dress from the armoire, ignoring the impulse to open the secret door and wend her way to the secret room for nourishment.

She was *not* that *thing,* that monster. The one under the bed draped in a shroud.

Dressed, she felt more like herself. Except she felt no hunger. No feeling for food or tea or—*anything*. But blood.

She tucked the obsidian rock in her pocket and ran downstairs to find Lady Augustine in the parlor.

Where the séance had been held another lifetime ago.

Lady Augustine had a guest and they were drinking tea. It was as if things were normal, when Senna knew they weren't.

She stopped short, horrified, as she recognized who sat with her. Charles.

Charles, who was dead.

The Countess had done it again—saved him against his will and sired another victim in the process. Only now, she was truly dead, sapped of blood and life, and there was nothing Dominick could do, no vengeance he could take, no retaliation, no retribution.

His eternal battle with his mother was over, and it would be said that she'd died valiantly trying to save the intruders at Drom.

Viciously trying to kill them, rather.

But that wasn't for public consumption. Nor was how Peter Augustine had died, stabbed and bashed, and his body consigned to the flames.

A fire was a purifying thing.

Dominick felt tempted to jump in himself and end all the psychic pain.

But then, Senna.

Turned and twisted by Peter and then his mother, and now she was of the blood. But which blood?

It was the all-important question and one reason he'd left her in the shadow of Drom with the piece of obsidian folded in her hand.

Because he couldn't know yet which clan's blood had taken, and where her loyalties would lie.

And Charles had vanished, a vampire at last, his untainted blood ripe for taking by the enemy clan, and now free to give in to his every bloody impulse.

Charles was now his brother's sworn enemy.

In one bloody night, alliances shifted and everything had changed.

Find your clan.

He could still hear his mother's last words to him.

Find your place, your home, your people. She hadn't said that exactly, but he'd understood. He'd been untethered for so long, tormented by dreams of revenge; his place had never been important to him, nor had he ever had a home.

In Senna, he'd found his home.

He never expected things to end with his leaving her to find her way until her blood provenance could be proved.

And if there was a child?

He'd find them, he thought. He'd find them because he'd lost his half brother to the enemy, and if he didn't have Senna, he had nothing to show for all the years he'd courted death and cursed life.

Find your clan. Dominick could almost hear the Countess's reedy, death-racked voice in his consciousness.

It was better than existing in some blood-soaked netherworld. It gave him a purpose after all the bloodletting and a road to find his way back to Senna.

A rebirth of sorts. He could become Nicolai once again, a man born of fire and cleansed by fire.

And he would bury Dominick forever.

"*Who* is she?"

Lady Augustine's question caught Senna as she stopped suddenly on the threshold of the parlor.

She looked at Charles. He acknowledged her confusion.

"Come in, Senna."

"I don't know this person," Lady Augustine said.

"She's a friend of mine," Charles said. "I asked her to come, Mother."

Senna's heart stopped. Charles, taking Peter's place deliberately?

"Sit down, Senna. My mother is a little leery of unknown guests these days."

"So I see," Senna murmured.

"She was taken in by a very clever sharper not long ago. The girl actually pretended she was my lady's ward—can you imagine the gall of it?"

"Unimaginable," Senna said, chilled by his words.

"I want to toast our newfound status, Senna."

"And just what is that, Charles?"

"We've been turned, Senna dear. We are of the blood. The thing I longed for all my life, which the Countess adamantly refused because she wanted to keep the blood of the Lazlarics pure. Really, can you believe it? When she was hiding her vampirism all along. As if a mother couldn't pass the taint to her unborn child. The Countess knew very little about those things. Lady Augustine is much more informed."

He poured a cup of tea and motioned for Senna to join them. "Here you are." He handed her the cup and poured another for himself and then lifted it in her direction. "To eternal life—you and me."

Senna took a sip and set the cup aside. "You were dead."

"What? My son died?" Lady Augustine interrupted.

"My body was absorbing the eternal bite," Charles said. "I was reborn when Peter pulled me back into this life. Of course, I owe it to Lady Augustine to take his place now that he's gone. I owe him my new life."

He turned to Lady Augustine. "I assure you, Mother—I am not dead."

He looked at Senna. "He took you too."

"I don't know."

"You are of the blood—I feel it."

"Where's Dominick?"

"How would I know? Why would I care?"

"I'm leaving," Senna said. "I need to find Dominick."

"You can't leave yet. You're not used to the change, or any of it. You haven't even fed yet. You can't go out in broad daylight. You have to—"

"I am *not* Tepes," Senna said angrily. "And I *am* leaving."

"Senna." He caught her arm. "You're not prepared. Maybe in a day or two . . ."

"Why should you care?"

"Because there's so much to absorb, so much you need to know. And he won't mate with you if you're Tepes."

"I'll take that chance."

"You're going to kill first."

"I'm going to find Dominick."

"The Countess is dead. He might well have left London. How will you find him?"

"I'll find him."

She didn't know where. She only knew that suddenly she was standing on the topmost step outside Lady Augustine's town house, and then she thought, *Dominick,* and in a blink she was standing on the top step outside Dominick's home.

The powers.

The damaged door was back in place.

She rang the doorbell and the butler answered just as before.

"Is Dominick here?"

"Mr. Janou is not here," Knoll said. "And I am just about to leave."

"May I come in? I'm certain he would want me to wait."

Say yes. She found herself forcing the words into his mind the way perhaps Charles now occupied Lady Augustine's mind and erased the memory of Peter.

Interesting.

"For a few moments," Knoll said grudgingly, opening the door.

She settled herself in the parlor anteroom. Everything destroyed during the Keepers' sweep of the house had been replaced. Everything looked just as it had been. So if Dominick was not here, he was certain to return to such a beautiful home.

But, of course, he didn't care about a beautiful home, really. Neither did she. Rather, she was thinking, with some longing, about the coffin cavity under Dominick's bed. She thought about going upstairs and lying down and wrapping herself in Dominick's shroud. He might even be there, and if he wasn't, perhaps he would feel her presence there and come back to her. He could be on his way even now.

Knoll said he was about to leave. The house was very very quiet. Was it possible Knoll was the only one here?

How tempting was that?

No. Nonono.

Rest first, feed later.

She didn't even notice how easily the idea came, and that she felt no revulsion at the thought.

She crept up the steps very quietly, and into Dominick's bedroom. The room was redolent with his scent. He was coming, she felt it. He could be here any moment.

She looked down at her belly, touched it, thought about the possibility of a child, their child, gestating there. He would come. Soon.

All she had to do was wait.

She got down on her knees, feeling for the edge of the cavity. She slipped down into its recesses, all alone, pulling the shroud around her body, and heaved a long, deep sigh of relief at having finally come home.

Printed in the United States
By Bookmasters